# CRASHERS

# DANA HAYNES

# *CRASHERS*

MINOTAUR BOOKS ♠ NEW YORK

CRASHERS. Copyright © 2010 by Dana Haynes. All rights reserved. Printed in the United States of America. For information, address St. Martin's Press, 175 Fifth Avenue, New York, NY 10010.

www.stmartins.com

Design by: Philip Mazzone

Library of Congress Cataloging-in-Publication Data

Haynes, Dana.
    Crashers / Dana Haynes.—1st ed.
        p. cm.
    ISBN 978-0-312-59988-1 (hardcover edition)
    ISBN 978-0-312-67656-8 (first international trade paperback edition)
  1. Aircraft    accidents—Investigation—Fiction.    2. Government    investigators—Fiction.
3. United States. National Transportation Safety Board—Fiction.    I. Title.
    PS3558.A84875C73 2010
    813'.54—dc22

                                                                        2009046155

First Edition: July 2010

10   9   8   7   6   5   4   3   2   1

To Don and Shirley Haynes.
Landy, Mary, Tyler, and I voted you Best Parents Ever.
The vote was 2–2 but a tie goes to the runner.

# *ACKNOWLEDGMENTS*

This book would never have been written if it hadn't been for Jonathan Harr's fabulous article "The Crash Detectives," in the August 1996 issue of *The New Yorker*. Some works of journalism stay with you forever.

# BOOK ONE

## FIRST PLANE DOWN

*1*

DENNIS SILVERMAN AND MEGHAN Danvers woke up almost
simultaneously.

As the rest of Portland, Oregon, was getting ready for dinner or making the commute home, Dennis and Meghan rolled out of their beds.
They had never met and would never meet. They were just two people
waking up in Portland, Oregon, on a sunny and glorious late-afternoon
Monday in March. Dennis, in the spendy, gentrified Pearl District, third
floor of a confectionary factory turned into half-a-million-dollar condos.
Meghan, in the Residence Inn at Portland International Airport.

Dennis had been so keyed up, he'd slept barely three hours. He started
his day by scanning a half-dozen blogs on his homemade laptop, while he
downed two Red Bulls and two Snickers, his traditional breakfast. MTV
played in the background but he hardly noticed. He was so nervous, his
hands shook. And every time he caught a glimpse of himself in the mirror,
he grinned.

This was going to be a day. A hell of a day. A day people would remember. A day the media whores would recount on its anniversary and people
would ask: where were you when you heard?

Meghan awoke to the sound of a travel alarm. She drank bottled water
she'd set out the night before, then went to work on one hundred crunches,

one hundred push-ups with her bare feet up on one of the hotel-room chairs. CNN played in the background but she hardly noticed.

She showered, called her husband, James, in Reston, Virginia. They talked for exactly two minutes about nothing in particular. The baby was fine. The weather was crappy in Virginia. March 7, and there was black ice everywhere. Meghan pushed aside the hotel-room curtains and squinted into the lovely evening, the sun peeking over the West Hills, illuminating the radiant Mount Hood to the east, topped year-round in snow.

They said "I love you" and hung up.


## PORTLAND INTERNATIONAL AIRPORT

Ninety minutes later, Meghan Danvers found herself standing in the shadow of her very own jet airliner. It wasn't "hers" hers, but she was the pilot and the senior officer, so, as far as she was concerned, the mammoth Vermeer 111 was all hers.

She breathed in the slightly salty tang of the Columbia River, just a little to the north, and studied the wispy hints of clouds that dotted the sky. *One octa,* she said to herself: only one eighth of the way toward being overcast.

"It's a looker." Russ Kazmanski noted the boss's attention on the sky.

"Sweet," Meghan said. She wore the navy Eisenhower jacket and matching trousers of CascadeAir. Tall and willow thin, the uniform hung nicely on her athletic frame. Russ wore the same, although he was short and paunchy, and she doubted that he had ever ironed his trousers.

"Almost no wind up top," she said. "Day like this, must be what it's like flying in outer space."

Russ squinted up at her, smiling. He knelt in the shadow of the landing gear of the colossal 111, about the size of a Boeing 737. Above their heads, the retractable gangplank of Terminal C4 began inching out, touching the skin of their four-engine wide-body. "You a NASA wannabe, Skip?"

"Damn straight." Meghan canted her head, running her hand through her hair, which she wore tightly cropped. She was African American; Russ was white. It dawned on her that less than one generation ago, no white pilot—especially one eleven years her elder—would have called a black woman "Skip." "Stewardess," maybe.

He grinned. "No kidding?"

"I almost made the program, eight or nine years ago. I never told you that?"

"Nope." The laptop at Russ's knee chimed. It sat on the cool, gritty tarmac, its infrared emitter aimed at a portal in the underbelly of the jet, ten feet directly over his head. The emitter, shaped like a penlight and shining in the invisible range, was attached to the laptop by a gooseneck flex tube. The underbelly portal was marked GAMELAN. "They screwed up, not taking you. You'd've been a hit with the Flash Gordon set."

She smiled at the kneeling man. "Why, Kazmanski. That's the sweetest thing anyone's ever said to me."

Russ made a fist and blew into it. It had hit fifty-two today, but with the sun going down, the temperature was getting ready to fall like a Warner Bros. anvil.

Russ Kazmanski had been the copilot with Meghan Danvers for a week now, running a three-legged pattern from PDX to LAX to Sea-Tac and back again. They were two days away from a four-day layover in Los Angeles, before starting the rotation all over. Russ had enjoyed his week of flying the right-hand seat with the skip and looked forward to staying on this assignment.

"What's the FDR say?" Meghan asked, and knelt, too, to get a better angle on the laptop screen linked by microwave to the flight data recorder. There was a solid, almost masculine quality to her movements, Russ noted. Like most pilots, she exuded confidence. Both kneeling, it was easier to speak over the sounds of the food-services truck that had just arrived.

"Nine hundred and seventy-one telltales are green-for-go," he said, tapping the keyboard at his feet, which was reading information from the Gamelan flight data recorder. "And we got two yellow. No reds."

"The yellows?" Meghan craned her neck to see from Russ's angle.

"Nothing major. The Gamelan says we need to have one of the nodes of the transponder looked at within the next seven thousand five hundred miles, or five cycles." A cycle is one leg of a journey; a takeoff, flight, and landing. "Also, we got a little blip on the port elevator. The box says check it within seven cycles."

Meghan shook her head. "That is the damnedest thing I've ever seen."

"No shit." Back in the day, checking out almost 2,000 systems would've taken a weekend. The new flight data recorder being released by Gamelan Industries made the preflight check in twenty minutes. Russ began disassembling the transmitter. "Let's hear it for technology. This gadget is made right here in Portland, you know."

He closed the laptop, picked it up. His knees popped as he stood straight.

"Okay, I'm on the walkaround," Meghan said. "You want to start on the preflight?"

"I'm on it." He glanced around, admired the cerulean sky and the snowy slopes of Mount Hood. They were an hour away from sunset and the mountain glowed like it was radioactive. "I could retire here."

"Tell me that when it's raining," Meghan Danvers said, and began walking around her three-story-tall bird.

## REST STOP, INTERSTATE 5

Dennis Silverman didn't bother hiding. He drove his Outback off the interstate and into the rest area. Harsh white lights on very tall poles illuminated the blacktop area. The only other vehicles in sight in were two double-long truck-and-trailer rigs, a handful of RVs and campers, and one dilapidated Volkswagen Bug with a couple of twenty-somethings in tie-dyed shirts and raggedly cuffed jeans, leaning on the hood and poring over a badly folded map of the Pacific Northwest. They looked like they'd just stepped out of 1972. *Proof of a fold in the time stream,* Dennis thought.

He was about equal distance between Portland and Salem, the state capital. A serrated copse of Douglas firs separated the rest area from I-5 but did a poor job of keeping down the drone of highway traffic. Dennis had come here many other times in the last few months. The first few weeks, he'd parked at one end and waited, then at the other end for a little while. He'd finally found exactly the spot he needed. He checked his waterproof, pressure-proof watch; he'd gone online twice that morning to make sure his watch was on the money. He had used a U.S. Navy Web site to confirm the time. There was very little room for error in this game.

Satisfied, he strolled to the rear of the Outback, opened the hatch, and pulled out a laptop computer and a device that looked like a long microphone attached to a short tripod. He returned to the front of his SUV and hiked himself up onto the hood, feeling the heat of the engine through his trousers. He set up the tripod on the hood next to him, attached it to the laptop via a USB port, popped the lid, and booted up. The twenty-somethings had stopped trying to read the map and were making out. The truck drivers cared for little that happened outside their cabs. If the RV crowd was paying attention, Dennis couldn't tell. And he wasn't all that concerned anyway.

A couple of squirrels were nosing around, three parking spaces away.

Dennis dug a Ziploc bag out of his REI ski jacket and sprinkled walnuts on the ground. Three more squirrels hopped in his direction.

As the laptop screen began to glow, he grinned and removed his wire-rimmed glasses, cleaning them on the untucked bottom of his *Farscape* T-shirt, which hung below the ski jacket. He'd thought about dressing up for the occasion, knowing something momentous was about to happen, even if no one else did. It's important to look businesslike when you're about to change history. But in the end he left the house with his one suit, one dress shirt, and one tie hanging forgotten from the hook on the bathroom door. He'd made it halfway to the rest stop before he remembered. He smiled, realizing that when he told the story of this day, he'd be wearing a really sharp suit.

He glanced at the hippies and the truckers. Let them stare. Sure, he was about to commit a crime. And in Oregon, it was a capital offense. But so what? No one here today would recognize his crime, or realize that anything bad was going on. Hell, Dennis thought, there wasn't even a good word for the crime he was about to commit. They'd have to come up with a name for it. Maybe they'd call it a silverman. Maybe he was about to commit first-degree silverman.

The images on the screen clarified themselves. Dennis tapped madly at the keyboard, making no mistakes, no type-overs or go-backs. He'd done this a thousand times in practice and he knew exactly what he was doing.

Time to change the world.

## CASCADEAIR FLIGHT 818, GATE C4, PDX

Fifteen minutes later, Annie Colvin, the chief flight attendant for Flight 818, rapped on the cabin door and poked her head in. "Got 'em corralled," she said, in the tone a preschool teacher uses to announce that naptime has commenced. "Ready when you are."

In the left-hand seat, Meghan Danvers nodded and looked back over her shoulder. "Thanks. Tower's giving us the hold sign but we're up next."

Annie Colvin started to back out, then stopped. "Anybody want anything before I buckle up?"

Meghan said, "No, thanks. I'm good."

Russ Kazmanski turned as far as he could in the cumbersome copilot's chair. "I'll take some coffee, if you've got it brewed up."

"Hang on," she said and backed out.

"Decaf!" Russ called, hoping she heard him. "That's all I need, the jangles."

"Careful," Meghan warned playfully, and rolled her eyes, the color of nutmeg, toward the ceiling panel equidistant between their seats. The cockpit voice recorder was housed above that panel. "Big Brother's listening."

"Then I probably shouldn't mention the ganja, mon."

He grinned, but Meghan frowned. "Not funny, partner. CascadeAir doesn't even allow joking about that."

"I know," he said soothingly. It had been a joke, and they both knew it. In the past six or seven years, a corporate policy of zero tolerance for alcohol and drug use had turned into a siege mentality. Substance-abuse posters were mandatory in all crew lounges, and pamphlets offering help and counseling seemed to arrive in employees' mail almost monthly.

Annie Colvin came back with the coffee; it was not in the plastic that passengers got, but a proper china cup. "Here you go," she said and handed it over the high-backed chair. "Decaf all right?"

He noticed that she'd put in milk and had provided a spoon and a saucer to put it on. He winked back at her. "Great, thanks. We're— Hold it."

Annie saw both pilots tilt their heads a fraction of an inch, hearing something over their headsets.

Meghan said, "Roger that, tower."

"Okay, we're rolling," Russ said to Annie. "We'll see you topside."

She said, "Bye," and headed back to her foldout seat in the galley.

Russ stowed the coffee cup and saucer on the recessed panel at his right knee, where it was out of the way. He knew the skipper was a real stickler for protocol, but the softly curved shroud was made of vinyl laminate over thermoformed plastic, all perfectly waterproof. In fact, the surface was intended for food and drinks during flight.

The moon shone down, illuminating the tarmac runway. A dull glow emanated from the south: downtown Portland. The moonlight made Mount Hood a little pink. The Vermeer 111's harsh white lights turned night into day, bled all the color out of the grass to the left and right of the runway.

Meghan queued her jet up to the line, ready to roll. She toggled her microphone. "ATC, this is CascadeAir Eight One Eight, in the blocks and ready to sprint."

The air traffic control voice that came back was surprisingly West

Virginian for Oregon. "Ah, roger that, Eight One Eight. Y'all got limitless ceiling tonight and little wind. You are cleared for takeoff on runway two eight lima. Have yourselves a good one."

"CascadeAir Eight One Eight, roger that." Meghan nudged the Vermeer 111 out into the wide runway. "Thanks for the hospitality, Portland. We'll see you next week. Eight One Eight out."

They began to pick up speed. Meghan glanced over just as Russ glanced at her. They winked at each other; kids with big, multimillion-dollar toys. Russ said, "Power's set."

"All right, then. Read 'em off."

"Seventy-five knots," Russ chanted. "One hundred . . . one twenty."

"Vee one," the captain said. V-codes represent aircraft speed, and V1 is the decision speed. Hit that speed and you're committed to taking off.

Which they did. Smoothly.

Russ said, "Positive climb."

"Okay, gear up."

He hit the landing-gear handle. They could hear the mechanism clamor beneath them. Both waited to hit a layer of turbulent air, as so often happens, and Russ casually put a hand over the coffee cup that Annie had brought him. When it happened that evening, it was as soft as the gentlest breeze. They doubted any of the passengers felt it.

"LNAV on auto?" Meghan said.

"Got it." The copilot put the lateral navigation controls on autopilot. "You've got good climb thrust."

Meghan waited for a moment, watching the lights of the city spread out beneath her. "VNAV."

Russ put the vertical navigation system on autopilot. "Gotcha."

"Good. Flaps go to one, gear handle off," she said, and they began chanting the after-takeoff checklist. For every term she used, Russ repeated it back at her, like a call-and-response sermon. Landing gear up and off. Flaps up. Checked up. Altimeter okay. Center autopilot on.

Meghan gently turned the sleek, massive aircraft, bringing it into a southerly direction. Russ reached for his coffee cup.

"Like a baby's butt," he said.

Meghan allowed herself a proud smile. "Damn straight."

Flight 818 found its course and began picking up speed. It was still climbing to cruise altitude as it passed over a rest area off Interstate 5.

·  ·  ·

With the press of a knuckle buster—shift, option, apple, and the letter *X*—the handmade computer on the hood of the Outback emitted a silly, cartoonish sound. Dennis Silverman had chosen the noise because he thought it was funny. He smiled at the noise now, almost drowned out by the sound from the airliner passing overhead. He smiled down at the squirrels.

Dennis logged off the computer, closed the cover, disconnected the emitter and tripod. He was careful not to step on the twitching forms of the poisoned squirrels as he hopped down off the hood.

He did so love to play with poisons.

# 2

Russ Kazmanski said, "Hmm. What's that?" He tapped the screen of the Gamelan flight-data-recorder monitor.

Meghan Danvers said, "What's what?"

"I've got a— Whoa!"

The cockpit began shaking madly.

"Shit!" Meghan barked, the avionics monitors dancing so badly in front of her eyes that she couldn't get a read on them. "Trimming rudder to the left! What've we got?"

"I— Dammit!" The bucking grew worse. Above their heads, four electronic caution tones sounded, followed by a siren.

"What've we got!" she barked.

"I dunno! Wait, check the— This doesn't make sense!"

The tones chimed again. The siren was going nonstop.

"Call it in!"

Russ toggled his transceiver. "Uh, PDX flight control, this is CascadeAir Eight One Eight! Mayday! We are declaring an emergency!"

In economy class, passengers gripped their seat arms or one another. The air masks deployed, just as they had in the safety video everyone had ignored.

. . .

The West Virginian drawl from the tower answered back immediately. "Roger, Eight One Eight. Do you wish to return to Portland?"

"Affirmative," Meghan cut in. She was holding the controls with both hands, the small clusters of muscles around her knuckles standing taut. A vein pulsed visibly at her throat.

"What is the nature of your emergency?"

"Unknown, Portland! Engine trouble! We're shaking apart!"

"Understood, Eight One Eight. Runway one zero romeo is available. We're clearing airspace for you. Contact one zero five point four for your lineup."

Russ fought down the urge to puke, switched the secondary communication array to frequency 105.4. He flicked a glance toward the captain, who didn't look frightened. She looked positively pissed off.

"One zero five point four, roger," he said.

"Ah, good, Eight One Eight. Come about one eight zero, altitude at your discretion. Would you like fire crews on scene?"

"One eight zero confirmed. Affirmative on the fire crews. We don't know what's wrong!" Meghan shouted to be heard over the warning sounds and the rattling of her vessel. She began the 180-degree turn as directed.

"Eight One Eight, you are, ah, seven miles from the first localizer."

"Meg, we got— Christ!"

The airliner yawed madly. Russ's coffee cup and saucer went flying, a clipboard rattled to the deck. The ship began rolling to the left. Meghan gripped the yoke, hauled with all her might to the right. The ship bucked like a bronco.

Both Meghan and Russ looked up as the "stick shaker" sounded; they were perilously close to stalling an engine.

Meghan reached down beneath her legs, toggled a switch. They heard a gurgling sound as fuel began dumping from the emergency vents, raining down on the farmland of Marion County, Oregon.

Something deep inside the plane snapped. The stick in Meghan's hands whipsawed to the left. She was holding on so hard, the sudden movement broke two bones in her left wrist.

"Dammit!" she shouted.

"Jesus, God," Russ muttered.

The Vermeer jetliner shrieked. It howled and jerked like a wounded animal, as the starboard wing began ripping away from the body. The ship rolled, pivoted, began its death dive.

"*Nooooooo!*" Meghan roared, demanding the beast do her bidding.

The negative g force hammered them into their restraints. Russ's face went white as his clavicle cracked under the pressure.

CascadeAir Flight 818 screamed toward the ground. Meghan Danvers pressed her feet to the floor, lifted her butt off the chair, and hauled back on the stick with all her might. She screamed as her broken wrist protested, the bones grinding together. She pulled and pulled, back arched, legs vibrating. The jet howled and she howled back, one wild animal challenging another.

Less than a hundred feet from the ground, the overworked elevators began responding to Meghan's herculean effort. The pitch leveled out, at least a little. When the giant aircraft hit the ground, it was belly, not nose, first.

Meghan Danvers wouldn't live long enough to realize how many lives she'd saved.

*3*

WEST LOS ANGELES: ANOTHER happy hour, another club.

The scene was a blend of nouveau riche and Eurotrash, corporate risers and high-end call girls. Half the room were players, and the other half had fucked the first half. The music was low and sensuous for now—with a promise of something rougher as the night wore on. The place was a ragout of money and hormones and booze and meth and coke. A high-octane cocktail of adrenaline and endorphins.

Daria Gibron had come there for a couple of reasons: one was to translate for a junior-junior member of the Saudi royal family in the market for a French chateau. The work had been easy enough, the negotiations simple and the vodka martini dry. The job complete, Daria bade both foreigners *adieu* and drifted deeper into the crowd, finding a place at the long teak bar and ordering another.

There wasn't much chance of going home alone, and that suited Daria just fine. She wore Dolce & Gabbana: a little black tank top with a matching jacket and a short skirt, with strappy spikes to show off her muscular calves. She'd spent lots of money to give her hair that poorly cut, haphazard look, very short in back, much longer in front, which looked as good in a boardroom or business luncheon as it did on the dance floor. She accepted the Belvedere martini and spent the next hour turning down invitations to "get the hell out of here" from men in Armani suits and women in Gucci.

The one who finally caught her eye was out of place. Faded blue jeans, lace-up military boots, and a maroon pullover sweater that was neither stylish nor weathered enough to be chic. Blond with blue eyes, he wore his sleeves pushed up to reveal tattoos on both sculpted forearms.

"How d'you do?" he asked, his accent Irish and rough-hewn.

"Well enough." Daria went with noncommittal. This man, with a half-day's stubble and lopsided smile, was far from the best-looking man in the room. But there was something about him, she thought, as he ordered a beer. It arrived and he took one sip, all but spitting it back out. Daria let loose a laugh that surprised the Irishman and herself.

"God, and that's rat piss," he said, and she laughed again.

"American beer? Undrinkable."

"Aye. Give us some of that, then." Without waiting for an okay, the Irishman took a sip of her martini, their hands brushing as he took the glass.

"That's passable. Name's Jack."

"Hallo, Jack. Daria," she replied, leaning toward him and speaking for his ears only. Her accent was Middle Eastern, but that's all he could tell.

He glanced into the mirror behind the bar and Daria realized what it was about Jack that had attracted her, in a room full of gorgeous men and women. He was scanning the room the way a pro does. He'd chosen his position to give him a view of both doors, and his eyes strayed to Daria's face only in passing, a touch-and-go before scanning the room again.

Much as Daria herself had been doing.

"What brings you to the United States?" she asked.

"Was hoping to get laid," Jack replied, his blue eyes gliding to hers for a moment, then sliding away to scan the room again.

She nodded.

"The table to your left," she said, catching Jack's eyes and locking them onto hers. "Seven o'clock. Two men and two women."

He squinted a little, but kept his eyes on hers. She stared straight back. "Aye?"

"The man facing us is left-handed and is drinking red wine."

He smiled, sandy eyebrows rising in mild surprise. "Am I that obvious?"

She nodded.

"Lass with her back to us is wearing a houndstooth coat and has a cocktail with ice," he said. "Why do Americans drink cocktails with ice?"

"I've no idea," she said, and slid off her stool. "Shall we?"


Jack was with two other men, both of whom had Irish accents; they had secured a table in another room of the restaurant and were watching a horse race on a gigantic TV screen. A fourth Irishman sauntered their way, making a big show of counting out the twenties he'd just won from some lawyer-types at the bar.

"Having fun, are we?" Jack approached, his fingers barely touching Daria's left elbow.

"Aye, tha'." The big man winked. "I'm winning. What'll yez have, then? 'Son me."

Jack turned to the big guy, nodded at the money he'd won. "Less of that, you. We're on the clock here. I need your head in the fucking game."

Daria noticed that the three other men treated Jack as their boss.

"Now," Jack said. "Be lucky, my lads. The lady is about to show me a good time."


It was almost 9 P.M. when Daria unlocked the door to her flat and escorted Jack through the door. Inside, she knelt and swept away a Persian rug, revealing a trapdoor. She opened the door. Beneath it was the face of a safe with a ten-digit keypad. She tapped in a code, then cranked the handle and hauled open the door.

Within was a stash of handguns. Glock 9s, a couple of Colt Pythons and a Colt Defender, three Springfield Armory V-10s, a brace of Para-Ordnance P10s, and an PDA P14.

Jack knelt, ran his hand lovingly along the profile of the Colt Python. "You do know how to show a lad a good time."

# 4

THE MEDICAL EXAMINER ACROSS the table said something that Dr. Leonard Tomzak disagreed with. In typical "Tommy" Tomzak fashion, he wadded up a napkin and threw it at the medical examiner's head.

"Stu?" he said. "That there is twenty pounds of horseshit in a ten-pound bag."

The medical conference had begun in a sterile, white-on-white conference room at Portland's Oregon Health & Science University, complete with PowerPoint presentations and color-coded handouts. The topic—blunt abdominal trauma and the effects on hollow viscus—had drawn specialists from throughout the United States. The panel discussion had been gentlemanly, collegial. The audience in the stadium seating had applauded at the right times, laughed at the right anecdotes, and hadn't seemed surprised that there would be laughing points in a discussion of blunt abdominal trauma.

In short, it was a perfectly dull seminar.

Later, a half dozen of the top specialists moved the conference to a brew pub in downtown Portland. They sat at a thick, varnished wooden table, cluttered with beer mugs and pitchers, and greasy baskets of home-made corn chips and salsa that could melt the enamel off your teeth. Tommy drank seltzer with a wedge of lime.

The bartender, when asked, had provided vast sheets of butcher paper. The physicians drank and marveled over the salsa and drew rough diagrams of spines and skulls and vector analyses. They argued and drew over one another's chicken scratches.

"There seems no doubt whatsoever," said the most scholarly of the group, a professor of emergency surgery at the Truman Center, University of Missouri. "Concussive damage is the most dangerous, period. The studies have been done again and again."

Which is when Tommy finished off the last of his seltzer and did the wadding-up-and-throwing thing.

"Tommy! How can you argue with the facts?"

"I'm not," Tommy drawled. He was leaning back, the front legs of his chair off the floor, his cowboy boots on the edge of the table. "I'm arguing with a guy who hasn't seen a real, live patient since Reagan was in office. Y'all got the American studies, sure, but the WHO stuff that's out right now points to the linear shearing of deceleration trauma. That there's your real killer."

The professor removed his glasses and smiled kindly. "For a pathologist, you seem to hold an awful lot of interest in live patients, Tommy."

Tommy brushed back an unruly hank of hair that fell near his left eyebrow. He wasn't really dressed for the professional lecture circuit, favoring khaki trousers, cowboy boots, and a blue denim shirt with a red-and-white-striped tie, loosened, the top shirt button undone. He also didn't make any effort to hide his Texas twang. "A whole lotta dead folks get carted into my operating room, Prof. I'm the guy digging around inside these folks. You can trust me on this."

One of the trauma specialists—a woman who'd come down from Seattle for the conference—watched Tommy carefully and tried not to make it obvious. He wasn't classically handsome, but he had a tight, leathery roughness to his skin, as if he had spent a lot of time working or playing in the sun. His hair was black but turning gray around his neckline, and it was cut poorly, a straight, black hank hanging over his forehead and occasionally scraping his eyebrows. Five-eight and wiry. Also, no wedding ring. The Seattle trauma specialist checked her watch and wondered when this confab would end. She definitely planned to ask him out for a drink.

Before the argument could come around—for the fifth time—to the same points, a pediatric trauma specialist from New Orleans stepped out of the women's restroom, her eyes darting to the TV screen behind the bar. She stepped closer, peered up at the screen. She waved down the bartender, asked him to turn up the audio, then turned to the debate. "Tommy? You better see this."

Tommy craned his neck around, wondering why they always put TVs so damn high in bars. The picture was grainy, a bouncy image taken from the air, probably from a helicopter. A banner in the upper corner read SPECIAL REPORT, along with the station's call letters.

Tommy squinted; he wasn't wearing the glasses he needed to drive and play golf. But he could make out the image well enough. The helicopter was hovering over a scorched, burning field of grass. A long, rough trench had been gouged into the earth. The camera shifted to the right and revealed the smoldering tail of a jetliner.

The front legs of Tommy's chair hit the floor with a thunk. "Ah, shit."

The peds expert at the bar took the remote from the bartender, upped the audio even more. "It just happened," she said. "It's near Salem, south of here. I know you're with those air-crash people, I figured—"

Tommy's face reddened. "I was. I quit."

One of the doctors at the table turned to him. "Crash people?"

"NTSB, yeah."

Someone said, "NT . . . ?" and the peds specialist said, "National Transportation Safety Board."

A neurosurgeon from Shanghai said, "When did you quit? I hadn't heard that."

Tommy watched the screen. "Three, four months ago."

The professor's eyebrows rose. "You're fifteen minutes away by helicopter. I always thought time was of the essence in these situations."

Tommy said, "You got a helicopter?"

The woman who had been checking Tommy out was one of the hosting physicians from OHSU. She reached for her purse and produced a cell phone. "We're a level-one trauma center. We've got one, sure."

Tommy watched the smoldering scene for a moment, then checked his watch. Almost 9 P.M. He felt his stomach tightening up and wondered if his ulcer was making a comeback. He nodded without looking at the woman beside him. "Get me there."

## L'ENFANT PLAZA, WASHINGTON, D.C.

Susan Tanaka dashed through the darkened halls of the National Transportation and Safety Board building, empty except for the night cleaning crew. The clocks showed midnight, Eastern Standard Time. She zigged around two guys with floor waxers. "Excuse me," she shouted. "Coming through. Pardon."

Susan was a small woman, only five-two, and she probably didn't weigh 110 pounds soaking wet. The men got out of her way all the same.

Her BlackBerry chirped. Susan wore it in a holster attached to the belt of her wool, camel-brown pin-striped trousers. She swept back the matching Max Mara jacket and snapped up the phone with the fast draw of an Old West gunslinger.

"Tanaka. Sorry, look out!" She zoomed past another janitor.

"Susan?" The shouting voice on the other end was tinny and hollow, the call definitely long distance. There also was an odd whooshing noise in the background.

"Who is this?"

"Tommy Tomzak. You heard?" She realized that he was shouting to be heard over that whooshing noise.

Susan rounded a corner, barely missed knocking over a security guard. "Oops. Sorry. The Vermeer in Oregon? We're on it. Where are you?"

"About five minutes from the site!" Tommy said.

Susan screeched to a dead stop, her Prada heels almost skittering out from beneath her. "What!"

"I was in Portland, at a conference! They're flying me out! I'll be on site in a couple of minutes! I can keep the site pristine until you build a crew! Susan? Can you fucking hear me over this racket?"

Susan swiped back her pitch-black hair, which she wore straight and shoulder length. Her suit was impeccably cut and her silk blouse was the color of brandy. She was a senior incident investigator. In a field dominated by men who wore jeans and steel-toed boots, Susan Tanaka had a reputation for her taste in clothes, wine, art; in short, in everything.

"Are you un-quitting?"

"Hell no! I'll handle the rescue work until your crew leaders get here."

Susan shook her head in awe. "Tommy, the eastern seaboard is socked in. There's a tropical depression off the coast of Georgia. We won't get out of here for hours. If you want in, you're in, but I'm going to make you my Investigator in Charge."

"Tanaka! You're as crazy as any five people I ever met!" he hollered. "No way, no how!"

"Tommy, this will be your fourth major crash investigation; one as part of the pathology team, one as leader of the pathology team, and one as Investigator in Charge! At your age, that's incredible."

"Yeah, but that last one was Kentucky," he replied darkly, "and that was a clusterfuck! Look, I'm not the guy for this work and we both know it. Get out here fast as you can."

And he hung up.

She closed her BlackBerry, started running again. She made it to her office just as one of her assistants arrived, wearing sweats and sneakers, pillow creases evident on her cheek. Susan waved a sheet of paper in front of her.

"We've got a liner on the ground. You call the names on the left, I've got the right. Hurry up; we're building a Go-Team."

## 5

SAN FRANCISCO: KATHRYN DUVALL sat on a couch with a bowl of dry Special K cereal and a tortoise-shell cat on her lap. She was watching *Chocolat,* which she'd Netflixed for the fourth time. The special pager she kept with her twenty-four hours per day chirped.

Lawrence, Kansas: another pager woke up Walter Mulroney. An early riser, Walter had been in bed by nine and fallen asleep with a copy of *East of Eden* on his chest.

Pensacola, Florida: Peter Kim had been making love to his wife when the pager went off at their split-level home overlooking the Gulf. It would not be making too fine a point of it to say that the call ruined the moment.

New Haven, Connecticut: Isaiah Grey was sound asleep, his legs tangled with those of his wife, a fat tabby cat, and the eighty-pound Irish setter that insisted on sleeping perpendicular to them. It took Isaiah a minute to heave the dog off him so he could reach his pager.

Thirty thousand feet over Illinois: John Roby was en route to Toronto. By FAA regulations, his satellite pager couldn't be kept active while he flew, so Susan Tanaka's call was patched through to the copilot of the Boeing 757, who called the senior flight attendant, who went out to first class and informed John that he was being rerouted to Oregon, once they touched down.

"Yeah?" He'd been asleep when the attendant came back. It took him a moment to get his bearings. "Where's Oregon, then?"

The woman smiled. John's scruffy English accent identified him as a resident of Manchester. "Pacific Northwest, between California and Washington. You're with the NTSB?" She kept her voice low, not wanting the others to hear.

"Yeah. Something must be up."

"I'll go up front and ask. The pilots usually hear from the towers. What are you, an investigator?"

"Aye."

"Are you a pilot or engineer?"

He said, "Mad bomber."

## MARION COUNTY

The Life Flight helicopter from Oregon Health & Science University touched down a little after 9 P.M. Tommy was sweating despite the cold, and the sour, acidic feeling in his stomach hadn't gotten any better. He wasn't dressed for the field, but at least his cowboy boots were better designed for fieldwork than the loafers he'd considered wearing. One of the other docs had loaned him a fully lined coat. The temperature had just dropped under forty degrees.

Fire trucks were just now arriving from both directions, Portland and Salem. Ambulances were on the scene, too, at least six, with more dome lights visible in the distance, inching through insane traffic to reach the scene. Traffic on Interstate 5 had slowed to a crawl in both directions, and the emergency vehicles were moving exclusively along the shoulders. State troopers were there, but they didn't have much work to do.

For all that frenzy, Tommy couldn't take his eyes off the blackened, still-smoldering gouge that had been clawed diagonally through a field of grass. The tail section and about a third of the fuselage lay nearby, the grass before the open end of the fuselage littered with overturned seats and human bodies and survivors. The rest of the fuselage was a quarter mile away. One wing was missing.

Once the helo was on the ground, Tommy unbuckled, gave the pilot a thumbs-up, and leaped out. He dashed across the grass, flagged down two of the state-police officers, and flashed them the badge he had never bothered to throw away when he resigned. "Dr. Leonard Tomzak, NTSB," he lied. "We got federal authority over any airplane- or train-crash site. You fellas okay with that?"

One of the troopers eyed him critically. "You're a doctor?"

Tommy nodded. "Pathologist. Are we cool?"

The trooper shrugged.

"Good. I've got to organize the rescue teams but I'm dressed like a fucking civilian. You guys have the badges and the guns and the cool hats, you come with me."

"Sure," the trooper said. He was happy to be able to do something. Anything.

A woman in work boots, jeans, and a Royal Navy sweater was standing nearby and overhead them. Her hair was pitch black and pulled back into a ponytail. "You're NTSB?"

Tommy said, "Close enough," but she hardly listened.

"Thank God! Angela Abdalla, Portland International Airport. We're supposed to oversee the rescue ops, but I've never, um . . ."

She waved blindly toward the wreckage. Tommy suspected that Angela Abdalla was petrified even to look in that direction. *Smart lady,* he thought.

"I have," he said. "I don't want to be stepping on anyone's toes, ma'am, but I'm glad to help, at least until the Go-Team is assembled."

Angela shook his hand, her almond-shaped eyes glittering with tears. "Thank God, Doc—"

"Tommy," he cut in. "Come with us."

"Here." She shrugged out of her NTSB windbreaker and handed it to Tommy. It fit well enough, and it made him look like the guy in charge. Angela accepted the coat he had borrowed in its place.

Tommy, Angela, and the troopers moved toward the cluster of fire trucks and ambulances just as the first foray of rescuers were about to head out into the field. Tommy leaped up onto the hood of a fire department incident-command station wagon, the shock absorbers making the car bounce under his weight. Every eye turned in his direction as he held up his folding pocket ID.

"I'm Dr. Tomzak, National Transportation and Safety Board. I'm gonna need y'all to follow my orders. All right?"

"Maybe later, bub." One of the paramedics surged to the front of the group, holding a med kit in one beefy hand and a litter under the other arm. He wore a baseball cap backward. "Write a memo. We got work to do."

"Officer," Tommy said, "arrest his ass."

The troopers didn't move, but neither did the paramedics. The guy with the battlefield litter said, "Are you shitting me?"

"Please listen to him!" Angela Abdalla pleaded.

Tommy nodded, understanding where the paramedic was coming from. "Sorry, folks. I've seen three major airliner crashes. I'm a pathologist now but I did two tours in the army as a field surgeon and before that I did my ER rotation at a downtown hospital in Baltimore. I've set up triage units from Kuwait to Kentucky. I know how to do this. Anyone else want to be in charge, or you want me to do it?"

It didn't take the crews long to figure out which they wanted.

"Good," Tommy shouted over the sounds of traffic and sirens and the hiss of burning grass. "We're gonna find three kinds of patients in there. And, God willing, maybe a fourth. Type one is the wounded. Ambos, you'll get them out of here as fast as we can. Type two is the dead. Don't move them. Repeat: do not move the dead unless it's to get to a wounded patient. Type three is the badly wounded and traumatized. How far are we, timewise, from trauma hospitals?"

An ambulance driver answered first. "When the plane crashed, half the rubberneckers on the highway slammed into each other. There's snarl-ups to the north and south. We'll have to use back roads. That puts Salem Hospital at least forty minutes away. Portland's nearest hospital is Meridian Park but it doesn't have trauma status. And it's an hour away."

Tommy shook his head. "We got enough birds to fly out the wounded?"

"There's only three Life Flight helos in Portland," a paramedic answered. "Salem doesn't have any."

Tommy rubbed the back of his neck. When dealing with the critically wounded, time was one of the biggest X factors. He watched an Itasca motor home crawl by in the molasseslike traffic. He turned to one of the troopers.

"All right. Okay. Ah, tell your people to commandeer the next couple three mobile homes or recreational vehicles that pass by. They've got beds, water, and electricity; like it or not, they're about to become a MASH unit."

One of the cops said, "Is that legal?"

Tommy shrugged. "The fuck should I know?"

The cop shrugged, too.

"Good. Firefighters, we're not going to dump water on this scene unless something blows up but good. That'll just make slogging through the mud harder, and it might hurt the wounded. Instead, I need you guys to set up a perimeter. Start walking this field and all the adjacent fields. Both sides of the freeway. If you find any type of debris from the crash, mark it with something. One of your helmets, a flashlight, a flare—anything. We're establishing the field of play and we need to know its exact dimensions."

Several of the firefighters cast glances at one another.

Tommy raised his hands. "I know: this sounds like scut work. You guys are used to being the lifesavers. Believe me, what you're doing will be pretty damn important in the weeks and months to come."

The firefighters agreed.

"Okay, let's do this. Half of the paramedics, follow me to the tail section. The rest of you, go ahead and try to drive your rigs a little closer to the main fuselage. Not too close. Don't go in. Check for survivors in the field, but don't go into the fuselage till I say it's cool. Another thing: I've got a feeling the captain dumped his fuel, but there's still a hell of a lot of stuff that can burn on these ships. And this is important: we're looking for two boxes, about the size of truck batteries. They're the black boxes. No matter what all y'all might've heard, they ain't black. They're bright orange. Sing out if you find them.

"One last thing: you people are professionals. You've seen it all, the worst of the worst. But there's going to be some shit here that you've never seen before and, God forbid, you shouldn't ever have to see again. If it gets to you: good, you're still a human being. Puke if you have to: I'm a canoe maker, and I always toss my cookies at these things. Just try to mark it somehow. Everything in this field is evidence, even your dinner. Got it?"

They got it.

"Good. Questions?"

A firefighter raised his hand. "You said we might find a fourth kind of person?"

"Right. The uninjured. It's rare, but it happens. More questions?"

The EMT in front, the one who'd challenged Tommy's authority, said, "Canoe maker?"

"Think about how you carve out a canoe from a tree. Now think about autopsies."

The guy said, "Oh."

"More questions? Okay, folks, let's do this."

The time was 9:10 P.M.

## WILSONVILLE, OREGON

Dennis Silverman found an International House of Pancakes that was open twenty-four hours a day. He took the home-built laptop in with him and ordered blueberry pancakes because, well, it said *pancakes* in the name, so it seemed rude to order anything else. Another customer had left a copy of *USA Today* and he tried to concentrate on the stories, while a cacophony of sirens rose and faded continually from Interstate 5.

At 9:30 P.M. exactly, Dennis went outside to the pay phone and fed quarters into the slot. He dialed the number he'd memorized. It was long distance. The phone rang three times, then an answering machine clicked on. No greeting, just the elongated beep.

"Did you watch the news?" Dennis said. "Did you like what you saw? If so, you sweeten up my offshore account and I'll drop the next jet in less than seventy hours."

He hung up.

## ELSEWHERE

A jetliner in Vancouver, British Columbia, waited a full ninety minutes for John Roby to land and switch planes before taking off for PDX. Airline officials are quick to help get NTSB officials wherever they have to go, no questions asked, although, secretly, few pilots liked having the investigators on board. It seemed like tempting the fates, somehow.

John was eager to get to the scene. As an explosives-and-fire expert, he could collect tons of data just by standing on the scene, lifting his nose to the sky, and sniffing. The smells of a crash site are essential clues.

Walter Mulroney, an ex-Boeing chief engineer, was a big-boned, rangy Kansan with wind-raw skin and permanent wrinkles in the leathery areas around his eyes. He looked more like a farmer than a man holding a doctorate in aeronautical engineering. He would be heading up the structures team.

The plane that had gone down was a Vermeer, not a Boeing. Made on the other end of the continent, in North Carolina, Vermeer was Boeing's major American rival. Even though he had worked for Boeing, Walter was pretty sure he could rebuild any Vermeer from the ground up. It might not be necessary; usually, a complete reconstruction isn't. But if they needed one, he was the best man for the job.

As Tommy Tomzak was leaping onto the hood of the incident-command vehicle, Walter was carrying his single suitcase with him up the ramp of a DC-10 at the Lawrence airport, en route to Denver and then on to Portland. In the bag were several changes of clothes, his NTSB wind-breaker and ball cap, and his well-worn Bible, King James Version.

Peter Kim was a civilian engineer who worked for the United States Air Force. His specialty was the power plant, including the engines and the engine mounts. Living down in Pensacola gave him the greatest distance to cover, but that wasn't a problem. The air force agreed to fly Peter in a trainer all the way to Los Angeles, where he could catch a direct flight to PDX. He'd be among the first crew leaders to arrive.

In New Haven, Connecticut, Isaiah Grey kissed his wife, LaToya, goodbye.

"Go fight the good fight," she said, helping him pack his dilapidated, mismatched luggage.

Isaiah checked himself in the hall mirror. African American and forty, he was as fit today as he had been in the air force. Lately, his close-cropped hair had begun to go salt-and-pepper above his ears. LaToya told him it was sexy, so he didn't do anything to stop it, but secretly, the gray hair annoyed him every time he looked in the mirror.

A former air force pilot—certified in fixed-wing jets and propeller aircraft as well as military-grade helicopters—Isaiah would be given the duty of handling the operations crew for the NTSB investigation. His arena would be the preflight and the flight itself.

Kathryn Duvall, known to everyone as Kiki, lived in San Francisco and had the shortest distance to travel. She was a former navy lieutenant, ro-tating out at the grand old age of thirty-three, with experience in subma-rines as an audio and sonar officer. In fact, she was one of the first five women ever to do long-mission service in an American sub. She'd gar-nered a reputation in the nuclear-powered fleet as a "sonar witch," an of-ficer who could see with her ears better than most humans do with their eyes. Within five hours of her honorable discharge, she'd received a call from a complete stranger who identified herself as Susan Tanaka, offering her a job with the NTSB. That had been two years ago. Susan discovered early on in her career that submarine sonar jockeys made the best cockpit voice-recorder specialists.

Susan Tanaka had no real hope of the weather letting up in Washington, so she climbed into her candy-apple-red Miata and zoomed to Philadelphia, where, she was assured, the weather was calm enough to get a plane off the ground. Although she would be designated the intergovernmental liaison for this specific Go-Team, she'd be the last member to get to the crash site, a fact that made her drive like a maniac.

Other specialists were on the road or in the air that night. There were crews assigned to handle hydraulics, electronics, air traffic control, and operations, such as preparation and the flight itself. There were experts in reading maintenance records, and in transcribing the invaluable flight data recorder, which, with the cabin voice recorder, made up the so-called black boxes.

There also were crewmembers who would report directly to Tommy Tomzak and John Roby and Kiki Duvall and Walter Mulroney and Peter Kim and Isaiah Grey. In all, 120 experts were called out of their beds that Monday evening. Each of them was being called to a spot on the map they knew little or nothing about. No one knew exactly what they'd find when they got there. But they each had a job to do.

6

THE IRISHMAN CALLING HIMSELF Jack picked two Glock 9s, a Para-Ordnance .45, and the Colt Python from the stash in Daria Gibron's West Los Angeles cottage, plus four boxes of parabellum rounds. She told him the going price and he paid cash without haggling. Very un–Middle Eastern, no bargaining, but she didn't complain.

She offered him a vodka. He accepted.

"Selling guns on American soil," he said, as she pulled the Grey Goose bottle from the freezer in the kitchen of her 1940s-style stucco cottage. "Please take this in the spirit it's intended, miss. That takes balls."

She poured a fingerful in two mismatched glasses, handed one to him. They clinked their glasses. "It does at that."

"How do I know they're any good?"

Daria picked up the Para-Ordnance. Keeping her eyes locked on Jack's eyes, she slid the full magazine from the beveled grip and jacked the single round out of the firing chamber. She pushed in on the recoil spring plunger and rotated the barrel bushing to free the spring and the bushing itself. She yanked back on the slide and removed the slide stop. Never taking her eyes off Jack, she pushed the slide forward and off the frame. She removed the recoil spring and its guide, pulled apart the barrel. Smiling, she spread out the stripped components of the automatic on her counter. Jack dragged his eyes off her. The components were clean and well taken care of. He could smell cordite and linseed oil. Smiling and with his eyes locked on hers, he proved that he could quickly reassemble the automatic without looking, too.

He said, "Been doing this long, have you."

She smiled. "I've got all the dates and sales, with receipts, in a folder in the bedroom."

Jack laughed, downed his drink in a gulp. "Aye, and that was a stupid question. I apologize."

"Forgiven."

He glanced around. There were no knickknacks in her apartment. A few photos, but they looked generic. Nothing was out of place and nothing showed a "feminine hand." It was a stopping point, not a home. Given any trouble, he realized, she could ghost from this place in a heartbeat, mourn nothing left behind. He liked that. A lot.

Unbidden, he grabbed the bottle and drank directly from it. He wiped his lips with the back of his hand and Daria noted scar tissue on the tips of his fingers.

"Now, about that good time . . ." Jack purred.

Daria finished her drink. "Go back to your mates, Jack. Tuck them into bed with visions of nine-millimeter angels watching over them."

Jack stood his ground. And Daria stood hers. Jack smiled and she smiled. And Daria got the sense that, had she quivered, had she demurred, he'd have grabbed her. But in the end, he nodded and set down the bottle and accepted the cheap duffel bag she gave him to carry his guns in. And said his gentlemanly goodbyes and slipped out the door.

Daria was just a little disappointed about how it went down, but there you are. *Land of milk and honey,* she thought. *Bloody lot of good it does you if you can't handle lactose and you've diabetes to boot.*

She watched him walk toward Crescent. When he was a good distance away, Daria slipped out of her stilettos, poured a much healthier drink, and dialed a ten-digit number from memory.

"Em," she said when the line hissed. "Zero, zero, nine, dee."

A male voice chuckled. "How's everyone's favorite gunrunner tonight?"

"A mark just left. Calls himself Jack. He bought four guns and ammunition." She described the make and model of the weapons.

"Okay," the voice said. "You're amazing. We really do appreciate this, Ms. Gibron. Are you okay? Anything you need?"

*A good hard ride by a man who looks like our Jack,* she thought. "No. I'm fine. He was positioned right for the CC camera. I'm fairly sure you'll get a good ID."

"No worries, ma'am. You hit your panic button, the Alcohol, Tobacco and Firearms team is at your door. You have a good night now."

She hung up.


The man calling himself Jack checked his watch. Ten till ten. He walked three blocks to Edinburgh Avenue, found a pay phone. He fed it, looked up a number scribbled on the inside of the paper wrapper from a stick of gum. The phone rang three times. When the recording machine came on, he hit the 5 button to play back messages.

A scratchy, long-distance voice on the machine said, "Did you watch the news? Did you like what you saw? If so, you sweeten up my offshore account and I'll drop the next jet in less than seventy hours."

Oh, fuck yes, the man calling himself Jack said. He'd liked it just fine. He unfolded a piece of notebook paper in his shirt pocket, studied the long string of letters and digits linked to a Cayman Islands account.

# 7

TOMMY TOMZAK WISHED THE NTSB jacket he'd borrowed were lined. The temperature was dropping fast. He had ditched his tie in the helicopter and would never see it again. He'd stuffed a box of thin plastic gloves in his right-hand jacket pocket and would swap them regularly throughout the night. He had a plastic garbage bag in his left-hand pocket, where he'd stuff the used, soiled gloves rather than dump them on the ground.

By ten o'clock, many of the easily moved patients were away, leaving only the more seriously wounded; the ones who would require triage on the ground before being moved. Tommy checked a note he'd written to himself. The jet had smashed to the ground at 8:41. They'd gotten the "easy gets," the ambulatory patients, out in under an hour and a half. That was remarkable.

Also, because he was there to direct traffic, the first responders hadn't messed up the evidence. In the months to come, that could prove crucial.

*There's no reason on earth this has to be Kentucky all over again,* he told himself.

Fire trucks and police cruisers were training more than twenty high-energy lights on the field. The wild array of low-to-the-ground light sources threw monstrous, stretched-out shadows every which way. Tommy's team slogged through the field, which wasn't as muddy as he'd feared, toward the gigantic tail section. Bits of shrapnel and luggage lay everywhere. As they drew closer, they could hear the crackle of burning grass on the perimeter of the gouge and the moaning of victims. Tommy had been lucky enough to miss a famed 737 crash near Pittsburgh, in which the jet had nosed into the ground at full throttle. Not only were there no survivors, there were damned few identifiable body parts. The entire scene had been a schmear of ex-plane and ex-human, and the teams had worked in full biohazard suits, since blood-borne pathogens could have been anywhere.

This liner hadn't augured in, it had pancaked in. That made all the difference in the world.

"What the hell is this field?" Tommy asked, glancing around. "It looks like the world's biggest lawn."

"We grow grasses all over Marion County," an emergency medical technician told him. "Grass is a profit crop around here."

"And you're not saying *grass,* as in primo shit, right?"

The med tech smiled grimly, nodded, too, as if to say, Thanks for the gallows humor, I appreciate the effort.

They found a body fifty feet from the tail section. It was a torso and two arms and one leg. No head. It wore an orange-and-black sweatshirt with the Oregon State University logo and blue jeans with tube socks and Nikes. Tommy marched past it, knowing that one of the NTSB officials heading their way would be bringing the flags that would be mounted beside each dead body.

The next body was a child, maybe age eight. A girl. She had a butterfly barrette in her blond hair. A very large section of her abdomen was missing.

Two more bodies, both female. They found an arm farther on. The arm wore a Mickey Mouse watch. Later, another team member would note that the watch was still ticking, the time exactly right.

Tommy heard moaning and sprinted ahead. The EMTs hustled to keep up with him, their flashlights bobbing in the night. The burning grass helped to illuminate the scene but, thankfully, wasn't burning enough to endanger them.

Tommy knelt. It was a man, in his eighties, lying on his back, eyes open and wide, mouth open and moving but with little sounds coming out. The man probably had false teeth but they were missing. His hair stood askew, at all angles. He was belted into a seat. The back hinge had snapped, and the seat lay flat like a dentist's chair, the safety belt still around the man's lap. In his hand was a paperback copy of a Grisham novel, clutched like a life raft in the Atlantic. One of his legs was badly broken, the bone exposed just above the knee. From the nasty angle of his foot, his ankle was broken, too.

Tommy had a penlight, which, along with a Swiss army knife, he carried at all times. He shone the penlight in the man's eyes, one after another. "Can you hear me, sir?"

"Wh-what . . ." The man was in deep shock.

Tommy stood. "Broken leg, broken ankle. Bleeder at the knee. No obvious damage to the head, neck, or chest. The seat's too heavy to carry and it won't support his legs, or I'd suggest using it as a backboard. Switch him to a litter."

Two EMTs hustled to follow orders. Others had leapfrogged ahead of Tommy and had found their own injured.

Tommy knelt by a woman who was doubled in two, holding her stomach, her chin and mouth covered with vomit. She was sobbing, bucking as if in seizures.

"'S okay," Tommy crooned. "'S all right, ma'am. Here we go." He gently probed her abdomen, stopped when she hissed in agony. "All right. Hang on. We'll get you out of here."

"M . . . m . . . m . . ." The woman struggled to stop sobbing, to speak.

Tommy said, "Shh. Hey! Get a litter over here. We've got a possible ruptured spleen."

Behind the oncoming EMTs, Tommy could see the first commandeered Winnebago arrive; his field hospital was taking shape.

"M . . . my d-daughter . . ." The woman on the ground spit the words out between sobs.

"Shh. We'll find her. You'll be okay."

They started loading her onto a litter.

Tommy moved to the next shape groaning in the grass, a man with neither leg attached below the knee.

# 8

SUSAN TANAKA DOWNSHIFTED AND zipped past a Porsche like it was standing still. She was on Interstate 95, outside Chester, Pennsylvania and was moving at thirty miles over the speed limit.

Susan would have looked like an early-twenty-first-century version of Emma Peel, if Mrs. Peel had been five-two and Asian American. Today she wore a black leather peacoat she'd purchased in Milan, a black pencil skirt, a metallic-gold ribbed sweater, and calfskin boots imported from Gucci. She was a size-two petite and could get away with the look. People tended to make fun of her fashion-plate sensibility. Susan didn't mind: she gave money to the United Way and National Public Radio, she adopted dogs from the pound, and she usually fed her change into those Special Olympics canisters at the checkout lane. And for doing all that penance, she indulged in her single greatest passion: she shopped.

Her Miata was Bluetoothed to the max, giving her global positioning capability as well as worldwide cell-phone service. Just in the last year, the comm system had become standard for all NTSB Go-Teams. The other section leaders couldn't use them in the air, of course, but several of them had been delivered to an FAA official at Portland International Airport. As soon as the section chiefs arrived, they'd be linked up.

Another unit was traveling via helicopter from PDX to Legacy Good

Samaritan Hospital, to pick up two emergency-room physicians who'd volunteered to staff Tommy's makeshift field hospital. Susan smiled as she smoked a Nissan Z car, passing on the right. According to the report she'd just received from her assistant, Tommy was using RVs as a field hospital. Brilliant. Illegal as hell, of course. The police might be able to commandeer private vehicles, but the NTSB sure couldn't and the sheriff's office was working at Tommy's behest. Susan sensed that there would be administrative hell to pay, maybe from Del Wildman himself, her boss and director of the NTSB. If that came along, she'd handle it. In the meantime, Tommy was saving lives, minimizing the catastrophe. She'd take that trade-off.

Saving lives isn't the domain of the Go-Team. The job, simply, is to find out why an aircraft crashed, then to make recommendations to the six-member board to keep other aircraft from suffering the same fate. Maybe the team would recommend that a part be added to the construction, or removed. Maybe they'd find a bomb and recommend some new airport safety procedure. Or maybe, like Tommy's last Go-Team assignment, they'd work for eighteen months and come away empty-handed. It happened. Flyers like to say that an airliner is two hundred thousand parts flying in close formation. Not all the parts are vital, but many are. Many can cause catastrophes only if they fail in tandem. That's called a binary problem: if part A works fine but part B fails, the plane won't fall from the sky. If B is okay but A fails, no problem. But if A and B both fail, the plane hits the earth.

Sometimes it doesn't take two malfunctions; it takes three. Or four.

Sometimes the part that fails is called the pilot.

The permutations were endless. Susan had heard a mathematician well schooled in chaos theory talk about infinite paths in a finite space. She knew that a crash investigation could take on that sort of mythical, never-ending life of its own.

Susan hoped that CascadeAir 818 wasn't going to be one of those.

She was still a mile from Philadelphia International Airport, traveling at eighty miles an hour, when her communications unit, designed for use by NTSB Go-Teams, chirped. She was wearing an ear jack and a voice wand, attached by a thin wire to a transmitter on her belt. The actual satellite phone sat on her matching bags in the passenger's seat. She toggled the belt device. "Tanaka."

"Susan? Tommy."

"You got your headset already?" That had been quick.

"Yeah, thanks. And a team of volunteers just got here from PDX and the FAA. They've got the flags, sticks, the outside markers; everything."

Almost every major airport in the United States has a storeroom tucked away in some corner, filled with crash-investigation equipment from the NTSB. The supplies include hundreds of pennant-shaped flags on short wire rods that can be shoved into the ground. Red flags mean dead bodies; green are injured who need to be moved; yellow are injured who can't be moved. Blue flags represent important findings, like the black boxes or obvious bomb debris.

The volunteers from the Federal Aviation Administration and the Portland International Airport personnel had been trained how to mark the circumference of a crash scene. As soon as they got started, they realized that the fire crews from adjacent cities, towns, and rural fire districts had begun the project already, outlining the scene with helmets and boots and flashlights and even lunch buckets.

"That's great news," Susan said, and skittered out from behind a semi, nearly shoving a delivery van off the freeway. She shot forward, snuggled back into the slow lane, crept past a Saturn, then swung out and pulled away. "What's it like?"

"Ah, we got two major sections down and separated. The fuselage split just aft of the wings. One wing's missing; damned if I know where. I just finished triage on the tail-section passengers."

"How many survivors?"

"I don't know. Twenty, maybe. Do you have a manifest yet?"

Susan had the information stored as a Word document on her Black-Berry. She activated it. "Ah . . . Okay, one captain, one copilot, three attendants, a hundred and forty-one registered passengers. That's one forty-six souls, if everyone got on board."

"Understood. We've stopped to get some water and to rest. I've got med techs working the forward section. I'm going to go check on them here in a— What?"

Susan could hear everything Tommy said but not much of the background noise. He sounded tired and he still had a hell of a night ahead of him. She checked her watch. It was two in the morning, Eastern Standard; 11 P.M. Pacific.

"Here you go," he said to someone. "Thanks. Susan? I've signed for the supplies, the volunteers are getting going. I borrowed an NTSB jacket, so for now, nobody knows I quit."

"Um. Right." She took the off-ramp at fifty-five miles per hour.

"Who're the section chiefs?"

"We've got Walter Mulroney on structures and Peter Kim on power plant. Do you know them?"

"Sure. Mulroney's good. He'll be your IIC?"

*No, you thick Texas hick. You're the Investigator in Charge!* "We'll see, Tommy. The team's still coming together. Oh! John Roby's coming."

She could hear the smile in Tommy's voice and guessed it was the first time he'd smiled in hours. "He's crazy but he's usually right. Also, he's a cop. Retired or not, we may need his creative eye for villainy."

She named several other section chiefs. Most he knew, some he didn't. There are many volunteers sprinkled around the nation who work for Go-Teams, but it's a small community. Most "crashers" know one another, at least by reputation.

"Hey, who's on CVR?" he asked.

Susan winced; Tommy rarely missed details, and the cockpit-voice-recorder specialist is a key player. She said, "Kiki," and left it at that.

"Ah," Tommy said.

"Okay, I'm here. I'll be in the air as soon as I can. Keep it together, Tommy."

"Okay," he said. "See ya."


The next time Tommy stopped long enough to gulp bottled water and glance at his wristwatch, an hour had passed.

It was 12:05 A.M.

The NTSB uses midnight-to-midnight to define a day. Even though the jet had only been on the ground since 8:41 P.M. Pacific, it was officially Day Two. The thought made Tommy's stomach roll. The clock wouldn't stop ticking.

It hadn't in Kentucky. It had ticked and ticked and ticked for eighteen months. He felt a sour taste in his mouth and feared that he was about to puke. *Thank God I didn't let Susan rope me back in,* he thought.

Slipping his ear jack into his shirt pocket, Tommy found the two ER doctors from Good Samaritan already at work, figuring out the order of patients they'd see in the recreational vehicles turned MASH unit. *Stop thinking about Kentucky,* he told himself. *Fuck Kentucky. This is Oregon. Get this done.*

Tommy introduced himself to the ER doctors.

"This should work," said the younger of the two men, a trauma surgeon with thoracic credentials. He patted the side of the RV lovingly. "I've never heard of it being done."

"Me neither, but we've already got a dozen people who can't be moved much. I figure you guys get them stabilized here, it'll mean that much less traffic at the actual hospitals. Good luck."

He left them, grabbed a restocked med kit from one of the EMTs, finished the last of the Gatorade someone handed him, and started jogging toward the front half of CascadeAir Flight 818.

He glanced up. Four helicopters from Portland TV stations hung in the air, capturing it all.

He looked at his luminous watch again. Midnight and change. They'd off-lifted more than a dozen survivors and transferred eight to the field hospital. How many more were waiting for him up front?

Not many. There were far more deaths in the front of the plane than in the aft sections.

Tommy could smell charred flesh and fresh vomit from the EMTs, as well as the acrid stench of electricity and burned plastic. He hadn't reminded the med techs to avoid the high-voltage lines. Just because the engines were off didn't mean that all batteries were dead. He hoped they'd have enough common sense to realize that.

The fuselage loomed over him, blotting out the stars. Everything was cocked at a fifteen-degree angle, one wing and its crushed engines on the ground, the other wing mysteriously missing. The lower deck, where cargo and avionics were stored, had been crushed, its contents spewed throughout the field. The inside of the vessel was dimly limned by the arc lights set up by the sheriff's troopers, a quarter mile away at the field hospital. Every time a cable sparked, it sent a harsh flash of pure white light into the belly of the beast. With each flash, Tommy caught a quick glimpse of a face, eyes and mouth wide open, or a severed limb or a splotch of body fluid. He didn't really see them at the moment of the electrical arc, but the afterimages burned into his eyes and bored into his brain.

*Ah, God. This is going to be a bad one.*

"Have y'all stayed outside of this thing?" he asked a med tech who was just rising from the hunched, back-twitching effort to dry heave.

"Yes, sir. Like you said, we don't know how dangerous it is."

"Good. Here's the rundown: that's one big-assed hot zone. There's blood everywhere. Gather everybody, would you? Gimme that."

He took the med tech's halogen flashlight. Inhaling deeply through his mouth, Tommy thumbed the light and shone it into the fuselage. The afterimages he'd glimpsed popped into view, all the colors washed out by the harsh light of the flash. Half of the interior seats had been ripped from the deck and scattered around the field. Greasy smears of blood had been daubed on every surface, glinting like oil. The dead were everywhere. Tommy walked sideways, circling the hulk at a safe distance, studying the scene within. He was going in there and he honest-to-God didn't want to.

Paramedics were jogging in his direction, awaiting orders. All resistance to an outsider telling them what to do had faded.

Someone was standing to Tommy's left, staring at the craft. Tommy glanced over. The man wore a suit coat and trousers, a white shirt and forest-green striped tie. His tasseled loafers and his cuffs were caked with mud. He was maybe fifty-five. He sure didn't look like a med tech.

"Sir?" Tommy said, praying that the guy wasn't a journalist who'd gotten onto the scene. "Are you supposed to be here?"

"No." The man shook his head but didn't take his eyes off the ruined craft. "I'm really not."

"If you're not part of the rescue effort, I'm going to have to ask you to leave."

The guy still couldn't take his eyes off the ruin. He shrugged a little and said, "Sure."

But he didn't move. Tommy flicked the beam of his light over the man's face. He was pale, eyes dilated, in shock. Tommy glanced back at the highway, saw the fire trucks and ambulances and police vehicles and incident-command vehicles and confiscated RVs. It didn't look like any other civilian vehicles had stopped.

He turned to the man who stared at the plane. "How'd you get here?"

The man nodded at the plane. The penny dropped and Tommy realized what the hell was happening. The man reached into his sports-coat pocket and withdrew the folder that contained his ticket and baggage-claim check. He handed them to Tommy.

"Um. Okay. Wow. These men are medics. Is it okay if they take a look at you, Mister—" He opened the folder and held it in the beam of light. "Mr. Weintraub?"

"Sure," the man said. And stared at the plane.

Tommy told the nearest med tech what had happened. Mr. Weintraub didn't put up any protest when the medic turned him gently and escorted him to the triage staging area.

"Jesus Christ," a paramedic hissed, and made the sign of the cross. "His hair isn't even mussed!"

Tommy looked at the ticket again. Seat 10-B. He tucked the ticket into his hip pocket. He played his flashlight around the ground and found a crumpled raincoat. He bent to lift it up and it was covered in gore. Explained how Weintrab looked so pristine.

"All right." Tommy raised his voice, roused himself from shock. "Who's got hazmat training?"

Half a dozen hands went up.

"Any of you guys ever in the military?"

Three hands stayed up.

"See any combat?"

Two hands.

"Okay, it's the three of us. Everyone else, hang back."

He turned to the two people whose hands were in the hair: a black man who looked like a linebacker and a woman, maybe five-five, with short-cropped hair and five rings in each ear. "There could be blood-borne pathogens on every surface in there but I don't want to drag out the biohazard suits if we don't have to. We also don't know how stable the craft is. It's going to be dangerous and it's going to be messy and it's going to be a little slice of hell. I'm not ordering you in, but I could use the help. Don't go if you don't want to. No questions asked."

The med techs glanced at one another, then nodded to Tommy.

Tommy inhaled deeply and led the way, hoping no one noticed that his hands were shaking.

# 9

KIKI DUVALL AND PETER Kim arrived at Portland International Airport within ten minutes of each other and were escorted by airport police to a flight attendants' lounge. Each carried one piece of luggage. Peter's was sturdy and stylish and made of space-age polymers. Kiki's was a navy-issue duffel bag.

The difference in their luggage was reflected in their demeanor. Peter was a civilian working with the air force, but he'd taken on a military air. He had very little sense of humor. He thought of himself as a diligent worker and a stern father and a good American. He'd emigrated from South Korea at age three. Not by nature a gifted student, he had worked his tail off to get through high school and Stanford and into his air force job at Pensacola and into the NTSB. He cut no one any slack, least of all himself.

Kiki had been a naval officer and had rotated out as a lieutenant, but she was much more casual than Peter. She tended to wear jeans and sweatshirts and scuffed hiking boots. At five foot ten, she was a jock who liked to sail and play volleyball. After years of discipline as a submariner, she'd moved to San Francisco and lived a life of luxury as an audio consultant for the arts community, as well as occasional jobs for the NTSB. She had sandy-red hair, the tips bleached blond by hours spent muscling a skiff through the Bay, pulled back into a ponytail with a simple rubber band. At thirty-five, she still had a sprinkling of freckles on her nose and cheeks.

She and Peter were the only people in Terminal C, with the exception of two janitors and Angela Abdalla, the airport official who had turned the crash site over to Tommy. She had stayed on the scene until around eleven, when it became obvious that the wounded were being evacuated in an orderly manner and safety crews had things well under control. The best thing she could do, after that, was to shepherd the NTSB crews into position.

She greeted them by shaking their hands. "How was your flight?"

"Better than the Vermeer's," Peter said. He wasn't joking. "Shall we go?"

"Can we hold off?" she asked. "We've got another one of your guys coming in, about five minutes out, and a fourth member will land in about twenty-five minutes. We only have the one helicopter available tonight."

"That's fine," Kiki said and flopped down on a couch, picking up a discarded copy of *The Wall Street Journal.*

"No, it's not." Peter looked at his watch. "I want to get out there now. You can send the helo back for the others."

Kiki rolled her eyes. "It's dark. They're still off-loading survivors. There were survivors?" She cocked a rust-colored eyebrow at Angela.

"Yes."

"So what?" Peter said. "I want to see my engines."

"Your engines will be there in an hour. We'll wait."

"Who made you the boss?" he asked brusquely.

Angela Abdalla was getting more and more uncomfortable.

Kiki looked up from her newspaper and curled her legs up under her. She smiled languidly. "You're right. I'm not IIC. Neither are you. Call Susan and ask her if we should wait a half hour, so four section leaders can be on site, or if your needs outweigh everyone else's."

Peter narrowed his eyes, and his lips went white. He wasn't used to being slapped down like that. Finally, with effort, he turned to Angela and granted her a single nod. Grateful, she rushed out.

Peter said, "I don't appreciate your tone."

Kiki said, "Oh," in the same way you'd react if someone in an elevator said, "My dog is a spaniel." She went back to her paper.


John Roby, the bomb expert from England, Walter Mulroney, who would head up the structures unit, and Isaiah Grey, the ex-pilot who would lead the ops crew, arrived within a half hour, were given their communication units, and were escorted out to the tarmac. Many of them had worked to-gether at one crash or another. Other section leaders, including Susan Tanaka, the intergovernmental liaison, were still hours away.

It was 12:20 A.M. Pacific.


## THIRTY THOUSAND FEET OVER WISCONSIN

There's a folding metal seat in the cockpit of Boeing 737s that can be used for a flight engineer or a visiting pilot or dignitary. The pilot let Susan Tanaka use the space, once she'd flashed her ID to the senior flight attendant. Neither the pilot nor the copilot was crazy about having a crasher in their cockpit.

She wore a headset, and the copilot had set up the secondary-communication array to the right frequency. Susan could talk to her staff in Washington, and they, in turn, could link her into the building's telephone system.

She heard a dial tone followed by ringing. "Chemeketa Inn, how may I direct your call?"

"Reservations, please."

"One moment please." Muzak. "Reservations."

"Yes, I need to book some rooms. My name is Susan Tanaka and I'm with the National Transportation Safety Board. Our people are investigating that plane crash, just north of you."

"Oh! I heard about that on my commute! My God, how many are dead?"

"We don't know yet."

"Well, how many rooms will you be needing?"

Susan said, "All of them."

"Um. Excuse me?"

"We need every room you have available. Book them for three weeks, please. And as other people move out, I'll take those rooms, too."

"Um . . . ah, well, yes . . . I see. This isn't really the high season and we are a rather large hotel, Ms. Tanaka. We have seventy-three empty rooms now and—"

"Perfect. I'll take them. How many total rooms do you have?"

"Two hundred and twenty-four, but—"

"Excellent. We'll take them all as they become available. My assistant is faxing you a credit-card authorization now. Good day."

## FORWARD SECTION

The fuselage had ended its journey at about ten degrees nose-up. The landing gear hadn't been deployed, and the avionics deck had been flattened on impact. Consequently, the opening was only about five feet off the ground. Tommy Tomzak and his two volunteers could step right into the wreckage with only a little help. Once there, they would have to walk uphill to the front of the plane.

The fuselage also was twisted to the left, so the ceiling of the passenger deck faced the eleven-o'clock mark, the floor at five o'clock. Walking up the aisle would be difficult, especially since they'd have to keep ducking every time an exposed wire sparked.

Tommy and the volunteers waited until firefighters scrounged up three yellow overalls for them, plus thicker gloves than the disposables they'd used so far.

The plane had cracked in two just aft of the wings, at row twenty-seven. The seats for rows nineteen through twenty-seven had been dumped out of the plane and had been found earlier in the field, with no survivors.

Rows eighteen through one were left in place. And almost immediately, the rescue party realized that they weren't going to find any survivors. The bodies were everywhere, some still in their seats, others sprawled. Men, women. Children. The big paramedic turned around after a dozen steps, marched back, and puked out the back of the aircraft. He knelt at the edge, eyes locked on the grass so he couldn't see the shocked, white faces of his cohorts, feeling ashamed. He heard Tommy draw up behind him and realized he was going to get his ass chewed, in front of his friends no less, for so unprofessional a display.

Tommy knelt beside him, gripped the edge of the vessel, and threw up, too. They knelt side by side, panting. The paramedic and Tommy made brief eye contact, nodded their understanding.

"Hey," Tommy said to the crews standing in a semicircle outside the ship. He pointed to their vomit. "Find a stick or something. Mark that."

Tommy and the medic returned to the woman paramedic, who nodded to them both. They went back to surveying the abattoir.

When they reached first class, Tommy was surprised to see sky ahead. The nose had sheared off; he hadn't done a walkaround before entering, which is standard operating procedure. He kicked himself for that. An engineer would have thought of that.

The cockpit and more bits of the fuselage lay in the field about thirty yards farther on. The cockpit was crumbled and scarred, and Tommy might not have recognized it if he hadn't known what he was looking for. *So much for either pilot walking away,* he thought.

He walked back through the darkened corridor of death, trying to touch as little as possible but still having to support himself because of the angle of the path. The thighs of his waterproof firefighter's outfit were soon smeared with blood and viscera, from supporting his weight by leaning against seats.

Tommy leaned over to the right-hand-cabin sidewall—starboard, he corrected himself. The fuselage was pocked with holes. He could stick his fingers through some, his fist through others. The metal and bits of thermoformed plastic around the edges of the holes were curved inward. They'd sustained an impact from outside, and probably while in flight. Weird.

The air masks had deployed, too. Some of the corpses still wore them. They'd had time to realize they were doomed.

"Let's get the hell out of here," he said, his voice echoing eerily in the tube-shaped space. The others nodded, eyes wide. They headed back toward the tail section. Tommy stopped, played his flashlight along the bodies. On his left sat a decapitated male in seat F, nearest the window. An infant and a woman in seat E, both of them mangled by debris and unrecognizable. In seat D, the aisle seat, was a teenager with massive blunt-force trauma to his torso.

Tommy swung the flashlight to the other side of the aisle. Seat C, an elderly woman, eyes and mouth wide open as if cut down in midscream. In seat A, he found a bloody pulp that looked to have been a woman, but the body was far too damaged to make that assessment, though she appeared to have been wearing a dress.

And between these two was seat 10-B. The seat of Bernard Weintraub, who'd unbuckled himself, walked to the back of the plane, stepped out, and waited for the crews to arrive.

Tommy felt a chill sweep down his spine. He almost dropped the light. Pushing on, he and his two volunteers exited the charred hulk of the aircraft.

## STAGING AREA

The PDX helicopter dropped off the first five section leaders and hurried back to the airport for more. Lower-level Go-Team members began showing up, too; some to the field of grass in Marion County, others to their assigned stations at the NTSB labs in Washington, D.C., and Seattle.

Kiki Duvall, John Roby, Peter Kim, Isaiah Grey, and Walter Mulroney wore windbreakers with NTSB stenciled on the backs and over their hearts. These they wore over heavier coats or pleated vests, plus scarves and gloves. It was almost 1 A.M. and very cold, hovering around twenty-eight degrees. Fortunately, it was neither rainy nor windy. Only later would they realize how unusual that was in March in western Oregon.

John strode out into the field immediately, leaving the others behind. Isaiah Grey sat on a big, plastic water cooler filled with emergency blood packs and began reading the initial report from PDX air traffic control. He grudgingly hauled out his reading glasses; at forty, Isaiah had just gotten his first pair of glasses and they galled him to no end. Like the salt-and-pepper splashes over both ears. Maddening.

Walter Mulroney studied the two pieces of the aircraft, limned in harsh white light that threw gaudy shadows across the manicured field. Folded his arms across his chest and squinted into the night, memorizing every detail of the fuselage and the one visible wing. His every breath plumed in the bright-white lights of the fire trucks.

Peter Kim made a beeline for a coffee dispenser set up near an ambulance. He brought back a cup. He hadn't asked if Walter wanted coffee and he didn't particularly care.

Walter said, "How are you?"

Peter Kim, never a conversationalist, shrugged.

"I'm a designated IIC. If you don't mind, I'll take point on this one."

Peter doctored his coffee with creamer and sugar. "Makes sense. Where the hell's the other wing?"

They both turned as Kiki Duvall made a very theatrical *ahem.* "You boys missed a memo or two. Tommy Tomzak has been here all night. He's IIC."

The engineers exchanged perplexed looks. "He quit," Peter said. "After fucking up in Kentucky."

Walter winced. "There's no need for the language, but Peter's correct. And even if he hadn't quit, they'd never let Tomzak run another investigation."

Kiki turned to him, eyes narrowed, and shot the engineer a look that would have melted a battleship's plating. "It wasn't a botched investigation. It just wasn't solved."

Peter nodded. "And thus, it was botched. Putting a pathologist—a jumped-up morgue attendant—in charge was a fiasco in Kentucky. He has no idea how to handle all the complications of a crash investigation of this magnitude."

"No?" Kiki swept unruly strands of sandy hair away from her face. "Look around. He seems to be doing all right."

And with that, she wandered out into the field, in John Roby's wake.

Walter put in his ear jack and tapped numbers on the surface of the satellite-communication-control device. "Well, that's just nuts. I'm calling Susan."

Peter blew on his coffee and said, "No."

Walter frowned at him.

"Tanaka always had Tomzak's back. Even when Kentucky went south," Peter said.

"So we should sit idly by while—"

Peter shook his head. "Wait till morning. Go over her head. Call Del Wildman."

Walter smiled with approval.


## THIRTY THOUSAND FEET OVER MINNESOTA

"Valence Airfield."

"Hello. My name is Susan Tanaka. I'm the liaison from the NTSB. My people are out there investigating that Vermeer One Eleven that went down."

The joviality drained out of the Latino voice on the other end. "Yes, ma'am. Jesus, that's bad. Me and Danny went up in a Piper 'bout an hour ago and checked it out."

"You didn't see the missing wing, did you?"

"No, ma'am, but we're going up again at dawn. You guys don't know where it is yet?"

"I don't know. I'm calling from the sidecar seat of a seven three seven; I'm not in Oregon yet."

"Well, how can we help?" Like any flyer, anywhere, the guy on the other end of the line jumped at the chance to assist a downed aircraft.

"I'm told you've just built a new hangar, to be leased by UPS."

"Yep. Finished it last month. They've run out of room at the Salem airport. We're closest and we just lengthened our runway last year."

Susan noted the singular, runway. "UPS called my office, offered to loan their new hangar to us for wreckage and reconstruction. I want to clear that with you."

"Outstanding. Anything we can do, name it. We've got some stuff stored in there now but it'll be empty by dawn."

"What's your name?"

"Ricky Sanchez, ma'am. I kind of run the office here."

"Mr. Sanchez, you've just become guardian of the Vermeer One Eleven. We appreciate your assistance."

"Yes, ma'am!" the man boomed. Any pilot in the world would have sounded the same.

# 10

KIKI DUVALL STEPPED UP beside John Roby, who stood and sniffed the bitterly cold air. Short and stocky, his hair cut very short, muscles taut under pale skin, anyone in the world would have recognized him as a cop. He sniffed again. It should have been a beautiful, earthy smell, but it stank of fuel and burned rubber and burned flesh. Kiki couldn't take her eyes off the wreckage, less than two hundred feet away now. This was only her second airliner, although she'd also fielded a Learjet crash that had killed three.

She said, "My God."

He suddenly slid his arm through her elbow and bussed her on the cheek. "Hallo, love. How've you been?"

"Doing good," she said. "You?"

"Handsomer than ever. Tommy's here, you know."

She froze for a moment, then nodded. "Yeah."

They were quiet for a while. Kiki broke the silence. "I don't envy you boys. All I want to do is get my black box and get the hell out of Dodge. This one doesn't look pretty."

John said, "You're thinking Kentucky."

Kiki didn't reply.

"I shouldn't be here long, meself," the Manchester native said, and took a moment to squint up at the stars. He checked his watch. "What time zone is this, love?"

"Pacific," Kiki said, and checked her watch. It was a Swatch that might have cost all of thirty dollars. John probably had paid as much for his as she had for her first car. John made more money in a year as a demolitions expert and consultant than he did in ten years as a deputy chief inspector for the Yard. And he liked to spend it as quickly as he made it. "It's about one eighteen."

He adjusted the time on his Swiss watch.

"You think this will be fast work?" Kiki asked.

"Will for me. I'm the bomb man."

"And?"

He sniffed the air again, just to be sure. "And there was no bomb," he said, smiled at her, and began walking back toward the coffee urn he'd spotted on the bumper of a ladder truck.

## STAGING AREA

It took Tommy's rescue teams the better part of three hours but, by 4:30 A.M., the last victims had been carted off, the "footprint" of the crash scene had been well documented by the firefighters, and all the Go-Team unit leaders had been assembled.

Realizing that there was terribly little they could do until sunrise, Susan Tanaka—calling from thirty thousand feet over Idaho—corralled them all to the hotel she had secured in the town of Keizer. Walter Mulroney, Peter Kim, and Isaiah Grey headed there to get some sleep. Kiki Duvall and John Roby stayed behind, just in case Tommy needed any help.

Just about the time that Susan's plane was landing at PDX, John looked up from a cup of particularly awful American coffee and saw Tommy Tomzak dressed in a firefighter's yellow outfit, trudging toward the staging area. John's eyes swept to the north and caught sight of Kiki Duvall moving to intercept Tommy. "This," John murmured to no one at all, "should be interesting."

Tommy and Kiki met halfway between the plane and the staging area. Kiki's bulky, high-top hiking boots were perfect for clomping through a field, but Tommy was wading around inside the too-large fireman's outfit, looking vaguely like an acrobat/clown from Cirque du Soleil.

"Hi," Kiki said.

"Hey," Tommy said.

They paused.

He added, "You look good."

"Thanks. You look like crap."

Tommy grinned and kicked at the soil with his boot. "Had better days."

"You look exhausted."

"That's just the exhaustion."

Kiki laughed. "Seriously. How've you been?"

"Good. I'm good. You?"

"Good," she said. "I'm good, too."

There was a space of about two feet between them, plus the ghosts of an affair that had ended badly and spawned enough guilt to light up a small city. They'd spent six months together in Kentucky, not quite two years ago, investigating the crash of an Alitalia Airbus. They'd hit it off right away and soon were making plans to get breakfast together to go over their findings, or just to chat. Later, they'd begun meeting before the nightly "postmortem"—when the crew leaders got together to reveal what they'd learned that day. Eventually, they were going out for coffee after the postmortem, and, inevitably, it became a sexual thing. They were both young (Tommy was five years her senior), both attractive, both single. It was as natural as walking.

But six months became eighteen months as the investigation stretched out and no answer appeared. The Go-Team's frustration began to manifest itself in a variety of unhealthy changes. Team members began showing up late for meetings. They snapped at one another. They burned out. Kiki and Tommy had been no different. Tommy, who'd sworn off booze shortly after his college years, started drinking again.

By the time the investigation team was disbanded, their romance had become indelibly linked to the Airbus investigation. And as one had failed, so, too, had the other. They'd turned to quarreling or simply annoying each other. And one night they agreed mutually to call it quits. Neither of them had seen or spoken to the other since.

Now, here they were in the weird, harsh light thrown by the emergency vehicles, their shadows stretching for yards, their breath misting. Kiki used her open palm, fingers spread, to sweep long, sandy-red hair away from her eyes. She breathed into her other fist, which she could barely feel. "Well, this has been fun. We should talk like this more often."

Tommy nodded, embarrassed. "Sorry. I'm tired. And I puked."

"You always puke."

"Yeah."

"Look," she said, and rested a strong hand on his forearm, being careful to avoid the bloodstains. "Let's just get through this thing. We were friends once. We're still friends. Cool?"

He made a fist. She did, too, and they bumped knuckles. "Cool," he said. "Susan must be glad as hell to have the Sonar Witch on this team. I got a bad feeling this one's going to go south on you."

Kiki thought, *On you?* but let it slide.

"Don't be pessimistic. I've looked over the section rosters. We've got a solid team. We'll get this thing."

He nodded, feeling the exhaustion like a scrim, covering everything, making things hazy. He'd been up for twenty-two straight hours now and had been on the scene for closing in on eight hours. "Then let's start with some good news: they found your CVR."

He cocked a thumb in the direction of a pennant that marked the location of the cockpit voice recorder. It lay near the tail cone. He could see Kiki brighten up.

"Cool!" She started jogging in that direction, revealing an easy athleticism that Tommy remembered well. "Take it easy, boss. Get some rest!"

Tommy thought, *Boss?*

John Roby walked over to him, wearing a thick, quilted parka under his NTSB jacket. Tommy grinned when he saw him. "You look like the Michelin Man."

John moved to hug him, then noticed the grisly bits on his turnout. They settled for a handshake. "Bloody cold out here, innit. How're you, mate?"

Tommy said, "Given the given . . ." and shrugged.

"Yeah." John shrugged inside his massive coats. "You done good, protecting the site. Pennants up, the firefighters haven't poured water over everything. Nicely done."

"Thanks, man. You've got bomb duty?"

"Yeah, but not for long. Have a butcher at that."

Tommy never got John's rhyming slang and had stopped trying years ago. John pointed to the fuselage. "There's some charring on the outside but it's all up and down, not horizontal. See? That came from the fires in the field. Nothing was aflame before the crash."

"Bomb coulda been inside."

"No. I'd smell it if there were an explosive. You'll see. The cadavers won't have any soot in their noses, their lungs. This wasn't a bomb."

"You're the expert." Tommy yawned.

John thought maybe it was a trick of the low, harsh lights, but he didn't remember Tommy looking so pale and drawn.

"Come on," he said. "Susan set up a hotel. Dunno where, but Kiki likely does. And Susan's called one of those fucking Allthings for the morning."

Both men rolled their eyes. They stood near one of the massive plastic coolers of medical supplies that the EMTs had brought. Tommy knelt and began stuffing supplies into his med kit. "Yeah, you head on out."

"You're knackered, mate. You should come along."

"Can't," he said, standing. Kiki joined them and handed Tommy a bottled water. "I'll follow you, soon as we get the pilots' bodies out of the flight deck."

"D'you have to do that now?" John asked.

"Yeah."

Kiki looked at Tommy's face and didn't like what she saw. "You're running on fumes," she said. "You've done a great thing here. This is the cleanest crash scene I've ever seen. The rescue teams were on tight rein, and we're going to appreciate that for weeks to come. Come on. Get some rest."

"Thanks. But I'm gonna get the pilots' bodies. It's . . ." He thought about it for a second, then turned and peered into the field. "I want to see them."

Kiki touched his arm. "If I know you, you're going to want to stay on and handle their autopsies, too."

He laughed. Kiki always could peg him. "This ain't your average autopsy situation. The local MEs are going to want to help, and thank God for that. But if they start hacking away before they understand NTSB protocols, they could contaminate the bodies, screw up the chain of evidence."

She nodded.

"'Sides, I want to do the pilots before the wolves start howling."

Kiki and John understood. In any major crash, people started asking about pilot error almost from the first moment. It just made sense: the various manufacturers assumed that their technology couldn't fail so dramatically, thus the pilot must have screwed up.

Go-Teams had learned to rush toxicology tests on the pilots; that is, whenever a sufficient amount of the pilots' bodies can be identified. Until alcohol and drugs could be ruled out, the media would steadfastly report that they hadn't been ruled out yet. Through no malice of their own, reporters would begin the process of maligning the cabin crew. A quick tox test could put a stop to that.

It hadn't happened like that in the Alitalia crash in Kentucky because the plane had nosed in. It had taken weeks to find enough body parts to DNA test for identification, and then to test for drugs or alcohol. By that time, decay made any such tests inconclusive.

Kiki patted his arm. "Go get 'em, tiger. I'll wait here. We'll head to the hotel together."

"Okay," he said, truly appreciating it. He took a swig of water and headed back into the field of grass.

Tommy Tomzak gathered his paramedical team. They looked as tired and brittle as he felt. Everyone stood on the asphalt of the blocked-off, north-bound slow lane, in the space between two fire trucks. It was close to 5 A.M.; the sun would be up soon.

"We're done with the first job," Tommy told them. "The survivors are away. I gotta tell you, we broke some kind of NTSB record for evac'ing the wounded. Y'all done good."

There was a smattering of applause and backslapping. Most of the med techs who'd arrived the night before had departed with the victims. About one in four had stayed behind to cart wounded away from the site. Now, as the sky began to lighten behind Mount Hood, the fatigued group guzzled bottled water and coffee and Gatorade. Some sat on the ground, others rested on the running boards of the fire trucks. Tommy sat on the bumper of a cherry-picker truck.

"Next is phase two," he said. "We gotta get the dead out of here in the same orderly manner as the living. The number-one thing we can do for these people—both the living and the dead—is to figure out why this bird crashed, and to see that it doesn't happen again. So far, we've left the crash site immaculate, and that's going to help a hell of a lot."

Beyond Tommy's field of vision, yet another helo landed in the area that the state police had roped off and designated "the LZ," the landing zone. Susan Tanaka stepped out of the glass-canopied bird.

"I'm gonna help retrieve the first two bodies but then I'm leaving you on your own," Tommy said. The paramedics didn't look happy about that, but nobody spoke. "It's the same rule as before. Touch as little as possible. Don't move any of the artifacts unless you have to. If you move something, tie a yellow ribbon around it and try to put it back where it was. Are the moon suits here yet?"

Someone sang out, "Suits are in the AMR incident commander's van, over there. We only got five of 'em. They set up a bleach-and-water-decon station back there by the pumper truck."

Tommy nodded. He didn't know what AMR stood for but didn't ask. The bright white biohazard suits were designed for work in dangerous, uncontrolled field conditions. The gloves were thick and impervious to punctures from needles, broken glass, or nails. The shoes had rubber treads for traction in dirt and mud. They came in two varieties: biosafety levels three and four. For this kind of operation, level three would probably be fine, which meant that Tommy wouldn't have to schlep an air tank around.

Now that he'd been inside the front section of the jet, he had no intention of letting anyone else in there without a full suit. He debated making them dig out the level-four suits with the self-contained breathing apparatus, but decided against it. The fuselage was coated with blood and viscera on every surface, but that didn't mean a high likelihood of aerosol-vectored agents. Getting blood on an open wound is one thing; breathing in a rare virus is a heck of a lot less likely.

"Please pick five people for the front section; people who've worked biohazard before. The rest take the tail section and the grounds. I need two volunteers to help me get the pilots out of the cockpit."

No hands went up. The female paramedic with the masculine haircut and multiple earrings said, "Um, have you seen the cockpit, sir?"

"The name's Tommy. And yeah, I saw it." He knew what they meant and they knew he knew. But he was going in anyway. The woman EMT raised her hand. Another hand went up, too.

"Thanks. All right. Get your second wind and plenty of liquids. Except you guys getting into the moon suits."

Everyone laughed, getting the joke. It was battlefield humor, the kind that keeps soldiers sane.

Tommy stood, his body aching. "And, folks? Nicely done."

## STAGING AREA, FORTY YARDS AWAY

Once the cockpit voice recorder was on its way to Portland, Kiki Duvall had little to do but wait. She stood in the field and jammed her hands into the back pockets of her faded, boot-cut jeans. The smell of the crash scene and the voyeuristic, almost hedonistic gawking of the passersby were making her queasy. She couldn't imagine staring, slack-jawed, at such a sight. If it hadn't been her job, she'd have averted her eyes from the slaughter in the field of grass.

*No,* Kiki quickly corrected herself. *Staring at a crash scene is human nature.* She'd have been as curious as any of the drivers inching past. If she hadn't been a curious individual, she probably wouldn't have joined the navy two days after high-school graduation.

John Roby stepped out of the back of an oversized, multiincident ambulance, big enough for four gurneys stacked two-by-two. He waved her over.

"Get your fancy tape recorder airborne, did we?"

"I'll get a digitized version for an MP3 player before noon," Kiki said. "Let's hope the insides of that baby are in as good condition as the outside."

"Let's." John nodded toward the ambulance. "Someone I'd like you to meet."

The back doors were open. A man sat on a stretcher, staring into a plastic coffee cup that he held in both hands, resting on both knees. He didn't seem injured. For that matter, he didn't even seem bothered.

"Meet Bernard Weintraub," John said. Being British, he put the accent on the first syllable of *Bernard.* "According to our Tommy, Mr. Weintraub was assigned to seat ten-B."

Kiki almost said, Of what plane? before it hit her. "He looks okay."

"Yeah. Passengers on either side of Mr. Weintraub are dead. Those in front and in back, as well. Seated amid a sea of death, and the lucky bastard hasn't a scratch on him."

The man still hadn't moved. He stared into the depths of the coffee cup like a diviner studying the eddies in a crystal ball.

"Why is he still here?"

"No room in the ambulances or helicopter for a man with no injuries. Plus, Tommy thought he might snap out of it and tell us a bit about what happened."

Kiki said, "Tabula rasa?"

"Beg pardon?" John smiled up at Kiki, who was a good four inches taller.

"Blank slate. A fugue state; walking catatonia."

"You know the oddest things for a wee slip of a girl."

From anyone else, the sexist comment would have earned a rude retort. But the "wee slip" part gave away John's weird sense of humor. Kiki had garnered a reputation on more than one naval base's coed basketball team as a power forward not to be screwed with in the paint. She could box out with the best of them. Now, though, she nudged him with her elbow and rolled her eyes.

"No. I've chatted with your lad here. He's in shock, but coherent. I wouldn't mind if the Sonar Witch gave him a listen."

"Sure," she said.

They climbed into the ambulance together, its heavy-duty shocks hardly budging under their combined weight. John and Kiki sat side by side on a stretcher facing Bernard Weintraub.

"Sir?" Kiki said softly.

He stirred, looked up, surprised. He hadn't seen them enter, although their knees practically touched in the narrow space between gurneys.

"Yes?"

"I'm Kathryn Duvall," she said, offering her hand. His palm was ice cold, and she noticed no steam rising from the cup. "Do you want a fresh cup?"

"No. Thanks. I'm trying to cut down." His voice was soft and a little raspy, like a lifelong smoker's. Or maybe he was just a shy person who had never learned to project his voice. Kiki had heard only eight words, but she pinned him as a Midwesterner.

"Are you injured, sir?" she asked.

"No. I'm fine." He expressed no shock, no fear, no outrage, no relief. If she had asked about the Boston Celtics or the Dow Jones leading industrials, he might have answered the same. Three more words, and Kiki guessed Kansas.

"Do you remember what happened?"

"You mean, on the plane?"

"Yes, sir."

"Yes."

*Not Kansas,* Kiki corrected herself. *Higher. Nebraska or South Dakota.* It was a gift she had, like her perfect pitch and her ability to play almost any song on the guitar after hearing it just once.

John said, "When did you realize something had gone wrong?"

Weintraub looked at him and blinked. "I fell asleep. I always sleep on planes. I was using my raincoat for a blanket. Something hit me on the head. I think it was that breathing thing."

Kiki said, "The air masks came down before the plane shook? You're sure?"

"Not really. I'm a heavy sleeper. The plane might have been shaking." His shoulders rose and fell. "Sorry."

*Nebraska,* Kiki decided. *And not rural. Maybe Lincoln.*

People in trauma can be like the hypnotized, she knew. They can be susceptible to suggestions, so Kiki and John worded their questions with exquisite care. But traumatized people also can have remarkably clear memories. She tried something that had just dawned on her. "Before that, were you dreaming?"

John's eyebrows rose, surprised by the question. A smile flickered across Weintraub's lips, his first hint of emotion. "Yeah."

"What about?"

"Ah, it was stupid."

"No, I want to know." She kept her tone light, conversational.

"I had a Mustang in high school," he admitted a little sheepishly. "A real muscle car, No muffler, just glass packs. You know?"

Kiki did; John didn't, but kept quiet, letting Kiki play her hand.

Kiki said, "Cherry bomb, sure. I haven't heard that noise in years."

"Yeah." Weintraub's smile broadened just a bit, then slipped away like a breeze on a hot summer night. "That Mustang roared."

John got it: the noise of the breakup had intruded into Weintraub's dream before he woke up. A lour roar, as in an explosion, and before the air masks deployed. Mr. Weintraub had incorporated the sound into his dream. John had been a very good detective in his day, and he knew how to run an interview. He'd also asked Kiki into the ambulance because the Sonar Witch heard things that other people didn't.

Kiki said, "What happened after you woke up?"

His eyes didn't wander, the way most people's do when they try to recall specific incidents. Instead, he seemed to stare at the questioner, but looking toward their throats or chests, not making eye contact.

"People were screaming." He spoke softly and without emotion. "Things were in the air. A book, one of them flimsy little pillows they give you. Lady next to me started chanting that thing."

John said, "Thing?"

Weintraub's eyes turned to John's chest. "That Catholic thing. What's that called?"

"The rosary."

"Yeah, that."

Kiki asked, "How long before you hit the ground?" even though she knew the answer would be meaningless. Time elapses in bizarre ways for people in the middle of a life-threatening crisis.

"A long time," Weintraub said.

"Did anything on the jet break? Anything big?"

"The overhead doors popped open. Stuff fell out. And there was . . ." His voice trailed off.

"Mr. Weintraub?"

"There was holes, over on the right side. Holes just appeared in the wall. Kind of like they weren't there, then they were. It sort of looked like a roll of film that freezes in a projector, you know? And the film starts bubbling and melting?"

Kiki nodded. "I know what that looks like, sure. And you saw that on the right side of the plane? *Your* right?"

He nodded.

"Then what?"

He cleared his throat. "Oh, there was lots of blood, I guess."

The plastic cup was shaking a little now, the surface of the coffee undulating in concentric rings. Weintraub wet his upper lip with the tip of his tongue. Kiki saw a single trickle of sweat escape from his scalp, course down his temple. She gently touched John's leg, nodded toward Weintraub. Without a word, John stood and hopped out of the ambulance.

"There was blood and people were screaming and there was this blood," Weintraub said. His voice cracked. Little peaks—the coffee equivalent of whitecaps—popped up in the cup. Kiki gently reached over, took the cup from his hands, set it down at her feet. He didn't protest.

"There was just so much screaming and crying and people were shouting and these holes, these holes, they just appeared, like film melting, holes in the plane and that's not right."

John came into view with a paramedic right behind him. Susan Tanaka was with them.

"It's just not right, holes in the plane like that, it isn't supposed to happen. I gotta be in San Diego for a sales meeting and it's starting real soon and I didn't bring an extra sports coat and there's just so fucking much blood! It's just fucking blood! It's bleeding! THE FUCKING AIR-PLANE IS BLEEDING! IT'S GOT HOLES AND IT'S *FUCKING BLEEDING, MA'AM! IT WAS BLEEDING!*"

That single, mannerly "ma'am" spooked Kiki as much as anything. The paramedic was in the ambulance now, seated next to Weintraub, sliding up the sleeve of his houndstooth sports coat, jabbing a needle into his arm. Weintraub turned to the younger man, eyes blazing, the full iris visible in both. His arm jerked, pushing the paramedic back. Kiki switched seats, sat on the other side of Weintraub, threw her arms around him, and pinned his arms at his side. Even in his livid, terror-stricken state, Kiki was too strong for him.

Kiki didn't know what was in the syringe but she felt the man's energy drain away from him. He leaned against her, losing form like an inflatable figure with a fast leak. She stood—as well as she could in the cramped ambulance—and Weintraub toppled over onto the gurney, his eyes rolling up into his head.

The paramedic nodded. "Thanks."

Kiki scampered past him out of the ambulance, eyes glittering with tears. Susan Tanaka stood with John.

"Oh God oh God I am so sorry," Kiki gushed. "I didn't mean . . . I don't . . ."

"Kiki!" Susan almost barked at her. "Calm down. He was going to spin out at any minute. That's why Tommy parked him in an ambulance. It's all right. You did okay."

"Oh, Jesus." Kiki hugged her, almost hyperventilating. She'd seen sailors with attacks of claustrophobia go nuts on nuclear subs, parked beneath the Arctic ice pack. But that had been different. She'd been an observer. This time, she felt like she'd caused Weintraub to lose it. "Susan. Thank God you got here."

"He was sleeping before the crisis," John told Susan. "He dreamt of a very loud sports car."

"Muscle car," Kiki corrected. She was regaining her equilibrium. "A car with glass packs instead of a muffler, to reduce back pressure. They make a heavy, bass sound. I think there was an explosion before the air masks deployed. He also said the starboard side of the fuselage seemed to melt."

Susan wrote everything down in her ubiquitous notepad. "Good. All right, it's something. Hey." She took Kiki by the forearm, stared up into her eyes. "You're okay?"

Kiki inhaled deeply, let it out. "Yeah. Freaked me out. I'm cool."

Susan bussed her on the cheek—not easy with their height disparity. "It's so good to see you. Both of you." Susan handed the investigators two sheets from her pad, with the name of their motel. "Here. It's in the town of Keizer, south of here, next to Salem. The debriefing for all the stakeholders is at nine, and we'll do our first press conference at eleven. But for now, you two should get out of here. Relax. There's nothing to do until the CVR comes back and we get bomb dogs from the Portland police."

"You're right." John nodded. "But there was no bomb."

Susan shrugged. "You're usually right, but Mr. Weintraub described an explosion. We've got to go by the book."

# 11

SUSAN TANAKA WAS ON her ear jack satellite phone, confirming more arrivals. The NTSB is one of the smallest bureaucracies in Washington, with fewer than six hundred employees in all. The only way to handle a major crash investigation was to bring in experts from the very manufacturers they were investigating. It was an uncomfortable partnership, the ultimate example of strange bedfellows, but it had worked like that since the 1960s.

Peter Kim was a gifted engineer and his crew was highly trained. But when it came to studying the Vermeer 111, they'd need the experts from Vermeer Aircraft itself to help them take apart the wings. And they'd need a crew from Patterson-Pate Electric to tear apart the four cowls on each of the four engines, which covered the intake, fan, core, and exhaust systems. Likewise, the hydraulic actuators, cascade segments, and sleeves of the engine were highly complicated pieces of technology, and only teams from the manufacturer could hope to truly understand it all. Some parts could fail if they malfunctioned by as little as two millimeters.

It was the perfect example of foxes guarding the henhouse. And it was Susan's job to make sure they helped but didn't hinder the investigation. Those experts—often called "hired guns" by the NTSB regulars—were beginning to arrive now. Susan had arranged for the offers of help to be routed through her. By booking every room at the Chemeketa Inn for her own people, she hoped to severely limit the casual interaction between the hired guns and her Go-Team.

Susan broke a telephone connection with a flick of the switch on her belt-mounted control unit and slipped her earpiece into a jacket pocket. She checked her ever-present notebook. Her to-do list was growing frighteningly long.

## FLIGHT DECK

Tommy's volunteers were named Gary and Sarah. The three of them stood outside the ruined remains of the airliner's nose for a couple of minutes, studying it from different angles. They wore firefighter turnout suits but not the helmets or breathing tanks. The first two sections of the fuselage had been easy to get into, having landed relatively flat, but the flight deck section had torn off and tumbled. The best way to get in looked like it was pointing straight up.

"We're going to need one of those ladder trucks," Tommy said. "Do you mind?"

Gary used his walkie-talkie to whistle up a truck. Tommy stepped closer to the crushed section and knelt in the crisp, ashy grass. The cockpit windows faced the ground. He bent low, his elbow in the muddy soil, and shone his flashlight into the window.

The ruined body of a white male, in his fifties, was pressed up against the window, his face distorted by the pressure. Blood was everywhere. His body ended after the third rib and Tommy didn't know where the rest of it was.

He stood and said, "Well, shit."

The fire truck edged its way slowly into the field, tearing up the nicely tended grass even further. It took a circuitous route, avoiding all debris. The driver parked twenty feet from the nose of the plane and extended a ladder, not up but straight out, over the flight deck.

Two firefighters climbed out on the ladder on their hands and knees, followed by Tommy and his two volunteers.

Flashlights shone straight down into the flight deck of the Vermeer. They were facing the galley, with its refrigerator and heating units and sinks. The rolling trays of food had miraculously remained in place, and Tommy could smell Salisbury steak.

The male volunteer sniffed. "Since when did they go back to serving real food on flights?"

"First class only," Tommy said. "It's a CascadeAir thing."

The woman volunteer, Sarah, swung her legs over the edge. "Let me go first."

No one disagreed.

She stood on the door of the galley refrigerator, holding on to the ladder. The two firefighters flanked her, holding on to the shoulders of her baggy, nearly indestructible turnout. She shifted her weight. Nothing gave. She said, "Okay, try it."

Tommy went next and stood on the fridge beside her. It all seemed sturdy. Gary, who was built like a fullback, stayed where he was, by unspoken mutual consent.

Tommy knelt. Beside the galley was a bathroom and the main hatchway, the one people walked through to get on and off the plane. The hatch door was missing; it lay about seventy feet away and had sliced into the ground like a giant arrowhead. Next to the fridge was the door to the flight deck. Tommy knelt, reached down, and turned the handle. The door didn't open. He shoved. Nothing.

"Let me try," Sarah said, and took the hands of both firefighters on the ladder. "You guys hold on to me. Ready?"

Tommy nodded. She lifted her right leg and slammed the sole of her boot down on the door. It creaked open about three inches. She raised her leg and stomped on the door again. It opened halfway. Another mighty slam and it swung in all the way, banging against the wall of the flight deck.

Tommy sat on the fridge and dangled his legs over the side, into the darkened flight deck. He beamed his flashlight in. Sarah did, too. Tommy said, "I don't see much blood."

Gingerly, an inch at a time, he lowered himself so that he was standing on the door frame, straddling the dark hole at his feet. He knelt slowly, gripped the edge of the door, and lowered himself like a spelunker into the darkness. Sarah's flash lighted the way for him from above.

Tommy's foot found a bank of computers. He put a little weight on it, then a little more. It held. He lowered himself farther and his other foot came to rest on the back end of the center control console, between the two pilots' seats. He looked up and squinted into Sarah's light. "Okay. I'm all the way down."

Standing, Tommy freed his flashlight from the sling at the small of his back and flicked it on. The first thing he noticed was the lower half of

Russ Kazmanski. The right-hand seat had snapped off its track and smashed into the console, shearing his body in two. His legs lay on the floor where the seat had been secured, the soles of his shoes facing Tommy.

Tommy turned to the left-hand seat. He knelt and bent over, his head going lower than his feet, poking down past the back of the captain's chair.

The captain had been impaled by the yoke of the jet, her chest caved in. Her eyes were open and staring at Tommy. It was a woman, Tommy noted. African American. She wore her hair very short. She looked athletic and competent. She looked like she'd tried very hard to save the lives of the people entrusted to her.

Tommy almost threw up again.

"Bad?" Sarah knelt on the upward-facing fridge and shone her light down into the flight deck.

Tommy reached through, touched the captain's lapel, turned her gold name tag in his direction. "Meghan Danvers," he said.

Sarah was quiet for a moment, waiting for Tommy's orders. Tommy sat up straight. "Can you rig a tackle and harness? We gotta get them out of here."

## STAGING AREA, FIFTY FEET SOUTH

Susan thought she had time for one more phone call before joining the others at the hotel.

"Hello?"

"Hi. Is this the security desk at the Lloyd Center mall?" Susan rarely knew how her executive assistant came up with these telephone numbers. She just did. Susan suspected her assistant used to be CIA. Or KGB.

"Yes?"

"My name is Susan Tanaka. I'm with the National Transportation Safety Board. We're investigating the downed CascadeAir flight near Salem."

The voice on the line said, "I heard about that!"

"Yes. Well, we're going to need the mall's help. Can you contact whoever you need to contact? Tell them we're going to need access to your ice rink."

"The skating rink? I'm sorry, did you say you need our skating rink?"

Susan said, "Yes, please. And time is of the essence. Can you contact whoever it is you need to contact? Now?"

"Uh, sure. Okay. Um, may I ask what you need our ice rink for?"

Susan said, "Cold storage."

## STAGING AREA

It took twenty minutes to rig a tackle and harness and to free the corpses of Meghan Danvers and Russ Kazmanski from the flight deck. It took six EMTs with three litters—one for Meghan, one each for Russ's two halves.

Tommy watched it all, sipping a stale, cold coffee. The sun rose behind Mount Hood, splashing soft yellow light on the field. It was a stark contrast with the harsh halogen lights he'd been working with since dusk.

He checked his watch. Technically, he checked his wrist, which didn't have a watch. He had no idea where the hell it was.

"Six thirty," John Roby said and put a hand on Tommy's shoulder and jutted his chin in the general direction of the crash site. "This wasn't half bad, this."

Kiki stepped up and put a hand on his other shoulder. "No kidding. Well done."

Tommy smiled at them both. "Thanks. Where is everyone crashing—"

The word caught in his throat, and after a second, Tommy choked out a rude little laugh.

"Shit. Can't believe I said that."

John smiled. "Susan secured a hotel in Keizer, Oregon. No idea which way that is or how far. I always thought Oregon was in the Midwest."

"That's Ohio."

"Nation's too bloody big, you ask me."

"C'mon. We'll get one of the state police to give us a lift. We'll go get a little shut-eye. Then the team can get started doing its mojo before noon."

The three of them trudged toward Interstate 5, past the troopers who stood on the sidelines, staring with awe at the scene of devastation. One of the troopers agreed to drive them to the hotel. Kiki asked the remaining units to guard the site until later that morning, when the NTSB would take over.

A cop with a bushy mustache said, "Take over? You guys are the NTSB."

Tommy shook his head. His neck made a snapping noise. He couldn't remember being this tired since he'd gotten out of the army. "Nah," he said. "This was just the rescue ops. NTSB isn't in the business of rescuing victims, it's in the business of solving crashes. This here? This was the overture. The curtain goes up now."

# BOOK TWO

THE CRASHERS

# 12

DARIA GIBRON WAS UP by six with just the slightest bit of a hang-
over. She slipped into vibrant blue biking shorts and a matching sports
bra, a stretched-out Avia T-shirt faded to a ghostly gray, and sturdy cross-
trainers. She wrapped a Velcro strap with a waterproof plastic pouch around
her upper arm.

She started jogging south through Los Angeles, down North Broadway, into the heart of the city. She cut into La Puebla de Los Angeles, past
the trucks delivering fresh tomatoes and peppers and freshly baked torti-
llas. The air was heavy with promised rain. Warmed up, Daria turned the
jog into a near sprint, pumping her legs like pistons, breathing through her
mouth, and feeling the constant tension in the back of her brain begin to
ebb, if ever so slightly. She was going at full clip, sprinting due west along
First Street, past the L.A. County Courthouse and the Dorothy Chandler
Pavilion. She was breathing with difficulty, her ribs protesting, her legs
really feeling it, as she cut around Bunker Hill toward Figueroa. Her lungs
gave out and she almost collapsed against an apartment building. She walked
two blocks, arms raised, fingers laced in her sweat-plastered hair, opening
up her aching lungs. The long muscles in her browned legs felt spongy and
untrustworthy.

She found the coffee shop on Fifth, on the fringe of the financial district. It had outdoor tables under a striped awning and a vendor selling biscotti and bagels. Ray Calabrese sat at a table with a cappuccino and *The Times*. The way he held the paper open in both hands, Daria could see the front page. The top story was about an airliner crash up north in Oregon.

Daria took a few crumpled dollar bills out of the plastic pouch strapped to her upper arm and bought a bottled water. She collapsed into the seat opposite Ray, gulped water, then poured some into her other hand and splashed it on her beet-red face. The coffee shop catered to a business-class crowd, lots of lightweight London Fog raincoats and attaché cases and day planners. At 7 A.M., most of the tables were empty. Daria had no sooner sat down than her sweat began to drip onto the iron chair.

"Hi," Ray said. "Chased by pit bulls?"

His tone was as usual: a blend of formal and friendly. The voice of a colleague. She'd met him once a week, more or less, for three years, and his tone had rarely changed. Only his eyes lit up whenever she entered the room. But that was a reaction Daria was used to from men and women alike.

Still breathing deeply, she smiled at him. "Hallo, Ray. What's the good word?" She'd been practicing her American vernacular.

Ray Calabrese sipped his foamy coffee. "Things are good. How're you?"

She shrugged, then pulled up the tail of her T-shirt to wipe her face, exposing the electric-blue sports bra. Ray was aware that every eye was on the exotic creature sitting opposite him.

"Things are okay," she said. "How's the business?"

"The business is busy," he said. "The L.A. field office is one of the biggest in the bureau. We've got so many guys, we're tripping over each other, and still we can't get it all done. You know how it is."

She smiled. "Yeah. I know. Or I used to."

Ray was a big man, six-two and still muscular at forty-four. He wore his suit coat well under the raincoat, the gun clipped to the small of his back invisible. He was a twenty-year man for the FBI and a senior special agent in the Los Angeles field office. He also was Daria's handler, and had been since she'd been smuggled into the States.

Sitting there now, across from her, Ray fought down an impulse to check his wristwatch again. He had an in-basket filled to the brim awaiting him at the office and probably thirty while-you-were-out messages. A typical Tuesday for a guy who usually ate a cold bagel and sipped coffee from a Starbucks cup in his car, rather than waste time on breakfast.

Sitting with a beautiful if bedraggled woman and sipping a cappuccino was an unparalleled luxury in the life of Ray Calabrese.

"Want something to eat?" he asked.

"No. I got a message on the special phone yesterday at noon," she said. Ray leaned forward. The special phone had been set up by the ATF guys. "I was to meet an Irishman in a specific bar. He was on time."

"Yeah?"

"This is him." She reached into the pouch on her arm and withdrew a single photo. It had been taken by the hidden camera that could catch whoever knelt next to her at the in-the-floor gun safe. She tossed it down onto the white iron table with its glass top. "He calls himself Jack."

Ray turned the photo, looked at it. It was a head-to-belt shot, straight on, of a blond man put together like a soldier. His sleeves were rolled up to show complicated tattoos on both forearms.

She put the heel of one shoe up on her seat, knee in the air, and gulped bottled water.

"He said he's from Dublin, but he met three other Irishmen at a bar and they all said *yez* for *you.*"

She waited.

Ray said, *"Yez?"*

Daria said, "Yes, *yez.*"

They both waited. He gave in first. "And that means . . . ?"

"*Yez* is a Belfast accent for the plural of *you,*" she explained, frowning slightly. "Don't they teach you people things like that?"

"I'm not an Ireland watcher," he said. "We have people who do that, but I'm not one of them. So you're saying this guy's from Belfast but claims to be from Dublin."

"Right."

He waited again. She gulped more water. The color in her face had returned to normal, which was good, because she'd looked like she was about to have an aneurysm when she arrived.

"And you know about the Good Friday Accord," Ray said gently.

"Yes; but you should watch this fellow anyway. He's in the States and claiming to be someone he's not. There's something else: he has scars on his fingertips. They obscure his prints. He's from a part of the world that, just a few years ago, was rated as a top hot spot for terrorist activity."

"A lotta years ago," Ray said. "Northern Ireland has been downgraded since the peace agreement. The IRA has put its weapons beyond reach,

Sinn Fein has taken its seat at the table. Things are as calm there as they've ever been."

She shrugged and said, "Still. You have the saying about knowing and not knowing devils, yes?"

Ray nodded and pocketed the photo. "Yeah, I know that saying. I know some guys who used to be in the Ireland shop, back in New York. I'll show this around. Did ATF get a copy of this?"

"Hmm." She nodded.

"Good." He sipped more coffee, watched businesspeople scurry past.

The first raindrops were beginning to drum on the awning over their heads. Ray hadn't been happy when ATF first came to him with this scheme. But it seemed that Daria—in her past life—had built quite a legend as a gunrunner. And apparently she'd offered to pick up her old "bad" habits for the feds.

Ray didn't like the setup, but he didn't have the juice to stop it. The boys from Alcohol, Tobacco and Firearms figured, Hey, the scumbags of L.A. would get guns one way or another. This way, they'd be toting guns that already had been test fired and could be easily matched.

While he thought about all that, Daria told him what she knew about Jack and the three Irishmen; about the bar where they'd met and that Jack seemed to be in charge, and he moved like a trained soldier. When she was done, Ray just nodded. Daria said, "What?"

Ray leaned forward, both arms on the round glass tabletop, and spoke softly, for her ears only. "You're not a spy. Not anymore. And not ever, for this government. You don't have to be watching for bad guys."

"I know. But I owe you." She'd lost very little of her accent during her time in the States and something about her voice always reminded Ray of Mediterranean spices.

He shook his head. "No. We owe you. You did a good thing for your country and for ours. You saved a lot of lives and you were injured in the process. I know the transition hasn't been . . . easy for you."

Daria looked away. She shrugged off the comment. It was a proper rain out there now, the noise on the awning almost a match for the traffic.

"It's just, I don't want you having any false expectations," Ray said. "You were on our payroll when you first got here, but just to provide you with some funds because it was the least we owed you. It wasn't a paycheck and you're not on the job. Anyway, these days you make as much as I do with your translating. You're not supposed to be spying on people and telling us who to watch."

"What am I supposed to do, Ray?" she asked, leveling those dark chocolate-brown eyes at him. "Hmm?"

"You're just supposed to get on with your life."

"My life ended when I betrayed my government," she said and stood. She reached for his cappuccino and drained it, leaving a foamy mustache on her upper lip. She leaned over the table and kissed Ray on the lips, then wiped her lips clean. "My life ended and I have the bullet wounds to prove it, Agent Calabrese," she said, her eyes still very close to his. "Get on with my life? What life?"

She headed back out toward the rain-slick sidewalk. Ray called after her, "Do you want to share a cab back to . . . ?"

But Daria waved a hand over her shoulder without turning around. She broke into an easy jog, already thoroughly soaked, catching the eye of every man on the street.

Ray Calabrese sat there for a while, feeling guilty and frustrated and not knowing why. His meetings with Daria always left him feeling off-kilter.


## KEIZER, OREGON

The Go-Team leadership had ordered wake-up calls for 8 A.M. That meant that Tommy Tomzak got about an hour of sleep before the phone in his room shrieked like a Harrier jet.

*Why do they make hotel-room phones so freaking loud?* he wondered.

"Good morning, Dr. Tomzak?" The voice on the phone was way too chipper. "This is your wake-up call. Mrs. Tanaka asked me to tell you there will be a van waiting in front of the hotel at eight thirty A.M., and that breakfast will be served when you get there."

Tommy said. "There? Where there?"

The chipper voice didn't say, and Tommy hung up. He got up, stood under the hot-hot shower until his brain kicked into first gear. He didn't bother to shave, just threw on jeans and his boots and an *Austin City Limits* sweatshirt. Somehow, during the night, Susan Tanaka had had his things moved from his hotel in Portland to this one in Keizer. Tommy wasn't sure why; maybe she wanted him to be debriefed by the Investigator In Charge, first thing this morning. He couldn't find his sports coat or his raincoat, so he threw on the NTSB windbreaker. *What the hell,* he thought. *For old times' sake.*

.   .   .

The van was waiting for him in front of the Chemeketa Inn. In it sat Isaiah Grey, John Roby, and Kiki Duvall. Tommy and Isaiah exchanged handshakes; they had not met before.

"I hear good things about the crash site," Isaiah said. "I can't believe you were on the scene so fast."

Tommy said, "It's good to be good but better to be lucky. We got fucking lucky. Hey, where we headed?"

John Roby, who sat in the back, drawled, "Del Wildman's famous Allthing."

"Yeah?" Tommy said, facing forward and thinking, *What do they need me there for?*

Kiki frowned. "All the craziness, I forgot to ask, do we have a head count?"

Tommy shrugged. "I was in the field all night."

John grimaced a little. "I asked Susan, first thing this morning. Thirty-five survivors, a hundred and eleven dead."

Kiki shivered. "A hundred and eleven dead on a Vermeer One Eleven. That's eerie."

# 13

SUSAN TANAKA CHECKED HER watch. Ten minutes until 9 A.M. The Vermeer 111 had been on the ground about twelve hours.

The setting was McNary High School in Salem. Susan stood in the middle of the set for *South Pacific,* watching people arrive. Most wore suits. Some were more casual. The place was filling up.

She glanced to the side stage and saw Walter Mulroney and Peter Kim. Walter was on his cell phone. Peter watched Susan.

The high school had a traditional proscenium stage facing six hundred seats curved like a fan, the seats elevated the farther back you went. About 250 of the seats were occupied. It was an Allthing, as Del Wildman, director of the NTSB, called them: the first meeting of all relevant parties to the crash. The first meeting could be long and annoying, but it also set some important ground rules. Most of the crashers hated them, but most also realized the wisdom of getting this meeting over with as quickly as possible.

## L'ENFANT PLAZA, WASHINGTON, D.C.

It was 8:50 A.M. Pacific Time, 11:50 A.M. Eastern, when the secretary in Director Wildman's office got the call from a Go-Team in the field. Everybody in the building had heard about the Oregon crash on the morning TV talk shows or drive-time radio news broadcasts. The secretary knew rule number one: time is more precious than gold after a plane goes down, and any call from an active Go-Team gets top priority.

She buzzed Delevan Abraham Wildman in his office and relayed the call.

Wildman, sixty-three, was the number-one man at the NTSB. He'd been a TWA pilot in the seventies—when being an African American pilot had been rare indeed—and an American Airlines executive in the eighties before joining the agency. He'd been on a record seven major crashes in his eighteen years before getting kicked up to the top echelons of administration.

When the call came, he snatched up the phone. "Wildman."

"It's Walter Mulroney."

"Walt?" he drawled. "You're in Oregon?"

"Yes, sir. Peter Kim, power plant, is with me. We're about ten minutes from one of your Allthing meetings."

"Give me good news, son." Wildman had been born and raised in Tennessee and he'd never made any effort to lose the accent.

"We'll know more in about an hour, after the meeting. But we've got a potential crisis. Someone made Leonard Tomzak Investigator in Charge."

Wildman said, "Tommy?" It was Del Wildman himself to whom Tomzak had given his resignation, only a few months earlier. Wildman wondered for a split second, but then the obvious answer hit him: silver-tongued Susan Tanaka had talked him into this. He wondered why Tomzak had agreed.

Walter was still talking. "Sir, he's a pathologist: he's never taken an engineering course, never flown an airplane. This guy's going to fold when the real media gets here. Imagine what he's going to be like when officials from Vermeer Aircraft and CascadeAir show up, not to mention the engine manufacturer and the danged lawyers. Sir, I don't know who dropped the ball here, but I'm offering to take control as IIC before this situation gets out of control."

"Walt? Where's Susan?"

"She's out onstage, getting people to take their seats."

"Stage?"

"We're in a high-school auditorium."

Wildman said, "Well, put her on."

"It's just, I think we need a more professional IIC than we saw in Kentucky. I think we need to—"

"Walter." Wildman let his voice dip an octave. "Put 'er on. Now."


At McNary High School, Walter Mulroney walked half the width of the stage and handed Susan a cell phone.

"It's Del."

Susan stepped well away from the microphone, covered her left ear with her other palm. "Hello?"

"Susan. Del. Did you get Tomzak to rescind his resignation and make him IIC?"

Susan glowered daggers at Walter Mulroney's retreating back.

"He was on the scene before anyone," she said. "I watched his work in Kentucky. He's brilliant and tenacious, and he gets amazing work from his crashers."

"Kentucky was—"

"A fluke," she cut in. "Nobody could have gotten to the bottom of that one. No one. I want Tommy."

"How 'bout going with a more traditional IIC. An engineer. You've got Mulroney. He's an experienced leader. Put him in—"

*"Screw Walter!"*

Delevan Abraham Wildman was one of the most feared and respected administrators in the aviation industry. The FAA and DOT had head-hunted him for years, but he remained loyal to the board. He was known alternately as The Bear and The Old Man, but to his face he was Mr. Wildman to most people, Del to a few, and sir to the world at large.

Nobody yelled at him. Not ever.

Susan Tanaka actually stomped her foot as if Del Wildman could see it. "God damn it!" she boomed into the cell phone. She paced the stage in short, choppy strides that threatened to buckle the wood under her Gucci calfskin boots.

"Susan, I—"

"Tomzak was my choice for IIC and he's done a sensational job, Del.

I'm the best intergovernmental liaison you've got, and if Tommy goes, so do I. Get your ass out from behind that desk and get out here to relieve me yourself, or else put Tommy back in charge and let me do my job!"

"Walter—"

"Blow him!" she boomed—as much as a petite woman can boom. "The jet pancaked in at eight forty-one local time. We had an IIC on site and controlling the rescue parties forty minutes later! That's a record, Del! The scene is in mint condition. The rescue teams were kept on a tight leash. This is the finest day one I've ever seen, and that wasn't because of me or because of Walter Mulroney. It was Tommy Tomzak. He's done a fantastic job and you can't just undermine his authority, not to mention my authority, by pulling crap like this! You can't!"

When he didn't respond, she plowed on through the silence.

"So Tommy was IIC for the Alitalia crash in Kentucky. So that was never solved. Are you thinking that Tommy was at fault? Are you questioning the actions of that Go-Team?"

"No," Wildman shot back. "Not at all. That was an awful crash. Nobody could have coaxed any secrets out of that pile of rubble."

"Right. Tommy drew the short straw, and his name will forevermore rest on a document that says: 'we don't know.' But he still ran a good investigation there, and he's got this crash site in excellent shape. I made the call and I back it up. Now, is Tommy in charge or do I head back to the airport and debrief my replacement?"

She stopped pacing, crossed her arms under her breasts, and held her breath.

The last thing in the world she expected to hear was the low, throaty chuckle of Del Wildman.

She said, "Hello?"

He kept laughing. When he could, he drawled, "Don't hold back on my account. Tell me how you really feel."

Susan said, "I always do."

"It's your scene. I won't pull Tomzak. Y'all do what you have to do. Find out why the bird's down."

She said, "Done. Can you stay on the line a minute?"

Tommy, Kiki, John, and Isaiah entered the theater through a side door, escorted by a Salem police patrol officer, just in time to see Susan march up to Walter and hand him a cell phone.

"It's for you." She smiled politely, turned on her heels, pointed to Tommy, and said, "You. Over here. Now."

Tommy glanced at John, who shrugged. "Jesus H. Christ on a bicycle," Tommy whispered, but did as he was told.

Tommy noticed that more than two hundred people were getting into their seats. A table had been set up over the closed orchestra pit with coffee, water, and pastries. He nodded to the crowd as he joined Susan.

"Good showing for so early."

"A midevening crash meant everyone was home from work, done with their commutes," she explained. "It saved us a day, contacting people."

Tommy rubbed his bloodshot eyes. "What's going on?"

She spoke for his ears only. "I picked an IIC and Walter Mulroney got bent out of shape because it's not him. He went behind my back, called Del Wildman."

"No shit?" Tommy frowned. "Gotta say, you shoulda gone with Mulroney. He's good."

"He has no imagination."

Tommy nodded, conceding the point.

"I'm the best there is at this." Susan said this as a matter of common knowledge.

"Hell yes."

"Don't you think my pick for Investigator in Charge should be respected?"

"Absolutely."

"Well, Del agreed. He's backing my play. I just wanted you to know."

"Okay, well . . . thanks." He hugged her. And because he was so addled from lack of sleep, it didn't even dawn on Tommy to ask who her pick for IIC was.

At 9 A.M. sharp, Susan stepped to the microphone and said, "Let's start by introducing ourselves. Larry? Want to kick this off?"

A man in the third row stood and, around him, twenty-three more people stood. "We're CascadeAir," he announced. He pointed to his people, who included some high-ranking brass, a few engineers, public relations specialists, the marketing department, and attorneys; lots of attorneys.

Tommy and the three he'd rode in with had stepped off the stage and were helping themselves to coffee and pastries.

Twenty-nine people stood and identified themselves as representing Vermeer Aircraft. The pilots' union was next, followed by the flight attendants' union and the engineers' union. People from Patterson-Pate Electric, who made the engines, were there. The insurance carrier for CascadeAir was present, as were the insurance carriers for the unions and for Patterson-Pate. The Federal Aviation Administration sent its representatives, as did the federal Department of Transportation and the Transportation Safety Administration. The Department of Homeland Security sent two people, just to observe. The Portland office of the FBI sent one woman. All air crashes are initially investigated by the NTSB until someone can prove that a crime was involved, at which time the case gets handed over to the FBI. The governor of Oregon had sent a handful of people to report back. And, of course, Marion County had sent Sheriff Alfredo "Al" Escobar and District Attorney Adele Bergman-James. The aircraft had crashed in Marion County, and if a crime could be proved, it actually fell under the purview of local law enforcement and prosecutors—as the constabulary in Lockerbie, Scotland, knew only too well.

The janitorial staff and the principal of McNary High School sat in, too.

It took twenty minutes for representatives of all the stakeholders to stand up and introduce themselves. In the past, NTSB investigations had begun by kicking all these people out, but it had been learned that pissing off the participants too early actually slowed down the investigation. So Del Wildman's now-infamous Allthings had been invented: first-day gatherings of all the "clans" to speak out, be heard, and feel appreciated.

From this day onward, these groups would be cut out of the link substantially. And they knew it. This was their chance to be heard.

"Thank you," Susan said into the microphone. "I'd like to thank Principal Mike Aleman for the use of this auditorium."

The principal waved to her from the back of the audience.

"Okay. I'm Susan Tanaka, intergovernmental liaison for the Go-Team leadership. These three are my people." She waved to three twentysomething assistants who stood off to the side. "Go through them to get to any one of us. You have their business cards with their cells and e-mail addresses. Before we get going, I'd like to introduce our Investigator in Charge."

Tommy took a very large bite of a bagel with cream cheese, and was wiping cheese off his *Austin City Limits* sweatshirt just as Susan waved to him and said, "Ladies and gentlemen: Dr. Leonard Tomzak."


An Allthing meeting generally can take two, maybe two and a half hours. Tommy really didn't want to wait that long to kill Susan Tanaka.

# 14

RAY CALABRESE STOPPED AT a drinking fountain on the third floor of the FBI's Los Angeles field office and took a sip, holding his tie carefully against his chest. He stood up straight, his lower back protesting a little, reminding him that he'd been slacking off at the gym lately.

Through a doorway halfway down the hall, he caught a glimpse of an agent sitting at a desk. He paused, then walked down that way, rapped twice, and entered.

The agent sat with his wingtips up on the desk, reading through a fat court transcript and marking passages with a yellow highlighter. He looked up and smiled. "Hiya, Ray."

"Hey, Phil." Ray perched on a corner of the desk. "Got a sec?"

Ray retrieved the snapshot from his suit-coat pocket and handed it over. "You used to work the Ireland book. Recognize this guy?"

Phil stared at the photo for about three seconds, then frowned. His eyes took in the tattoos on the man's forearms. He shouted, "Yo. Lucas?"

Lucas Bell, a black man in a natty suit and an Oxford tie, strolled in. He slapped Ray on the shoulder. "Ray Calabrese. The Kid Complete."

Phil looked at Ray and said, "Please, for the love of God, don't ask about his tie."

Ray turned to Lucas Bell. "Nice tie." It was, in fact, a damn fine tie. Lucas could put together a suit like nobody else in the Bureau.

Phil said, "You're killing me here, Calabrese." He handed the photo to the newcomer. "Who's this look like?"

Lucas took the photo, blinked several times.

Ray said, "You know him. See, this is why I like playing poker with you."

"Tell me that's O'Meara!" Phil said, a little shock in his voice.

Lucas said, "How the hell'd you get a photo of this guy?"

"I have a source who knows him as Jack, that's all."

Lucas Bell studied the bigger man for a second. "Since when do you have contacts in Belfast?"

Ray's stomach dropped. He had a very bad feeling. "This source is in L.A. So's your boy here."

"Bull!"

Ray shrugged. "This guy's trouble?"

Lucas said, "This guy's Ebola on a bad day!"

## PORTLAND, OREGON, PEARL DISTRICT

Dennis Silverman wanted to watch his masterpiece unfold but he wasn't stupid enough to show up at the crash site. No one knew there'd been a crime yet, but he had no intention of getting photographed as a rubbernecker anyway.

He sat in his recliner, wearing boxers, fuzzy slippers, and a flannel robe, the remote in his fist switching between the ABC and NBC affiliates, then to CNN. All three offered aerial views of the crash, with the fuselage separated into three sections; the aft and wing, the fore section, and the crumpled remains of a cockpit. The brown, burned trail behind the jet was obvious for all to see. There seemed to be something missing, and it took Dennis a few minutes to realize that it was a wing.

That engine he'd cooked must have blown the entire wing to kingdom come, he thought, and snickered.

The phone rang. Dennis hit the speakerphone function, his eyes locked on the TV.

"Denny?"

"Hi, Mom."

"What are you doing at home? Aren't you going to work?"

"No," he said, eyes on the screen.

"Den-ny," she said, drawling the name out, which she did whenever she was annoyed with him. Which was always.

"I'm on flex time," he explained for the thousandth time. "I'm working at home today. Telecommuting. They understand."

"This is a corporation," she wheedled. "Bosses notice who's at the grindstone and who isn't, Denny. How do you hope to advance if you don't get noticed?"

He switched from ABC to CNN, which had a better helicopter view of the crash.

"Denny?"

"Hmm?"

"I asked, how do you hope to advance if you don't get noticed? Because you've been with the company for eight years now, and you're still just an engineer."

He tried the CBS feed. Yes, that was better. His cell phone dingdonged. He picked it up from the end table. Incoming text message.

"It's important to move up, Denny. You move up or you move down. That's life. That's how it is. God knows your father tried to teach you that."

Dennis okayed the acceptance of the text message and glanced at the television. Fire trucks lined the freeway for almost half a mile, he estimated. Troopers were trying to keep the traffic moving but it was at a snail's pace. He wondered why three RVs were parked so close to the scene.

He looked down at the cell and grinned. His bank in the Cayman Islands confirmed that his account had just ballooned by one hundred thousand dollars.

"You know Irene, from temple? Her husband works at Intel. He moved from engineering to marketing, what was it? Three years ago? He's the assistant manager now. He drives a Lexus."

Dennis hadn't been to his mother's synagogue in twelve years and didn't know any Irene. He squinted, noting that several people wore dark blue windbreakers with words stenciled on the back, but with the overhead views, he couldn't tell what the words were. He switched to ABC.

". . . And he's no smarter than you are, not by a long shot. It's just that he has drive, Denny. . . ." He wondered if she was going to stop talking anytime soon. He used to wonder that a lot, growing up. She'd talk and talk and talk, and sometimes, when she wasn't even there, he'd hear that same nails-on-chalkboard voice, talking and talking and talking. He'd be in the wooded ravine beyond their house, watching some neighborhood dog he'd caught in one of his traps, being electrocuted to death in his inge-nious devices. *I'm Dr. Doom,* he'd think. *You'll never escape my trap this time.* And the squeals of the dying animal would morph into his mother's voice, talking and talking and talking.

". . . And drive is what makes it. I mean, I do what I can. I scrimped and I saved for you. . . ."

*Scrimped and saved.* It was her favorite expression. Dennis thought back over the years, tried to remember when she'd scrimped on anything. Or what *scrimped* even meant. He made a note to look it up. He couldn't read the words on the jackets from that angle, either. Back to CNN.

". . . Always the best clothes. Always the most expensive shoes. And you outgrew everything so fast. Now look at you. Stuck in the same job, year after year. That's why it's important to get to the grindstone, Denny. Get in there and show them how hard you're working. Let them know you're interested in advancement."

NTSB. That's what the jackets said. *Of course, makes sense.* Dennis won-dered when they'd arrived.

"So you'll go in? Today? You'll get to work, let them see you? Denny?"

"I'm on flex time," he said. "I'm telecommuting."

"Den-ny!"

## 15

Assistant Director Henry Deits of the Los Angeles FBI field office turned a corner with a cup of decaf in one hand and a cheese Danish in the other to find three of his agents waiting outside his conference room. It was 10:15 A.M.

"Did I miss a memo?" the AD asked.

"No, sir," Agent Lucas Bell said. "But we've got something to show you."

The conference room had a computer-generated overhead projector and a document scanner. A minute later, the photo of Jack kneeling over the gun safe dominated one wall. Three more top brass had been called into the impromptu meeting.

"Donal O'Meara," Lucas said. "He's a known terrorist with a long list of assassinations under his name. He served time in Britain's Maghaberry Prison and, we thought, he'd been holed up in Belfast for the last year or so. But Agent Calabrese here has a contact who shot this photo of O'Meara last night in Los Angeles."

Assistant Director Deits sipped his coffee and said, "IRA?"

"Other side. The Red Fist of Ulster, a hardline Protestant group that opposed the Good Friday Accord and the power-sharing agreement. O'Meara runs his own cell, or he used to."

"My contact says he's traveling with three other men, all with Belfast accents," Ray cut in.

One of the brass asked, "Who's your source?"

Ray played with his legal pad for a moment, knowing that he really had no option but to answer. "Daria Gibron."

Two men gawked at him. The others vaguely recognized the name but couldn't remember why.

AD Deits said, "Are you out of your mind?"

"No, sir. I've been in contact with Ms. Gibron, on and off, since she came to the States."

"She's a drug addict!" Deits laughed. "She's unreliable!"

"With all due respect, sir, she's not a drug addict."

"Your own report said so, Calabrese."

Ray reined in his annoyance. "No, sir. My report said she has an addictive personality. She smokes too much, drinks too much. She works too hard and plays too hard. She doesn't jog, she runs marathons. She doesn't do calisthenics, she kickboxes at a competitive level. If she's addicted to anything, it's adrenaline. And granted, that makes her dangerous and unstable. But not wrong; not this time."

One of the other brass said, "I remember something about Vicodin?"

"Yes, sir. She was shot badly when we brought her to the States. After her recovery, she developed an addiction to painkillers. She's beaten that."

Deits turned to Lucas and said, "Could this photo be wrong? Could it be someone who looks like your whatsisname?"

Lucas paused, and Ray cut in. "She ID'd his accent as Belfast; that's why she brought the photo to my atten—"

"An adrenaline addict." Deits sneered. "What're the chances she was schtuping this guy, didn't like how it ended, and turned him in to her pet FBI agent?"

Ray let his anger settle before answering. His poker face never wavered. "I don't think so, sir. As you may recall, ATF started using Ms. Gibron and a cover that she'd established when she was with Israeli intelligence. She hooks people up with guns; guns that can be traced and, if need be, have been LoJacked. I've got a call into the ATF to see if they tracked this guy last night. Ms. Gibron said he calls himself Jack and is from Dublin but she recognized the accent as Belfast. I showed this photo to Agent Bell and he immediately recognized a known terrorist from Belfast. That's evidence enough for—"

"Okay, okay." Deits stood and buttoned his suit coat. "Ray, drop everything else and get going on this. I want to know if we've got a serious threat here or if we have an overly horny ex-spook who's about as stable as a hyperactive eighth-grader."

Lucas cleared his throat. "I was on the Ireland Watch, back in the New York field office. I'd like to lend a hand."

Deits said, "Fine. It's ten thirty now. I've got tickets tonight for some concert or play or something with my wife, which means I'm out of here by six. Let's meet at, say, five thirty. Tell me O'Meara's in town, or not."

And with that, he and the other brass filed out.

Ray pointed to the projected photo. "Do you believe that's O'Meara?"

Lucas studied the wall a moment. "Yes," he admitted, sighing. "God, I hope we're wrong."


## LOS ANGELES

Donal O'Meara knelt by the TV in a dark, condemned apartment and manually flipped from the ABC affiliate to CNN.

*NTSB. That's what those wankers' jackets said.*

He sighed with relief. He'd been afraid they were FBI. Although, what was he afraid of? There was nothing connecting him to this crash, even if the FBI had been there. Just as there wouldn't be anything linking him to the next crash, either.

He wondered what the fuck NTSB stood for.


## WEST HOLLYWOOD

After her strenuous workout, Daria Gibron showered and changed into a little black skirt and open-toed slingbacks with four-inch heels and a black Versace shirt and matching black leather biker jacket. She was just about to leave for a translation job when her phone rang. It was *her* phone, not the ATF phone. She answered. It was the private secretary for a Saudi businessman for whom she had done a little translating.

"He will host a party next Tuesday. And has asked you to do him the honor of attending. There will be some Israelis there."

This particular businessman cared little for the hatred and woes of the Arabs and Jews. He came to America with only one plan: to make money. Which he did, spectacularly.

Daria wasn't the only translator in town, or the cheapest, but she knew the consul liked how she looked. She could stand being eye candy for an evening. Besides, there were material rewards. "I would love to, but I have nothing to wear," she replied forlornly.

The private secretary may have been smiling, because the pitch of his voice changed. "That is a small problem, easily solved. Arrive around eight and one of our people will find you something." She knew they would, too. The Saudi businessman liked to surround himself with beautiful things and beautiful people, and he was willing to pay a high price for his fun. Daria would end up with a designer dress out of the deal.

She agreed, and he said goodbye.


Twenty minutes later, she sat in an elegant restaurant, doing what she was paid to do: translate.

The FBI had had no trouble getting her work in the United States: she spoke fluent English, French, High Arabic, Hebrew, and Spanish, with a smattering of German and Italian. There were a thousand corporations in the financial district alone that could use an instant translator.

She was still a little weak at the knees from that morning's very hard workout. Fortunately, neither the Egyptian gentleman to her left nor the English gentleman to her right realized it when she entered, or when they stood and shook her hand.

The translation duty was easy enough and barely occupied her mind. Half of her brain was on the night before. There was something wrong about the Irishman, something off. She knew it. It probably wasn't any of her business; she wasn't a spy or a law enforcement agent. Now she was just a freelance translator for several West Coast investment houses. The contact had left her energized, nonetheless.

In the end, the Egyptian sold something and the Englishman bought it. Or the other way around. Two filthy-rich snobs, exchanging something nobody in the world needed. The whole transaction left Daria bored beyond words.

As they bade each other adieu and she was handed a check for her translation services, Daria thought, *Screw Calabrese.*

On the street, Daria suddenly remembered an Americanism she had read in the newspaper. "Being benched." She thought she knew what that meant. *Bench me, Ray?* she thought, slid on her Prada sunglasses, and headed out to find Jack.


## McNARY HIGH SCHOOL, SALEM

Kiki Duvall's cell phone vibrated. She adjusted the ear jack and answered.

"Miss Duvall? This is Brian, from Sonic Broom Label."

She used her splay-fingered palm to push red hair away from her sandy eyebrows. "Yes. You have it?"

"Yes, ma'am. There's a guy here says he's a marshal."

Good. Proper evidence protocols. Last night, she'd arranged for a deputy from the U.S. Marshal's office to take her black box—the cockpit voice recorder—to state-police headquarters and to lock up the box until morning. Now, it was in the hands of a recording engineer at Sonic Broom Label records. The marshal would stay with it the whole time and would deliver it back to the NTSB when the engineer had done his magic.

Before Kiki had joined the NTSB, the standard operating procedure for all crashes dated back decades. As soon as the cockpit voice recorder and flight data recorder were captured, they were instantly transferred to NTSB headquarters in Washington's L'Enfant Plaza, where they'd be analyzed. At Kiki's insistence, a new protocol had been established for the CVR. She'd been able to convince the brass that the federal government's audio equipment was vastly inferior to that of major record producers and Hollywood soundstages. Technology in the entertainment industry tended to improve at a dizzying clip and showed marked improvement every few months.

Kiki had gained permission to have CVRs sent to New York, L.A., Nashville, Austin, or Portland, depending on where the jet went down, to take advantage of the best audio technology on the planet.

Rather than speed off to D.C. and separate herself from the downed aircraft and the rest of the Go-Team, Kiki would have digital recordings of the cockpit voice recorder delivered to her within hours. Her process shaved days off crash investigations and had resulted in a fourfold improvement in the audio quality.

She talked to the engineer for a moment, then hung up, detached her ear jack. As she did, Isaiah Grey said, "Good news?"

It was 11:30 A.M. Susan Tanaka's Allthing was all but finished, and now Susan was about to step out and hold her first press conference. Kiki and Isaiah were backstage at the high school theater. She told him about the CVR.

"Sweet. You were a hell of a pickup for this team. You know that?"

Kiki threw her arm over his shoulder. "You're a nice man, Mr. Grey."

"Tell that to the PDX ground crews."

She nodded. "You have crew duty?"

"Yeah," he said, but didn't elaborate. It was a task few of the crashers ever wanted. He got to be the guy who rooted through the protocols and procedures of the ground crew and the flight crew and tried to figure out who, if anyone, had screwed the pooch. It was not a popular role.

Kiki squeezed his shoulder. "Good luck."

"Gonna need it."


Thirty feet away, Susan smiled her most charming smile and said, "Feel like punching a petite person?"

Tommy shook his head. "You are an evil, manipulative, lying sack of shit."

"Yes," she said, ramping up the smile a few watts.

"Suze! Hell's bells, I can't—"

"Shut up, stupid boy. You can and you have. You've been IIC for more than fourteen hours and didn't even realize it. You've done wonders."

"But Kentucky—"

"—Is a place with good college basketball and good bourbon. This is Oregon. They have neither."

Tommy's shoulders sank and Susan slipped her arm through his. "Admit it. You secretly want to do me right now."

"Well, yeah. But I'm still gonna throttle you."

She kissed him on the cheek. "Come meet the media."

Tommy groaned.


## McNARY HIGH SCHOOL, GYMNASIUM

"All right, show of hands," Susan shouted to be heard. There were eighty-plus journalists clustered in the McNary gym. "How many daily-print people do we have here?"

Hands went up.

"Morning or evening papers?"

"Morning!" someone shouted. "We've got a ten P.M. deadline."

"Mine's eleven!" another voice piped up.

"Okay, how many weeklies?"

More hands. People shouted, "Wednesday!" and, "Thursday!"

"Do we have a weekly from, ah, Tigard?" She consulted her ubiquitous notepad.

"Um, yes." A twentysomething woman with blond bangs looked surprised.

"Good. Radio? What kind of airtimes?"

"Drive time!" someone said. "NPR wants our feeds by eleven for the East Coast!"

"Well, it's eleven forty-five now, so you've blown that deadline." The reporters laughed. "Okay, do we have TV?"

Again, deadlines were shouted. Susan wrote it all down in the palm-sized notepad, then checked her notes. The janitors had pulled out a set of bleachers and Susan stood on the second row so that everyone could see her. "All right. The Go-Team will meet each evening to compare notes. Now—"

"Can we sit in?" a newspaper reporter asked.

"No. But I'll hold a press conference every day. Late mornings or noonish. Times will vary, depending on our schedules. My assistants are handing out fact sheets with a Web site. The press conferences will be posted at least two hours in advance."

Tommy handed her a bottled water and she took a delicate sip. "As I said, I'll hold a press conference every day. Sometimes two, if anything breaks. I may not have anything to tell you, but we'll meet daily anyway. If you've got any questions about the investigation, I'm the person to see. I'll ask section leaders to attend the press conferences on a rotating schedule, or as needed to explain technical details. Is that going to work?"

They begrudgingly admitted that it would.

"This is Dr. Leonard Tomzak. He's our Investigator in Charge. I'll have him available for as many of these as I can."

"Though not sober," Tommy said for her ears only.

"Okay, then, here's what we know: CascadeAir Flight Eight One Eight declared an emergency last night at approximately eight thirty, Pacific time. She carried five crew and a hundred and forty-one passengers. Portland International air traffic control immediately cleared airspace and the captain began trying to turn the aircraft. . . ."

Twenty-five minutes later, the press conference broke up. As the media began packing up, Susan called to the young reporter from the Tigard weekly. Surprised, the blond woman struggled her way to the front of the crowd. She wore blue jeans and sneakers and a bulky sweatshirt, her hair pulled back in a butterfly clip. No makeup. It was obvious she'd leaped out of bed upon hearing the news and had hurried down to the crash site.

"I can't help the weeklies all that much," Susan said. "I know how to schedule releases so that the dailies, the radio, and the TV guys are happy, but you don't come out until . . . ?"

"Thursday," the woman admitted. It was Tuesday morning.

"Right. You're gonna get smoked. But when I can, I'll try to throw some bones your direction, just to keep things equal. Okay?"

"Sure," the reporter said. "We always get beat by time."

The way she said it made Susan cock her head to one side, questioningly.

"We can't be first, so we just have to do a better job," the woman replied. She looked all of twenty-three. "And we do."

Susan smiled, liking her. She handed her a business card. On the back was a name and phone number. "This is a paramedic. One of my assistants got his name. He's from Tigard. He wasn't even on duty last night because he has a broken arm, but he showed up anyway, in a cast, just to help."

The reporter's eyes glowed. This was a genuine human-interest story, and with an angle handpicked for her town's readership.

"Thanks! Um, can I ask you a question? Why are you treating us so respectfully? We don't get a lot of that."

Susan shook her hand. "In the weeks to come, you reporters are going to alternately loathe me and assume I'm either lying to you or that I'm an idiot. It's early days. I need all the good markers I can get."

# 16

BUD AND IRENE WHEELER walked gingerly down the stairs of their farmhouse. Bud wore corduroy jeans, a plaid flannel shirt, and floppy slippers. Irene was in her nightgown and robe. They were both seventy, and the stairs had been a lot friendlier to them once upon a time.

"Didn't sleep a wink," Bud growled for the third or fourth time.

Behind him, Irene Wheeler said, "I know, dear."

"Thought for sure I heard someone down here. Thought for sure!"

"I know, dear."

In the kitchen, Irene put on the kettle for a little lunchtime tea and got the makings of tuna fish sandwiches out of the fridge. Bud went to the back door, opened it, stepped outside, bent gingerly, and retrieved the dog's water dish. Irene turned from the fridge, glanced over her husband's stooped back, and realized that a gigantic airplane wing had scythed into the ground, destroying their barbecue pit and part of the porch. It stood up at a ten-degree angle and was taller than their old maple tree.

Bud walked to the sink and began filling the dog's bowl. "Thought for sure I heard something last night."

. . .

In the high school parking lot, the crashers discovered that Susan had arranged for four Sentra rentals, all identical. Isaiah Grey took a set of keys. "I'm heading to the airport. Anyone else?"

"You'll pass the crash site," Walter Mulroney said. "Give me a lift?"

Tommy's satellite phone chimed and he answered it as Kiki Duvall announced that she was heading back to the hotel to get the digitalized cockpit voice recording, then would head to the crash site. John Roby said he would join her, since he had determined in his own mind that there would be no bomb residue to look for at the crash site.

Tommy disconnected and turned to Peter Kim, tossing him one of the sets of keys. "Petey? They found your other wing. Farmhouse, couple miles away. Trooper's waiting for you at the crash site and will take you there."

Peter nodded, wordlessly, and climbed into the sedan.

That left Tommy and Susan Tanaka. "I'm heading into Portland, too. Gotta autopsy the pilots."

"On one hour of sleep?"

He shrugged. "It's why I love being a pathologist. No small talk. No asking polite questions. You just open 'em and poke around inside."

"You're a highly demented person, Dr. Tomzak."

He climbed into the third Sentra. "Maybe you oughtn'ta put me in charge of this circus!"

## LOS ANGELES, OCEAN PARK

"So tell me about this Daria," Lucas Bell said.

Ray Calabrese made the turn onto Pico and shrugged. The dashboard clock said it was noon, straight up. The lunch-hour traffic was a bear and the rain was coming down lightly. The storm would burn off soon. "She came into the country three years ago, after a career as a spook. She'd have been a terrific asset for the CIA or even the Bureau, if she wasn't such a flibbertigibbet."

Lucas studied him for a moment. "You straight people say the damnedest things."

"Yeah." Ray nodded. "We tend to look a lot alike, too. You ever notice that?"

They cruised past the bar Daria had told them about, looking for a place to park.

"Gibron. She's what? Lebanese?"

"Israeli," Ray said. "She was a deep-cover Shin Bet agent, assigned to live in the West Bank, which she did for several years. She found out that a right-wing contingent in her own operation was afraid al Qaeda was going to get a toehold in Jerusalem, maybe even split the city like Berlin. They decided to have a liberal member of their own Knesset assassinated and to blame Islamist extremists. Daria didn't think that was right, and she didn't know who in her own agency she could trust. She didn't know who was CIA and who wasn't, and she didn't know if she trusted them, either."

"Smart girl."

"Yeah. Fortunately, there was an FBI operation in Beirut, there to train Israeli soldiers how to hunt for bodies in blown-up buildings."

Lucas snorted. "You wouldn't think they'd need help with that. They should be experts."

"We had some new heat-source-seeking technology. I was with the team. Anyway, she found us and we made a sort of crazy decision. The hit was happening within a couple of hours, so we informed Washington, then interceded ourselves. We stopped the plot and we won the thanks of the Knesset and Washington and all was well. But Daria took two bullets in the midsection. We didn't know who to trust any more than she had, so we evac'd her to Ramstein, and once she was better, she asked for asylum in the U.S. The brass said yes."

He stopped at a space and slid the dark blue Caprice into place. But before they stepped out, Lucas turned to Ray and said, "You've got a thing for her?"

Ray barked a laugh. "No. I'm her handler."

"As it were . . ."

"No! Seriously. She's . . . she's a hand grenade in high heels. Who needs the trouble?"

"Sure." Lucas let it slide. They stepped out and joined each other on the sidewalk. He glanced up, realizing that the rain had stopped.

They both checked the sky. The radio had said that L.A. was in for some hot weather by the end of the week. Still, they stashed their umbrellas for good luck.

# *17*

WALTER MULRONEY STOOD BACK, fists on his hips, and studied the three visible sections of the jetliner. Four of his structures crew stood with him, two of them drawing sketches and trying to calculate the stress factors, for when they brought in cranes to pick up the fuselage. He checked his twenty-year-old Timex. It was going on 12:30 P.M.

The six-two Kansan looked around, found one of the state-police troopers, and waved him over. "Officer, know where they found the other wing?"

The cop pointed across Interstate 5 and upward, to a two-story farmhouse atop a small hillock. "Dropped straight down in some guy's barbecue pit."

As Walter squinted in that direction, he caught a glimpse of two state-police cruisers and a white Sentra arriving at the farmhouse. That would be Peter, he thought.

## WHEELER RESIDENCE

Peter Kim took three of his power-plant team and four state-police troopers to the home of Bud and Irene Wheeler to begin the process of securing the starboard wing. They couldn't move it, of course, but they could make sure it remained untouched.

Bud Wheeler met them at the front gate of his property. Behind him, they could see the white-painted, two-story house with its majestic stand of oak trees. The Vermeer wing wasn't visible from where the cars had stopped. Peter and the others climbed out.

Peter walked up to the gate. "Excuse me. Are you the owner of this property?"

The elderly man on the other side of the wooden gate glowered at him, arms folded across his ample chest. "I am. Bud Wheeler. And you are . . . ?"

"My name is Peter Kim. I'm a chief investigator for the National Transportation Safety Board. We're here to check on the wing, and we want to leave one of these troopers here to secure the area, if that's all right with—"

"Nope," Bud Wheeler said. "You can turn yourselves around and get off my property. Right now."

Peter blinked at him. "I beg your pardon?"

"Just turn your little Japanese butt around and get off my property, Mr. Safety Transportation Board. I've contacted my lawyer in Portland. He's on his way. And until I speak to him, nobody's stepping on this property."

Peter's face slid into a soft, predatory smile. He enjoyed confrontation. "First, sir, I'm Korean American. Second, this is a federal investigation. You can't keep us out. And third, what do you need an attorney for? You haven't done anything wrong, have you?"

A thought fell into place and worry flickered in Peter's eyes. "You haven't, have you? You haven't touched anything or tried to take any souvenirs. Right?"

"Get the hell off my property," Bud Wheeler repeated. "Somebody's gonna pay for destroying my barbecue. I'm going to sue the airline company and the people who made the wing and the people who made the engine. I'm gonna sue the Portland airport. I'm gonna sue the captain and his crew. And in about ten seconds, I'm gonna sue your ass, too. Now get off my property before—"

"Officer," Peter Kim turned to one of the troopers, "arrest this man."

The troopers eyed one another. "I'm not sure we can—"

"This is a federal investigation," Peter almost growled back at him. "Yes, you can. Do it."

And they did. Irene Wheeler stood in her bedroom and watched through her window as troopers handcuffed her husband and eased him into the back of their prowl car.

She hit the Redial button on her cordless phone and called their attorney.

## FIELD OF GRASS

Susan said, "Has anyone seen Peter Kim? He went after the missing wing."

One of the engineers shrugged. "He and his guys aren't back yet."

Susan had just arrived at the crash site. She'd picked chocolate suede boots today. As usual, her ensemble was splendid and stylish. Absolutely nobody noticed.

She turned and found a stranger approaching. He was a tad overweight, wore thick glasses, corduroy slacks, tennis shoes, and a frayed green sweater. He carried a largish computer bag slung over one shoulder. "Are you Miss Tanaka?" he asked.

"Yes. You are—?"

"I'm here about the Gamelan," the man replied and smiled broadly.

As far as Susan knew, a gamelan was an Indonesian musical instrument. She said, "Excuse me?"

"The Gamelan," he repeated. "It's the flight data recorder. It monitors all the automated, preflight, and in-flight indicators on board the jet. My company makes the interface controls right here in Oregon. Beaverton, actually. Anyway, my company sent me to help the systems crew figure out what went wrong."

"Good. Do you have a card?" He handed her one. Susan dug out her notepad and pen. "Your crew chief is Walter Mulroney. I'll introduce you. We'll have our first major debriefing this evening around eight. I don't know the venue yet. We'll be in touch, Mister—"

She read the card. "Mr. Silverman."

"Dennis," he said, and smiled.

## 18

SUSAN! HOW ARE WE doing?" Kiki Duvall asked as she and John Roby climbed out of the rental. They had just arrived, and with Kiki was the digital recording of the cockpit voice recorder. Susan had been talking to an overweight, nerdy-looking guy with a laptop-size messenger bag. She was pointing across the field toward Walter, and the nerdy-looking guy headed that way.

John Roby moved off into the field, too.

Susan Tanaka removed her ear jack and frowned.

Kiki blinked at her. "What's up?"

"That was Peter on the line. He's got the missing wing but there's a complication. He said he didn't want to explain over the line. All he said was, we should expect a call from Farmer Sloyer."

Kiki said, "Who's Farmer Sloyer?"

"I don't know. Peter sounded royally pissed off."

"Whose farm did they go out to?"

Susan said, "Wheeler. Bud Wheeler."

Kiki said, "Not Sloyer?"

"No, Wheeler."

Kiki's ability to discern patterns in acoustical signatures kicked in. She said, "Oh, crud."

Susan said, "What?"

"Not Farmer Sloyer. Farmer's lawyer."

Susan said, "Oh, crud."


## FIELD OF GRASS

Walter Mulroney squinted up at the darkening sky and said, "Crab cakes."

"'S all right." John Roby stepped up next to him. "You can say *crap*. We're in a farmer's field. People will think you're making an observation about the soil."

Walter glowered at the small, compact Englishman. "Tomzak is a pathologist. He can't run this Go-Team."

John shrugged. "You think?"

Walter said morosely, "What do you know?"

"I know there was no bomb."

There was something about John Roby's casual certainty that drove Walter nuts. "You can't know that until you've done a forensic investigation. Dang it, Roby, this is serious business! We're not goofing around out here."

John patted him on the shoulder, not in an unfriendly manner. He really didn't want to be the enemy of the crew boss of the structures team. "If there was a major explosive on board, I'd smell it. It's a distinctive aroma, that."

"This field stinks of oil and death."

"True. But high explosives also leave fairly obvious visual clues behind, and there's none to be seen on the fuselage. Don't care if you're talking about the CIA's fanciest designer explosive or five-for-a-penny fuel-and-nitrate pipe bombs made in someone's flat. I've walked the perimeter of this beast," he said, and motioned toward the three major sections of the Vermeer 111. "No soot deposits higher than the burning grass. No radial streaks on the surface. No blast cratering. No gas wash." He shrugged. *Elementary.*

Walter didn't know what most of that information meant, but he had to admit that Roby seemed casually adamant about his knowledge. They both looked up as a younger man approached. He was egg shaped and wore thick glasses and wrinkled, baggy clothes. His hair was disheveled.

"Sorry, mate," John said. "We can't blame any terrorists for bringing down this jet."

· · ·

The tubby man with thick glasses approaching Walter and John now offered his hand and smiled big. "You're Walter Mulroney?"

Walter shook his hand, nodded his jowly head.

"Dennis Silverman. Gamelan Industries. We design the—"

Walter smiled. "A Gamelan! I've been hoping to see if these are all they're cracked up to be."

John said, "Sorry?"

"John Roby, bomb expert. Dennis Silverman. His company makes a state-of-the-art flight data recorder that stores a thousand telltales."

Dennis shrugged. "About two thousand, really."

Walter pointed to the Vermeer. "Best of my knowledge, this is the first jetliner with a Gamelan recorder to go down."

Dennis beamed. "Y'know? You just might be right."


Five minutes later, Walter Mulroney and Dennis Silverman knelt in the churned-up soil, Dennis on his haunches, Walter down on his hands in the dirt, his head only ten inches off the ground. He was staring at the surface of the twisted gob of aluminum, steel, and glass that had been the nose of the jetliner. John Roby had walked to the other end of the field and was doing yet another walkaround of the empennage, or tail cone, looking for any signs of a midair detonation and finding none.

Dennis said, "Do you see it?"

"No good news," Walter said. "The infrared input node is there but it's busted up. No way you can access the FDR from here."

Dennis smiled amiably. He stood, hands stuffed into the pockets of his cords. "That's all right. I can hardwire the Gamelan and take out all the information she's carrying."

Walter stood up and clapped the caked dirt off his hands. "Thank God for that, son."


## MULTNOMAH COUNTY MEDICAL EXAMINER'S OFFICE, PORTLAND

One does not get to be an intake clerk at a medical examiner's office without having a strong stomach.

Today, that was being put to the test. The day-shift clerk for the medical examiner's office for Multnomah County had never seen so many bodies at once. His intake area held fifteen corpses. And he knew that this was a small percentage of the cadavers heading his way.

Before his brain could begin to register those numbers, double swinging doors burst open and the medical examiner entered, along with a wiry guy with an NTSB jacket, lanky hair that hung into his eyebrows, and the kind of buzz about him one gets from too little sleep and too much caffeine.

The medical examiner, Dr. Ellis Ridgeway, carried a clipboard and his reading glasses. "We've got pathologists and coroners from every corner of the state, as well as Washington, volunteering to help. If we keep our suites operating around the clock, I can autopsy the victims in . . . three, maybe three and a half days."

"Good," said the stranger with a Texas twang. "Y'all got mass spectrometers?"

The examiner nodded. "We have one that—"

"You're gonna need more. Every bit of metal that entered these folks, we gotta take out."

"Ah . . ." Ridgeway started to respond.

"Got X-ray machines?"

"Again, we have one—"

"That's gonna be a choke point for getting these folks through," the Texan said, then made eye contact with the intake clerk. "Hi. Tommy Tomzak. NTSB. You're . . . ?"

"Jeff Tr—"

"Jeff, call some hospitals. Get us portable X-ray equipment." He turned back to Dr. Ridgeway. "Everyone gets X-rayed twice. From two angles."

"Twice? I don't—"

The Texan picked up a slim metal ruler from the clerk's desk. "There's aluminum inside these poor, dumb bastards. This thin, maybe thinner. Shoot the X-rays from the wrong angle . . ." Tommy turned the ruler sideways.

Dr. Ridgeway nodded.

Tommy eyed the intake clerk. "How you doing, Jeff?"

He wet his lips. "That's, ah, a lot of bodies."

Tommy slapped him on the shoulder. "Fuckin' A." He turned back to the coroner. "First thing up, we need tox tests for both pilots. Check for everything: alcohol, street drugs, meds, poison."

"Poison?"

"Rule out nothing. Also, we're getting the medical files for 'em both. Check the pilot, Meghan Danvers. Find out how tall she's supposed to be."

"Supposed to be? I don't—"

Tommy said, "I got five bucks says she's two, three centimeters short. Wanna know why?"

Both the medical examiner and the intake clerk nodded, realizing that they were in way over their heads here.

Tommy mimed holding the yoke of the jetliner. "If she was trying to bring up the nose of that plane, she'd've planted her boots and hauled on the stick like a sumbitch. When the plane hit, it would break her spine in enough places to shorten her. If she's presenting compression fractures, it'll tell us shitloads about the last seconds."

Dr. Ridgeway and Jeff looked at each other. They were in the tall weeds.

"'Kay, folks!" Tommy checked his watch. "Let's rock 'n' roll."

It was 1:30 P.M.


Traditionally, autopsies go like this: X-rays, visual inspection of the epidermis, open the chest, then open the skull.

After an airplane crash, it's slightly different. First comes a proper videotaping of everything, plus a sketch of all external wounds. That's followed by a mass spectrometer or metal detector, to look for fragments. Then come the X-rays and the rest. The process is time consuming. But the trajectory and resting patterns of the shrapnel are as important in a crash investigation as the bodies themselves.


The medical examiner's team started on Captain Meghan Danvers by taking samples for the toxicology screening. They drew blood directly from her heart to check for bacteria. They also drew urine, bile, and a little of the fluid from her left eye.

The morgue was crowded. Half of the MEs who had traveled to Oregon Health & Science University for the convention had called their bosses and spouses and told them that they would be staying on. Most of them looked like physicians and dressed like physicians. They drove expensive cars and lived in fancy homes. Tommy Tomzak dressed—and swore—like a dockworker half the time. The other medical examiners played golf or yachted. Tommy played pickup ball at the Y; half-court, three-on-three, make it–take it and call your own fouls. He was an atypical doctor, but there was absolutely no question about who was in charge.

He changed to scrubs, then sketched Captain Danvers's external wounds, front and back, as the morgue attendant shot video of the whole scene. When he was done, Tommy reached for the heavy scalpel. He began by making the classic Y-shaped incision from shoulders to midchest, then down to the pubic bone. Normally, he would have used shears to snip through her rib cage and breastbone, exposing the abdominal organs. In this case, the airplane yoke had staved in her ribs. The existing wound finished the downstroke of the Y incision.

Carefully recording everything into the dangling microphone, Tommy snipped out the heart and lungs and inspected their mass. They were severely deformed or perforated from the cracked ribs and hydrostatic shock. He weighed them. Next, he took out the kidneys, liver, and spleen. Each was visually inspected and weighed, and each was put in its own Tupperware-like plastic container. Each of the containers went into a self-sealing biohazard bag.

Tommy removed the smaller organs, the adrenals and thyroid, and a medical technician weighed them on a much smaller, triple-beam balance. Tommy removed his goggles and wiped his brow. His gloves were fairly clean; there's almost no bleeding in an autopsy because the fluids have settled and there's no blood pressure. After gulping water from a bottle, he moved up to her head.

"The scalp is reflected, revealing contusions with associated subgaleal hemorrhaging over the right occipital region," he said into the mic. "The basilar skull is lined with fine fractures. The calvarium has fewer fractures. We got us one big, badass hematoma on the right side. Subdural, covering most of the right temporal lobe. Figure that alone would've killed her. The spinal cord is intact. Okay, someone want to do the honors?"

He stood back as a lab assistant powered up the skull saw.

## 19

IT WAS GOING ON 2 P.M. when Daria Gibron found the first of the Irishmen. He was a massive, thick-boned man with no neck. The night before, the others had called him Johnser. He was the one who had won a bet in the bar. Daria started asking around the neighborhood and heard where a couple of standing poker games could be found. That had produced nothing but the names of some bookies who could be counted on to run some lines. She'd had no luck there, but had been pointed to a sports bar. No luck, but another tavern was named. This one had five television sets showing five sporting events. And there was Johnser, at the grungy, Formica-on-particle-board bar, slapping down a hundred bucks and grumbling about a just-completed golf game.

"Fucking wanker!" he bellowed at the set. No one in the bar seemed to disagree.

Dressed up for her meeting with the Egyptian and the Englishman, Daria was as conspicuous in the dingy sports bar as a clean glass would have been. She found a booth near the women's restroom and ordered a vodka straight up and watched Johnser bet on a bowling tournament.

During the next hour, three men tried to pick her up. She told each that she was waiting for her husband. Johnser was so absorbed in his winnings and losings, he never came close to noticing her.

Just a little past three in the afternoon, a man slid into the booth opposite Daria. He was blond and had a crooked smile and a chipped tooth and a nose broken and badly repaired, but he was handsome for all that, and he knew it. He wore a Blue Devils sweatshirt under a black leather biker jacket, the sweatshirt hood hanging outside the jacket. He held a plastic, ivory-colored toothpick in his mouth. It was the kind that came in some pocket knives, along with little scissors and a screwdriver. "I am madly in love with you," he announced.

Across the bar, Johnser stood up and paid his bar tab.

"I've got to go," Daria said.

"Hey." The blond man reached across and trapped her hand on the table. He winked at her. "You've been here for at least forty minutes, and I can't take my eyes off you. C'mon. This place is a shit hole. Let me buy you a nice drink."

"Please," she said, and smiled at him, shrugging in apology. Johnser was halfway to the door. Daria pulled her hand back but the blond man didn't let go.

"Ah-ah," he said, still smiling. With his tongue, he shifted the ivory toothpick to the other corner of his mouth. "Come on. One drink. We could go around the corner, to my place. It's clean."

Johnser was nearer to her now, so Daria leaned back into the booth, hiding from him, and pretended to think about the offer. "Well . . ."

"There you go," the blond man said, winking. "We'll have a couple of shots, you'll tell me your life story."

Daria heard the little bell over the door, knew that Johnser had stepped outside. She leaned forward and laid out her other hand, palm up. The blond man smiled contentedly and moved his hand, grasping the one that she offered.

Daria said, "Maybe another time." She twisted sharply, her elbow in the air. The blond man's thumb broke. Two thin bones in his wrist sheared. His eyes bulged, his tongue moved as if to warble but he made no sound.

Daria stood and was across the room, her hand on the door, when she heard the blond man puke.

The most disturbing thing about the encounter, Daria knew, was that on another day, she might well have said yes the first time he asked.

## LOS ANGELES

Donal O'Meara set two six-packs of Samuel Adams on the middle of the little round table and said, "Help yerselves, then." Back home, of course, it would have been Harp or Guinness. But he'd soon figured out that the horse piss they passed off as Guinness in the States was a faint fake compared to the real thing. He vowed not to taste the deep, dark brew until his feet touched the soil of Northern Ireland again.

An Ireland free from the grasp of Rome.

"Ta," said the smallest in the group, a wiry little man from Derry named Feargal Kelly. He was a fine gunman, O'Meara thought, both a gifted sniper and good at up-close wet work. A little crazy, but then who wasn't? Next to him sat Keith O'Shea, who'd been born on the beautiful Antrim Coast and who'd learned to hate the Catholics after his father and older brother were slaughtered by a bomber in Kilkeel. O'Shea was a fighter, pure and simple. He liked a knife but could use the machine pistol with the best of them. These two, with Johnser Riley's bulk, fighting skills, and pure meanness, made for a good quick-strike team.

"So it worked," Kelly said, draining a third of his beer.

O'Meara nodded. "Our friend sounds like a right wanker but he delivered. Simple as that."

They clinked the necks of their beer bottles together.

"But can he do it again?" O'Shea asked. "Can he bring down the plane we tell him to?"

"Fella says he can," O'Meara said, and shrugged. "Got no reason to doubt him so far. The flight happens in a couple of days. When it does, we let our friend deal with it. That'll put things right."

"Aye," the others chimed in, just as the door of their hole-up opened. Johnser Riley rolled in with that John Wayne walk he was perfecting.

On the street below them, Daria made note of the address. The building looked like it was deserted. No life was evident from the street, but this was where the big Irishman had gone.

She tried the door, found it locked. He must have had a key.

She found a space between the apartment building and the next one, too narrow to be called an alley. The space was cobwebbed and no wider than her shoulders. The narrow shaft of air was dark, the ground cluttered with beer bottles and bricks. She started edging her way down the space, walking sideways, the front and back of her sporty jacket quickly growing filthy with soot. Rats squealed, dodging over and around her open-toed slingbacks. She wished she hadn't worn a short skirt. The thin space smelled of urine. She got to the end and found a narrow courtyard tucked among all the tall buildings. No sun had touched the ground back here in genera-tions. A rail-thin cat arched its back and hissed at her. Stained mattresses were stacked up, reeking of mildew. A child's Big Wheel lay on its side under a fine layer of dust. More rats skittered away; some stood their ground and stared at her with red eyes.

Daria found a window low to the ground and broke it with her elbow. She used a bit of brick to clear it all away. She buttoned up her black leather Versace jacket—it was ruined anyway—then got down on her stomach and climbed into the rank darkness of the condemned apartment build-ing, wiggling through the window headfirst, her body blocking all light.

# 20

"EXCUSE ME?"

The bartender, a thick cube of a man with a cauliflower ear and a marine buzz cut, turned to the two men in blue suits. One suit was off the rack and generic. A big guy wore that one. The other was hand-tailored and unique. A black guy wore that one. Both held badges.

"Yeah?"

Ray Calabrese pulled the photo of O'Meara out of his jacket pocket. "We're with the FBI. We're looking for this man."

The bartender slipped on a pair of bifocals, the earpieces held together with black tape, and took the photo, holding it at an angle to negate reflections from the overhead lights. "He's a mick?"

Ray said, "Yes, sir."

"Yeah, he and his buddies come in here a lot this week. Real full of themselves, you know? All piss and vinegar. Sometimes they pick up ladies, sometimes they just sit in the back and make fun of American beer and baseball and shit."

Lucas Bell pulled an envelope out of his pocket and produced eight more photos, all taken at British prisons. It hadn't taken him five minutes on the computer to come up with O'Meara's likely collaborators. "Do you recognize any of these men?"

The bartender scanned them all. He selected three. "Yeah. These guys hang around with the first guy."

Ray said, "Were they in here last night?"

"Yeah." The bartender didn't seem too happy about it.

"Was there trouble?" Lucas asked.

The big man shrugged. "One of them made a bet, is all. He cleaned at least three hundred out of my regulars, made 'em look like chumps, really laughed at 'em. People come in here to relax, you know? They don't want to be made fun of or nothing."

Ray said, "Sure. Any idea where we can find these guys?"

"I don't know what they do for a living but they been hanging out in this neighborhood for about a week now. They buy groceries down at the corner and they eat at Mario's, across the street." He pointed out the front window. "They're like cockroaches. Big, mick cockroaches. They're everywhere."

He paused, his eyes narrowing. "No offense. You're not Irish, are you?"

Ray said, "Well, I'm not . . ." and nodded toward Lucas.

While the bartender pondered that, Ray slid the first photo back into his pocket, then handed the bartender his business card. "If you see these guys, call this number, please. And don't tell them we're looking for them."

The bartender said, "You got it. Ship 'em back to fucking Ireland, I say."

The FBI agents started to turn away. Ray turned back. "Out of curiosity, which guy won the three hundred bucks off your regulars?"

"That big blond guy."

"Yeah? Can I ask how?"

It was a good question. It was the kind of detail about a suspect that could lead to an arrest.

"Damnedest thing." The bartender shook his head. "This guy bets us that the top story on TV would be a disaster. Some kind of crash, he said. Lots of deaths. I'll be damned if they didn't break in to the news with a . . . what do you call it? A breaking story. Seems some airplane crash up in Oregon or Washington or some such."

He smiled and shrugged. His smile wilted when he realized that the two FBI agents were staring at him, their mouths open.

The bartender said, "What?"

Ray turned to Lucas and said, "Christ almighty."

# 21

THE AFTERNOON-SHIFT GROUND CREW at the airport wore bright orange jumpsuits with THE SULTANS OF SWING stenciled on the back. As they arrived for that day's work, they were greeted by a shift leader, officials from the airport, and representatives of their union. Angela Abdalla, of the Port of Portland's incident-investigation team, was there with a black guy who was going a little gray and wearing the windbreaker and ball cap of the National Transportation Safety Board. The black guy thumbed through a stack of papers the crew recognized as the Vermeer's transit check: the routine maintenance reports, consisting of not much more than walkarounds and topping the fluid levels, which occur every seven days or thirty-five flight hours.

"People," Angela Abdalla said, getting the ball rolling. Those who knew her, or who just had seen her around the airport, thought she appeared exhausted and rumpled, rather than her usual, sleek executive look. "This is Isaiah Grey. He's with the NTSB. We need to figure out what happened with the Vermeer yesterday, and he's going to need your help."

"He needs to figure out how us dumb ground crews fucked up?" one of the men shouted back. The others rumbled, too.

"Yup," Isaiah cut in mildly, and the honesty surprised everyone. Not looking up from his clipboard, he gave it two beats. "Maybe you did screw up. Maybe you didn't. Maybe the pilot was stoned. Maybe she wasn't. Maybe the plane missed its last maintenance rotation. Maybe it didn't. Maybe a guy named Yousef was sitting at the end of the runway with a Stinger missile in the back of a Jeep Cherokee that he bought, cheap, in Uzbekistan."

Isaiah clicked open a pen. Signed something. He still hadn't looked up. When he did, he said, "The Stinger, not the Cherokee. And maybe the guy's name was Jim Bob and he fired it to protest gay rights. What I'm saying is: we don't know what the hell happened yet. But we've got to figure it out, and you know I'm right. For good or bad. Okay?"

The crews weren't happy about it, but their crew chief stood up and crossed his arms across his barrel chest. "Listen up! We're gonna help this guy and get back to work. That's the plan. Got a problem with it, tough. Let's get busy."

And they did.


## LOS ANGELES

From their sedan, Ray Calabrese and Lucas Bell called the federal building and got Assistant Director Henry Deits on the line. Deits turned it into a conference call, with all of his top brass.

"The bartender identified O'Meara and three known associates of the Red Fist of Ulster," Lucas said into the handheld radio. "All four were in a bar down here, near the garment district, last night. One of them, John Padraic Riley, DOB nine four seventy-seven, made a bet at the bar. He said the top story on last night's news would be a major crash with lots of deaths."

The agents could hear FBI brass mutter a couple of curses.

"Are you declaring this a terrorist incident, Agent Bell?" Deits asked.

Ray and Lucas exchanged glances. Ray took the handheld unit. "Sir, we have a correlation between known terrorists and the downing of an airliner in Oregon. Again, it's a correlation. We don't know for sure that they caused it, but one of them predicted it. We don't want to declare a known terrorist incident yet, but we want to bring these guys in as soon as humanly possible."

"Agreed," Deits said. "Liz is here. Liz, how many agents can you get down to the garment district?"

They heard the voice of the deputy assistant director in charge of terrorist activities, Liz Geddes. "I can have thirty-five people in your position in ten minutes, Ray. I'll have LAPD SWAT back them up."

"Okay, here's the deal." He told the brass about the bar, the corner grocery store, and the restaurant known as Mario's. He also described the general neighborhood and recommended that teams dress down in civilian clothes ("ditch all the navy blues and wingtips") to begin canvassing the scene.

Everyone agreed. Ray and Lucas checked the ammunition in their 9-mm Glock automatics, then opened the trunk of their sedan. Ray also checked the small, matte black Kahr K9 clipped to his right ankle.

"Little somethin'-somethin' should the need arise?" Lucas asked.

"Something like that." They doffed their neckties and suit coats and found a couple of blue microfiber jackets with Velcro-covered shoulder patches that covered the letters FBI. There also were Kevlar vests and riot guns, but they left those where they were. They left the walkie-talkies, too, relying on their cell phones. They checked the batteries to make sure they were charged. "I'll go east," Lucas said. "You go west."

Ray nodded and they headed off in opposite directions, to see what could be seen before the cavalry arrived.

When they ran out of beer, Donal O'Meara sent the wiry little Derry man, Feargal Kelly, to get some more from the grocery down on the corner.

Daria scrounged through her purse for the disposable Bic lighter, found it, and illuminated the basement she'd landed in. It stank of old garbage, human shit, and rats. Red eyes blinked around her when the flame appeared. She couldn't see more than five feet ahead of her and slowly scanned the room. It was musty. Someone had drawn outrageous graffiti all over the walls; not the creative, urban-message stuff, but obscenities and cartoons. A fine layer of soot and grease covered the graffiti, suggesting that it was at least a decade old. She walked into a spiderweb, felt something skitter through her hair. She stumbled backward over an old carton and almost lost the Bic, the flame going out. She thumbed the mechanism, got the pale yellow light back. She found a doorway with no door, blackness beyond. She edged that way and entered, with no idea what lay beyond.

Daria felt more alive than she had felt for three years.

# 22

NEITHER RAY CALABRESE NOR Lucas Bell found the first of the Irishmen. Instead, it was two FBI agents in an unmarked prowl car. They passed Feargal Kelly without slowing down or even appearing to look at him. Kelly took a key out of his pocket and ran up the three steps to an abandoned tenement building. Abandoned it might have been, but the key fit and the door opened. He disappeared inside. The two agents rounded a corner and immediately spotted Lucas trotting down the sidewalk. They pulled over.

"Got one of your perps," said the driver, rolling down his window. "Round the corner on Twenty-eighth. Went into one of those abandoned apartment buildings, the big brick job on the right side."

Lucas knelt. "Okay, good. Ray Calabrese is four blocks from here. Go get him and bring him back. I'll keep my eyes on this guy. Hey, in Ireland, these assholes regularly monitor emergency bands. You go eyeball Calabrese and tell him what you told me, but face-to-face."

The driver said, "Got it. Watch your ass," and pulled away.

Lucas crossed the street and hit the sidewalk, heading down Twenty-eighth. He checked his watch. He scanned the windows carefully, then jogged across the street and dug lock picks out of his wallet.

. . .

Daria made it up to the ground floor as quietly as she could and put the Bic back into her purse. This floor had been turned into a shooting gallery, each room littered with stained box springs, syringes, used condoms. It stank to hell. Maybe, she thought, it stank of hell.

In the gloom, Daria doffed her ruined coat, threw it into one of the rooms. She tossed her purse in, too. It contained no weapons, and she wanted her hands free. She was dressed entirely wrong for crawling through windows and skulking through drug dens—the four-inch heels would have to go, not that she hadn't been fully trained in how to move in the stilettos better than most people could in sneakers. Besides, her years in the Israeli army and Shin Bet had taught her to be nothing if not resourceful.

She heard noises above and crept up the first flight of stairs she found, stepping on the risers near the wall, not in the center of the stairs, where they were more likely to squeak. The noises from the supposedly abandoned apartment building were coming from the ground floor. Daria paused at the top of the stairs, noted that heavy foot traffic had scraped away a layer of dust and dirt. She was close enough to recognize the voices now. One of them was Jack's. She didn't know how much farther she could creep without being noticed. She glanced up. Much of the ceiling on the first floor had disintegrated, and she caught glimpses of light from the next floor up. The question was: go up to the second floor and try to listen to the conversations happening below, or try to get closer to them on this floor?

The decision was taken out of her hands. A key rattled in the ground-floor entryway and hinges squealed.

Daria bolted up the next flight a little faster than she should have. A length of handrail had fallen off. She stepped over it carefully, trying not to send it clattering down the stairs. Risers groaned ominously under her weight and a fine salt of dust floated down onto the landing where she'd been crouching.

She made it to the next landing and skidded to a stop—most of the floorboards were thoroughly rotted away and clearly wouldn't hold her weight. She teetered, almost falling through, and took the risk of planting one shoe on each of the only two floorboards that looked sound. Daria straddled a gaping hole leading to the floor below. She was fully exposed, should anyone choose to look up. She flattened herself against the cobwebbed wall as best she could.

Below her, someone clomped up to the second floor. Daria looked down between her feet through the gap in the floorboards. The man she knew as Jack approached, a silver Colt Python in his hand; he spun around the corner, pointed the massive .357 revolver at the man ascending.

"Jay-sus!" the newcomer squawked.

"What are you playing at, ye fuck!" Jack boomed.

"Put that cannon away, you!"

Jack tucked his gun into a shoulder holster. "You made enough noise to raise the dead."

"Pff. If isn't Donal himself O'Meara, acting like me mother. Don't piss yourself, you."

The newcomer trudged the rest of the way up. As he passed below her, Daria saw that his grocery bag was filled with beer.

If either man looked up, they would have been treated to a very unladylike vision straight up Daria's short skirt.

Neither man looked up.


Daria was still standing there, thirty seconds later, when the scratch of lock picks reached her ears. The hinges squealed again.

She waited, pressed against the wall. A spider skittered across her shoulder and clavicle. She plucked it away.

Below her, through the holes in the floorboards, she saw a black man skulking up the stairs.

*Now what?* she wondered.

Below her, directly beneath her patent-leather heels, Daria saw the stranger kneel. He gripped a matte black Glock in his left hand. With his right, he quietly peeled a Velcro-laden flap off the arm of his dark blue windbreaker.

Daria squinted. Beneath the flap were the letters FBI.

Still straddling the gap in the floor, the floorboard under her left shoe squeaking a little, she craned her neck, peering through the rotted floor. The space below had been a living room, once upon a time. She saw the four Irishmen there now. They'd set up a table and chairs and a couple of couches. They were pirating electricity from somewhere. Probably the next apartment building over. But they were being smart about it; electricity for space heaters and a hot plate and a small fridge, but not for lights.

As she watched, the man she knew as Jack held a finger to his lips. He gestured in the direction of the stairs. Two of Jack's men disappeared from Daria's line of sight, moving off to the left.

Daria mouthed the word *shit* in English and in Hebrew.

Where one FBI man is, can others be far away? She concentrated, listening hard. Where the hell was this man's backup? Where the hell was Ray Calabrese?

Jack and the biggest of his cronies had drawn their weapons in the room beyond. They were moving cautiously toward the second-story landing. Daria couldn't see, but she was sure the other two were circling around for the same destination.

Daria mouthed the word *shit* in Arabic and in Italian.

Ray Calabrese parked himself half a block and across the street from the building that the two agents in the prowl car had told him about. Ray's cell phone vibrated. He was sure it would be Lucas, but the alphanumeric code that appeared read SWAT, followed by a seven-digit number.

Ray dialed the number and was connected to the special-weapons commander, FBI. He was assured that three unmarked cars had just entered the field of play—a panel truck with the decals of the L.A. Department of Water and Power, a UPS delivery van, and a battered Ford Econoline. Ray could see all three and thought they blended nicely into the down-on-its-luck neighborhood.

His cell phone vibrated again. Again, he assumed it would be Lucas. And again, he was wrong. It was Assistant Director Henry Deits.

Ray told Deits that they had the place under visual surveillance and that the cavalry (mechanized, of course) had arrived.

Satisfied, Deits wished him good luck and rang off.

Ray went back to watching the building, assuming that Lucas had tucked himself into another doorway or alcove along the block.

Standing on the last two decent floorboards of the second-story landing, Daria Gibron made a decision.

Lucas Bell crouched. Since hitting the first-floor landing, all noises had died away. Lucas wasn't very happy about that.

*Concentrate,* he told himself. *Do your job. Find O'Meara and the others and get your ass back down to the street.*

.   .   .

Donal O'Meara and Johnser Riley approached from the bivouac they'd carved out of the abandoned apartment. They'd definitely heard something near the stairs. O'Meara had sent the other two around through a hole they'd found punched through a bathroom wall; a classic pincer trap.

They were on the verge of greatness. Now wasn't the time to fuck up.

Lucas Bell had just decided to push forward when a flash of flesh caught his eye at the very edge of his peripheral vision. He turned. The woman he recognized from Calabrese's files as Daria Gibron stood behind him with a length of handrail the size of a pool cue. Before he could react, the muscles of her shoulders bunched and she jammed the blunt end of the rail into Lucas's side, right above his kidney.

The pain was instantaneous and paralyzing. Every muscle in his body spasmed. He stiffened, couldn't inhale. He saw the rail spin like a bo staff, saw the other end swing down and around. It caught him under the chin. With a grunt, Lucas went sprawling, his Glock clattering to the floor.

Donal O'Meara stood, stunned. A black man slid into view only a few feet off the floor. He slammed into the far wall, all but unconscious, blood flowing from a split lip.

The next instant, another figure appeared over the fallen man. It was a woman in an absurdly short skirt and heels and a black shirt with blousy sleeves. She carried a length of wooden dowel, one end wet with a splatter of blood. O'Meara didn't recognize her at first. Then his eyes narrowed. "It's you!"

The other two men appeared at the women's left, four guns trained on her, four shocked faces. Keith O'Shea said, "The fuck?"

She dropped the length of rail. It clattered and sent up a little puff of dust. The man at her feet groaned.

Daria turned to the men and smiled. "Hallo, Jack. Introduce me to your friends."

O'Meara stood his ground a second, trying to figure out how things had gotten so deeply fucked so very quickly. He looked down at the unconscious black man and aimed his 9-mm at him.

"Don't be stupid," Daria said, not revealing that her heart had skipped several beats. An FBI agent was about to be killed by a gun that she and the

ATF had sold to this bastard. "You can't shoot him. He's FBI. He's probably not alone."

"She's right." It was the big man, Johnser Riley, moving smartly away from the bombed-out living room. "They're right outside."

The stunned men stood at the top of the stairs in a semicircle, trying to figure out what to do next. They'd been ready for the unexpected. Or so they'd thought. But the smallish woman in the stylish outfit was so far outside their wildest expectations that they just stood there.

"Well?" She shrugged. "Do you have a back door or don't you?"

Donal O'Meara led the three men and Daria Gibron down the hall to an apartment at the far end that smelled even worse than the rest of the building. He hit the door with his shoulder and it bounced open.

A sledgehammer had been taken to the external wall and created a human-size gap, open to the elements. The room reeked of mold and pigeon droppings. Two of the men grabbed long planks hidden behind the door and shoved them out through the hole in the wall, to a similar hole smashed into the next building over.

Daria had shimmied in between these buildings a little while earlier but hadn't noticed the holes in the walls over her head.

They walked the wobbly planks into the next building, which also had been condemned. They pulled the planks after them, dashed through the apartment, guns drawn, then hustled down the stairs, all the way to the basement. They'd left flashlights along the way.

Led by the bobbing ovals of light, the five of them hurried through the cluttered basement and found a metal door, already opened. This led to the next apartment over and, if Daria's sense of direction was any good, across the street.

Before anyone entered, O'Meara turned and shoved his forearm against her throat, slamming Daria back into the metal door. Her head ricocheted painfully off the surface. He cocked his Colt Python, stuck the four-inch barrel against her left cheekbone. She smelled cleaning oil and cordite. "Pat her down," he ordered.

Keith O'Shea ran a meaty hand over her front and down her sides, lifted the front of her skirt, and flashed her tarty, black panties. He yanked her blouse out of the waistband and made sure she wasn't wearing a wire. He enjoyed his work immensely. Daria stared directly into O'Meara's eyes throughout, never blinked or complained.

O'Meara eased the pressure on her throat. "Who the fuck are you?"

"I'm Daria," she croaked. "You're Jack. Although that one called you *Donal*." She nodded to Johnser Riley.

He cocked his gun, pressed harder against her cheek, creating a half-moon depression. "Do not fuck with me, little girl. What are you doing here?"

"I was at a disco," she lied. "That man came looking for you, asking questions. I followed him."

"Discos aren't open this early."

"It is for me," she said simply and left it at that. It was the perfect kind of lie: too ambiguous to disagree with.

"Why attack that FBI bastard? Why would you do anything for me?"

Daria stared right into his eyes and said, "Because right after I sold you that gun—the one you're pointing at me?—my place was raided. I didn't know if you led them to me or if I was under surveillance. Which means I'd led them to you. Either way, I had to find out."

The lie sounded good to her own ears.

O'Meara glared at her, towered over her. He searched her eyes for fear and found none; for untruths and found none. She seemed totally at ease in the bizarre setting.

"Who are you?" he repeated.

"I'm a businesswoman. My work has little to do with the law. The less, the better. I think maybe you're the same."

He stepped back and she relaxed, her hand going to her sore throat. O'Meara softly lowered the hammer of his handgun.

"Where's your purse? Your ID?"

"In a Dumpster," she said. "When I decided to follow the agent, I didn't want any ID on me."

O'Meara would have done the same. It made sense. Of course, if she had a badge or a gun in her purse, there'd be no way for him to know now.

On the other hand, why throw away a gun before entering this scene?

"Right," he said, and shoved the gun into his belt. "I snagged this from that FBI wanker before we left."

He reached behind his back and produced Lucas Bell's handcuffs and key. He snapped one link around Daria's right wrist and connected the other one to his left, leaving his shooting hand free.

"We might kill you later. Probably will. For now, you just might be of value."

He turned to the darkened tunnel and took two steps before he disappeared into the gloom. Before she was dragged in, Daria made eye contact with the three others, holding her gaze on Keith O'Shea for a moment.

Johnser Riley tapped Keith O'Shea on the shoulder and whispered, "God, but she's a ride!"

O'Shea nodded, thinking the same.

Ahead of them, O'Meara wondered if he should call the cut-out phone and answering machine in the rented apartment in Atlanta, to alert the necessary people that there'd been a change of plans. *Plenty of time for that,* he thought.

## ATLANTA, GEORGIA

The tropical depression off the coast made it official. The first storm had socked in Washington, D.C. The next, in what was beginning to look like a never-ending string of storms heading toward the States, now took its toll on Georgia and Tennessee. By 6 P.M.—3:00 Pacific Time—all power went out for large sections of Atlanta.

Including the rented apartment with Donal O'Meara's cut-out phone and answering machine.

# 23

KIKI STOOD IN THE field of grass on the side of Interstate 5 and stared at the downed wreckage. She shivered a little. In her left hand was an MP3 player. In her right were a pair of foam headphones that fire-truck drivers use to limit noise damage to their ears.

"Miss Duvall?" A beat, then she turned to the firefighter standing behind her. "I talked to the guys from Silverton. You can use their rig."

He pointed to a pumper truck with a fully enclosed cab. "That'll do," she said. "Thanks."

A minute later, Kiki was snug in the cab of the pumper truck. She tucked the earbuds from her MP3 player into her ears, then put on the "Mickey Mouse ears."

She could have done this from the comfort of her hotel room. She could have done it from L'Enfant Plaza in D.C. But she was convinced that it would be better to stare at the downed jetliner while she listened to the last minutes in the lives of Meghan Danvers and Russ Kazmanski.

Across the field, Dennis Silverman watched the tall, lanky redhead climb into the fire truck. He wondered what that was all about.

His laptop pinged. Dennis had downloaded all the evidence from the

Gamelan flight data recorder. He rubbed his palms together in gleeful anticipation. *This is going to be so fucking fun!*

He stepped away from the crushed cockpit. It was taking all his concentration to avoid giggling or even booming his laughter for everyone in the field to hear.

He detached the coaxial cable that linked his laptop to the external controls of the aircraft, then searched the field until he found Walter Mulroney. "The FDR is pretty badly smashed, but I'll compile the data and have it to you by noon tomorrow."

"Outstanding," Walter said, and shook Dennis's hand. "Thank God we've got you on the team."


## LOS ANGELES

A team of heavily armed agents in Kevlar vests, helmets, and face shields led the way into the abandoned apartment building within thirty seconds of the time the planks were being pulled across, into the next apartment over. They fanned out, covered the first floor, and found Lucas Bell as he began to push himself to his knees.


On the street, Ray Calabrese had changed into a flack vest and had picked up his walkie-talkie. His jaw was clenched, and a vein in his throat stood out. He was angry at Lucas Bell and angry at himself. And he almost jumped out of his skin when his walkie-talkie squawked and a voice said, "Agent down! Agent down!"

Ray crossed the dark street, gun drawn, and burst into the apartment building. He saw agents on the first-floor landing. "Calabrese!" he announced and took the stairs three at a time.

He just about burst into song as two of the agents in SWAT black helped Lucas to his feet. Lucas's chin was wet with blood and he looked nauseated, but *nauseated* translates as *alive,* and that was all that mattered.

Ray threw a bear hug around the wounded man, who groaned in pain. In Lucas's ear, Ray whispered, "You asshole."

When he disengaged, Lucas nodded his head. "You got that right," he said in fine agony.

.  .  .

It took the SWAT unit, plus Ray Calabrese, twenty minutes to search the condemned apartment. When they were done, and realized that the joint was vacant, Ray called for a forensic team to tear it down to the granular level.

He took Lucas Bell into the ruined remains of a bedroom—the walls were lined with *Star Wars* wallpaper, so faded that it was almost unrecognizable—and closed the door.

"Jesus, Lucas."

No one was angrier at Lucas than Lucas. "Look, I fucked up big time. But this?" he pointed to his split lip, "came from Daria Gibron."

Ray's blood pressure dropped. "You're sure." It wasn't really a question.

"Yeah. She coldcocked me with, I don't know, a bo staff or something."

Ray stared at the other agent. "Deits finds out about this, he's gonna have a fucking seizure."

"I know."

"Did she say anything?"

Lucas thought about it for a couple of seconds. "They didn't know . . . *they* being the Irish assholes, and there are four of them, by the way. They didn't know she was there. They were as surprised as I was. Also, she stopped O'Meara himself from shooting me." From the way he steadied himself on the cobwebby wall, it was clear that his jaw and his gut were killing him.

"She kicks your ass, then saves your ass?"

Lucas shrugged. "Doesn't mean she isn't running with them. Doesn't mean—"

"Hey, guys?"

The voice in the otherwise empty room almost made Ray jump out of his suit. He turned and found a SWAT officer, a Thai woman he'd worked with a few times before. She was on the floor above them, on her knees, peering down at them.

"Chanpong! I damn near capped you!"

"You'd have tried," she observed with a smile. "Hey, I heard you guys talking. This chick you're talking about? She was up here. I'm finding shoe prints up here. High heels. Size five, five and a half."

Ray digested that. "Could she see the entrance? She's about five-four."

The SWAT officer disappeared, came back. "Yeah."

Ray played it out in his head. "She was up there, spying on the Irish. She heard you enter. She might have seen them react; maybe they heard you, too."

"Yeah, I supp—"

But Ray was on a roll. "She clocks you to avoid the Irish shooting you. She's not running with them! She's pissed that I put her on the bench and she went after the Irish on her own! Jesus Christ!"

Lucas paused. "It . . . it could've gone down like that."

"She's a player. She was a spook living undercover in a hostile land; a deep-cover Israeli agent surviving in the West Bank as a Palestinian. Then she blew the whistle on an illegal assassination, got herself shot by her own side, became expatriated. All before the age of thirty. Since she's been in the U.S., she's been nothing but bored and antsy to get back into the game. This O'Meara prick shows up, she figures boom, this is her chance."

They heard a knock on the door. Lucas opened it. A second SWAT officer, still wearing his vaguely Nazi helmet and chin strap, said, "Got something to show you. C'mere."

He led them to the "living room," which had morphed, through neglect, to the Ulstermen's bivouac. The room was littered with space heaters, a cooking stove, a ping-pong table turned into a dining-room table with greasy buckets of KFC and empty beer bottles. Four mismatched chairs and a futon with stains that nobody present wanted to think about. The agent knelt and pulled a pile of newspapers out from a moth-eaten futon.

Ray picked up one article, unartfully ripped out of a newspaper. Then another. And another. "What the fuck is this shit here . . ." he whispered to no one in particular.

They were articles ripped from the *Los Angeles Times,* the *Santa Monica Daily Press,* and *USA Today.* All of them focused on CascadeAir Flight 818.

# 24

FIFTEEN TECHNICIANS FROM THE power-plant crew, led by Peter Kim, began the process of disconnecting the outboard engine from the starboard wing of the jetliner. Peter checked his watch: going on four o'clock. The sun would set in a little while. He considered bringing in generators and industrial arc lights on tripods to illuminate the Wheelers' backyard. With him was a crew from Patterson-Pate Electric. Unlike many of the NTSB crew chiefs, Peter wasn't bothered by their presence. They had the expertise and the personnel necessary to tear apart the formerly missing engine.

Besides, Peter didn't actually like his own teammates all that much.

The inboard engine was still missing.

It took two orange Caterpillar tractors with crane attachments to disconnect the engine. The gate into the Wheeler residence wasn't large enough, so the crews ripped up part of the white picket fence, then plowed the Cats through the Wheelers' lawn to get to the backyard, gouging up grass and shrubs in their wake.

They began by sliding two titanium steel crossbeams between the underside of the wing and the pylon sling attachment. Heavy-duty chains hung from the ends of both crossbeams. The Patterson-Pate crews had brought along a custom-designed cradle with wheels, like a gigantic Radio

Flyer Wagon, which they positioned under the wing. It was difficult to do, since the wing wasn't parallel with the ground, as it normally was. Instead, the tip had pierced an elaborate, half-circle barbecue pit/picnic area, and the widest part of the wing poked into the air at a one-o'clock angle.

The fuel lines, control cables, pneumatic system, electrical lines, and anti-ice ducting, all of which linked the engine to the airplane, had been sheared when the wing broke free. Workers clamped them anyway. The dangling chains were connected beneath the hanging engine. They fit snugly around the roughly barrel-shaped engine. While spotters watched from five different angles, crews on stepladders disconnected the engine-pylon rear mount. The whole thing didn't fall apart, so they disconnected the forward mount. Now, only the crossbars and the chains kept the engine and wing together.

The chains were connected to a ratcheting gear. By cranking the handle, the engine was slowly, gingerly lowered into the wheeled cradle.

While the Patterson-Pate crew worked to free that engine—engine number four—Peter and three of his people climbed up on two stepladders they had borrowed, without asking, from the Wheelers' garage. They started at the wider end of the wing, at the torn and twisted pylon, upon which the inner engine normally rested. There was no engine now, and no signs of it anywhere they could see at the Wheeler residence.

Shining a penlight, Peter ran his fingers over the warped metal of the pylon, the penlight trained on his finger like a follow spot on a tenor. A small smile flickered across his usually stolid features. He pointed his penlight and said, "Do you see that?"

The other men focused their lights on the pylon.

"Oh, yes," Peter said, standing. He shoved back the sleeve of his jumpsuit and checked his diver's steel watch. "Four twelve. This bird was dirtside at eight forty-one," he said. "Plane's only been on the ground for twenty hours. And we just solved this thing."

Peter and the power-plant crew were so excited, they didn't notice Irene Wheeler catching it all on the video camera her grandsons had chipped in for last Christmas.

## MULTNOMAH COUNTY MEDICAL EXAMINER'S OFFICE, PORTLAND

Tommy Tomzak slowly snipped the conduits linking Meghan Danvers's eyes to her brain, then cradled the brain in one double-gloved hand. He pulled, gently. There was a slurping suction sound as the brain slipped free of the cranium. Tommy gingerly slipped the brain onto the scale, noted the weight, then turned back to harvest the eyes.

The man who threw up at every crash scene was unaware that he was whistling a Lyle Lovett tune as he worked.

## FIELD OF GRASS

Kiki Duvall reached the end of the digital recording and hit the controls to listen to the CVR recording for the eighth time. She checked her manly, waterproof wristwatch. It was going on four thirty.

# 25

DONAL O'MEARA, HIS THREE men, and Daria Gibron traveled four and a half blocks, either through basements or by quickly ducking through alleys, before emerging onto Somerset. Luck was with them: a bus was just pulling to a stop. O'Meara said, "Get on," and let his men lead the way. He kept his hand inside his jacket, not far from his gun. He yanked hard on the handcuff linking himself to Daria, who stumbled forward. He put his lips near her ear and said, "Don't think about it."

Daria climbed on board without making eye contact with the driver.

They moved to the rear of the bus, finding five seats in two rows. O'Meara sat with Daria. He pulled his gun loose from his jacket, just for a peek. "Don't fuck with me," he whispered.

"I'm not fucking with you. I just saved your life."

O'Meara sneered. "From your man, that FBI bastard? Not much."

The bus started moving. "Now. Who are you? Tell me the truth, ye cunt, or I'll kill you."

The bus began moving away from the FBI cordon.

"Daria Gibron. You've been to my apartment, you know wh—"

"What were you doing in the flat?"

"I've no love lost for the police or FBI. When they raided my apartment—"

"You said you found that fucker at a disco. What were you doing in an after-hours club in the middle of the afternoon, then?" The questions were being peppered at her in a staccato rhythm. O'Meara never released her hand.

The bus continued moving through the streets of L.A. It was maybe eighty degrees; warm even for Los Angeles on March 8.

"I have a business arrangement with the disco," she lied. "I provide . . . certain supplies for them."

The Irishmen exchanged glances. "She's a fucking drug runner," Keith O'Shea said with a sneer.

O'Meara said, "Is that so, then?"

Daria nodded. Why not? It was as good a story as any for her anti-authority alibi.

"D'you know what we do with drug runners in Belfast, girl? We knee-cap them. You're scum, you are."

"Scum who can help get you out of the city," she said calmly. "Look at you. You have the clothes on your back and four guns between you. Do you have a stash of different clothes? Money? More weapons."

She could tell by their eyes that they didn't.

"Look," she said, speaking for O'Meara's ears only. "I don't know what you're doing in Los Angeles. I don't care. Whatever you're here for, I'm betting it's better news for me than any FBI operation in my own backyard. What I did, back there? That was more for me than you. What is it the Americans say? Covering one's ass?"

O'Meara studied her eyes, worked his jaw as if he were chewing something. They rode in silence for while.

"I can help you, Donal," she whispered.

He barked a laugh. "Help us how?"

"I'm willing to bet I know L.A. better than you. I can get weapons and money and clothes in a heartbeat."

"How?"

She shrugged. "Do you want my help or not?"

## FBI, LOS ANGELES FIELD OFFICE

Assistant Director Henry Deits listened to the story that Ray Calabrese and Lucas Bell spun. He made them tell him three times. Then he picked up the phone and dialed a District of Columbia area code.

"Gail? Henry Deits in Los Angeles."

"Hi, Henry. You just caught me." It was nearing 8 P.M. on the East Coast.

"We filed a preliminary report this morning of four suspected Irish terrorists in Los Angeles. Did you see the circular on that?"

"Yes," the D.C. officer of the watch said simply, slipping into a more official voice.

"We had contact with them but they escaped. One of our guys sustained minor injuries. He got a good look at them and is sure they're with the Red Fist of Ulster. And there's evidence to suggest they knew about the downing of that Vermeer One Eleven in Oregon last night."

Deits's D.C. counterpart didn't waste time commenting. "Go on."

"We're declaring a terrorist incident. We suspect the Irishmen were involved in the crash of a major civilian airliner. We request an interagency alert. And we want to take over the crash investigation."

"Give me your evidence."

Deits did. When he was done, the woman on the line said, "That's . . . a little thin. NTSB will fight us until we come up with more. I happen to know that Del Wildman himself is keeping an eye on this investigation, and he isn't going to hand over an investigation like that without pitching a fit."

"I know. We're putting all available resources of the Los Angeles field office into this situation. We should have trace evidence from the latest scene processed within two hours, and we've got LAPD locking down the city. Gail, please. We want this."

Deits waited.

"All right. For now, I'll call NTSB and tell Wildman what we know. I'll stick around and wait to hear. You'll send a liaison to Oregon?"

"Done," he said. "He's going to assist in the investigation and, as soon as we've thrown together some serious evidence, something that would stand up to a court challenge, we'll take the reins up there. Fair enough?"

"Fair enough," the woman on the East Coast said. "Send someone who's familiar with the investigation to Oregon. Then get on top of this thing."

"Done. Thanks, Gail. I'll keep you guys in the loop."

Deits depressed the phone's tine and turned to the two men who hadn't bothered sitting down. "Calabrese? Pack light. You're in Oregon first thing tomorrow."

## 26

Bᴇᴄᴀᴜꜱᴇ ᴏꜰ ᴛʜᴇ 5 ᴘ.ᴍ. rush-hour traffic, it took Daria and the Ulstermen a good hour to reach Beverly Hills. Daria led them—through two buses and finally by foot—to a palatial mansion on Beverly Park Terrace, with a sprawling five acres of lawn, a lush garden, and a colonnade-studded monstrosity of a house that would have looked vulgar in downtown Las Vegas. Donal O'Meara didn't know much about architecture but he knew shite when he saw it. "What's this, then?"

Daria smiled up at him and, single-handedly (her right wrist was chained to Donal's left), opened the heavy, wrought-iron gate and led the lads up the winding brick pathway to the gaudy mansion. She noticed that the phalanx of seven or eight high-end European cars that normally stood on the lawn like grazing cows was missing today. Perfect.

It was almost 6 ᴘ.ᴍ. and Hassan Al-Rouaf was most surprised to hear the doorbell. Hassan was executive secretary to Abdul-Hakam Bakshar Farouk Abdel-al, a businessman who had done exceptionally well for himself in America. The boss was in Vancouver, B.C. that week, at a film shoot, along with his bevy of hangers-on, which included his cousins from Cairo and Damascus, his multitude of girlfriends, his assistant executive secretary, the assistant executive secretary's aide, the macro-biotically inspired new cook, and the new life coach, a zen master who claimed to have recently escaped from China-controlled Tibet but who had actually grown up in Minidoka County, Idaho, and gone to Washington State University on a golf scholarship. (Hassan Al-Rouaf knew all this, but he didn't think Abdul-Hakam Bakshar Farouk Abdel-al necessarily needed to be told the truth, because the faux-zen life coach seemed to make the boss happy these days, and who needs more grief?)

An executive assistant to an insanely rich Egyptian businessman doesn't usually answer the door at 6 P.M. on a Tuesday, but Hassan found himself alone that evening. He had been sipping the boss's brandy and smoking one of the boss's cigars when the deep, lyrical chime sounded. He wrapped a long robe around his portly form and stepped into leather slippers, then hurried down the gently curving stairs to the fine, marble hall that dominated the first floor of the mansion (which had belonged to such illustrious owners as an MGM CEO and the drummer for Whitesnake). He opened the massive oak inner door, leaving the ornately carved, black wrought-iron outer door closed. He found four men and a small, dark woman waiting in the lighted vestibule. The men were clearly not Middle Eastern, yet, oddly, they didn't look exactly like Americans, either. The woman, on the other hand, had Semitic skin coloring and the almond-shaped eyes of the Mediterranean. There was something most familiar about her.

"Good evening, Hassan Al-Rouaf," she said, in perfect High Arabic with a slight Lebanese accent. "I hope all is well with you and your house."

"Do I know you, madam?" he asked, also in Arabic.

"My name is Daria Gibron. I have been prevailed upon by your employer, Abdul-Hakam Bakshar Farouk Abdel-al, to serve as an interpreter from time to time."

He studied her some more. Yes; of course. Daria, the Lebanese woman who had been helpful on a few occasions. And the boss fancied her, although—to Hassan's knowledge—he had yet to, as the Americans say, score with her.

He bowed his head politely but did not open the iron outer door. "How may I be of service to you this evening?"

(Silently, Donal O'Meara ground his teeth together. The Arabic conversation was getting on his nerves.)

"I have had occasion to help your employer in some extremely sensitive negotiations, as you may know," the small woman said.

"What of it?" Hassan prodded. The sun was setting, and Beverly Park

Terrace is a nice neighborhood, but still: L.A. is L.A., the men were strangers, and he owed no allegiance to a Lebanese. "I'm afraid my employer is away in Canada at the time and won't be back un—"

"Yes, I know," the woman said. "I have helped Abdul-Hakam Bakshar Farouk Abdel-al speak to officials from British Petroleum on two occasions, as you may recall. I've also helped translate a conversation between himself and banking officials from Zurich."

"I wouldn't know such details, madam, but—"

"And, on a few occasions, I've translated between your employer and a businessman who has arranged for several young girls to visit this very fine home."

Hassan froze. What the hell was she hinting at? "I am not privy to Mr. Abdel-al's private life, madam. I'm only his secretary," Hassan replied stiffly.

"I received a call from . . . the agency that places the young women. Abdul-Hakam Bakshar Farouk Abdel-al has again requested their presence, in Canada. My friends and I are to pick out some . . . suitable clothes for them, from your employer's most humble ensemble."

Hassan mulled it over. His boss's appetites were ravenous, and just because he had taken two—make that three—girlfriends with him to Vancouver did not rule out that he had grown tired of them.

"I will have to call and confirm this," he said.

Daria said, "Of course. May we wait inside?"

Hassan unlocked the wrought-iron door and led them in. The front parlor was circular, with a spiral staircase climbing along the curved wall to the second floor, fifteen feet over their heads. The floor was polished black and white parquetry. A dazzling chandelier glistened above, and the center of the parlor was dominated by a truly awful, full-figure female nude, twelve feet tall, in a pose that would most likely be found in an issue of *Penthouse*.

"Please wait here," Hassan said.

And in response, Daria rose up on the ball of her left foot, her right leg scything around from behind, her slingback arcing higher than her head. The toe of the shoe clocked Hassan at his temple. His body waited a second for his brain to send some more electrochemical signals, and, when those signals failed to arrive, the body decided to crumple like a stringless puppet.

Daria's kick had been even more impressive given that she was handcuffed to Donal. The pirouette ended with his left arm wrapped around her petite frame, their chained wrists behind her back. She smiled up at Donal.

"Hallo."

Donal's eyes went from the fluffy pile of robe and human on the floor to the small-boned woman in his arm. "The fuck was that, then!"

"It was quick," Daria said. "I told him his employer had invited us into his home to secure clothes for some teenage hookers he was ordering. If he had called his boss, he would have found that to be a lie, and I would have had to deal with him then. My way was quicker."

She pivoted on the ball of her left foot again, retro-pirouetting out of the embrace of Donal's arm.

Johnser Riley studied the deeply bad statue, nodded approvingly. "What is this place?"

"The home of Abdul-Hakam Bakshar Farouk Abdel-al, who has made fat stacks of money since moving his business from Cairo to Los Angeles."

Donal unlocked the cuffs and Daria rubbed her right wrist.

Keith O'Shea whistled, high–low. "Oil?"

"Porn," Daria said. "Video. Online. What the Americans call peer-to-peer services. I don't know what that means, but apparently there's money to be made."

"Well, the deal took long enough," O'Meara growled at her.

Daria ignored him and crossed to a marble-and-iron side table with a cordless telephone on it. "I want to find out about my apartment. See if the FBI is still there."

Donal drew his gun and tapped the barrel on her left clavicle. He shook his head, and she took a step back.

"No phones. And all this?" His head gesture took in the mansion. "This better not be some sort of trick."

"No trick," Daria said. "I've been to a few cocktail parties here. I got bored once and snooped around. You'll find food and clothes. And Mr. Abdel-al has been known to be generous with his spare cash. Look." She took him aside. "Your boys look like what they are: street fighters. Let's get them showered and shaved and into some fine suits. Dress everyone up as gentlemen. No one will be looking for them hiding behind pinstripes."

It made perfect sense, which didn't please O'Meara all that much. He didn't want to trust this woman.

# 27

Susan Tanaka checked her silver Movado watch. Eight forty-five.

Cascade Flight 818 had been on the ground for twenty-four hours and change. Susan felt a small shiver. In a crash investigation, time's arrow points in only one direction: further from the incident. The clock was not their friend.

*It's only one day,* she reminded herself. No reason in the world why this had to be Kentucky all over again.

Susan had reserved a suite for herself on the top floor of the hotel that overlooked the freeway, not because she was the boss but so that she'd have room to host the nightly debriefings. The room was soulless, generically decorated, but it would suffice. It had an oval conference table and a minibar with a coffeemaker and a small fridge.

Tommy Tomzak arrived from Portland, dressed in sweats and sneakers he'd borrowed from the Portland Police Department about ten hours into supervising the first round of autopsies. He'd slept for an hour between the rescue operation and taking over the Go-Team. He walked into the room and collapsed on his back on the couch, one arm crooked over his face.

John Roby and Isaiah Grey came next. They picked chairs around the oval table in the center of the room. With a knock, Walter Mulroney peeked in and stood aside. "Folks? Have you met Dennis Silverman? He's with the flight-data-recorder company."

Dennis waved to the room at large. "Hi."

John and Isaiah shook his hand and made room at the table. Tommy stayed on the couch, his arm folded over his eyes. He might have fallen asleep.

Susan reintroduced herself to Dennis and said, "Thanks for coming by. Has anyone seen Peter?"

Walter said, "He should have been back by now." He nodded toward the couch. "Tomzak? Anything useful in the autopsy?" He was still angry about losing the feud for the IIC position. He didn't realize it, but Tommy didn't know that there was any bad blood to get over.

"We'll have tox tomorrow," Tommy murmured, not removing his arm from his face. His voice was hoarse with fatigue. "And that's rushing the tests ahead of everyone else in the Northwest. Suze, the locals are being incredibly helpful. There's no turf bullshit whatsoever."

Susan said, "I'm finding the same."

Tommy continued to speak, his eyes hidden. He'd been awake for thirty-five of the last thirty-six hours. And he hadn't slept all that well before his lecture at noon at OHSU or his panel discussion that afternoon. "Anyway, I weighed the livers and we don't have any big drinkers. There are no track marks. That only tells us we don't have alcoholics or IV-drug users; it doesn't tell us if either pilot had a highball before the flight. As for the captain, Meghan Danvers, she's got the muscle tone of a pretty serious athlete. I'm going to be shocked if I find out she's got booze in her system."

Susan turned to Walter. "Can your crew get the Vermeer out of that field?"

He pulled on his lower lip, frowned. "We think so. I've had structural engineers running simulations all afternoon. We should be able to lift the primary sections onto flatbeds. Do we have a hangar?"

"Yes. Little town called Valence has a brand-new, as-yet-unused UPS hangar. It's ours."

Walter nodded his approval.

Isaiah, who was leaning well back in his chair, the front legs off the mushroom-colored carpet, removed his reading glasses from their case. With his eyes cast downward, he glanced at the others to see if anyone had noticed that he needed glasses. He was still that pissed about it. "How about Kiki?" he asked. "I want to know what's on that black box."

Susan turned to him. "Did you find anything at the airport?"

"Yes." He pulled out the steno pad he'd been using. "Captain Danvers was apparently a by-the-book flyer. The ground crew said she watched them like a hawk. She and her copilot both did walkarounds, and they both checked the Gamelan."

"Why is the data recorder called a Gamelan?" Susan asked.

"It's the brand name, is all," Dennis spoke up, then cleared his throat. "Somebody in marketing did polling on a few names, came up with this one. It's the latest in flight data recorders. It checks almost two thousand electronic relays and pneumatic actions throughout the ship, without taking off cowls and unbolting engines and, you know, whatever it is you electrical-engineering types usually do. They're installed in many of the major liners these days."

There was a soft knock at the door and Kiki Duvall let herself in. She carried a manila folder under one arm and her portable MP3 player in the other hand. She was dressed in low-rise jeans and a hoodie, but she was barefoot. She'd come straight from her room. "Hi, guys. Sorry I'm late." She started handing out transcripts that had been faxed to her. "The CVR," she announced.

Peter Kim entered the room, and nobody noticed that his usual, self-confident swagger had kicked up a notch. They did notice that he looked cool and unemotional, his suit nicely pressed, Hugo Boss tie snugged firmly under his chin. Everyone else, except Susan, looked rumpled. Kiki handed him a copy of the transcript but he hardly looked at it.

She waited until everyone had their copies, then poised her finger in midair an inch over the control for the MP3 player. "Ready?"

CHIEF FLIGHT ATTENDANT ANNIE COLVIN: Got 'em corralled. Ready
   when you are.
CAPTAIN MEGHAN DANVERS: Thanks. Tower's giving us the hold sign but
   we're up next.
COLVIN: Anybody want anything before I buckle up?
DANVERS: No, thanks. I'm good.
COPILOT RUSS KAZMANSKI: I'll take some coffee, if you're got it brewed up.
COLVIN: Hang on.
Sound of door closing.
KAZMANSKI: Decaf! That's all I need, the jangles.
DANVERS: Careful. Big brother's listening.
*(In the hotel room of the Chemeketa Inn, Susan Tanaka blushed, realizing that these dead people had just made reference to herself and to everyone else in this room.)*

KAZMANSKI: Then I probably shouldn't mention the ganja, mon.

*(Walter Mulroney frowned and pursed his lips. Isaiah Grey smiled.)*

DANVERS: Not funny, partner. CascadeAir doesn't even allow joking about that.

KAZMANSKI: I know.

Sound of cockpit door opening.

COLVIN: Here you go. Decaf all right?

KAZMANSKI: Great, thanks. We're— Hold it.

PDX AIR TRAFFIC CONTROL: Ah, CascadeAir Eight One Eight, you're loaded and fine. We have you at one-forty-six with three laps. You can leave the terminal now. Please queue up for runway two eight lima and await further instructions.

*(Kiki reached over and hit the Pause button on the machine. "One-forty-six and three laps?"*

*Isaiah said, "A hundred and forty-six passengers; three of them are children young enough to ride on their parents' laps."*

*Kiki said, "Oh," and eyed Tommy's prone form.*

*Without uncovering his eyes, he knew she was looking at him. He just shook his head. Kiki, who was naturally pale, blanched, then hit the Play button again.)*

DANVERS: Roger that, tower.

KAZMANSKI: Okay, we're rolling. We'll see you topside.

COLVIN: Bye.

Sound of door closing. Sounds of increased ground speed.

DANVERS: ATC, this is CascadeAir Eight One Eight, in the blocks and ready to sprint.

PDX ATC: Ah, roger that, Eight One Eight. Y'all got limitless ceiling tonight and little wind. You are cleared for takeoff on runway two eight lima. Have yourselves a good one.

DANVERS: CascadeAir Eight One Eight, roger that. Thanks for the hospitality, Portland. We'll see you next week. Eight One Eight out.

Sounds of increased speed.

KAZMANSKI: Power's set.

DANVERS: All right, then. Read 'em off.

KAZMANSKI: Seventy-five knots . . . one hundred . . . one twenty.

DANVERS: Vee one.

Sounds of jet leaving the ground.

KAZMANSKI: Positive climb.

DANVERS: Okay, gear up.

Sound of landing gear being stowed. Sounds of light turbulence.

DANVERS: LNAV on auto?

KAZMANSKI: Got it. You've got good climb thrust.

DANVERS: VNAV.

KAZMANSKI: Gotcha.

DANVERS: Good. Flaps go to one, gear handle off.

Sounds of systems being operated.

DANVERS: Landing gear up and off.

KAZMANSKI: Landing gear up and off.

DANVERS: Flaps up.

KAZMANSKI: Flaps up.

DANVERS: Checked up.

KAZMANSKI: Checked up, aye.

DANVERS: Altimeter okay.

KAZMANSKI: Altimeter reading A-okay.

DANVERS: Center autopilot on.

KAZMANSKI: Confirmed center autopilot on.

Sounds of airplane in flight.

KAZMANSKI: Like a baby's butt.

DANVERS: Damn straight.

*(Around the hotel room, the NTSB investigators glanced nervously at one another. They felt like voyeurs as they listened to the dead chatting. No one was sure if Tommy was asleep or not.)*

More sounds of standard flight.

KAZMANSKI: Hmm. What's that?

A tapping sound.

DANVERS: What's what?

KAZMANSKI: I've got a— Whoa!

Sounds of violent shaking.

DANVERS: Shit! Trimming rudder to the left! What've we got?

KAZMANSKI: I— Dammit!

Sounds of extreme turbulence. Four electronic caution tones sound. A siren sounds.

DANVERS: What've we got!

KAZMANSKI: I dunno! Wait, check the— This doesn't make sense!

Sound of chimes. The siren continues.

DANVERS: Call it in!

*(In the hotel room, Dennis Silverman rested his elbows on his knees, hands clenched before him, head bowed. He might have been praying or he might have been nauseated.)*

KAZMANSKI: Uh, PDX flight control, this is CascadeAir Eight One Eight. Mayday! We are declaring an emergency!

PDX ATC: Roger, Eight One Eight. Do you wish to return to Portland?

DANVERS: Affirmative.

PDX ATC: What is the nature of your emergency?

DANVERS: Unknown, Portland! Engine trouble. We're shaking apart!

PDX ATC: Understood, Eight One Eight. Runway one zero romeo is available. We're clearing airspace for you. Contact one zero five point four for your lineup.

KAZMANSKI: One zero five point four, roger.

PDX ATC: Ah, good, Eight One Eight. Come about one eight zero, altitude at your discretion. Would you like fire crews on scene?

DANVERS: One eight zero confirmed. Affirmative on the fire crews. We don't know what's wrong!

PDX ATC: Eight One Eight, you are, ah, seven miles from the first localizer.

KAZMANSKI: Meg, we got— Christ!

Sounds of extreme turbulence. A crash, several thuds. The siren continues to sound. The stick-shaker begins.

*(Isaiah closed his eyes and whispered, "Christ almighty." The stall had begun.)*

Sound of emergency fuel venting.

A dull snap within the aircraft. A yelp, from one of the pilots.

DANVERS: Dammit!

KAZMANSKI: Jesus, God.

Sounds of damage to airframe.

DANVERS: No!

Sound of pilot howling.

End of tape.

In the hotel room, everyone stayed silent for a while. Meghan Danvers and Russ Kazmanski had spoken to them, had relayed to them what few details they knew about the last moments of their lives.

It was up to the Go-Team to take this message from the grave and to figure out what went wrong.

Dennis Silverman sat with the others, his head bowed. He was biting his lip. In his head, he was chanting, *Don't laugh don't laugh don't laugh. . . .*

He stood and said, "I've got to go."

The others saw his pained expression. Walter patted him on the shoulder as he left.

"You did well today. Thanks."

Dennis nodded and left the room. In the hall, he held his hand over his mouth and leaned against the wall and waited for the hysterical laughter to subside before heading for the elevator.

He realized that he had a massive erection.


Everyone remained quiet for a time. Tommy lay on the couch, Peter leaned against a wall, studying his fingernails. The others sat around the table, looking at their photocopied transcripts or staring out the window at the blackness beyond.

"There's something you should know," Peter said to the room at large. His tie was firmly knotted at his throat and his cuffs were buttoned. "There's a very strong likelihood we're looking at pilot error."

Isaiah's frown grew deeper. Tommy said, "Why?" without moving his arm.

"Engine number three," Peter said. "It's preliminary, of course. We haven't even found it yet. But the primary pylon is torqued inwardly. I've seen metal strain like that before. It's evidence of a partial thrust-reverser deployment."

Walter Mulroney's eyebrows rose and he let loose a low, slow whistle.

Kiki said, "What's that?"

"You're in a jet and it's landing," Isaiah explained. "You know how, right after you touch the ground, you start to hear a loud scream from the engines? It's the loudest sound they've made the whole trip."

"With any luck," Peter muttered.

"Anyway, that's the thrust reverser," Isaiah said. "Metal slats block the flow of air through the engine, actually making the air move the wrong direction, slowing down the plane."

Walter scratched his neck. "But that makes no sense. If thrusters reverse in midair, the aircraft would break up instantly. We would have found debris over a thirty-mile area, not in a single field."

Peter shrugged. "Not if it was a partial deployment, rather than a full one. Just enough to make it nose over. But even if it was only partial, it would have shown up on the flight-deck's monitors. The pilots should have realized what was going on and manually corrected for it. They didn't: pilot error."

"I don't know." Tommy lowered his arm for the first time and squinted in the light. He hadn't shaved in more than a day and his hair stood up, spiky. "Did Captain Danvers sound panicky to any of you? She didn't to me."

Walter turned a baleful eye on him. "Yes, well, you've never flown an airplane."

Tommy sat up. "What's that supposed to mean?"

Susan whispered, "Oh, God," and rolled her eyes.

"It means what I said: you've never flown an aircraft and you've never been an engineer. Maybe if you had, you'd know how people react in mid-air disasters."

"So you're saying the captain sounded panicky."

"No, I didn't say that. I'm—"

"That was my point, Walter. She sounded pretty fucking levelheaded, considering the situation. Peter said she should have seen a monitor telling her what was going wrong. But she didn't. That implies panic, and I'm not buying it. Kiki?"

"Not panic, no." Kiki had heard the recording an even dozen times and made notes on her copy of the transcript. She had covered three pages with doodles and scratches that meant nothing to any other living human. "I don't get fright from her, either. The dominant emotion in that voice is anger."

"Yes." Susan nodded. "I heard that, too. Her aircraft is supposed to obey her every command. And it's not. So she's angry at it."

Peter shook his head, a sneer making his thin features hard and unpleasant. "Whatever. The point is, she has a monitor to her right, to the copilot's left. If she had a partial reverser deployment on engine three, it would have shown up. She should have seen it. She didn't. *Quod erat demonstrandum*— pilot error."

"If it's a reverser deployment," Isaiah Grey cut in, his chair tipped far back.

Peter checked his air force wristwatch. "At first light, I've got a team covering the ground from the Wheeler farm back along the flight trajectory. We'll find most of the engine along the way. As for the three other engines, there's a Boeing operation east of Portland, in the suburbs somewhere. They've offered us the use of their shop for the strip-down."

The term *strip-down* wasn't an exaggeration. Before the full diagnosis would be offered, every tiny part within the engines would be separated and scanned, some with X-rays, some with a mass spectrometer, and some with a microscope.

Kiki stood, placed her fists on the small of her back, and bent to the left. Her spine let loose an audible series of cracks. "This monitor—does it have an audio signal?"

Peter looked to Walter and Isaiah. They both shrugged. "Some do," Isaiah said. "We'll have to see what brand they installed."

Kiki bent to the left and her spine popped. A runner, she hadn't exercised in two days and was beginning to feel it. "Susan, can we get a swap-out?"

It was an expensive request. Kiki wanted an exact duplicate of the Vermeer 111, made the same year and with more or less the same number of air miles as the one that had crashed. They'd have to lease such a jet, probably from CascadeAir, to make sure the same equipment had been loaded in each aircraft. CascadeAir would agree, of course, but the company would charge the NTSB dearly for it.

To Kiki's surprise, Susan smiled. "Already done. Del okayed it this morning. We'll have a swap-out here in the afternoon."

Kiki headed for the door. "Thanks. I'm going to bed."

Tommy's eyes were bloodshot and he looked like the walking dead. He stood, too, yawning. "I'm gonna catch some sleep."

Walter stood. "We'll start playing pick-up sticks at dawn." The structures crew had a task ahead of them that was very similar, in a macabre sort of way, to the children's game. They would begin moving the Vermeer 111, bit by bit, to the hangar that Susan had secured for them in Valence, Oregon. It was tedious, arduous work, and his was the largest single section of the Go-Team, with more than sixty people in all.

Susan started to tidy up the room. "Everyone remember to eat and get some rest. We have a long, long way to go."

Glumly, the fatigued group trudged out and headed to their rooms.


Nobody had planned it this way. It was a complete coincidence that Tommy and Kiki ended up on the same floor of the hotel, their rooms right across the hall from each other's. It was just after 10 P.M. when they fumbled for their keys and stepped off the elevator together. The corridor was abandoned, the other guests asleep. Tommy's hair stood on end and the bags under his eyes were turning the color of eggplant.

"This is me," Kiki whispered, halfway down the hall. She matched the number on the envelope of her magnetic swipe-key card with the number on the room door.

"Huh. I'm right across the hall."

Kiki said, "Guess so. Well . . ."

Tommy shrugged. "Yeah."

They stood for a moment. Tommy played with his key.

Finally, Kiki let out a soft, quiet laugh at their predicament.

Tommy grinned. "Yeah. See you in a couple."

They turned away from each other and opened their doors.

In his room, Tommy fell onto his bed, fully clothed, the key in his hand, and fell asleep instantly.

## 28

THE BEVERLY HILLS HOME of Abdul-Hakam Bakshar Farouk Abdel-al was massive, and a huge amount of the space had been turned over to the luxury of the staff.

O'Meara's people found walk-in closets that ran the length of the building, featuring literally hundreds of suits, from polo uniforms to evening clothes to a wide array of business attire. Everyone on staff was expected to dress impeccably, and even the massive Johnser Riley found a Calvin Klein suit that fit his frame. When they emerged from the dressing rooms, Daria Gibron directed them to the immaculate kitchen and told them to help themselves.

"This is the fucking life," Feargal Kelly said around a mouthful of turkey and havarti on rye.

Down in the south wing, in one of the spare bedrooms, Daria discovered that the consul general liked the beautiful young things (accent on *young,* as in legally underage) who were draped on his arm at social events to be dressed to the nines. There were enough clothes to be found in the room-long wardrobe to handle a decent-size fashion show.

Daria slipped on a snug pair of black leather jeans. She had stripped down to her bra and held up two tops, a gray-and-black sweater and a maroon jacket that buttoned to the neck. She held each up in front of her, studied herself in a tri-fold mirror. Either would complement her small, athletic frame, she thought. Spikes should have been a must for the leather trousers, but Daria planned on doing some running in the next few days, so she toed around in the floor of the closet for something a bit more sensible, found a pair of black leather boots with a Spanish heel.

*My God,* she thought. *I'm enjoying myself way too much.*

"You look the fucking ride." O'Meara startled her, speaking from the doorway of the dressing room. He wore gabardine trousers in a natty camel brown, with wingtip shoes to match. He wore an undershirt. He'd thrown a plain white shirt and brown tie over his arm.

Daria said, "Is that a compliment?"

O'Meara gave her that same crooked smile she'd seen when they first met. Then he raised his other hand and pointed the silver Colt Python at her midsection.

"You've helped us this far and I'm grateful. But I don't trust coincidences. And you showing up like that, kicking the shite out of your FBI lad, that was just too coincidental for my taste."

Daria nodded knowingly. "Besides, they're looking for four men and one woman. Changing our look helps, of course, but killing me also alters the group profile. That's smart."

O'Meara hesitated, a little crease forming on his forehead. He hadn't thought about "changing the group profile" but he understood what she meant. And her passionless, logical recitation of why killing her made sense was unnerving.

"You have been helpful," he admitted, stalling as much as anything else.

Daria sighed and tossed both tops onto the bed. "Keeping me around would be a tactical error. I understand thoroughly."

She reached behind her back and unsnapped her bra with a casual flick of her thumbnail. The cloth fluttered to the floor. "If only I could think of a good reason to keep me around."

O'Meara grinned. "You figure, flash a man a bit of that and he'll think with his dick?"

She pretended to think about it a bit. "Yes," she said with a decisive nod.

The grin widened. "You may be right. Let's even the odds a bit." And he produced Lucas Bell's handcuffs again.

.   .   .

Downstairs, Keith O'Shea finished off a sandwich and twisted the cap off an expensive microbrew. "Where's O'Meara, then?"

"Probably shagging your lass there," Johnser replied, snorting a laugh.

"Jay-sus, you!" Feargal Kelly threw the remains of his turkey and havarti sandwich at the big man. "O'Meara's a professional, isn't he? Don't you worry, lads. His mind's on the game."

# 29

ON WEDNESDAY, THE 6 A.M. briefing started on time, in the same executive-level briefing room of the FBI headquarters as before. Once again, Donal O'Meara's photo was being projected onto the wall. This time, it was a surveillance shot courtesy of British intelligence.

Lucas Bell stood at one end of the table, holding the remote control for the projector and a laser pointer. He was the least senior of the agents and executives in the room, which was packed. He wore a double-breasted black suit with a perfectly pressed white shirt. The overall look was smooth enough to cover the swollen lip and discolored mark on his jaw. The hunt for the Irishmen had just become top priority for the entire Los Angeles field office, and Lucas Bell had been the top man on the Ireland Watch unit back in the 1990s, charged with looking for illegal, partisan activities in the United States.

"O'Meara," he said and nodded toward the face projected on the wall. "Donal Liam O'Meara. Age forty-two. Born and raised on the west side of Belfast, within the shadow of Belfast Castle."

He tapped the remote. Another photo of O'Meara appeared. He was walking through a city street, glancing over his shoulder in the direction of the long-distance lens, smoking a Silk Cut cigarette. "He never made it out of what we'd call high school. He started out as a juvenile delinquent with no specific political inclinations. Arrested for assault at age sixteen, arrested twice for armed robbery before he was eighteen. He did a year in a juvenile jail for armed robbery, after he knocked over a grocery store with a sharpened screwdriver. O'Meara hooked up with right-wing Protestant paramilitary groups while in juvie. When he got out, he started joining Ulster groups during the marching season. He was suspected of kicking a couple of Catholic boys to death, but that was never proven. He did two more years for assault. After that, he drifted further and further to the right, eventually joining a cell of the Red Fist of Ulster, a rabid anti-Catholic fringe group that opposes the Good Friday Accord."

Lucas checked his legal pad. "After the power-sharing agreement was put into place, the Red Fist went quiet. I've talked to some guys in MI6 who think the crew just drifted into drug running and prostitution. There was always a fine line between the most radical elements in The Troubles and would-be mafiosi."

"How long has he been in the U.S.?" someone asked.

"Unknown. Maybe for weeks."

"Who's he running with?"

Another face popped onto the wall. "Riley, John Padraic. Forty, from Belfast. Three arrests for murder, including beating to death a Protestant woman who married a Catholic man. She was pregnant at the time."

*Click*; another face. "Kelly, Feargal. No middle initial. Thirty-five. From Derry. He allegedly threw a grenade into a Catholic bar, killed two, and injured twenty more. He's supposed to be a gifted marksman. In fact, he was trained in the Irish army."

*Click*. "O'Shea, Keith William. Also thirty-five. From the northeast coast, up near Scotland. His father and brother were killed by a Catholic bomber. He started out as an enforcer for a bookie; just a classic knee breaker with a penchant for knives. Somewhere along the line, he drifted into the Red Fist movement. His rap sheet is a little long to go into here, but it includes rape and assault and murder."

The executives glanced at one another around the table. "Are these terrorists or street thugs?" someone asked.

"In the anti-Catholic movement, those are two sides of the same coin," Lucas explained. "I did three years on an exchange program with British intelligence, based in Belfast, before the power-sharing agreement. Some of the paramilitaries really did care about the religious conflict, but for a lot of them, Protestant and Catholic, the fighting was just a good excuse to rob banks and kick people to death. The Good Friday Accord took away a lot of their fun."

Someone asked, "What about the Gibron woman?"

Lucas cleared his throat. He wished Ray were there; Ray could tell her story a lot better.

"Special Agent Ray Calabrese has been her liaison," he said, casting a picture of Daria onto the wall. The photo was five or six years old. She looked all of twenty-five and wore the uniform of an Israeli soldier, her night-black hair chopped short and lacking all style, her face more rounded, more girlish, with a hint of an overbite, her front teeth showing white against her dark complexion. Her eyes seemed much more innocent, Lucas thought.

"According to Agent Calabrese, she's one of the good guys. I . . . believe he's right. She sucker punched me yesterday to save me. We think she's running with the Irish cell. We haven't turned up her body yet, and we have her place staked out. If she is with O'Meara, Agent Calabrese is convinced it's to keep an eye on him for us."

"What do you think?" asked Assistant Director Henry Deits.

Lucas took a moment, adjusting the files in front of him.

"I agree, to a point. She brought O'Meara to our attention to begin with, and she may represent our best chance of reacquiring him."

"But . . . ?" Deputy Director Liz Geddes pushed.

"Trust but verify," Lucas said. "I think we should take everything we hear from her with a grain of salt. She could be perfectly accurate. She could be feeding us disinformation planted by O'Meara. Or she could be on his side. Agent Calabrese doesn't think so and I trust his judgment. I'm just saying we should be careful."

"Agreed," Deits said. "That's if we hear from her."

"She'll have to find a way to contact us. Agent Calabrese seems convinced she will. We've put an active trace on his cell phone, his home phone, and his desk phone."

"And as for Calabrese," Deits spoke to the room at large, "he should be halfway to Oregon by now."

"So we're sure these Irishmen knocked that plane from the sky?" an administrator asked.

Deits said, "No. But there's enough evidence to suggest it. We don't have that nailed down yet, so we're going to let the NTSB keep the investigation. Calabrese is going to be our point man with them until we declare this a terrorist incident. Then he'll take command of the crash investigation."

More questions were peppered at Lucas and he answered as best he could: the CIA and Los Angeles police were in on this; the FAA had been informed of their suspicions; the National Transportation Safety Administration was brought in and their Washington headquarters knew. In a few hours, the crash investigators would know. Until then, Los Angeles was being bottled up and every resource was being thrown into finding the Protestant Irish cell.

As the meeting broke up, Deits cornered Lucas. "Has Ray seen these guys' jackets? Does he know how bad they are?"

"He knows."

"Jesus," the assistant director moaned. "He has this image of himself as the Gibron woman's rescuer, kind of a father-figure thing. He must be going through hell."

Deits walked out of the room. Lucas whispered to himself, "Father figure my ass."


## LAX

Ray Calabrese pinched the bridge of his nose and willed himself to calm down before he started busting heads. He was not a man given to bad moods. Today was the exception.

"Listen to me, please. I am an FBI agent. This is my ID. I really, truly have to be in Portland, Oregon, as soon as possible."

The woman in the blue blazer and red ascot behind the service counter gave him her most non-organic smile. "Yes, sir. Everyone has to be somewhere. But Flight Seven Twenty-five to Portland and Seattle has been grounded with a minor mechanical problem. There's nothing I can do."

"Can you get me on another flight?" Ray forced his voice to remain even and low. She was the third person he'd asked. Hope springs eternal.

The woman studied a screen at Ray's belt line, on her side of the counter. "Umm . . . N-no. No, I'm sorry. We don't have another flight to the Pacific Northwest until one this afternoon."

"Oh, God." Ray glanced at his watch. It was almost 6:30 a.m. He couldn't wait half a day in limbo.

"You're the third airline I've tried. Look, can you get me to Denver? I'll try my luck there."

"Let's see . . ." Ray could see the reverse image of the computer monitor flickering on her glasses.

"Excuse me?" A man in the navy blue, Eisenhower-cut jacket of CascadeAir stepped up beside Ray. "Did I hear that right? You're FBI and you need to get to Portland?"

Ray nodded, hope flaring. "Have you got a flight to Portland?"

The captain smiled. "You could say that."

# 30

TOMMY TOMZAK AWOKE WITH a mouth lined with pool table felt and a head that weighed more than a boat anchor. He had a severe cramp in his right wrist, which came from gripping a scalpel too hard for too many hours.

He scored aspirin from room service and downed six of them, not caring that they'd burn through his stomach.

He stripped and stood yawning in the shower until the cobwebs cleared away, then changed into his "flying clothes"—comfortable khaki trousers, driving mocs, a weathered denim shirt with many pockets. It was the ensemble he wore whenever he had to fly significant distances and wanted to be comfortable.

He wondered where the clothes he'd worn to the trauma conference had ended up. He remembered changing into a firefighter's suit. But he couldn't remember what he'd done with his clothes.

A little restaurant downstairs just off the lobby offered selected pastries, coffee and tea, and juices each morning. Tommy headed there and grabbed a plain bagel and a plastic container of low-fat cream cheese with a plastic knife. He was in line for coffee when Kiki Duvall skimmed past the window outside, her tawny hair held in a ponytail, an iPod strapped to the elastic band of her running shorts. She must have risen before dawn for her morning run, Tommy thought. A flash memory skittered through his brain: the way Kiki smelled in the morning after running. It was a clean, musky scent. A sexy scent. Tommy ground his teeth together, told himself to concentrate on the job.

He grabbed a cup of coffee and just about dropped it when the muscles in his right hand cramped. Tommy had never worked such an arduous autopsy schedule before, not even in Kuwait. He found a round, iron table near the window and set down the cup as fast as he could, then flexed his fingers, spreading them wide, forcing the muscles to tense and relax, tense and relax.

He dug into a jacket pocket and came up with a small notepad, the size of his palm, opening it and scanning the notes he'd made in the middle of the night. Looking for parallels, looking for errors. He picked up the coffee cup gingerly and sipped.

"Cramping up?" Kiki plopped down in one of two chairs at the table. A hotel towel hung around her shoulders and she'd wiped the sweat off her face and arms. She wore a navy sweatshirt, the sleeves ripped off, with teal shorts and cross-trainers. She swept her feet up onto her chair, her knees sticking straight out in either direction of her torso.

Tommy said, "Hey," and sat.

"Hey, yourself." Kiki had grabbed a glass of grapefruit juice and a poppy-seed muffin on her way in. She gulped the juice, picked off a minute bit of the muffin and chewed on it.

"No tall decaf mocha with cocoa sprinkles?" Tommy asked.

Kiki grinned. "You remembered. Not right now, but I bet I'll find one before the day is out."

Tommy sipped his coffee, using his left hand. He scanned his notepad again, shaking his head at something.

"You still look exhausted," Kiki said. "Did you get any sleep?"

"I'm good." Tommy put the pad aside. He was well aware that he looked more like a cadaver than some of yesterday's patients. The skin under his eyes resembled three-day-old bruises. He'd turned over and over throughout the night, trying to find a comfortable position, but his lower back hadn't wanted to play ball. He'd almost fallen asleep standing in the shower that morning. In fact, he suddenly realized Kiki's relative calm and the healthy flush lighting up her cheeks after her run mildly annoyed him. How dare she look so good when he felt like death on melba toast? The fact that her good health was a source of annoyance only made

Tommy feel guilty, and guilt on top of fatigue on top of annoyance made for a nasty combination. *Snap out of it*, he spat silently at himself.

Kiki said, "What?" and nibbled on her muffin.

"What, what?"

"What-what's buzzing around in that thick skull of yours? Something's on your mind."

She licked pulp off the edge of her glass and Tommy made an effort not to stare at her darting, pink tongue.

"Just hoping everyone gets their act together today," he said.

"They didn't yesterday?"

"Peter Kim," Tommy said. "That was the amateur hour, going after that cracker farmer like he was invading Normandy. Did you see the local paper this morning? We look like the Marx Brothers."

Kiki said, "Didn't see it. We were the top domestic story on NPR, though."

The peel-away lid of the cream cheese container wouldn't budge and working on it was only aggravating Tommy's hand. Kiki took it from him, both of them noting the quick spark as their fingers touched. She peeled the lid back easily, put the packet in Tommy's palm.

Tommy stared glumly at the little packet. "Screw it," he said, and tossed it into a nearby garbage can. The untouched bagel followed. "We gotta roll."

Kiki grabbed his hand, kept him from rising. Her green eyes were flecked with gold from the window light.

"Tommy, yesterday was outstanding. The team is doing great."

"Let's celebrate when we solve this thing." His voice sounded tense, even to himself.

"This isn't Kentucky," Kiki said.

Tommy stood. "You don't know that."

He moved off to a coffee carafe, refilled his cup. As he did, Kiki reached for Tommy's notebook, turned it around to check the notes.

It took her about ten seconds to realize that they were notes on the Kentucky crash, not the Oregon crash. She thought about yelling at Tommy to get his head in the game. She thought about telling Susan Tanaka. But as Tommy winced and flexed his cramped right hand again, she simply turned the notepad back around.

Tommy and Kiki compared their thoughts for a few minutes, then Kiki ran upstairs to shower. Tommy moved toward the exit, where he found

Isaiah Grey drinking decaf and pecking away at a MacBook Pro. He wore a deep navy V-neck sweater over cargo pants and hiking boots. Plus the reading glasses. He waved Tommy over.

Tommy said, "Research?"

Isaiah finished typing and hit Enter. "E-mailing my wife. She teaches ninth-grade civics. I agreed to blog for her class, next major crash I caught. You know, a few years ago I would have sneered at that word. *Blog*."

Tommy frowned. "What are you telling them?"

Isaiah looked up, took a second, removed his reading glasses. "Well, I'm going with the theory that the pilot was a mule for a Columbian drug cartel, and they killed her for stiffing them on their cut."

It took a two-beat, but Tommy sat and shook his head, tossing out a shy, lopsided smile. "Okay, had that one coming. Sorry. You know your protocol."

"Nah. It's cool."

Tommy looked at the screen of the laptop, noticed the photo of a handsome black woman that served as his screen wallpaper. "She's pretty."

Isaiah smiled. "Yeah."

"You married out of your league."

Isaiah ratcheted up the smile a bit. "And a big fuck you, too, Lone Star." He glanced back to where Tommy and Kiki had been sitting. "Trouble in paradise?"

"No," Tommy replied too quickly. "We better get rolling. Today's likely to be as psychotic as yesterday. Are you off to PDX?"

Isaiah nodded.

"Mind dropping me off at the Multnomah County ME's office? I know where it is, now."

"You insult my marriage and you want me to do selected scenes from *Driving Miss Daisy*?"

Tommy sipped his coffee. "Play nice, and I'll try not to kick your ass on the golf course, first day off we get."

Isaiah stowed the laptop in its carrying case, deciding then and there that he and the Texan were going to get along. "You're on."


Peter Kim was up at dawn. He called his wife in Florida and got an update on their son's sixth-grade Invention Convention experiment. He did twenty minutes of calisthenics, then showered and changed into a crisp blue shirt with a dark blue tie and darker blue suit. He took another rental car and headed north to the Portland suburb of Gresham, to oversee the strip-down of the Patterson-Pate engines.

Walter Mulroney got up and read a passage from the Bible to himself, his morning tradition for the past thirty years. Today it was a passage from the Book of Luke. He showered, dressed and ate a bowl of hot cereal with a glass of orange juice from room service. Fortified in body and spirit, Walter felt ready to begin the task of picking up the pieces of the Vermeer.

His spirits fell when he opened the curtain and saw the wall of storm clouds marching over the mountains to the west.

John Roby's job was to determine whether there had been a bomb on board the $79 million wide-body jet. He felt he'd accomplished that well enough for his own purposes. That done, John could have headed back to his sublet in New York and waited four or five days until the NTSB chemists were done testing the plane and its content for explosive residue. Then he could have typed up his report and e-mailed it to Del Wildman's office in Washington.

But instead, John opted to stay. Before joining the agency, he'd been a cop, a deputy chief inspector for the Yard. As such, he was an experienced hand at debriefing witnesses and victims.

He downed a cup of coffee—he couldn't abide the toxic waste Americans called tea—and took a rental car south to Salem Hospital, where a third of the surviving wounded were being treated. It was time to find out what people other than Bernard Weintraub, Mr. 10-B, had seen and heard and felt before the crash.

Susan Tanaka tossed aside *The Oregonian*. It landed atop the *Salem Statesman Journal* and *USA Today*, which she'd already scanned.

The news was worse than she feared.

The Oregonian led with the crash and, on the front of the Metro section, ran a story headlined: INFIGHTING PLAGUES INVESTIGATION. Someone at the NTSB had leaked the story of Walter's attempted insurrection and bid to be Investigator In Charge. *The Statesman Journal* had missed that little byplay but led with the story of Bud Wheeler's arrest and the destruction of the Wheelers' lawn, fence, and hedges by heavy-handed investigators for the NTSB. "Bastard," she muttered; Peter admitted that he'd pissed off some farmer while retrieving the starboard wing but he hadn't bothered to tell her he'd taken the almost unprecedented step of having a civilian arrested. The old man, Bud Wheeler, hadn't been shy when giving his quotes to the reporter. Worse, there was a three-column photo of tractors in the backyard of the house, the destruction in their wake evident to all.

"Oh God," Susan moaned. She thumbed through the rest of the pages absently, not reading more than the headlines. That's when she saw the second, worse bit of news.

"Dammit!" she said, and scrambled across the room, yanking open the curtains of her window. There it was, just as the paper predicted. A dark gray mass of clouds forming over the Coast Range. A storm was moving in.

## 31

Everyone on the airy, glass-walled sixth floor of Gamelan Industries, Inc., hovered around Dennis Silverman's low-walled cubicle. Everyone, from his fellow engineers to the secretaries to the well-dressed preppies from marketing, who normally wouldn't be caught dead near the Dilbert cartoons and *Star Wars* models and unruly piles of computer components and Nerf hoops that decorated the engineering unit.

Everyone wanted to know: what had it been like? Were their dead bodies everywhere?

"Yeah." Dennis had parked his butt on his desk, feet up on his ergonomically correct chair; he was the star around which the sixth floor orbited. At least, that morning. "They'd begun clearing away the bodies before they let us at the plane, but they weren't half done. And the blood? Oh, man . . ."

He shook his head in mock sorrow. His cohorts lapped it up.

How about the interface? He shrugged. "Fried. I had to almost climb into the nose of the plane to hardwire the Gamelan."

Was it an L-19 unit? He winked at them. "D-Forty," he said, and the crowd made *oooh* noises. The L-19 was an older, less reliable Gamelan diagnostic computer, which monitored fewer servos. The D-40 was the Cadillac model.

How was the data stream? Dennis removed his tortoise-shell glasses, rubbed his eyes, gave them the I've-been-slaving-all-night look. "We'll see."

It went on and on. Everyone had questions, even the receptionist with the long blond hair and the great legs and the killer rack had hand-carried a while-you-were-out note to his desk. *Hand-carried it.* She hadn't stuffed it into his pigeonhole without so much as glancing in his direction, the way she had for the past two years.

Even she wanted in on the story.

## OVER ROSEBURG, OREGON

Ray Calabrese was sitting in first class, nursing the mother of all headaches. But at least it was first class—tons of legroom, seats big enough that he didn't feel like he was sitting in a bear trap. There was a small movie screen built into the seat back before him, along with a credit-card-driven telephone. And there was no problem with elbow room either. Nobody sat to his left. Nobody sat to his right. Nobody sat anywhere at all in first class, in business class, or in coach. The nearest humans were the two pilots; the three of them were the only people on board the Vermeer 111.

It felt weird, being the sole passenger on the plane. The pilot had told him to sit wherever he wanted and to make himself at home. "There's no food, but I put on some coffee," he said before disappearing onto the flight deck. "Have at it."

Ray wandered around the plane a little. He didn't have any idea why it was empty and, frankly, he didn't care. It was getting him to Portland. That's all that mattered.

He checked his watch. Going on 8 A.M. Wednesday. He went back to the seat he'd picked at random and grabbed the telephone out of the seat back, swiping his Visa card through the slot. He punched in a number he'd memorized.

"Bell."

"Lucas? It's Ray." The connection was static-ridden. "Can you hear me?"

Lucas said, "Yeah. Where are you?"

"In a jet. We're about halfway there. I'll be in Portland inside an hour. Have you found O'Meara?"

Lucas had to shout to be heard as the static suddenly got worse, then got better. "No. But we've got the city sewn up tight. We don't think he got out of L.A."

"Any word from Daria?"

"Sorry, no."

Ray squeezed his eyes shut. "Shit. Lucas, you've got to get her away from that psycho bastard."

"I know, Ray."

"I'm serious, man. O'Meara is a short-circuit wearing skin. Daria's an adrenaline freak. That is a bad combination. She's probably trying to help, but she's a civilian."

Lucas said, "Ray—"

"I know. A civilian with a spook's training, but a civilian all the same. And she's supposed to be living under our protection. Under my protection."

Lucas said, "I know, Ray. We—"

"I think I see what she's playing at. Trying to run with O'Meara gives us an in. But she could go from mole to hostage in a heartbeat. If that happens—"

Lucas shouted, "Raymond!"

Ray blinked, surprised. "What?"

"Inhale!"

It took Ray a moment to get the point. He forced his shoulders to settle, tried to drain a little of the tension out of his spine. "Um, yeah. Okay. Sorry."

"Good. Now listen. The Gibron woman isn't at home and she isn't in the morgue. We've got taps on your home phone, your office phone, and your cell phone. We've got live surveillance at her apartment, your apartment, and this office. We've informed our people and the cops that she's a civilian cooperating with us on an investigation. Protecting her is everyone's job number one. Okay?"

Ray sank into the plush seat. "I hear you. I'm sorry. You know what you're doing."

Lucas said, "Gee, thanks. Are you okay?"

"Yeah. I can't believe they're sending me to Oregon. O'Meara is in Los Angeles. Daria is in Los Angeles. The fucking case is in Los Angeles."

"Yeah, but the plane crashed in Oregon."

Ray thought about that awhile, watching a low layer of overcast float by beneath the empty jetliner. "You know these assholes better than I do. Do you think O'Meara's responsible for this?"

"Could be. We just don't know enough."

The Vermeer's shadow rode a vapor roller coaster outside Ray's window. The more he thought about it, the more Lucas sounded right.

"Okay. I'll check in from the Portland field office. We'll go over the jet's roster, see if any names set off alarms. Buzz me if Daria surfaces, will you?"

Lucas said, "You got it. And, Ray?"

"Yeah?"

"We're taking this seriously. Serious as shit."

## FIELD OF STRAWBERRIES

The air was heavy with the threat of rain. Clouds the color of bruises hung in the air, low and dark, packed tight enough to make complex, structured cloudscapes on their underbellies. And although no one had felt the first drop of rain yet, all the searchers in Peter Kim's crew wore heavy raincoats and hats and rubber boots.

The crew carried metal detectors. They were one farm over from the Wheelers' and walking gingerly through a strawberry field, looking for pieces of the missing engine number three, sweeping the ground with their oval sensors. They had picked up scads of old tin cans, coins, and assorted screws and bolts. One of Peter's team pulled up a steering wheel that looked for all the world to have come off a Model T. But so far, nothing that looked like it had fallen off a Patterson-Pate aircraft engine.

Forty minutes into their search, they began to find the fuel Captain Danvers had dumped just before impact.

## SALEM HOSPITAL

A seventy-year-old grandmother, Mrs. Nora Washington had been thrown from the rear of the jetliner—she'd been in the next-to-the-last row of seats—and had shattered her pelvis. Yet, somehow, she was awake and coherent at eight o'clock Wednesday morning, and the pain medication didn't seem to make her loopy. Detective Chief Inspector John Roby decided to start his interviews with her.

"Once a bloody cop . . ." the retired DCI muttered to himself.

After getting her permission to enter the semiprivate hospital room, John pulled a chair over and began the interview. He had a notepad and a pen but he didn't write anything down; that was for later. For now, his style was calm and conversational. He didn't try to play down the bizarre events, didn't try to lead her anywhere. There'd be time enough for that.

For now, he just wanted to get her talking.

"I was reading," she said, her brow creasing but the large, square bandage on her forehead remaining flat. "I don't know what happened first. I think I heard the explosion."

"My God." John shook his head and made *tsk* noises. This interview would take more than an hour, but he'd go at her rate. That was the best way to get the whole story.


## FBI, LOS ANGELES FIELD OFFICE

Lucas Bell hung up the phone and glared at it. He didn't know why he glared at it, but it felt good. His office partner was tossing a plastic basketball straight up in the air, catching it, and tossing it again. It was how he concentrated.

The dayside deputy assistant director—the commander of that Wednesday's active investigations—rapped on the door frame and poked her head into their perfectly tidy office. "Any good news?"

Lucas said, "No. No sign of the Red Fist of Ulster. No sign of the Gibron woman. Nada."

The assistant director shrugged it off. "It's a big city, Bell. Be patient. Did Calabrese call in?"

"Yeah. He's in the air, almost to Portland. Do we have any link between the Irish and the CascadeAir crash?"

"The Portland field office has gone over the roster. They say no. But it's early days. They're still looking."

"Good, good." Lucas continued glaring at the telephone.

Phil stopped tossing his basketball. "Here's a question: why that plane?"

The day chief shrugged. "What say we find out?"

The men smiled ruefully at her. Phil turned to Lucas. "Since it got all peaceful and shit in Ireland, we let our Rolodexes get a little rusty. What say we call Dublin and Belfast, call in old markers. Make some new friends. See what's shaking."

Lucas stopped scowling at the phone. "Now you're talking."


Lucas Bell spent the rest of that Wednesday morning on the phone or clattering away with e-mail, contacting the Ireland watchers at the CIA, British Military Intelligence, Interpol, the Royal Ulster Constabulary (or whatever the hell they were calling themselves these days) in Belfast, and the Gardai headquarters in Dublin. He asked each of these agencies if they knew of any Irish nationals with ties to the IRA or the Ulster leagues who were flying into the United States in the foreseeable future. He asked if they knew of any American supporters of the Catholic or Protestant sides who were currently making waves.

The agencies agreed to keep their eyes open and to get back to him.

British Military Intelligence was the first agency to get back to Lucas. And they had news, although the relevance was questionable. It seemed the next stage in the Ireland/Northern Ireland peace talks was set to begin in two days. In the States.

# 32

THE MARION COUNTY MEDICAL examiner waved a hand to the girl standing in front of Tommy. She wore a black T-shirt with an illustrator's rendition of Neil Gaiman's comic-book character Death emblazoned across her narrow chest. Accompanying that was a long, black lace skirt and a black shawl, plus black Doc Martens. Her hair was as black as fresh tarmac. Her eyeliner, black, looped and swirled across her temples. Her lipstick was matte black.

The ME said, "May I introduce my daughter, Arachnia."

Arachnia popped a gum bubble. Tommy offered his hand and said, "Arachnia?"

She blushed and Tommy thought a good Goth should learn not to blush. Her cuteness got in the way of her cool. "Laura. Arachnia is my tag."

Tommy said. "You're a Goth."

Her eyes lit up. "You know about Gothic?"

"Yeah, but in Texas, our Goths are even blacker."

She took a beat, then snorted an unladylike laugh, getting the joke, deciding she liked this disheveled Texan with the unruly hank of hair hanging over his left eye.

"Nice to meet you, Laura. Your daddy says you're good with computers."

She shrugged. "Pretty good."

"Know what a GIS is?"

She said, "Geographic information system. Used in cartography."

Tommy relaxed. She looked all of sixteen but she seemed to know her stuff. "Right. We're pulling shrapnel out of these bodies and out of the survivors. Now, it's really important that we map the trajectories of the shrapnel."

Arachnia, or Laura, wrinkled her nose.

Tommy said, "I know. It's pretty gross. But it's vital. We asked for a computer technician to join us, but the guy we were expecting is about to become a father."

The girl didn't look too sure. "I don't know. . . ."

Tommy's heart sank. "I understand. If you know of anyone else who—"

"Dad," she cut in, and popped another bubble. "Do you have the Microsoft suite installed here?"

The ME nodded.

"If you've got the Microsoft Access software, maybe we could do it. If I could slave that to the map-making GIS stuff, we could run it all off my MacBook Air. I added some serious RAM to it."

Tommy had a MacBook Air laptop. He could barely compose a letter using Word. "You can do that?"

She shrugged. "You're not supposed to be able to, but . . ." And again with the shrug.

Tommy grinned and held up a fist. "Give us a bump, Arachnia."

She touched her knuckles to his and grinned. Again, her studied coolness was shot to hell by her innate cuteness.

Laura excused herself to go get the needed hardware.

Tommy turned to the medical examiner. "Goth?"

He shrugged. "That, plus International Baccalaureate. She's a high school senior and already has seventy credits at Portland Community College." He shrugged again. "Daddy cuts up cadavers for a living."

## INTERSTATE 5, VANCOUVER, WASHINGTON

Monstrously huge flatbed trucks barreled south on I-5. There were three in all, each preceded and followed by wide-load-warning cars. State police also rode shotgun. The trucks were so big, they took up two lanes. Behind the entourage came three smaller flatbeds, these carrying massive cranes. The ground rumbled as they passed. Washington State Police were getting ready to shut down the Interstate 205 bridge that leads into Portland. When the dinosaurlike trucks arrived, they'd be the only vehicles allowed on the bridge at a time.

The entire entourage was on loan to the NTSB and was making good speed, heading toward the field of grass.

## PORTLAND INTERNATIONAL AIRPORT

There are lockers at the airport that flight crews can rent. Both pilots of the doomed Vermeer had taken advantage of them.

Isaiah Grey met Angela Abdalla of the PDX incident-investigation team, along with a lawyer who represented ALPA, the Air Line Pilots Association, in the crew lounge. Together, they followed an airport official with a bulging, jangling tumbleweed of keys on a thick ring. He unlocked the locker rented by Russ Kazmanski.

Isaiah had brought a sturdy banker's box with a removable lid, the kind used by police and prosecutors to keep evidence. With the lawyer and Angela Abdalla watching like hawks, Isaiah removed a raincoat from the locker. The pockets contained Kleenex, a lip balm, and thirty-five cents in change: a quarter and two nickels. He folded the coat and stuffed it into the box. Next came a gym bag containing gym shorts, two T-shirts with the CascadeAir logo on the breast, clean gym socks, clean underwear, and well-worn Adidas cross-trainers. There also was a toiletry bag with shampoo, deodorant, toothbrush and toothpaste, and a comb. A half-empty box of Airborne, which some people think can stop a head cold from happening, though Isaiah doubted it.

Isaiah stuffed the bag into his evidence box and returned to the locker. He found two issues of *Scientific American* magazine and a paperback copy of *The Brothers K,* which looked like it hadn't been read yet. He riffled through the magazines and the book, found nothing of interest. At the back of the locker shelf was a box of Good 'n Plenty, unopened.

Isaiah threw it all into his box. Satisfied the locker was empty, Isaiah sealed the box with masking tape, then he and the lawyer signed the tape with a Sharpie.

"I fall from the sky," the union lawyer said, "I hope I leave behind something more interesting than *Scientific American* and Good 'n Plenty."

Isaiah gave him the bent eye. "Shit like this? Interesting is bad. Dull is good."

The attorney blanched, then nodded his understanding.

Isaiah, the lawyer, and the PDX representative headed next to Meghan Danvers's locker, bringing along a second evidence box. They opened the locker and took out an umbrella with a collapsible handle.

"What are you doing?"

They turned. A man stood at the entrance to the lounge. African American, maybe thirty-five, he held an infant less than a year old. Beside him was a woman, five years younger, also black.

"What are you doing?" the man repeated. His eyes were puffy and red, and his voice was scratchy from fatigue and from sobbing. Isaiah's heart dropped. "That's Meghan's locker. That's her umbrella. What are you doing?"

"Mr. Danvers?" Isaiah stepped forward.

"Yes. What is this? Who are you?"

Isaiah had an exceptionally bad feeling about this. "I'm Isaiah Grey, sir. I'm with the National Transportation Safety Board. We're—"

"Oh my God." Mr. Danvers was trembling, and Isaiah feared for the infant in his arms. It was a little boy in OshKosh B'Gosh overalls and tiny Nikes. He was starting to grow fussy, absorbing the emotions from the man holding him. "You think Meg did this. You think she's to blame."

"No," Isaiah said simply. "No, man. We don't—"

"Don't *man* me! You're riffling her locker! You're looking at pilot error! Aren't you?"

The baby started crying, a panicky, high-pitched wail.

The woman next to him was red-eyed, too, but quiet, staring.

Isaiah said, "We really don't—"

"Meg wouldn't just crash. She was a pro." His voice broke. Angela Abdalla and the union lawyer looked like they hoped to untack the carpet and crawl beneath it. The baby shook his little, wrinkled fists and howled.

"How could you think that? Jesus. That's insane. Meg was a responsible pilot. She was conscientious."

"Sir, I—"

He was crying now, the baby picking up his sorrow and squealing louder.

Isaiah took another step forward. "Look. We don't know what happened. We've ruled out nothing. We're focusing on everything. That's our job. That's what we have to do."

The woman next to Danvers scooped the baby from his arms. The two of them had the same build, the same cheeks: Isaiah was sure they were siblings. She bounced the baby, patted his back, spoke over his howling.

"I understand," she said, turning to her brother, whose his face was crinkled in grief, his hands balled, his lips pulled back to reveal his gums. He made a keening noise, almost exactly two octaves below the baby's wail.

"James?" The sister rubbed the baby's back, then rubbed her brother's shoulder. "Hey, James? Shh. It's procedure. They're checking everything."

James Danvers all but collapsed against her. The child shrieked and kicked his legs. The sister turned James around and led him to the door.

He exited, sobbing. She turned back to Isaiah, Angela Abdalla, and the union lawyer. "Meg's my sister-in-law." She had to speak loudly over the baby's shrieks. "You'll find out what happened?"

"Yes," Isaiah promised. "We will."

"Meg was a good flyer. She . . . this is what she was, flying. She loved my brother and she loved her baby, but flying . . . it's . . . this is what she was."

Isaiah approached the woman, cupped the baby's head in the palm of his too-big hand. He could hear James Danvers crying in the corridor.

"Hey there," Isaiah said to the sobbing infant. "Hey, little man."

The sister-in-law jiggled the baby, tried to get him to squeeze her little finger in his fist. She made eye contact with Isaiah.

"I heard . . ." he started, feeling his own eyes mist up. "There's a tape. A cockpit tape. She fought hard to save her ship, save her passengers. She fought *hard*!"

The woman leaned in, kissed Isaiah on the cheek. "Thank you," she said, and followed her brother out of the locker room.

## MULTNOMAH COUNTY MEDICAL EXAMINER'S OFFICE, PORTLAND

The deputy medical examiner from Yamhill County had come into Portland to hear Tommy's speech on Monday. He'd volunteered to stay on in Portland and help with the crush of autopsies.

It was going on 10:00 A.M. Wednesday and the man had cut more Y incisions in the past twenty-four hours than he had in the previous year. He stood up straight, felt his shoulder muscles protest, and held up a metal mechanism the size and shape of a car's spark plug, wet with viscera. "What the hell is this?"

Tommy Tomzak was two tables over, working on another passenger. He glanced up. "Damned if I know."

"Then why am I charting its path through this poor dumb schmuck?" This was the umpteenth piece of unfamiliar metal or glass or plastic that the young assistant ME had taken from a body that morning.

Tommy straightened his spine and swung his shoulders, hearing his neck pop. "That widget? It went somewhere. It was part of an engine, or a wing, or it came from the cockpit, or from the coffeemaker or the toilet. It came from somewhere. And it ended up in Mr. Seven-C, there." They had taken to referring to the dead by their seat designations. "If we know where that thing started, and where it ended up, it'll tell the engineering geeks something about the crash. Something major, something minor; hell, I don't know what. But it'll tell 'em something."

He went back to his autopsy. "We tell 'em enough of the little things, maybe they'll figure out the big thing."

"Which is?"

"What got fucked up."


Once the metal mechanism the size of a spark plug was washed clean, it was put in a self-sealing plastic bag, which was designated 7C-14: the four-teenth foreign object taken out of that particular dead body. The bag was taken out of the autopsy room and into the office of the Multnomah County medical examiner, where it was given to Laura, the ME's Goth daughter, along with a crude drawing of a human body. Arrows showed the direction of impact and an X showed where the mechanism had been lodged, just under the left lung.

Laura had lashed together an interface between the map-making soft-ware of the geological information system with the report-making capabil-ity of the Microsoft suite. Using the amalgam, she made a three-dimensional representation of the victim from seat 7-C.

## 33

So you're not ruling out pilot error?"

Susan Tanaka made a herculean effort to keep the smile on her face. The noon press conference was only ten minutes along and it was already clear that the press was unimpressed by her answers. It was always this way. The uninitiated expected answers right away. Some understood that the process was time consuming. Some looked for a cover-up. Others assumed incompetence. She was dressed to the nines in a black-and-white-patterned Diane von Furstenberg wrap dress.

"We have ruled out nothing," she replied. "An investigation of this magnitude can take a year. Can take two years. CascadeAir Flight Eight One Eight crashed on Monday. This is Wednesday."

The room was hot and crowded. The Keizer Chamber of Commerce had offered the NTSB the use of this space for the morning debriefings, and apologized that it wasn't larger. But the smallness of the room played in Susan's favor by limiting the number of reporters and how long they were willing to hang out in the muggy confines.

Another reporter elbowed her way to the front. "Have you ruled out a bomb?"

*Are you deaf?* she thought, and smiled serenely. "Too early to tell. We have ruled out nothing whatsoever. Again, we know the Vermeer One

Eleven is on the ground. We don't know why. I can tell you that in the past decade, nearly a third of all U.S. aircraft accidents have resulted from a loss of control, suggesting mechanical failure. About twelve percent have been categorized as 'controlled flight into terrain,' suggesting pilot error or an error with the avionics instruments. Naturally, we're keeping an eye on both possibilities, and an eye on all other possibilities. I don't know how many of you know this, but we tend to think of Arthur Conan Doyle as the patron saint of the NTSB. We're guided by his famous dictum: when the impossible has been ruled out, whatever remains, no matter how improbable, must be the truth. So for now, we're in the ruling-out-the-impossible phase."

The next volley of questions, predictably, focused on terrorism: bombs and missiles being the villains du jour. "Why is the FBI interviewing survivors?" someone asked.

That would be John Roby at the Salem Hospital, Susan realized. "They're not. The passengers are being interviewed by our team. Next?"

The questions went on for another twenty minutes. As the press conference was breaking up, the devastatingly handsome anchorman for one of the local network affiliates walked up and flashed Susan his thermodynamic TV smile. "Hi. Quick question?"

Susan smiled politely.

"We're always looking for experts who can appear on our newscast, to lend a little authenticity to the reports."

"Yes?"

He flipped open a notepad. "How do we contact this Arthur Doyle guy?"

## SALEM HOSPITAL

"I don't remember much," said the fourteen-year-old girl in the spinal brace. Her words were slurred by painkillers and the fact that three of her teeth were missing. "I was reading *People*. There was an article about Rob Pattinson. Then I woke up here."

The interrogator asked her three more questions, but gave up as her eyelids fluttered. She was asleep before the man stood.

He turned.

Another man, smallish, maybe five-eight, stood in the doorway. He wore khakis and field boots, plus a navy-blue NTSB windbreaker.

"Cheers. John Roby. We met?"

The interrogator swore to himself and presented his own ID. "Tom Daystrom. FBI."

The newcomer, an Englishman, frowned. "Yeah? To what do we owe the honor?"

Agent Daystrom held up both hands. "Hey, don't bust my chops, okay? I know I'm poaching here. But I've never worked a major disaster before. You know? I figured it'd be good training. Besides, I thought you guys could use the help."

"Decent of you," the Englishman replied. "You don't mind if I call this in to the powers that be, do you?"

Agent Daystrom winced. "You do, and my supervisor will yank me out of here. He's a real by-the-book type."

John Roby paused, then smiled. "Sure, mate. The help's appreciated, init. I'll take the other side of the corridor and we'll compare notes in, say, two hours?"

"You got it," Daystrom said and offered his hand.


As soon as Daystrom was gone, John slipped on his satellite phone headset and called Kiki Duvall, who'd been interviewing victims at hospitals in Portland.

"Oh God, John," she said after he identified himself. "This is horrible. Most of these people don't remember diddly-squat. And those who do are trying to forget it. Until I get into their faces, that is. I hate this."

John chose not to remind her that, like himself, she'd volunteered to interview survivors. "Same here. By the by, any sign of the FBI?"

From the short pause, he knew the answer before she spoke. "Yes. I just ran into an agent who said he was volunteering to help because—"

"Because he'd never worked a disaster before?"

"Exactly."

"Same here," John said. "Something's not right."

"You think? FAA's doing more than they're legally required to do. Tommy had those firefighters and paramedics working through the night. Maybe the FBI really wants to help."

John shrugged, as if she could see him. "Dunno, love. Could be. I never poached on another agency's investigation without clearing it, though. Stupid. Kind of thing that gets court cases all smudged up. Think I should call Tommy, just to be on the safe—"

"Hold it," Kiki cut in. "I've got a call coming in. I'll be right back."

A subtle hiss of white noise told John he'd been put on hold. The line clicked. "John? That was Isaiah. The swap-out plane is here. I'm heading out to the airport."

"Right. Good luck. And sing out if you bump into any more FBI."

Kiki said, "You bet," and rang off.

## PORTLAND INTERNATIONAL AIRPORT

Isaiah Grey waited for the pilot to open the door of the swap-out Vermeer 111. They'd parked the giant airliner near the Alaska Airlines maintenance hangar, within the airport's security perimeter and out of sight of the passengers and other civilians in the terminal. Isaiah had ridden a motorized ladder attached to the equivalent of a golf cart out to the site. The wind was brisk and he held on to the steel railing until the door opened.

"Isaiah?" The swap-out pilot beamed and offered a hand. Isaiah stepped into the jet and pumped the man's hand, pulling him in until their chests touched.

"Jesus, they let you in the left-hand seat? Hell in a handbasket."

The pilot grinned. "Retiring next year. The steelheads are calling my name. So what are you doing hanging out with these ghoulish crash chasers?"

Before he could reply, Isaiah noticed a passenger standing up in the first-class section. The man was athletically built and wore a white dress shirt with a black tie. He was turned with his back to the door, and Isaiah saw something he had never before seen on any civilian airplane: the man had a small, matte black automatic pistol clipped to his belt.

The man approached. The swap-out pilot said, "Isaiah Grey, NTSB. Ray Calabrese, FBI. Ray, Isaiah."

They shook hands. Isaiah put a smile on his face. "FBI?"

Ray said, "You the IIC?"

"No, but he's here in Portland."

"I need to talk to him."

They turned and found Kiki Duvall dashing up the stairs. She wore a navy-issue T-shirt under a blue denim shirt, unbuttoned and untucked, sleeves rolled up to her elbows. Her long, rusty hair was pulled back and tied with a leather thong, and she wore almond-shaped sunglasses. "What's this? Did you say FBI?"

Ray said, "Yes, ma'am. Ray Calabrese."

Kiki said, "You guys get around. There was FBI at Good Sam Hospital and John said they were at the Salem Hospital, too."

Isaiah tried for nonchalant, got pretty close. "Really?" He appraised Ray.

Ray shrugged into his sport coat. "We're just one big, happy federal family. If someone can direct me to your IIC . . . ?"

## 34

THE GARGANTUAN FLATBEDS AND cranes arrived before 2 P.M. Walter Mulroney was a taskmaster that afternoon, running his troops at full speed, as the ominous, low clouds marched eastward, pregnant and bulbous with rain that hadn't begun to fall in earnest yet. When it did, everyone knew, the field would become significantly tougher to maneuver in.

The agricultural consortium that owned the field was represented that morning, along with their insurance provider. They stood on the right-hand, northbound lane, once again closed to traffic, and watched tires as tall as a man gouge rough trenches out of their cash crop.

The trucks and cranes made a slow, straight line for the biggest piece of the wreckage, the middle of the fuselage. Under Walter's watchful eyes, specially trained crews heaved metal-mesh belts around the jet. Another crew carefully carved away the remaining wing—it would be reattached later: moving the Vermeer with one wing sticking out would be impossible.

As the first drops of rain splattered onto the ground, crews dug trenches under the fuselage and slipped the heavy belts underneath at four places. The belts were attached to the cranes.

Walter wore rubber boots, oilcloth trousers and jacket, and a cowboy hat. It was his standard bad-weather getup. He carried an electric bull-horn in one hand and a walkie-talkie in the other. His NTSB-issued ear jack was in his jacket pocket. When he gave the nod, the cranes began gingerly lifting the body of the jetliner. It groaned, protesting under the new pressure points formed by the metal belts. But it didn't break up any further. That was vital.

With infinite care, the cranes set the fuselage down onto one of the massive flatbeds. As soon as it was down, Walter lifted the megaphone to his lips, his voice echoing across the field. "Okay! Empennage and tail cone are next! This weather's only getting worse, people! Let's get to it!"

He put down the bullhorn, picked up the walkie-talkie, and thumbed the Send switch. "Truck. How's the catalog going? Over."

## FIELD OF GRASS

A long panel truck the size of the largest U-Haul, with the NTSB logo on both side-sliding doors, sat on the edge of Interstate 5. In the back sat five computer operators with five computers. Displayed on each of the five monitors was a section of the grassy field, the edges of each section denoted by neon-green lines that didn't exist in reality but that marked the infrared tags on the global-positioning-system transceivers. The computer operators stared at small squares of the field, each being videotaped live by five automated cameras, mounted on the roof of the truck. Each operator wore a headset with a microphone.

A walkie-talkie stood upright on one of the monitors. When Walter Mulroney's voice sounded, the computer operator said, "Okay, time out," into his microphone, then picked up the walkie-talkie and keyed it for transmission. "Truck here. We're a little ahead of schedule, boss, but that's good. Over."

"Roger that." Walter's voice came back flat, harried. "Keep them at it, but don't let them get careless. We pick up everything. Over."

"Roger. Out."

The operator set down the walkie-talkie and jiggled his voice mike into position. On his screen, he could see two men and a woman standing in his prescribed sector of the field. The operator had stuck masking tape on his Dell terminal, and had scribbled 5J onto the tape: that was his sector. All three of his team were holding something in their hands. He said, "Okay, Tammy, whatcha got?"

He squinted at his monitor. The woman in the field held up something he couldn't define from that distance. Her voice came back over his headset: "It looks like a bundle of coax wiring, three wires colored blue, red, and green. They're connected to some kind of junction box, about the size of a paperback."

The operator logged that information into the Dell and said, "Roger. That's marked Five-J-eighteen. Paulie, what've you got?"

One of the men in the field held up something white. "A roll of toilet paper," he said. "Never been used. The end's still adhered."

"Toilet paper. Five-J-nineteen. Right. Bill?"

"Um, got an arm bone here. A femur, maybe."

"Femur's in the leg, Bill. We'll call it a long bone, human. Five-J-twenty. Check. What's next?"

Around him, the other four operators were going through the exact same drill, each with three of their own people standing in the rain. By the end of the day, they hoped to pick up and catalog every item of debris in the field.

## FIELD OF STRAWBERRIES

A mile and a half away from the flatbeds and cranes, the searchers from Peter Kim's power-plant crew began finding bits and pieces of the missing Patterson-Pate engine number three, strewn among the plants ruined by the rain of jet fuel.

## COVINA, CALIFORNIA

Donal O'Meara, Johnser Riley, and Daria Gibron stepped off a bus, drawing no particular attention, except for glances from a few women who recognized the expensive cut of their suits.

Reaching the sidewalk, Daria realized, to her amazement, that O'Meara hadn't tried to kill her. Yet.

She had fully expected to be attacked before leaving the porn czar's mansion that morning. If O'Meara was any sort of tactician, he would have taken advantage of her skills to get out of Los Angeles, then should have taken her to a quiet, isolated alley, broken her neck, and left her. Or at least he should have tried that. One of them would have ended up on the ground in that alley, and Daria was pretty sure it wouldn't have been she.

But he hadn't tried to kill her. Daria wasn't sure why she was alive, but she was having a hell of a good time.

She studied the little row of storefronts on San Bernardino Road. Three doors down was a hotel that featured a sports bar called Hot Shots. Johnser's eyes lit up when he saw it.

"What now?" the big man asked.

"Find a car we can steal," O'Meara said, squinting into the afternoon sun. The temperature had spiked that morning, and it was already a dozen degrees warmer than Tuesday's high. "We have half a day to kill before we meet up with the others."

"That's a long fucking wait," Johnser groused.

"Find hotels," Daria said. It was the first time she'd spoken since leaving the mansion. "Two of them. We need to split up again."

The two men looked at her. They looked at each other. Then back at her. With a shrug, Daria stepped over to a kiosk vendor outside a drugstore and started rummaging through sunglasses on a spinner rack.

Johnser leaned in to O'Meara and said, "Why split up?"

O'Meara backhanded him on the arm. "Gobshite. It's so we change our bloody profile again, isn't it." He drew a cigarette out of his pocket, eyes narrowed and never leaving Daria.

It had been Daria's idea to send the other two—Feargal Kelly and Keith O'Shea—on a different route to their final destination, because finding four big, tough, fair-skinned men and one small olive-skinned woman would be a "walk in the forest," as she'd called it, for the police. "Walk in the park," O'Meara had corrected her, but got her gist. She was right. Again.

So now the three of them were in Covina, waiting for . . . what? Daria didn't know and didn't ask. At the kiosk, she wondered how O'Meara would play it. He'd obviously enjoyed the sex back at the mansion and probably wouldn't mind some more time alone with her. But he also didn't trust her and, Daria sensed, he was beginning to lose his trust in himself. He should have killed her some time ago and they both knew it. But he hadn't and he didn't know why and it bothered him.

She picked a pair of tiny round sunglasses with blue lenses; they were either very 1960s or very 1880s, she wasn't sure which. She had found plenty of money stashed in the porn czar's home, and each of them was carrying close to five hundred dollars. She paid for the glasses and returned to the men, as O'Meara took a deep puff of his cigarette, exhaling slowly.

"All right, then. Johnser, you and the girl take that one." O'Meara pointed to a little mom-and-pop hotel at the southern end of the block.

He covertly handed Johnser the handcuffs and the key. "Here. Use these if you don't trust her."

Johnser grinned. "That's a bit of all right."

O'Meara stepped up to the bigger man, nose to nose. Johnser took a hesitant half step back. "You don't fucking touch her, do you, boy. No, you don't. That's right."

Johnser nodded. There was absolutely no question who the alpha male was here. Daria tried hard not to grin, although she was enjoying the testosterone fest.

"Right." O'Meara checked his watch. "Two hours. I'll meet you right here." And he stalked off to find another motel.

Johnser glowered down at Daria. "Come on, you."

## FBI, LOS ANGELES FIELD OFFICE

The FBI's liaison with the Los Angeles Police Department and the California Highway Patrol reported back to Lucas Bell, saying he had nothing to report back. No one had seen a sign of the four Irishmen or the Israeli woman who could pass for Lebanese.

Lucas took the news stoically but he could feel his stomach acids working their way up to a lovely ulcer.

He called FBI headquarters in Washington, D.C. and it took him five transfers, five *can-you-holds* before he got his opposite number.

"About damn time," he said. "We're on a clock here."

"Yeah, and we've got a low-pressure storm hitting the coast like the Packers' front line. No power from Florida to the Carolinas, and we're next."

"Okay," Lucas cut in. "I understand. Have you heard anything on the Ireland-watch front?"

Four more transfers. Four more *can-you-holds*. Nothing.

Next, Lucas called the various Ireland watchers again, both in the United States and Europe, to see if anything had broken.

MI5—British Military Intelligence, domestic side—was the only agency with a nibble. "The IRA and Ulster types are quiet," the soft, Eatonian voice over the phone assured Lucas. "However, did you know we had an American lawmaker in Dublin and, briefly, in Belfast?"

"Who?" Lucas reached for a notepad and a pen.

"Let's see. A, ah, Representative Dan Riordan. Californian, so it says. Republican, which I take to be the equivalent of a Tory."

"Right. What's he doing in Belfast? Business or pleasure?"

"Business. Met with some of the delegates from both sides. While in Dublin, your congressman stayed to himself. Rarely surfaced. Even turned down an invitation to lunch with the Taoiseach."

Lucas chose not to ask what the hell a *tea-sack* was. "Do you have a checkout date for the congressman?"

"Yes. Leaving this evening. Dublin to Heathrow, Heathrow to Washington, D.C., Washington to Los Angeles." He pronounced it with a long "e" in the last syllable. "He should be off the ground by nine, GMT."

Lucas did the math: leaving Dublin at 4 P.M., Pacific Standard Time. He asked about a flight number and jotted that down, too. "All right. I'll do a check on the congressman, see if he's had any strong ties to The Troubles. Thanks."

He hung up and called Assistant Director Henry Deits. "This is a pretty weak lead, sir, but Representative Riordan of California is in Dublin. He's flying back to L.A. this afternoon. Should I run a check on him?"

Deits said, "Sounds like warm beer to me, but what the hell. Do it. Also, alert the state police. I'll call the field office in Sacramento, fill them in."

Lucas said, "Got it," and hung up. He looked up an extension in the building directory and called a friend in the politics-watch section, asking for a standard backgrounder on a Representative Dan Riordan, Republican from California. He hung up.

Within ten minutes, the collective eyes and ears of the FBI began turning to Sacramento and Los Angeles International Airport.

Neither of which is anywhere near Covina.

# 35

"SUSAN TANAKA."

"Susan?" It was John Roby's even-keeled voice, coming over her satellite-linked headset. "John here. There's a bit of a complication you should know about."

Susan had just arrived at the staging area and was standing in the rain, under an umbrella, watching the cranes lift the tail section of the Vermeer 111 slowly off the now-muddy ground. She wore a long, belted raincoat, the collar turned up, and a beret. "Now what?"

"I just heard from Kiki. The swap-out's here, but it came with a passenger, didn't it. FBI agent. Says he wants to speak to Tommy."

Susan's radar for trouble snapped on. "FBI. And not local. Oh, hell."

"There's more. I found the Bureau volunteering to help interview survivors at the Salem Hospital. Kiki found the same at the hospital in Portland." His voice was heavy with sarcasm when he said "volunteering." "Kiki and Isaiah sent this new lad on to see Tommy. Thought you should know."

Susan was no longer watching the cranes. She was climbing into her rented Nissan Sentra. "I'm on my way, John. Thanks."

## COVINA, CALIFORNIA

The hotel room was an exact replica of ten thousand other rooms up and down the West Coast. Windows facing the San Gabriel Mountains and a fine layer of air pollution the color of a manila folder. There was a couch and a bed and two chairs and the small table. The TV was chained down and came with a complimentary HBO monthly guide.

Johnser Riley opened the door with the swipe key he'd gotten from the office. He shrugged out of his suit coat, revealing the Glock he wore in a shoulder holster with no chest strap.

"Sit," he growled and slipped the chain lock on the door. He pulled a chair up to the TV, turned it on, and started scanning channels.

Daria said, "I have to use the bathroom."

Grumbling, Johnser rose and led the way into the bathroom. He checked the window, which couldn't be opened without shattering it. The bathroom would have been tight with only one of them in there; with both, it was very snug. Johnser sidled past her to get out, their bodies touching. Daria made a point of looking up at him, over the tops of her tiny sunglasses and through her long, black lashes. Johnser paused, turned a little bit pink, but kept on going.

Daria stripped to the waist and washed her face, neck, and shoulders in the sink. She studied her reflection. She'd availed herself of a hot shower at the mansion, after having sex with O'Meara, but she didn't have on any makeup. Her hair was short enough that she could get away with toweling it dry and brushing it.

Daria had picked up a Furla purse at the mansion and, rummaging through the half-dozen bathrooms, managed to find a lip gloss that would suit her skin color, a used eyeliner, and a little tube of balm. She applied the lipstick, the eyeliner, and shrugged at the just-okay effect. She opened the tube of lip balm. She climbed up onto the bathroom counter, on her knees. She held the balm to the mirror and wrote her name at the very top of the mirror. She climbed down, walked back and forth, checking to see if it was visible. The distortion was there if you were looking for it, but tough to see if you weren't. And she'd written it up high, higher than either Johnser Riley or Donal O'Meara would naturally look.

The balm letters were invisible now. But take a shower and steam up the room, and everything on the mirror—starting at the top—would turn misty. Everything except her name, which would stand out in sharp relief. It was a trick she'd learned in Israeli intel.

Climbing back up onto the counter, she wrote, "Emergency. Call FBI," along the top of the mirror, followed by "Calabrese" and Ray's L.A. telephone number.

It was a message in a bottle, with lots of opportunities to never be seen. What if nobody rented this room for the next two or three nights? What if they didn't shower? What if the maid cleaned the mirror first? It was a long shot, but that was okay. Daria was enjoying playing cloak and dagger with these Irishmen until Ray caught up to them. She didn't mind dragging it out a bit.

She wondered idly what the Irishmen had done or were planning to do. What had drawn the wrath of the FBI? *Bank robbery,* she thought. They were a bit too thuglike to be terrorists. In the Middle East, criminal types and terrorist types were vastly different creatures. She assumed it was the same everywhere.

She ran a hand through her hair, then returned to the other room, waiting to button the black and charcoal sweater until Johnser Riley could see. Playing head games with the big man seemed like a fine diversion. She found Johnser planted in front of the television, arms folded over his barrel chest.

Something was amiss, although it took Daria a minute or two to realize what it was. The TV. It wasn't turned to sports. Instead, the big man with the penchant for betting on athletics was watching CNN. Daria pivoted around the bed to see what the story was. They were covering the ongoing investigation of a jetliner crash on the West Coast somewhere. She watched for a couple of seconds. The footage had been taken from a news helicopter, the scene showing monstrous flatbed trucks and daisy-yellow cranes lifting the tail section. Words scrolled across the screen: 111 DEAD; 35 INJURED.

Daria watched the news clip, then turned to Johnser. He sat back, arms folded, a look of smug contentment on his square face.

He looked at her and winked.

Her fingers froze on a shiny black button. The blood rushed out of her head, leaving her feeling wobbly. "Oh, God."

Johnser's smile turned predatory. "Shut it, woman."

"You did it," she whispered. "You brought down that jet."

He sneered. "You think we're a bunch of useless wankers, don't you. You know shite, you do. Now I said shut it and go sit on that fucking bed, or so help me I'll shut your mouth for you."

Daria turned back to the TV set just as the story ended. She caught one last glimpse of the words on the screen: 111 DEAD; 35 INJURED.

She looked back at Johnser and thought about the long-shot message scripted in lip balm on the bathroom mirror.

The fun in her grand little adventure turned sour in her stomach.

## MULTNOMAH COUNTY MEDICAL EXAMINER'S OFFICE, PORTLAND

Tommy washed his hands and arms with unscented soap, then changed from scrubs to his comfortable street clothes. He stepped out of the changing room just as a big, athletically built man with a solid tan and short-chopped hair flashed a badge at the receptionist. Behind the newcomer, the exterior door opened and Susan Tanaka entered, folding an umbrella.

Tommy glanced into the ME's private office and caught a glimpse of his deputized Goth girl, Laura, poring over her geographic information system. Gothic affectations notwithstanding, the girl had proven to be a gem and had made easy work of mapping the shrapnel patterns in the cadavers.

Tommy circled the receptionist's counter. "You're FBI?"

The newcomer produced his ID. "Ray Calabrese, L.A. field office. You are . . . ?"

"Dr. Leonard Tomzak," said Susan, stepping up beside Ray. "He's our IIC. I'm Susan Tanaka, intergovernmental liaison with Washington. To what do we owe—"

Tommy held up a hand. "Wait a minute. I've been cutting for hours. I'd kill for some coffee and a sandwich."

The receptionist overheard and suggested a place half a block away.

The diner, called the Deco Penguin, had been carved out of an old warehouse. The walls were stone, thick enough to make a fine bomb shelter, and the floor was badly poured concrete, uneven and rippling. The teak bar was massive and the tables were honed from thick, knotty timbers. Ray stared at the menu behind the bar and whistled. "What the hell's this?"

The menu featured no fewer than eighty-five varieties of independent-label beer from scores of microbreweries. Ray recognized about five of them.

"Yeah," Tommy said. "These people take their beer a little too seriously. Also their coffee. Plus, near as I can tell, every third person has one of them Mini Coopers. It's kind of a weird town."

Ray looked at him. "You're from the South?"

"Texas, yeah. You're from New York?"

Ray said, "Queens." Ray ordered a corned beef sandwich and a Diet Coke. Tommy got a large bowl of clam chowder with a thick slab of fresh-baked oat bread, plus a cup of coffee. Susan ordered a glass of water.

They made with the small talk until the food arrived. "Here's the situation," Ray said, taking a mouthful of sandwich and swigging his cola. He was used to lunch meetings and didn't bother separating the business from the food. "Four known, anti-Catholic Irish terrorists popped up this week in Los Angeles. We traced them to an abandoned apartment building but they booked, maybe thirty seconds before we took down the door."

He didn't feel any particular need to mention Lucas Bell's boneheaded play of entering solo. "What we found in their bivouac were clippings from every single newspaper sold in the city, each an article about your downed CascadeAir flight."

Tommy looked up from his soup and waited a moment, assuming more was to come. He said, "And?"

Ray frowned. "And, they're connected."

Tommy said, "How?"

"We don't know yet. The entire resources of the L.A. field office have been put on this. Police, sheriff's office, and state police are helping out, too. We've got Homeland Security lending us personnel and time on their mainframes. We will reacquire these guys. But in the meantime—"

"In the meantime what?" Tommy cut in. "These guys were reading newspapers? That's the crime you're investigating?"

"No, Doc. We're investigating a case of international terrorism and more than a hundred counts of homicide."

"Agent Calabrese," Susan spoke up and smiled politely. "We have some good news for you. There was no bomb on board the Vermeer."

Ray munched on his sandwich. "You're sure?"

She said, "About ninety percent sure. We don't have the chems back yet, but we've got the NTSB's best fire-and-explosives man on the Go-Team. He says there's no sign whatsoever of a bomb."

"And no bomb means no terrorism," Tommy added. "Besides, my MEs have been studying the bodies, looking for chemical residue in the skin and hair, signs of inhaled carbon monoxide and soot, that sort of thing. So far: nothing."

Ray said, "So what? Lockerbie, the bomb was in the cargo hold. Nobody breathed in any carbon monoxide there, either."

He was right, and it annoyed Tommy that the FBI man knew his topic so well.

"That doesn't change the fact," Susan replied softly. "Our bomb man says there's no bomb. So I'm sorry you came all this way, but—"

Ray said, "Don't sweat it, Ms. Tanaka. I've been assigned to you as FBI consultant. And that's what I'm going to be, until my people back in L.A. come up with the Irishmen."

"And then?" Tommy asked.

Ray smiled. "Then, I'm taking your job, Doc."

Tommy groaned. "Ah, shit. It'll be the amateur hour. Susan, call Del, tell—"

Ray said, "Delevan Wildman? He's been informed and he's signed off on this."

Susan's shoulders sagged.

Tommy's face turned red. "Am I not making myself understood, Agent? We got no bomb. That means you got no terrorists. Which means we got the FBI dicking around the scene, trying to interrogate survivors, muddying the waters for the real investigators. That's against procedure and it's contrary to the laws of this country, which say a plane crash is the domain of the NTSB until terrorism can be proven. Since it can't, I want your people out of the hospitals and away from the survivors. And I want you as far away from the Go-Team as possible. It's our job to figure out how one of the world's most sophisticated pieces of aviation technology ended up as a fucking lawn ornament. Stand clear and let us do that job. All right?"

Ray studied the man sitting opposite him for a while. He patted his lips with his paper napkin and pulled out his wallet, leaving a twenty on the table. "Doc," he said, smiling. "The sun will rise. Children will disagree with their parents. Politicians will lie. And I'll be your second shadow from here on out. That's not a threat or a promise. It's just physics. It's the way the world works. You got a problem with that? File a protest. You got any other problems? Stick them up your ass. Now, what say we get to work?"

## COVINA, CALIFORNIA

Daria stared at the smug Johnser Riley for maybe two minutes and felt something change in her gut. Her romp, her fantasy-camp version of her old life, evaporated the moment she realized Johnser was preening about killing 111 people on that airliner.

Johnser, for his part, was dying to brag about their big caper, but he wasn't stupid enough to actually tell her. O'Meara would gut him like a fish.

Daria sat on the bed, willed herself to breathe normally. Dark skinned, she knew she didn't blush visibly. She had that going for her. She inhaled quietly, through her mouth, filling her lungs, then exhaled, also quietly. Johnser grew bored with CNN and searched for a sports channel, any sports channel. Daria did the deep-breathing exercise again, felt her pulse slow down, felt her fingers stop trembling.

She put on the character of the glib, Lebanese gunrunner and said brightly, "Well, we better do something about that bathroom window."

The big, pink-faced man turned to her, his small, close-set eyes narrowing. "The what?"

Daria said, "The escape route."

His frown deepened.

"Mr. Riley," she said, speaking slowly. "If the FBI shows up at our front door, you do want an escape route. Don't you?"

"Would you fucking shut your mouth, woman?"

"What would O'Meara do? Would he have an escape route?" It was a rhetorical question: she'd seen the escape route at their apartment building. She stood. "Come on. There's bound to be a large bin out back. We'll move it under our window. If we have to scramble out, that'll give us something bulletproof to hide behind. It's what O'Meara's probably doing right now."

Johnser Riley didn't look particularly bright, but even Daria was a little surprised when he lumbered to his feet. "All right. But don't you fucking try to get away."

She said, "Have I so far?"


Outside, they circled the hotel and found themselves in a secluded alley that faced a cinder-block wall. Johnser and Daria shoved the freshly emptied Dumpster under the window of their bedroom, hearing the casters squeal. Daria shoved and Johnser pulled. "That'll do," Johnser said, standing between the Dumpster and the window.

Daria came around to his side. "I hadn't realized you and the others brought down an airliner."

He preened a bit, then remembered to look threatening. "Less of that. Let's go."

"I need to get a message to someone," she said.

His glower turned electric. Johnser stepped up in front of her, crowding her space. "Thinking of running out?"

Daria said, "No," and raised both hands, lightning fast, palms inward and cupped. She clapped both of his ears, pulled her hands back quickly.

Johnser was so angry, he decided to give the bitch a good beating. That thought lasted for all of a half second, until his body realized that she'd shattered both of his eardrums and shot tiny bits of his eustachian tubes, cochlea, and ampullae ricocheting into his brain. His equilibrium permanently ruined, Johnser collapsed to his knees.

Daria gripped his head with both hands and shoved downward, bringing her knee up and connecting with his throat, crushing his windpipe. Johnser Riley's body was still struggling to fight off its certain death as Daria took the room key from his pocket. She also took his wallet, then carefully turned out his pants pockets, as if he'd been searched. She stood and hurled the wallet over a tattered chain-link fence and into a dry gully. It landed out of sight.

Daria hurried down the windswept street to the bigger hotel with the sports bar. The wind was hot and arid, stinging the eyes. Once there, she ducked into the bar, retrieved one paper napkin with the bar's logo emblazoned on the front. Stepping back outside, she spied a pay phone in a grocery, halfway back to the hotel.

## MULTNOMAH COUNTY MEDICAL EXAMINER'S OFFICE, PORTLAND

Ray Calabrese stood at the observation window and watched the snotty mortician from Texas remove and weigh a human kidney.

"The guy's a piece of work," Ray said into his cell phone.

"Do you blame him?" Lucas Bell sounded tired. He had called Lucas at the L.A. field office, to check on Daria. There was—Bell assured him—no good news, which equated to no bad news, either. Daria Gibron and the Irishmen had ghosted.

"Yeah, I blame him. Guy's a pathologist. He can't run a criminal investigation."

Lucas sighed. "You're trying to take his case from him. You're undermining his authority."

"When'd you get all Mister Sensitive?"

"Well, I'm gay, so . . ."

Through the observation window, Ray could see that the Texan was wrist-deep in some guy's chest now. Ray, who'd served in the marines and who'd seen his share of corpses, winced. "Oh. So that's what you mean when you say *Special* Agent Bell."

Lucas said, "You're a homophobe."

"Isn't that two things, sound alike but are spelled different?"

"Yes, Ray. That's what *homophobe* means. I have to go do, like, investigative work now, okay? Bye-bye."

*Click.*

Ray folded his cell phone in half, watched Tomzak remove something—metal, the size of his palm, what was that?—from the victim's lung cavity. Ray squinted, almost recognizing the viscera-covered thing. Ray was standing in the doctors' lounge, a cluttered cyclone of medical texts and trade publications and dirty coffee cups. Seated beside him was Morticia Addams's kid sister, typing away madly at a keyboard and using a mouse to draw lines freehand through a three-dimensional representation of a human body. Charting entry and exit wounds, Ray figured.

His cell chirped.

"Calabrese."

"Hallo, Ray."

He damn near dropped the phone. "Daria! Jesus Christ, where are you?"

"Ray. The Irishmen. Did they crash an airplane?"

Ray's knees buckled a little and he sat on an end table next to a stained, concave couch in the doctors' lounge. "We . . . we think so. I'm up here now, in Oregon. Give me your exact address."

"They're not done," the tinny voice on his cell said. Ray's fingers slid over the smooth surface of his cell phone, feeling its contours.

"What?"

"The Irish. They are not done."

"Daria, you're not making sense. Look, Special Agent Lucas Bell is standing by at the L.A. headquarters with, like, an army of guys. Tell me where you are, he'll land like an anvil on their asses."

"Ray. Please to listen," she said, her voice preternaturally calm. "They do not move like men who have accomplished a mission. They do not plan an escape route. They are not lying low. They are moving *into* position."

"Into . . . what? What position?"

"The aircraft that crashed? They treat it as . . . what is the English word? Not *audition . . .*"

Ray's heart trip-hammered. "Rehearsal?" He prayed he was wrong.

"Yes. They had a good dress rehearsal. That is all."

He wet his lips. "Christ. All right. Okay. Tell me where you are?"

"I've made them split up. Two have gone ahead. I don't know where. I'm with the man they call Donal O'Meara, but it might not be his real name."

"It is."

"There was another. Johnser something."

"Riley," Ray said.

"Yes. He is dead."

"Where are you?"

"No. We do not know where they are heading, or why. I will stay with them, will contact you."

"Daria, no! Do not—"

"We need to know their staging area." She rode over his shouting. "We need to know their target. They are soldiers, Ray. So am I. Trust me."

"Daria." He rose now. "Do not do this! These guys are fucking butchers!"

"I know." She sounded more tired than Lucas had. "You never understood that."

"What? What don't I understand?"

"I am the butcher, too."

And she disconnected.


Ray burst into the autopsy room. Four tables were set up. Three volunteers worked with the small-boned Texan with the unruly hank of hair in his eyes.

"It's New York," Tomzak drawled.

"Daria. My contact with the Irish bastards? She's convinced they brought down this jet."

Tomzak was cleaning the object he'd removed from the victim's chest, running a low stream of water over it, turning it this way and back to get it clean. Ray looked at it again, then looked down at his own hand. The foreign object in the vic's chest cavity was a cell phone; same make and model as his own.

Tomzak bagged it, wrote on the bag with a grease pen. "You got proof?"

"Jesus, asshole!" The other docs stopped working, stared at him. "Daria Gibron is working these guys! Any one of whom would gut her over lunch and think nothing of it! In order to get a message to me, she had to kill one of them, which just increased her chances of being blown by a factor of ten! She says they brought down this fucking liner. Are you listening to me?"

Tomzak studied the larger man while drying his hands. "The rules ain't, like, ambiguous. They're written in goddamn stone. It's not a criminal investigation. Not yet, anyway."

"Okay, and I understand that. But these assholes killed the guy whose chest you were just in. And they killed the next guy comes sloshing in here, and the next. What did that report from Tanaka say? How many *laps* on that plane?"

The Texan stiffened. The act of drying his already-dry hands slowed down. He stared into Ray's eyes.

"Three," he said. "Three toddlers, small enough to fit on their mothers' laps."

Ray waited, gripping his cell phone, his knuckles white.

## MARION COUNTY SHERIFF'S OFFICE

"This is Susan Tanaka."

"Susan? Tommy."

Susan turned to the sheriff and said, "Can you excuse me a second?" She had been debriefing Alfredo Escobar and his top aides on the crash. Now she stepped into the corridor of the Marion County Courthouse. "Tommy?"

"Calabrese has an agent running with the Irishmen. She says they downed the jetliner."

Susan pushed the voice wand aside and bent at the waist to sip from a water fountain, returned her comm gear to position. "The rules—"

"I know the rules, crazy lady. And we're keeping the goddamn case.

I'm just saying. We've been keeping Calabrese at arm's length. I think that's gotta stop."

Susan considered it. Tommy wouldn't recommend it without reason.

"He's there with you now?"

"Yeah."

"What do you think?"

"I think we're the babysitters, Suze. I think the evidence is going to tell us that the Irishman crashed the jet."

"There was no bomb. And the cockpit voice recorder; there was a thrust-reverser deployment in engine three. The pilots—"

"They didn't miss it, Suze. They didn't sit there for three minutes and forget to check their monitors! You heard the recorder. They didn't panic."

"Then how—"

"I don't know, but all the engineers and pilots and pathologists in the world won't figure that one out. I think maybe the FBI might. I want Calabrese at the table. With the Go-Team."

Susan said simply, "Done."

"Okay. Tell Del? Gotta go." And she heard him hang up.


Forty miles to the north, Ray Calabrese extended his hand to shake. Then remembered where Tommy's hand had just been.

## 36

DARIA RETURNED TO THE alley in Covina. Johnser Riley's body lay hidden behind the Dumpster. She planted the bar's napkin and the magnetic room key on him, retrieved his gun and the handcuffs.

She returned to the hotel room; she'd left the door unlocked by blocking the bolt with the HBO guide. She put Johnser's Glock and the handcuff key on top of the TV, climbed onto the bed, and chained her left wrist to the aged radiator.

Then she closed her eyes and willed herself to sleep. Just as she used to do in the field.


## FBI, LOS ANGELES FIELD OFFICE

Lucas Bell said, "Yes, ma'am. Covina? . . . Closest intersection? . . . Thank you, ma'am," and hung up. He checked his watch. Almost 4 P.M. In a little over four hours, the crash would hit the forty-eight-hour mark.

He dashed from his office, rapped on the door of Henry Deits, who looked up from a deep pile of paperwork. "What?"

"The Gibron woman called Ray. I checked with Ray's cell provider. They traced her end of the call to a pay phone outside a hotel in Covina."

"Okay, let's move."

Lucas showed Deits the palm of his hand. "Hang on. She killed one of the four. Johnser Riley. And she says the Irishmen definitely downed the jetliner."

"Ray?"

"He's told the NTSB guys. They're giving him full access to the investigation."

Diets stood. "Now we're talking. Covina. I want boots on the ground."

But Lucas was already gone from his doorway.


## PORTLAND INTERNATIONAL AIRPORT

KAZMANSKI: Confirmed center autopilot on.
*Sounds of airplane in flight.*
KAZMANSKI: Like a baby's butt.
DANVERS: Damn straight.
*More sounds of standard flight.*
KAZMANSKI: Hmm. What's that?
*Tap.*
DANVERS: What's what?
KAZMANSKI: I've got a— Whoa!
*Sounds of violent shaking.*
DANVERS: Shit! Trimming rudder to the left! What've we got?
KAZMANSKI: I— Dammit!

Kiki stopped the MP3 player and removed her thick foam headset. She was sitting in the copilot's seat of the swap-out, the exact replica of the doomed Vermeer 111, provided by the airline. Officials at the company assured the Go-Team that this plane was a clone of Flight 818, down to all the retrofitted specialty avionics.

The copilot, Russ Kazmanski, had seen something odd, something that caught his attention. That had been followed by a tapping sound.

Using the knuckle of her forefinger, Kiki reached for the nearest monitor and tapped it once. She frowned, cocked her head to one side. She reached over and tapped the next monitor once. Another frown.

She methodically worked her away around to every monitor and control surface within arm's reach. None of them produced the same tapping sound she'd heard on the digital recording.

She leaned back, thinking about it, absently twirling an escaped strand of her red-brown hair. She tapped the first monitor again, this time with the tip of her finger. She wore her nails clipped short, so that wasn't a problem.

The sound was wrong. She tapped the next one waited, frowned.

Tap. Wait. Frown. Tap. Wait. Frown. The whole circuit again.

Isaiah Grey entered. Without turning around, Kiki said, "Close the door, please." The door to the flight deck had been closed during the crisis; opening it changed the acoustics of the deck.

"What are you doing?"

"There's a tapping sound on the CVR, just after the copilot said, 'What's that?' I figure he saw something that wasn't kosher. And a second later, everything went ka-blooy." She turned in her seat. "You got a minute?"

"I'm just doing some paperwork. I can do it here as well as anywhere."

"Good. Sit down. I need your body."

"A guy never gets tired of hearing that." Isaiah snugged himself into the pilot's left-hand seat, rested his clipboard against the yoke.

Kiki smiled. "I need your body *and* your clothes. To alter the acoustics, just like the captain's did."

Isaiah said, "It's nice to be needed."

Kiki dug her headset and control pad out of the pocket of her denim shirt and punched in a number. "Tommy?"

"What!" his voice snapped back over the line.

"Um, it's Kiki. Are you all right?"

"Hell no. My back's killing me and my hands are cramping like a sumbitch. 'Sup?"

"Do you keep a list of the personal belongings of the bodies?"

"Course."

"What did the copilot have in his pockets?" Kiki looked down at the shoulder harness, which she'd strapped on to approximate how far Russ Kazmanski had been able to reach. She noticed that the pockets of her jeans were inaccessible. "Just his shirt and jacket."

"Hang on. . . . Let's see, let's see . . ." Kiki heard pages flipping. "Kazmanski. Yeah, got it. Two sticks of gum. Sugar-free. One pen."

"What kind?"

Tommy said, "Big Red."

"Pen, Tommy! What kind of pen."

"Bic. Disposable, fine point. Black ink."

"Thanks, bye." She rang off, distracted. "Isaiah, do you have a Bic pen?"

He felt through his pockets, found two pens. "Both Pilots. Naturally."

She sighed, rubbed her forehead. "Can you get me a Bic pen?"

Isaiah smiled and eased himself back out of the chair. Normally, he didn't like anyone wasting his time, but Isaiah found it fascinating to watch Kiki. She had an intuitive understanding of the science of sound, the way a musical wunderkind can pick up a violin and play a sonata without practicing. He had been secretly studying Kiki on the one other crash they'd investigated together.

"Be right back," he said.

## FIELD OF STRAWBERRIES

The searchers from the power-plant crew were working in full breathing apparatus now, the stench of the jet fuel making it otherwise impossible to work in the field.

Three of the searchers gathered by a drainage ditch and showed one another what they had found. Each carried a piece of tempered steel, thin and about the size of a legal pad. Each was designed to be curved, and they were. But each had also been torqued, twisted in a way their designers had never intended. Each twist was clockwise.

The leader of the search flipped open a cell phone and dialed.

## BOEING PLANT, GRESHAM, OREGON

Peter Kim slipped on his ear jack and voice wand, then said, "Kim."

"Sir. We've found four blocker doors and a couple of reverser sleeves in the field. Each has a clockwise warp."

Peter stood in a lab the size of three handball courts, with very high ceilings and a spiderweb of air ducts and pipes hanging from the ceiling tiles. The room vents maintained a positive air pressure to keep out contaminants. In the center of the room was a worktable, belt-high and as large as the key of a basketball court. A crew of eight—some of Peter's people, some from Patterson-Pate, the engine manufacturer—were slowly stripping apart engine number four, taken from the wing found at the Wheeler residence. Each piece was measured with calipers and the measurements were checked against the "bible" from Patterson-Pate. It was slow, meticulous work.

Peter had lost interest in the process the moment he heard the news over his satellite phone. Engine number four seemed in relatively good working order considering that it had been taken from a backyard barbecue pit. Now his attention was squarely on the remnants of engine number three, found on the field two miles from the crash site.

"Clockwise torque," Peter repeated into his voice wand. "That fits with the twists we saw in the engine mounts."

"Yes, sir. We've got a partially deployed thrust reverser in midflight."

"Which the pilots didn't correctly identify in time to fix," Peter added. "Classic pilot error. Okay. Keep on it until you've found every last micron of that engine. I want it all."

## COVINA, CALIFORNIA

Donal O'Meara rapped on the door three times. Assuming the worst, he waited until the street outside the hotel was empty, then drew his steel Colt Python with the black grip and kicked in the door. He entered low, the revolver aimed in front of him in a two-hand hold.

Johnser Riley was nowhere to be seen. Daria Gibron sat bolt upright on the bed, eyes wide with shock. It took O'Meara a moment to realize she'd been sleeping. She was shackled to the radiator.

Gun aimed at her midsection, O'Meara rose. "Where's Riley?"

"Here and gone," she said, her shock disappearing quickly.

O'Meara cocked the stocky steel gun. "Talk sense, woman."

"Riley was here for about five minutes, before he put this on me and left." She rattled the handcuffs. "He was gone maybe forty minutes, an hour. I asked him where he was going. He told me to shut up. Then he fiddled about with the window in the bathroom, trying to open it or something. Now, will you please get me out of this damn thing? The key's on the TV."

O'Meara looked. It was, but so was Johnser's Glock 9. He'd gone out unarmed. O'Meara moved to the bed and touched her forehead with the barrel of the Colt. "If you're fucking with me . . ." He let the threat go unfinished and turned to the door.

"Donal?"

He turned back.

"Can I at least have the remote control?"

He left.

.   .   .

*That fucking Gibron woman,* O'Meara fumed. There she was, shackled and unarmed. Certainly she couldn't have done anything to that 230-pound package of violence that was John Padraic Riley. Still, she'd been a wild card ever since she'd shown up. Everything she'd said and done seemed to help their cause. But all of O'Meara's finely honed soldier's senses seemed slightly off-kilter in her presence. She was like a lodestone in a shop full of compasses.

Daria had said that Johnser had fiddled about with the bathroom window. O'Meara circled the hotel, counted off the windows until he came to the back of room seven. A grimy, sun-beaten Dumpster had been shoved up to the window. It looked out of place, that close to the wall. O'Meara pried open the lid and peered inside. Nothing. He looked around at the other side.

Johnser Riley's eyes were wide open, hands wrapped around his own throat, mouth open in a perfect O, revealing two gold teeth. He was curled up, almost in a fetal position, and flies buzzed around a trickle of dried blood that ran from his exposed ear to the collar of his fine, white shirt.

O'Meara knelt, his face red, his breath coming in shallow gasps, the air seeming hot as hell as it escaped his lungs. His vision blurred as tears arrived.

*Johnser. Jesus, God. Johnser.*

He wiped tears off his cheek. He'd drawn his gun but couldn't remember when. He was holding the black grip so tight that his wrist cramped up. Willing himself to calm down, O'Meara breathed in as much air as he could, filled his lungs to capacity, held it, exhaled. He swatted at the flies buzzing around his lifelong friend.

He tucked his Colt back into his belt. He closed Johnser's eyes. He checked the man's pockets and found nothing but a napkin embossed with the logo of a sports bar. None of the money stolen from the Egyptian's mansion. No wallet.

"Oh, God, Johnser," he whispered. "Who'd you piss off this time, my lad?"


O'Meara returned to the hotel room. Daria sighed theatrically and made a show of rattling the handcuffs.

He stared at her, unmoving. She stared back. Could she have killed Johnser Riley? Maybe. She'd kicked the shite out of that FBI fella back in Los Angeles. Also the fat Arab at the mansion. And that, while handcuffed.

But could she have moved that massive Dumpster to hide Johnser's body? Not bloody likely.

Daria gave up the staring game first. "What?"

"Nothing." He went to the TV set and grabbed the handcuff key, tossing it to her. One-handed catch. Daria unsnapped the cuff, rose from the bed, and flexed her knees and back. "Where's the big man?"

"He went ahead."

O'Meara crossed to the bed stand, picked up the phone, and dialed eight for long distance, then a ten-digit number.

Daria said, "If it's room service, I could kill for a bloody Mary."

O'Meara ignored her. Over the line, a mechanical voice said, "We apologize, but telephone service has been disrupted. Thank you for your patience."

"Gobshite!" He hung up, turned on the television, found it already on CNN. He moved one station down, to CNN Headline News.

And five minutes later, discovered that phone service was out for all of Georgia and the Carolinas.

His Atlanta telephone exchange was useless.

He hung up, turned, found Daria sitting on the bed, slipping into her Spanish boots, dark eyes studying him. "Change of plan?"

"Here." O'Meara showed her how much of the stolen money he had left. "Think that'll buy us another change of clothes?"

## PORTLAND INTERNATIONAL AIRPORT

Isaiah Grey sat down in the pilot's seat of the Vermeer swap-out and handed Kiki a pen.

"Bic," he said. "I hope blue ink is okay."

She rolled her eyes at his sly smile.

Holding the pen with the capped end in her hand, she tapped the nearest monitor. She frowned. Isaiah waited quietly, fascinated.

Kiki tapped the next one, waited. Then the next one. She hit each monitor within her reach.

She reversed the pen, cap facing away from her, and went through the ritual again. It took ten minutes.

She took off the cap, tapped the monitors with the metal nib.

After the last monitor, Isaiah said, "Anything?"

"Not a pen," Kiki said. "What the hell did he see? And what was that tapping sound?"

## INTERSTATE 5

The Oregon Department of Transportation and state troopers worked in the rain to close off the ramp from Interstate 5 to the rural community of Valence. The rain was coming strong now, bouncing off the asphalt and turning the borrow pits along the sides of the highway to mud. An independent contractor had been hired to move the remains of the Vermeer 111 to the leased hangar in Valence, and the crews were experienced enough to know that if the six-foot-high wheels of the huge trucks hit that mud, they'd have to transfer the cargo off and get hauled out. It would cost them a day.

Walter Mulroney rode ahead of the convoy in a rented Sentra. The first thing he noted about Valence was that the downtown had been designed for highway traffic, not for the residents. The main strip featured a dozen fast-food joints, each with its logo-bearing sign perched precariously atop metal poles at least a hundred feet up; hard to see from the sidewalks but readily visible from the highway.

Troopers were just beginning to close off the main drag—the massive trucks were far too wide for two-way traffic through town—as Walter took the well-marked turnoff for the airfield. A short, stocky man in jeans, cowboy boots, and a poncho ran out to open one of the two big gates for him. Walter rolled down his window and flashed his ID.

"Ricky Sanchez," the man said as he leaned down, elbows on the window frame of the driver's door. He was maybe twenty-five, Walter thought, and his accent was strong enough to suggest that he was an immigrant or first-generation in the States. "Where's the Vermeer?"

"Five minutes behind me."

The armrest inside the door was getting wet. Ricky Sanchez pointed to a row of hangars and said, "Park it over there. I'll meet you in hangar five." He dashed away to open the other gate.

The airfield was a bit of a surprise. It included one well-kept runway, easily long enough for multiengine takeoffs. There were five hangars, and, to Walter's experienced eye, they clearly delineated the history of the field. The first two hangars were rusty Quonset huts, barely big enough to park a Hercules transport plane. The third one, also a tin Quonset, was twice the size and half as old as the first two. The fourth hangar couldn't have been more than five years old. It was frame constructed and wide enough to provide cover for two UPS jets, side by side, along with wiggle room for ground crews to perform maintenance. As Walter drove past, that was exactly what he saw going on.

The fifth hangar was brand-new and freshly painted sky blue and white. The UPS logo adorned the doors. This building had more space than the first three hangars combined. It was a top-of-the-line facility that would have looked right at home at O'Hare.

Walter parked just inside that hangar. The barn doors had been thrown open. There was room inside for three Vermeer 111s, but currently his Sentra was the only vehicle within. Walter got out and shut his door, and the sound echoed crazily around him.

Ricky Sanchez hustled in and shoved back the hood of his poncho. His face was square and his smile was like a neon light. He was maybe five-six, and the hand that gripped Walter's could have belonged to a boxer.

"Walter Mulroney, NTSB. You have a fine facility here."

Ricky beamed as if he'd built it himself. "I'm the day foreman. It doesn't pay much but they're giving me free flying lessons."

"Want to be a pilot?" Walter asked.

Ricky said, "I am a pilot."

Walter smiled. Most pilots considered themselves born that way. "We're going to need outlets for a dozen computers, not to mention all the power tools. Will that be a problem?"

Ricky said, "We got enough power strips for that, and UPS had us put in three data drops. You can surf the Net right from the workstation."

Walter's fears of a podunk airfield with 1950s technology evaporated. "Outstanding. We're also going to set up a microwave relay from your tower, if that's okay."

He glanced outside. The control tower was a simple wooden box on stilts. It could have doubled as a fire-watch facility in a national forest or a spotlight guardhouse at a prison.

"Power's no problem," Ricky said. "UPS says you got the hangar for as long as you need. We don't got a lot of luxuries or nothing but there's a Coke machine and a candy machine in the office. And a couple restaurants around here deliver. My sister owns one. Best enchiladas in town, guaranteed. We also—"

He paused, eyes going wide, feeling the ground vibrate beneath his muddy boots.

Walter felt it, too, and smiled. "That's no earthquake, son. That's CascadeAir Flight Eight One Eight."

The first of the mammoth trucks turned into the airfield.

# 37

ISAIAH GREY SAID, "AH, roger that, ATC. We've got a yellow light. Holding at the line for your word. Over."

A crackle of static, then a woman's voice: "Confirmed November Tango Sierra Bravo One. Hang tight. We'll get you guys airborne in a minute. ATC out."

Hayden, the pilot who'd flown the swap-out—and Ray Calabrese— from LAX to PDX sat in the copilot's chair. Kiki Duvall sat in the fold-away seat behind Isaiah. Her teeth were working her lower lip and she was pulling absently on the frayed cuff of her jeans. Normally, Kiki loved to fly. But cruising in an exact duplicate of the jet whose shattered corpse she had so recently helped to examine was an unnerving experience.

"I didn't realize you could fly these big commercial jobs," she said, speaking up to be heard by Isaiah, who wore a headset.

"If it's got wings, I can fly it," he replied over his shoulder. "You ready to rock?"

The plane inched toward the painted stripe, its waiting position. Isaiah tapped the brake, bringing the plane to a full stop, and a loud *thump-thump* sounded from within. The men jumped, eyes alert.

"Relax, boys," Kiki said. "Something just fell over, amidships."

The copilot, Hayden, began to unbuckle his seat belt. "More than something. I heard two thumps, ma'am."

"Hmm." Kiki was staring out the window absently. "One thing fell. You just heard it twice."

He stopped before exiting the flight deck and smiled down at the seated woman. "Come again?"

Kiki sighed. "One thing fell. It'll be about halfway back to the tail. It's not metal. Rubber or plastic, maybe. We heard it land twice."

Hayden stepped out of the flight deck. Isaiah adjusted his voice wand and said, "Portland ATC, this is November Tango One. Be advised that copilot has exited the flight deck to check on a noise. Expect him back up here in thirty seconds. . . . Roger, tower. Thanks. November Tango One out."

The copilot returned with an odd, artificial smile painted on his face. Isaiah restrained his own grin. "Well?"

"Ah, a flashlight was stowed badly in an overhead bin. It bounced free." He retook his seat and turned to Kiki. "It's waterproof, rubber coated, not metal. It was just what you said and right where you said. You mind me asking how you knew that, ma'am?"

"I'll tell you if you stop calling me ma'am. It's Kiki."

"Hayden," he responded.

"Glad to meet you. Sound travels through the air. But it also travels through metal. Aluminum is a particularly good medium for sound. Even better than air. That means sound travels first through the skin of an aircraft, then through the air in the fuselage and the wood of the cockpit door. When the flashlight hit the deck, we heard the thump through the skin of the plane first. I knew it wasn't metal because the thump lacked that resonant quality. And I did a little calculation in my head, figuring out how far apart the thumps were, to gauge how far back the thing landed."

Hayden gaped. "How the hell did you learn something like that?"

Kiki blushed, enjoying the act of showing off. "I was a sonar officer on a nuclear sub. Want to know how to tell a Russian boomer from two whales making love?"

"Not really, no. Since when do they allow women on board subs?" Hayden asked.

"Since me. Well, me and four others. We were the freshman class. And we were only allowed to serve on the big, nuclear boomers. Attack subs don't have enough room for mixed housing."

Hayden exchanged impressed grins with Isaiah. "I've practically lived half my life inside jets and I never knew that thing about sound traveling through walls."

Isaiah inclined his head, hearing something over his headset, then toggled his Send switch. "Ah, roger that, tower. We're cleared and rolling. Thanks for the hospitality. November Tango One out."

He turned to Hayden and jerked his thumb back to Kiki. "And you wondered why I took this job."

## GAMELAN INDUSTRIES, BEAVERTON

Dennis Silverman was putting the finishing touches on the false data for the flight data recorder when his phone rang. "Dennis? Walter Mulroney here."

Dennis smiled and kicked back, his feet up on his cluttered desk. "Mr. Mulroney. Hey, how's it going?"

"Good. We've moved the fuselage to a hangar at the Valence Airfield and most of the detritus will be here by sunset. I just heard from Susan Tanaka. We'll debrief here, tonight. Any chance the data from the FDR will be ready?"

"You bet." Dennis sucked apple juice through a straw punched through the top of a waxy box. "We've got better data than I hoped. The Gamelan should explain a lot of things tonight."

"Really?"

"Trust me. I can make this box tell me anything I want," Dennis said. He meant it literally.

## BOEING PLANT, GRESHAM

One of the searchers from the fuel-soaked field arrived around 6 P.M. and presented the three thin, twisted pieces of metal, each in its own sealed evidence bag.

"Excellent," said Peter Kim. "Partial thrust-reverser deployment, as predicted. Good old-fashioned pilot error."

"We've swept three adjacent fields," the searcher said. "We haven't found even half of the engine."

Peter nodded. "I suspect some of it hit the fuselage. Have you found the hydraulic isolation valve yet?"

The man frowned. "I don't think I know what that is."

"Here." Peter walked him over to the massive workbench. A team of engineers from Boeing, Patterson-Pate, and Peter's own crew had engine number four almost completely stripped down. Peter picked up a piece of metal approximately the size and shape of a desk stapler. "Hydraulic isolation valve. This has to open before the reversers can deploy the blocker doors. The blocker doors check the airflow and reroute it, slowing down the plane. Here, see this?"

He held up the valve and pointed to a thin wire at the top. "This triggers a signal to a monitor on the flight deck. One of the pilots should have seen that. With a partial deployment, they could have cut power to that engine and flown fine on the other three until they could stow the reversers again. You find me this valve and we'll have the smoking gun. After that, we'll write our reports and head on back home. Case closed."

The searcher said, "Yes, sir," and left.

## ATLANTA, GEORGIA

The tropical depression that had beaten the crap out of Georgia finally skipped off the eastern seaboard and began lumbering toward New England and Canada. Power was quickly restored to much of Atlanta.

At the apartment with the Red Fist of Ulster's answering machine, phone service was finally back in operation.

## MULTNOMAH COUNTY MEDICAL EXAMINER'S OFFICE, PORTLAND

"Can you take a look at something?"

Tommy Tomzak was taking a break in the outer office of the ME's building, watching traffic glide past the front window. His hands were cramping up and his lower back vibrated with a dull, red ache from leaning over gurneys. He'd have killed for a sauna or a couple of laps in a pool, and he realized that he hadn't looked to see if their hotel offered either amenity. He was leaning against the back of a couch in the waiting room, sipping his sixth cup of coffee, his mind flitting from the cadavers awaiting his attention to the FBI consultant, to Kiki Duvall. He wondered what she was up to today, wondered if either of them would be free for dinner.

He wondered how she'd react if he asked. He wondered if he'd really ask her. Was there any point in pursuing a relationship that had already gone south once before?

He checked the wall clock. A little after 6 P.M. At 8, this crash would be forty-eight hours old.

He thought about the autopsies in Kentucky. About finding enough of a dismembered thigh to do a DNA test on the pilot. The muscle was far too ruined by jet fuel for a drug test. But was there something he'd missed? Hadn't someone written a paper about—

"Ahem." The voice of Laura, the ME's black-clad daughter, snapped him out of his reverie. "I said, can you take a look at something?"

Tommy smiled ruefully. "Sorry. My brain's slowly leaking out my ears. 'Sup?"

She waved off the apology with a good-natured pop of her bubble gum and led him to her dad's office. She plopped herself down in the rolling chair, facing the MacBook Air. Tommy parked his butt on the edge of the desk and watched her hands flash across the keyboard.

Simple outline drawings of male and female forms appeared on the screen, one after another. Each contained a scale accounting for height and weight. Each had a designation based on their seat selection aboard the aircraft. Each showed one or more bright red marks for entry wounds and bright blue marks for exit wounds. Yellow lines—some straight, most curved—linked the wounds. Where limbs were missing, the body parts were marked in dotted outlines.

The images flashed onto the screen, stayed for about five seconds, then were replaced by the next. Tommy watched, sipping his coffee.

Laura said, "See it?"

Tommy snapped out of it. "Um . . ."

The girl rolled her black-lined eyes. "The pattern?"

"Ah . . ." For a split second, Tommy thought about salvaging his ego by lying. "Nope. Sorry."

She started the sequence again.

"What am I looking for?"

"Watch the curve of the yellow lines and the progress of the seat numbers. Okay?"

She ran it again. Tommy concentrated on the screen. He brushed a curved hank of hair away from his gray eyes. He set down the cup. He folded his arms and rested his chin in one hand. The body language was designed to make him look and feel less like a doofus.

Laura said, "See it?"

"Ah. Well. No."

She sighed. "It's a pattern."

"Yeah?"

"Well, yeah."

Tommy still didn't see any pattern. "Can you link this program with any kind of . . . I don't know, slide-show software or something? Anything that will demonstrate the pattern better?"

She popped a bubble. "I can do better than that. I can overlay the images, especially if you get me an overhead view of the jet. I could superimpose all of it into one dynamic image."

"Done." Tommy slid his ear jack out of his pocket and reached for the controls on his belt. "Arachnia, huh?"

The girl blushed, pleased that Tommy had remembered.

# *38*

IN ONTARIO, CALIFORNIA, DARIA Gibron and Donal O'Meara caught a Greyhound east on Interstate 10. Dressed in jeans and matching UCLA T-shirts, they looked like a romantic couple. They switched buses, vectoring north and east on the 15, curving around San Bernardino.

Donal never spoke. Daria asked no questions.

The temperature began to fall a bit, but there was enough heat and dust in the wind to suggest that tomorrow would be a scorcher.

## STATE HIGHWAY 99E, OREGON CITY

Ray Calabrese wondered if the small Asian American woman in the designer jacket and skirt was practicing for the time trials at Daytona. She kept the rented Nissan at thirty miles over the speed limit whenever she could, and she handled the car as if she'd passed the Bureau's Automobile Pursuit Course at Quantico with flying colors.

"So where are we going?" Ray asked as they zoomed out of the downtown core that looked like it had been frozen in the early 1960s. They were on a winding four-lane highway parallel to the Willamette River. Fir trees towered over the roadway—green up close, the farther ones turned black by the night. On the opposite shore, lights shone from the windows of shiny new mansions.

"Valence," Susan said. She kept both hands on the wheel. "We've moved the Vermeer to a hangar on loan from UPS."

"This seems like a funny route."

Susan just shrugged. She'd pored over a Triple A map the night before and was convinced that this route would shave five minutes off the drive time.

"Your IIC doesn't like me much," said Ray.

"You come on a little strong, Agent Calabrese." She scooted the Nissan past an SUV, hitting eighty.

"I'm just here as an adviser."

"Ha!" She cast a quick glance his way. "Sorry, but you all but handed Tommy his hat and told him not to let the door hit him on the butt on his way out. Tommy can be forgiven for being defensive; you're on offense."

They were quiet for a while. Ray hadn't expected the land outside Portland to be so forested, so pretty. He'd been looking for sprawling suburbs, he guessed. But passing from Oregon City into unincorporated Clackamas County had been like passing through some kind of magic portal: before, there had been urban-style development; now, there wasn't.

"Besides," Susan said. "There's something else."

"What's that?"

She blew past a log truck. "I mean, there's something else about you. Something on your mind. You're in a bad mood, sure, but not just a bad mood. You're worried. Or maybe scared."

Ray studied her. Susan's hair was expertly cut. Her clothes were tasteful and expensive. She wore a diamond engagement ring and a platinum wedding ring, and both looked like antiques. Her almond-shaped eyes reminded Ray of Daria. He said, "You're good with people, aren't you?"

Susan said, "Yes."

"You married?"

She knew that he was deflecting her question, but she went with the flow. "Fifteen years, this August."

"And he doesn't mind you bopping all over the country every time a plane drops out of the sky?"

Susan said, "Kirk is a pilot. United. Every time one of my Go-Teams figures out what downed a jet and we order the companies to fix something so it doesn't happen again, I'm doing it for Kirk."

Ray grinned. "He's a head pilot?"

"Yes."

"Do they call him Captain Kirk?"

Susan laughed, the notes high and musical. "He's heard that once or twice, yes." She drove for a while, slowed down as the town of Canby drew near. "I called him last night. He knew Meghan Danvers, the Vermeer's pilot. They'd met at a couple of training sessions over the years. He liked her, said she was a pro."

"So you're hoping it wasn't pilot error."

"Yes." Susan's voice held no equivocation, no doubt. "Absolutely. I'm always pulling for the pilots. I admit that. But don't misunderstand. Our report will reflect the evidence. If it's pilot error, we'll say so."

Ray settled back in his seat, glad that their speed was down to forty. "Don't worry about it, Ms. Tanaka. This wasn't pilot error. It was a goddamn low-life terrorist."

"Your Red Fist of Ulster theory." Ray had explained it to Susan and Tommy over lunch. "Have they taken credit for it? Have they made any threats or demands?"

"No, but it's them."

"You're sure?"

*I have to be,* Ray thought. *If it's not them, then Daria is risking her life for nothing and I'm screwing around on the wrong end of the West Coast.*

"My asset is sure," he said. "Me, too."

## VALENCE AIRFIELD

Walter Mulroney rubbed his hands together like a little kid ogling a Christmas tree. "Excellent," he said. "The carpenters are here."

The UPS hangar was abuzz with activity. They hadn't unloaded the major pieces of the Vermeer from the flatbeds yet, but much of the smaller detritus was showing up, and crews were sorting fat plastic bins of shrapnel and personal belongings.

The three cranes were being backed off their carriers, their reverse beepers blaring. Hired security guards were keeping out all the roustabout fliers and mechanics who tend to hang around airfields everywhere, but Ricky Sanchez and a handful of airfield staff had been let in to watch. They couldn't have enjoyed Disneyland any more, but every now and then they glanced at the devastated cadaver of the jetliner and remembered that this was no lark. Sanchez's friends had each made the sign of the cross the first time they caught sight of Flight 818.

A couple of dozen long folding tables had been set up along one wall and Susan Tanaka was busy helping technicians set up computers with Internet links. Several telephones were also being set up. Tommy Tomzak had called ahead from Portland and had asked for a projector hooked up to a Mac with PowerPoint software. Susan didn't know what for, but she'd asked one of her assistants to get the equipment.

Ray Calabrese stood in an isolated corner, arms folded across his chest. He'd taken off his jacket and his Glock 9 hung from his hip in a leather scabbard holster. No one spoke to him.

Now came the carpentry crew, led by a foreman who'd worked with Walter for several years. She eyed the ruined remains of the jetliner. "Hey, Walt. So, where do you want this thing?"

Walter pointed to the southern end of the massive hangar. "Over there. I want it in diagonally, nose to the barn door, tail section in that back corner. I want the belly at least thirty feet up off the floor, so the forklifts and scissor lifts can be driven under it."

The foreman—calling her a "forewoman" to her face always resulted in a scowl—studied the hangar and made measurements in her head. "We can do that."

"Have you seen the nose yet?" Walter warned. He pointed to the front end of the jet, which looked as mangled as a bullet dug out of a brick wall.

"Yeesh. That's a mess. The pilot . . . ?"

Walter's face turned dark.

The foreman cocked her head, studied the nose of the aircraft. "We can set her up."

Walter said, "Outstanding."

"Hey!" They turned. One of the airfield ground crew with security clearance shot into the hangar like he'd been fired from a cannon. "The other Vermeer is on final!"

## OVER VALENCE

"Roger, Valence tower. We're on final. November Tango Sierra Bravo One out."

Isaiah Grey turned to the copilot seat. Instead of Hayden, Kiki Duvall sat there. She was tapping monitors with a Bic pen. She'd deduced that the acoustic signature of the tapping sound on the flight data recorder might have been altered by the pressurization of the aircraft, so she'd switched seats with the copilot.

Isaiah caught her eye. "Any luck?"

Scowling, Kiki shook her head.

Tommy Tomzak arrived at the hangar just seconds before the eight-o'clock debriefing was scheduled to begin. Laura, the medical examiner's daughter, borrowed her dad's car. She'd toned down the Goth look, changing into black jeans and a black T-shirt beneath a glossy black rain slicker. The lace and theatrical makeup were gone, and she looked even younger than her sixteen years.

"What's this?" Kiki Duvall asked as Tommy and the girl carried in two heavy boxes.

"Hardware," Tommy said. "How was your d— Whoa."

He looked around at the now-crowded hangar. The gigantic pieces of the Vermeer were being positioned to one side, while a truck with a long, steel tow bar was backing an identical—but unruined—Vermeer 111 into the other corner. The truck moved at a snail's pace, gingerly backing the aircraft into place. Isaiah Grey stood near the front wheels, holding a sensor with an infrared scanner. He flashed the beam at the Gamelan input controls, on the belly of the plane.

Kiki said, "We've been busy around here, jefe."

"Yeah. Any luck with the CVR?"

Kiki perched atop one of the folding tables as Tommy and Laura began to unpack the Mac computer liberated from her father's office. "The lab in Portland is running a digital analysis. We should know every organic clank, hoot, and whistle by tomorrow."

Tommy attached a cable to the Mac. "Organic?"

"All of the sounds made by the plane itself. We have thousands of acoustic samples on file in D.C. We'll ID all of that stuff, or nearly all of it, by week's end. It's the nonorganic sounds—the people sounds, or luggage hitting luggage. That stuff's tougher to identify. There's this sound, right in the cockpit, that's driving me bonkers."

Tommy laid a hand on her knee. "Put it on the back burner. It'll come to you."

Kiki smiled. "Hey, you're the Investigator in Charge."

"Damn right I am."

"Folks!" Susan Tanaka shouted above the clatter of the carpenters, who were building scaffolding to hold the major sections of the Vermeer in place. "Can we gather over here, please?"

The crew leaders gathered around the table where Laura was booting up the MacBook Air. At the barn doors, a security guard checked a list of names on a clipboard and stepped aside so Dennis Silverman of Gamelan Industries could enter. He wore a Columbia Sportswear microfiber jacket with the Gamelan logo on the breast, a hood up over his head. His eyeglasses fogged over the moment he entered.

People scavenged chairs. Some sat on the tables. Walter Mulroney caught Ricky Sanchez's eye and waved him over. The smile on the younger man's face warmed up the hangar by a few degrees.

Susan waved to Tommy. "You want to go first?"

"Sure. Folks, this here's Laura, newly promoted to be my technical adviser." The girl blushed, her fingers almost invisible as they glided over the keyboard. "My medical examiners have been taking shrapnel out of the bodies and charting wounds. We're more than halfway done, which sets some kinda record. Laura, here, has been logging them, using map-making software. Laura, show them what you showed me."

Her eyes went wide. "You can run the program. I'll get out of your—"

"No. This is your gig. Show them."

Laura gulped. Even though she dressed as a Goth on the streets and at her high school, being center stage was anathema to her. Tommy stepped away from the monitor, fully aware that the images on the screen presented some kind of pattern. What kind, he didn't know. He hoped the others would figure it out.

Laura started the slide show of body outlines, with blue and red wounds and yellow trajectory lines. She ran it through once, recycling it back to the first image.

"Anyone see it?" she asked. "It's like—"

"It's a spiral."

Every eye turned to Ray Calabrese. He glanced at their faces, then shrugged. "Like one of those seashells. A what-do-you-call-it? A nautilus. The trajectory lines spiral out from the bodies. Clockwise."

Laura swiveled in her folding chair. "Right. That's it."

Susan laid a hand on the girl's shoulder. "This is a wonderful bit of work. If you can give us the data on a flash drive, we'll have analysts at our headquarters blend these images into—"

"Oh, I did that already," Laura said, and double-clicked on the Cinema icon. "I hope that's okay."

The screen went black. Then the outline of the Vermeer appeared. It was an overhead view. Bright white numbers and letters began appearing, filling the interior of the outline.

"This is the plane. There are the seat numbers," Laura said. "I'm superimposing the trajectory lines, but not the wound marks, onto this. Oh, and I rotated it ninety degrees for a bird's-eye view. These are the same yellow lines as before."

She tapped the mouse. A single, curved yellow arc appeared. It began at seat 6-F—the first body to be autopsied—and arced off to the right.

"It's running backward," Laura explained. "It was easier to extrapolate by starting at the wound and tracing the trajectory backward."

The yellow line curved away from the seat. It passed through the outline that represented the starboard wall of the plane. It passed on through the wing, about a third of the way from the body of the jet.

Another yellow line formed, from seat 16-B. It, too, curved to the right, went through seat 9-E, through the fuselage wall, and through the wing, where it intersected the first yellow line.

The third, fourth, and fifth lines bloomed. Each had a right-hand curve. Each intersected the others out on the wing.

Peter Kim said, "Got it."

"I'll be darned," Walter murmured.

Kiki whistled two notes. "Engine number three."

"Right." Peter was tugging at one earlobe, analyzing the data in his head. More yellow lines were making a mishmash of the airplane's outline. Each intersected out at the wing. "That's why my searchers haven't found more of the engine. It's inside the Vermeer."

Tommy thought about the finger- and fist-size holes he'd seen punched through the starboard hull when he'd walked through the corpse of the jetliner. He opened the second box he'd carried in. It was filled with evidence bags. "Some of it is. The rest I pulled out of the bodies."

"Tommy?" John Roby had entered during the show, his NTSB cap sodden with rainwater. "I've talked to the hospitals. The shrapnel from the wounded is en route here, now."

"Then that should be all of it," Peter said. "Once I've reassembled the engine, it'll be confirmed. But here: my people found these."

He walked over to an evidence table and selected the three flat blocker doors from the engine, each twisted with a clockwise curve.

Isaiah Grey took one look at them and his face became pinched. "Partial thrust-reverser deployment?"

Peter nodded. "Engine number three released a few of these blockers, cutting off the flow of air through the turbine. Somehow, the pilots didn't see the signal on their monitor."

Kiki nodded. "Did it have an audio tone?"

"The swap-out doesn't," Isaiah said, his voice soft, sad. "I haven't been on the flight deck of Flight Eight One Eight yet, but they're supposed to be identical."

"So what?" Peter set aside the blockers. "They should have had ample time to see the signal on the monitor. They could have recycled the reversers, or shut power to that engine. Either would have saved their lives."

Tommy sat on the table beside the Mac. "I'm still trying to wrap my brain around pilot error. Captain Danvers just doesn't seem like a screw-up."

"Whatever," Peter said dismissively. He moved to the box of shrapnel and carefully began taking out the evidence bags, one by one. He peered at each piece. They'd been cleaned of all blood and viscera. Walter joined him.

Susan turned to Dennis Silverman. "Have you had an opportunity to analyze the flight data recorder?"

Dennis adjusted his tortoise-shell glasses. "Yes. Um, I could run this on that Mac, if it's okay."

Laura used the apple-Q keystrokes to shut down her programs, then stood and waved to the folding chair, pleased to be away from the center of the circle. She sat on a table, her Doc Martens up on the surface, and hugged her knees to her narrow chest.

Dennis inserted a thumb drive, then waited for the icons to come up on the screen.

"Here we go." He glanced up at the people clustered around him, enjoying the spotlight. "The Gamelan is the most sophisticated FDR on the market, and CascadeAir bought the top of the line. There was some damage to the input monitor itself. But the recorder was in the tail cone, and it escaped unscathed. I got some good data here. Watch."

Rows and rows of raw numbers scrolled down the screen, far too fast to read. "This is just the DOS shell," he said. "We've got a graphic interface. Here."

He tapped the keypad. The numbers blinked into oblivion, replaced by an illustration of a perfectly formed Vermeer 111, seen from a side angle.

He moved the curser to a bar of tools on the left side of the screen and rotated the plane's image. Once again, it was a bird's-eye view.

Pinpoints of green light flickered all across the body and wings of the jet. Many were clustered around the tail section, the wings, all four engines, and the cockpit, but other green lights glistened elsewhere, too.

"Green is good," Dennis said. "All of these servos and circuits are reading green-for-go."

Tommy said, "A few are yellow."

"Yes. A briefly misfired circuit. A joint that's misaligned, even by a few millimeters. Nothing to worry about, but the Gamelan marked every yellow light and would have reported them to the pilots, after the flight. Hey, who flew in that jet?"

He pointed to the swap-out. Isaiah raised his hand.

"Did you download the FDR when you got here?"

"Sure."

"We'll run that one next, show you guys what an uneventful flight looks like. But for now, watch this."

He turned back to the screen. More green lights popped on, disappeared. There were hundreds of them.

Dennis said, "Wait for it."

A light flashed candy-apple red on the right wing, right atop engine number three. It stayed red.

"Note the time," Peter Kim said.

Tommy noticed a clock reading off hours, minutes, seconds, tenths of seconds, and hundredths of seconds, in the upper right-hand corner of the screen. They were moving very quickly, ten times their real speed. The destruction of the Vermeer was on fast-forward.

The red light didn't disappear. It stayed on. Another appeared beside it. The seconds ticked away maddeningly. A third red light.

"Ah, damn," Isaiah muttered.

"If the pilots had corrected, those lights would have blinked off," Dennis explained. When the clock read 20:40.15, the entire engine turned bright red. More red lights spread like a virus into the fuselage.

Kiki Duvall said, "Is that your shrapnel?"

Tommy nodded.

A bouquet of bright red lights, more than a dozen, appeared in the nose of the plane at 20:41.06 exactly. The images froze.

Dennis said, "Impact."

Everyone was quiet for a time. The carpenters continued to work madly at the other end of the building, their hammers and power tools echoing, forklifts beeping in Reverse. Walter and Peter returned to emptying Tommy's box of evidence, but didn't speak. Laura, the youngest person in the room, looked from face to face. Some still watched the motionless screen. Others averted their eyes, studying their shoes or their hands. She looked at Dennis Silverman, and her stomach roiled. For a split second, a gleeful grin flitted across his face, more like a brief seizure than a true smile. The face seemed to glow, if only for the time it took Laura to blink. Then it was gone.

She looked at Tommy Tomzak. He was rubbing his eyes, fatigue playing across his face.

Susan Tanaka cleared her throat. "The pilots had, what? Two and a half minutes?"

"Almost three," Isaiah said. "Their monitor was hot for three minutes."

"Well, it's not here," Peter said, removing the last evidence bag from the box.

Tommy said, "What isn't?"

"Hydraulic isolation valve," the smaller man muttered, mostly talking to himself. "Last piece of the puzzle. Doesn't matter. I've got enough to begin a report. Walter, when can I start getting shrapnel out of the fuselage?"

"The carpenters will have it secured by morning. I'll go in first, test it for steadiness. Your team can sweep for evidence by, say, noon?"

Peter nodded. "I think we're close to done here, Susan. And on the second day, too."

He clapped dust off his hands and approached Tommy. "I was against you as IIC, Tomzak. But we're going to set some kind of record here. I admit: you kept the field immaculate. Congratulations."

Tommy nodded, not enjoying the compliment in the slightest.

## 39

LUCAS BELL CLOCKED OUT and drove to a Taco Bell. He downed a stuffed steak burrito and a Pepsi in the parking lot, hoping nobody he knew would recognize him. Lucas liked to brag about his state-of-the-art kitchen and his culinary skills. He had taken cooking classes in Paris and Avignon. He loved to throw parties with four, five, six courses of international cuisine. How embarrassing, then, if his secret craving for Taco Bell ever got out.

It was going on 9 P.M. but he had field agents all over the town of Covina, looking for the Gibron woman and the Irishmen. They'd been combing the town for more than four hours, with no luck to show for it. He pulled out his notepad and reread what the field team had reported: Daria and one of the Irishmen, Riley, had stayed at a flea-bitten motel off the freeway. The leader of the group, O'Meara, had stayed three blocks away. Breaking up their profile, Lucas assumed. No word yet on the other two—O'Shea and Kelly. But agents had found the body of Riley, behind a Dumpster at his motel. A severe blow to his windpipe had killed him. He had also bled from his ears, but they'd have to wait on the autopsy to figure out what that was all about.

And since then: zip. O'Meara and the Israeli ex-pat ex-spy had vanished.

Lucas was dead tired but he was the ranking investigator in the case, ever since Ray Calabrese had been repositioned in Oregon. He turned his Lexus around and headed right back to the Los Angeles field office.

As he walked in, an investigator with a shaved head and stud earrings said, "Hey, you're back."

"Miss anything?"

"Yeah. Forensics found a scrunched-up paper wrapper for a stick of gum in the abandoned tenement. Inside the wrapper was a phone number."

Lucas started to say, What's the number to? but the shaven agent said, "You know, where you got your ass kicked."

"Yes. Thank you. I vaguely remember the abandoned tenement. What's the telephone number?"

"It's an answering service in Georgia. Atlanta. We think maybe it's how the terrorists communicate with each other. We're getting a court order from a night judge in Atlanta right now. Give us a half hour, we'll have these pricks' communications link."

*Jesus,* Lucas thought. *Go get a burrito and all hell breaks loose.*


## VALENCE AIRFIELD

Isaiah Grey handed the Gamelan monitor from the swap-out jet to Dennis Silverman, who linked it via a USB drive to the Mac.

Ray Calabrese wandered away, not interested in seeing what the data from a normal, successful flight looked like.

The first piece of technology installed for the Go-Team—before the computers, the microscopes, the faxes, the telephones—was a coffeemaker, one of those big aluminum beasts that could double as a torpedo. Ray grabbed a chipped mug touting the 1988 Oregon State Fair. It looked relatively clean. He poured a cup, watching the carpentry crews mount a scaffolding to hold up the wings of the damaged craft.

The wiry pathologist from Texas, Tommy Tomzak, walked over and poured himself a cup. He, too, turned to watch the workers.

Tommy took a swallow and winced. "I gotta cut down."

Ray said, "Yeah."

They watched the crews on the far side of the hangar, listened to the whack of hammers and the whine of saws.

"You heading back to L.A.?" Tommy asked.

"I guess so. I don't know." Ray glanced at his watch, willing his cell phone to ring.

Tommy said, "I'm not happy with a ruling of pilot error. But hell, it could've been worse. It could've been terrorism. So, in a sense, this is good. Right?"

Ray wanted to think so. He wanted to get the hell out of the Northwest and get on the trail of the Irishmen. If those shits hadn't done this, they had done something bad. He knew it. He wanted Daria to check in again.

"Yeah," Ray said. "It's good news. You'll be rid of me in no time."

They watched the work for a while, sipped their coffee.

"You remember that Italian airliner, hit the ground in Kentucky two years ago?"

Ray nodded. "Seven Thirty Seven?"

"Yeah. I led the Go-Team. Kiki and Susan were with me. First time a pathologist ever led one of the teams. Before, it'd always been engineers. We worked the site for eighteen months."

Ray squared his shoulders, thinking, *Okay. This I understand.* "That one wasn't solved."

"Nope." Tommy finished his coffee. "Cause of accident: unknown. I was up at the lectern when Del Wildman told the media, and later when he told the families of the victims."

Ray said, "Shit. Unsolved cases are the worst. You figure: I start this investigation, I see it through. I point a finger and say, *he did it.* But unsolved ones . . ." He shrugged. "For me, it's a bad guy. Guys like you, it's a bad rivet or a substandard part. Or pilot error. But the point is, you start it, you solve it."

"Exactly," Tommy said into his coffee cup, not looking over at Ray. "If I came on a little strong, about handing over the crash—"

"Sure." Ray shrugged it off and Tommy was grateful that he didn't have to go through the full apology.

Ray sipped his coffee, hoisted himself up so he was sitting on the coffee table. Tommy leaned back against it, bent his neck so his chin touched his chest, and rotated his aching neck in both directions.

"I was never a hundred percent about the Irish terrorists," Ray said. "I mean, they are in L.A. That's for certain. The biggest hurdle for me? It's the whole hate thing. That four Protestants hate anyone or anything enough to take out *that.*"

He gestured toward the Frankenstein airliner on the far side of the hangar.

"Guy kills a guy for money. That I get. Guy kills a guy for love of a woman. Sure. One extremist of faith puts a twenty-two to the back of another extremist's head, double tap to the skull. Happens. But to hate Catholicism enough to knock a Vermeer out of the sky? It never added up."

"Given what we just saw . . ." Tommy said, nudging his chin in the direction of the Mac.

"Yeah," Ray said. "Pilot error sucks, but it makes more sense than thinking anyone *hates* anyone or anything enough to do this."

They sipped their coffee, just two guys.

Tommy said, "I dunno. I fuckin' hate the Lakers . . ." and Ray snorted a laugh.


Susan Tanaka looked over at Tommy cracking up Ray Calabrese and shook her head in awe. Who saw that happening?

Behind her, Dennis Silverman said, "Is there a phone around here?"

Susan pointed toward the airfield's office. As the pudgy little engineer walked away, Susan noted the medical examiner's daughter, who was repacking her computer. Susan crossed to her. "It's Laura?"

The girl nodded.

"What do you do?"

"I'm in high school, but I'm taking classes at Portland Community College. Web page design."

Susan slipped a business card across the table to her.

"Give me a call when you get your degree. I might have something a wee bit more challenging than that for you."

The girl blushed. "Thanks!"

Susan smiled, turned away.

"Ms. Tanaka?"

She turned back. The girl shifted her vision from Susan to the retreating back of Dennis Silverman. The quicksilver image she'd seen earlier, of Dennis grinning madly, seemed too fantastic to have been true.

"Nothing," she said.

# 40

THE PHONE RANG THREE times before the computer-generated voice said, "Leave a message." *Beep.*

Feargal Kelly said, "Finally! Fucking thing hasn't worked all night. It's us. We're heading out to the rendezvous site."

They were in the Greyhound station in Indio, California. Standing next to him, Keith O'Shea kept watch, on the lookout for cops or the FBI. He wished the two of them weren't haloed by the glaring overhead light in the parking lot. It was like a damn stage spotlight. The station had wound down for the night, the graveyard crew starting their rotation and the commuter traffic long dried up. The only remaining travelers were O'Shea and Kelly.

Kelly slammed the receiver back into its cradle. "So what's wrong with the message phone, you figure?"

"Dunno, do I. The shite don't work, then all of a sudden fixes itself."

They thought about that for a moment; and thinking was neither man's forte. "D'you fancy the FBI has the machine? That that's why we couldn't use it before?"

A quick look at the weather page of the discarded *Los Angeles Times*, plunked down on a bench not three feet from them, would have solved the mystery. Neither man thought to look at the paper.

O'Shea shrugged. "Donal says rendezvous in the Mojave and use the phone to keep in touch. We do as the man says."

That was good enough for Kelly.

## L'ENFANT PLAZA, WASHINGTON, D.C.

It was well past midnight, EST. The last living souls on the sixth floor of the NTSB headquarters were one janitor and Delevan Wildman, whose in-basket was only now shrinking to match the height of his out-basket. Due to the hour, when the phone rang, he picked it up and said, "Susan?"

"Don't you ever go home?"

Del threw down his pen, removed his half glasses. "Home, home. That word rings a bell. What's up?"

He noted the pause before the answer. "We're looking at pilot error, Del."

The retired pilot grimaced. "What are you talking about, child? You're only forty-eight hours into this thing."

"We're more sure than I ever expected to be. The Vermeer had a Gamelan FDR. Have we worked a crash site with one of those before?"

"No." Del Wildman had facts like that tucked away in his brain for every crash that had been investigated over the last five years. "We've heard reports that the new data recorders are incredible. Are they really that good?"

Susan said, "We just saw a graphic display of the data. I'm talking comprehensive data, Del. It normally takes our techs weeks to gather this much information. We have a rep from Gamelan on the Go-Team, and he downloaded the data onto a Mac. He said he'd have had the stuff for us yesterday, but the recorder interface was damaged. It's amazing technology."

Del whistled two notes.

"When I get back," Susan said, "I'm going to recommend Gamelan FDRs become standard issue on all major carriers."

## VALENCE AIRFIELD

Dennis Silverman looked at the telephone receiver as if it were alive. All day long, he'd gotten an out-of-service chime whenever he tried the Irishmen's Georgia-based answering service. At first, when this call had gone through, Dennis was overjoyed. But before he could even speak, anxiety hit him.

What if the phone had been compromised? Why had it not worked, and now suddenly it was fine?

He set the receiver back in its cradle. He hadn't spoken a word.

Better safe than sorry.


Dennis hurried out into the drizzle and climbed into his Outback. He'd been so excited, so jubilant, over the success of his little charade. He couldn't wait to share his good news with Donal O'Meara. But the answering machine spooked him. What did that mean? He'd seen a story on CNN about a storm on the East Coast. Maybe phone service had been disrupted. Maybe it was nothing more than that.

Still . . .

Dennis sat in the brightly lighted parking lot, wondering if the plan was off.

*If it is, who cares?* he decided. His plan had worked; worked brilliantly, if he did say so himself.

Gamelan Industries had been making a fine profit selling flight data recorders to airlines. But sales had been flat of late. Some people in the company wanted to blame marketing (which, despite the department's name, never seemed to be marketing much of anything). Others said that the FDRs were just plain too expensive when compared to digital recorders that didn't provide immediate infrared access and a graphic user interface. Not to mention the diagnose-and-repair technology. Still others blamed Boeing and Airbus, which had been slower than their smaller competitor, Vermeer, in adopting the Gamelans as standard equipment.

Dennis Silverman knew the real reason for the slowdown. In the six years that jets had been equipped with Gamelan FDRs, none of them had ever crashed. Since they hadn't crashed, the FAA and the NTSB hadn't seen how damn good the devices were.

No crashes; it was just bad luck that had stalled the company, not to mention stalling Dennis Silverman's profit-sharing contract.

It had taken Dennis weeks, working evenings and weekends in his workshop at home, to create the necessary programming. Rather than fix avionics problems, he'd devised an upload program that could cause them. Big or little, it hardly mattered, as long as it was computer driven. And hell, everything in modern airliners was run by computers.

He could do everything from turning off the lights in the bathrooms to shutting down the engines. Best of all, he could do it all from the ground below a passing jetliner. And since the transmitter used a widely dispersed infrared beam, he didn't have to worry about hitting some obscure target.

He'd tested his contraption on five flights landing at Portland International Airport. They'd been little gremlins, each time. Something small enough not to cause a disaster.

And when the FDRs were recalibrated—which Gamelan engineers did as part of their service contract, every five hundred flight hours—Dennis had made sure to get the boxes delivered to his cubicle.

All five Gamelans had registered the inconsequential errors that Dennis had whistled up for them. The tests had been 100 percent successful.

But when it came time to save the company, Dennis began to have second thoughts. Sure, increasing corporate profits was a pretty good motivation. So was increasing his own profits. But Dennis wondered who else might be interested in his ability to crash an airliner. Surely the world was chock-full of people who had an interest in causing such accidents.

He began reading everything he could find about terrorists and terrorism. He scoured the newspaper and the evening news, taped TV programs on the subject. He did Internet searches on the Pentium-fast computer at his office.

It was on the Internet that Dennis first heard about the Red Fist of Ulster. At first, he thought the "red" in their name meant they were socialists. More research revealed the Ulster myth of a warrior-king who, sailing up to Ireland, promised great honor and riches to the man who first set hand on the island's soil. One of his bravest warriors proved his valor by chopping off his own hand and hurling it onto the beach.

The red hand, apparently, had remained a symbol of bravery in Northern Ireland to this day. Dennis doubted that it had ever been a symbol of long-range planning, but that was beside the point.

According to one knowledgeable chat room on the Net, two cells of the Red Fist brigade had run afoul of the Royal Ulster Constabulary and were doing time in British prisons after bombing plans had failed. Their goal had been to disrupt the power-sharing government and to revert Northern Ireland to the bad old days of the twentieth century and The Troubles. The group appeared to be violent enough, and in need of a victory. To Dennis, they seemed perfect.

With his skills as a programmer, it was child's play to tap in to AOL and create a fictional user ID and account for himself, one with no ties to his real life. Surfing under the alias, Dennis drifted deeper and deeper into the online world of the anti-Catholic movement. When he found lurkers—people tapping in to the chat rooms but not chatting—he again hacked their Internet service providers to get their account backgrounds.

He eventually found one lurker who turned up again and again under different tags, each an alias. He traced the lurker's account and determined that the person was a man living in Long Beach, California. Dennis sent him an e-mail—encrypted and traceable to a retirement home in Durham, North Carolina, which he'd picked at random. The e-mail read, "Two swings, two misses. I can assure the Red Fist a hit. If interested, log in on Friday with a brand-new ID. I'll find you."

On Friday, a different name popped up in one of the anti-Catholic chat rooms. Again, Dennis's home-grown programming showed the true account name of every person logged in. The newcomer was his lurker with a new pseudonym.

Over the next week, Dennis explained his proposal to the lurker: pick a jetliner. If it's equipped with one specific bit of technology, Dennis explained, he could bring it down.

Dennis set up a dummy e-mail account with a real estate firm in Minneapolis—again, picked at random—so that he and the lurker could communicate. It turned out that the lurker was a U.S. government official who had secretly been leaking intelligence to the Red Fist. Given the opportunity to play broker between the anonymous Dennis Silverman and the Irishmen, the lurker was only too pleased to oblige. He offered Dennis five hundred thousand dollars to drop an airplane, but (naturally) demanded proof that the technology worked.

Eventually, they'd had to take the risk of meeting in person. The lurker had picked Las Vegas. It hadn't been love at first sight—they were vastly different coconspirators—but they got along well enough to put the whole plan together.

Dennis had agreed. A date had been set. He'd get one hundred thousand for dropping a random jet, and the remaining four hundred grand for dropping a very specific jet.

"Watch the news," was the message he sent to the lurker.

"Give me three months," Dennis's new coconspirator wrote back. "I can get the right people into an airplane, and get some of our like-minded people into the States to make sure nothing goes wrong."

*Like-minded.* That had made Dennis laugh. He wasn't particularly anti-Catholic, and if he'd found an IRA lurker first, that's who he'd have dealt with.

And now, here it was, three months later, and the test jet had crashed, just as advertised. The good guys had raced to the scene and had promptly handed the most vital piece of evidence to Dennis Silverman himself. He'd doctored it up nice and pretty, handed it right back to them, and had been patted on the head.

He couldn't wait to drop the real target.

Dennis and his lurker could have continued using the Internet but, over the last few months, *The New York Times* and *The Washington Post* had run stories about supersecret government agencies that illegally monitored Internet communications, looking for al Qaeda and other Islamist forces. Dennis and his lurker agreed to terminate their chats and, instead, opted for a much older form of communication—one that had stood the test of time for organized crime for many decades: an answering service, paid in cash, in a faraway city.

Only now, that communication link seemed to be on the fritz. *Could be a coincidence,* Dennis thought. But did he dare take that chance?

The timing was critical. The target was a day away and in California. The Red Fist of Ulster would be on scene to make sure the right people failed to survive the flight. All Dennis had to do was get himself to California and take care of business. He'd already been given permission by his bosses to attend a conference in San Diego. After th—

Someone rapped on the window of his Outback. Dennis freaked, his heart trip-hammering.

A man stood out in the rain, an umbrella shadowing his face. He twirled his finger in mid-air, the symbol for "roll down your window."

*What, what, what?* Had the FBI agent found out something? Had the teen chick in the black jeans been fiddling around with his doctored FDR file? Dennis rolled his window down a few inches. The man tilted back his umbrella. It was the pathologist. Tomburg? Tomquist?

"Hey. It's Dennis, right?"

Dennis wet his lips. "Yes?"

"A few of us are going to grab a beer at our hotel in Keizer. Want to come?"

Dennis almost started to giggle with relief. "Ah, sure. Why not?"

"It's the Chemeketa Inn," the pathologist said. "It's right on the highway. I'll see you there." He turned and darted over to his rental.

Dennis rolled up his window, the surge of fear-turned-relief making him shake.

He turned over the engine. *Calm down!* he chastised himself. There was no way the Go-Team could be onto him. Same for the big FBI agent he'd met. He was absolutely sure of that. After all, if the FBI had been on his trail, his friend the Internet lurker would have said something.

## FBI, LOS ANGELES FIELD OFFICE

Lucas Bell called the night shift at the Atlanta field office and asked how soon someone could get to the apartment with the answering machine. It would be secured before midnight, the agent in charge told him. They'd have a forensic unit scour the place for prints, too.

Lucas wasn't too worried about the Atlanta agents finding fingerprints. He knew he hadn't left any when he'd set up the telephone and answering machine for Donal O'Meara and his crew.

# 41

IT WAS HALF PAST eleven by the time Tommy got to the Trail Head Bar and Grille, on the ground floor of the Keizer hotel. He was bone tired; too tired to just go to bed, he knew. A quick drink with some of the crew leaders would loosen the knotted muscles in his shoulders and back.

The group he found was plenty quiet. They'd ordered two pitchers, but none of their glasses had been touched. Kiki and Isaiah were there, along with John Roby and the FBI liaison, Ray Calabrese. Dennis Silverman arrived within seconds of Tommy. As they walked in, Kiki pushed back her chair and walked to the bar.

"Glad you could make it." Isaiah shook Dennis's hand. "That's a cool contraption you guys built."

"I can only stay for a quick sip," Dennis told the group. "I'm flying out tomorrow for a business trip. Hey, can I see one of your comm systems?"

Smiling at Dennis's techno-geek excitement, Tommy handed him his ear jack and belt-clip control box. Dennis immediately pried the back off the control unit and peered into it. Tommy realized the gang had picked a table next to the room's baby grand piano. "Wonder if this thing's got any gas in it," he said, sitting and lifting the keyboard cover. He began noodling, no real song in mind.

Isaiah was about to put a glass of beer in front of Tommy when Kiki returned, handing the pathologist a glass of seltzer with a lime wedge. Tommy smiled up at her.

Susan lifted her drink and said, "To Meghan Danvers. A good person and a good pilot."

Ever since they'd heard her speaking on the cockpit voice recorder, every one of them had become her advocate. They hadn't realized it at the time, but they had. And now they were about to collectively sign a formal report that would end her reputation just as surely as Flight 818 had ended her life.

"To Meghan Danvers," Tommy repeated, stopping playing long enough to toast. They clinked their glasses.

Dennis cleared his throat. "Um, she did screw up the flight. Didn't she?"

"Suppose so." John Roby patted the engineer on the shoulder. "But the whole picture's a different kettle of fish, innit. The good captain lived a fine life. She was a mother and a wife and a pilot with hundreds of hours of perfect flying to her name. She was a good person who made a bad mistake. That shouldn't be forgotten."

"Speaking of her mistake," Kiki cut in. "That was a good presentation, Dennis. That FDR of yours is pretty impressive." Tommy let loose with a little fanfare on the keyboard, echoing Kiki's compliment.

Dennis grinned and gulped beer. "Thanks. We're pretty proud of that puppy."

"It'll revolutionize the industry," Isaiah predicted.

"That's the idea. Believe me, you didn't see half of what that baby can do."

Some of the crashers seemed to be listening. Others stared into their beers. Tomzak noodled at the keyboard. For an Austin resident, his tastes ran to show tunes and lounge standards.

Susan said, "What do you mean?"

Dennis absently put Tommy's communications gear back together. "The Gamelan doesn't just track problems and monitor them, it can fix some."

Everyone glanced around, except Ray Calabrese, who seemed to be studying the head on his beer with rapt attention.

"So why'd the jet crash?" Tommy asked, hammering out a dirgelike "Moon River."

"Oh, it can only fix small, electrical problems, and ones that have been noted and fixed in the past. Like a word-processing system that knows, from past experience, that if you type *t-e-h,* you really meant to type *t-h-e,* so it corrects it whenever it sees it. The Gamelan can do that, too. So long as it's a minor fix."

Isaiah shook his head. "Damn, man, I'm getting too old for this. Planes that repair themselves?"

Tommy said, "Yeah, you're gettin' a little gray up there. . . ."

Isaiah said, "Fuck you, Bobby Darin."

Dennis Silverman—who had never, ever, traded bon mots with another person—looked up quickly to see if there would be a fight. He couldn't figure out why Isaiah tilted back his chair, held his beer closer to Tommy. Tommy lifted his seltzer and clinked glasses with Isaiah. *How do people do that?* Dennis wondered. He had never mastered that level of human connection and had long ago considered that a good thing.

"Well, anyway, it's a remarkable machine," Kiki said. She gingerly clinked her glass against Dennis's. He blushed and took a sip.

Ray—who had not spoken since the group had gathered—took a long gulp of beer, brushed his lips with a napkin, and said, "Could the Gamelan crash a jet?"

Dennis performed a picture-perfect spit-take, à la Danny Thomas, beer particulate floating across the table. Everyone backed up.

"Well, shit, New York," Tommy drawled, switching to "Lullaby of Broadway." "Give the fella a heart attack, why don't you."

An easy laugh circulated around the table. John Roby shook his head and smiled. "You're an investigation in search of a crime, mate. You're bloody near as stubborn as Tommy."

Tommy winced. "Yeah, but I know when to cry uncle. It's pilot error. I wish to hell it weren't, but it is."

Dennis's mind had been racing a thousand miles an hour, trying to come up with an appropriate answer to the agent's devastating question, when it suddenly dawned on him that the conversation had moved right on. Nobody had expected an answer, because nobody seriously thought the question deserved one. Apparently, not even Agent Calabrese.

"You're grasping at straws," Kiki said to Ray, and grasped his forearm, giving it a friendly shake. "We like that around here. To the fraternity of straw-graspers!"

The crashers raised their glasses. After a sip, Kiki added, "Of course, I agree with Agent Calabrese."

"Ray," Ray said.

Kiki nodded. "Something about this doesn't track."

"Don't disagree," John cut in. "But that child whose curfew Tommy helped break showed us what happened. The number-three engine tore itself to bits in midair, didn't it, and peppered the fuselage with shrapnel.

Peter's a complete prat but he's not often wrong. That twisted pieces of metal—what did he call 'em, blocker doors? He and Walter say that's a reverser in the act of, y'know, reversing. And, Dennis? That visual display of the flight data was brilliant. I'm not taking a piss with you, Kiki, it's just . . ." He shrugged.

Kiki sighed. "Yeah. I guess so. But look: the pilot and the copilot didn't see the reverser warning? Sure, I can buy that. So what did the copilot see? What made him say, 'What's that,' and tap on something? I've got to figure that out, or I'm never going to be satisfied."

Ray looked perplexed, so John explained about Kiki's hunt for the tapping sound. "Did the copilot wear a ring?" Ray asked.

"No. I checked that." Kiki finished her drink. "I'm exhausted. I'm going to bed."

With a murmur of agreement, Susan and the men drained their drinks, too. Money was tossed onto the table, more than covering the bill.

As they stood, Tommy lowered the cover over the keyboard, then clapped Dennis on the back. "Hey. I meant what I said, kid. Nice job today. I hope we get to work together again, sometime in the future."

Dennis grinned. "Well, you never know when a jet's going to crash, do you?"

Once again, as they had the night before, Tommy and Kiki ended up on the same elevator to the same floor. Tommy leaned against the wall of the elevator, yawning. Kiki reached over and rubbed his shoulder. His muscles were knotted and twitched.

"Poor baby. You know, you could have delegated the autopsies. You are the Investigator in Charge."

"That's Susan's nutty notion," Tommy said as they stepped out and fumbled for their keys. "I don't know what the hell I'm doing, trying to run this show. Most of the time I feel three-fourths foolish and a quarter flash."

"Well, you did a good job," Kiki said as they reached their doors. She leaned in and pecked him on the cheek. "Good night, Doctor."

"Good night, Lieutenant," Tommy said, throwing her a sloppy salute. He kissed her back.

And kissed her again. This time on the lips. Kiki touched the stubble on his cheek, ran her finger down the length of his jaw.

They parted. Tommy's face was flush, his gray eyes sparkling. After a moment, he looked down and said, "Yeah. Look, I'm sorry. I—"

"Oh, for God's sake," Kiki said. She took his key from him, swiped the lock, and led Tommy by the hand into his hotel room.

## CHEMEKETA INN, KEIZER

Tommy slept like the dead, curled against Kiki's long, narrow back.

He climbed out of bed around six, stretched and groaned, and sighed contentedly. Steam escaped from the half-open bathroom door. Tommy crossed to the telephone and shouted, "Hey! I'm calling room service. How do you take your coffee?" He was slightly embarrassed to have to ask. They'd been together all those months in Kentucky.

He hit the button and the line connected. "Hi. I'm in room five seventeen. Can I get two coffees and—"

He turned, stunned, as Kiki Duvall burst out of the bathroom, stark naked, water pouring off her long, muscled frame and darkening the carpet under her feet.

She stared at him, green eyes wide with shock and understanding. "Milk!" she shouted. "Milk! Tommy, it's milk!"

Tommy stared at the nude madwoman a moment, then spoke into the phone. "Can I get milk with one of those?"


Tommy and Kiki dressed and made it to one of the rentals in ten minutes. Kiki brought a towel and dried her hair in the car. "Shit," she said. "Shit, shit, shit, shit, shit."

"Not your fault," Tommy said, slipping on the glasses he wore to see distances. He reversed out of a parking space and zoomed toward the parking lot exit. "We all missed it."

"I was so busy listening to the sounds on the recorder, I forgot to listen to the words," Kiki said, raking a brush savagely though her hair. The scowl on her face almost cracked the mirror on the passenger-side sun visor. "I mean, we heard Kazmanski ask for a cup of coffee! I should have known he'd have milk with it, plus something to stir it with."

They hit the freeway. Traffic was still light at that hour but the rain had picked up during the night. "Kiki, don't get your hopes up. It still looks like pilot error, even if we find a spoon up there."

## VACAVILLE, CALIFORNIA

It was only six thirty in the morning, Thursday, when Donal O'Meara and Daria Gibron stepped off the bus. "Jay-sus!" O'Meara sneered at the newly appeared sun. "It's got to be eighty bloody degrees out here."

Daria inhaled the dry air, smiled wistfully as the promise of heat filled her lungs.

If she closed her eyes, she could have been back in Tel Aviv.


## VALENCE AIRFIELD

The weather pattern that drove the heat up from Mexico into California was heaving a major-league storm onto the shores of Oregon and Washington. By the time Tommy and Kiki reached the airfield, the rain was slicing down at a sharp angle. They saw it wash in discrete waves across the tarmac.

Tommy pulled into the covered car park. "Look," he said. "Last night was great, but let's not tell everyone. You know . . . ?"

"God, no!" Kiki touched his arm. "Absolutely. Besides, it'll complicate things. And . . . it was one night."

"Right," he said.

"Right."

"Okay."

They climbed out and sprinted for the hangar. Once inside, they stopped, staring at the ruined Vermeer 111. The crushed nose cone, which had been resting nose down on the flatbed truck the night before, now hung three stories in the air. More than ever, it looked to Tommy like a bullet dug out of a wall.

The fuselage rested on its own web of scaffolding, a gap of an inch or two separating it from the crumpled flight deck. Behind that, the empennage and tail cone had been mounted, also in close proximity to the fuselage. Both damaged wings—but only two of four engines—had been mounted during the night and rested in place. One was torn apart in a lab in Gresham and the other had disintegrated.

Tommy squinted, almost shutting his eyes. Through his eyelashes, the jetliner looked almost whole, missing only its landing gear and engines three and four, on the right-hand wing.

Despite the hour, Walter Mulroney was overseeing the work. He turned to see the newcomers, who were heading across the vast interior of the hangar in his direction. Tommy had retrieved a large cardboard box from the trunk of his car and carried it under one arm. "You're up bright and early."

Tommy pointed to the flight deck. "We need to get into that cockpit."

Walter yawned, looking haggard. Tommy realized Walter had burned through the night with the carpentry crew. "No chance. I don't know if it's stable yet. We haven't tested the scaffolding."

"Fine. We'll test it." Tommy set down the cardboard box. Its four flaps had been folded over one another like the petals of a flower. He yanked on one flap and they all opened. He withdrew a sealed plastic bag containing a stark white biohazard suit, which he tossed to Kiki. He ripped open a second bag, unfolded his own suit.

To Walter's amazement, Kiki toed off her deck shoes and shimmied out of her jeans. She wore tiny briefs with a floral pattern. He started to protest but realized that Tommy had stripped down to his BVDs, too.

Walter turned to the Vermeer, studiously not looking at either of them. "Tomzak, I don't know what's gotten into you, but I can't let anyone up there yet."

"File a protest with the Investigator in Charge. Oh, wait. That's me." Tommy stepped into his coveralls, which were connected to clunky boots, and tugged them up. In a less cocky voice, he added, "I'm sorry, man, I don't mean to flip you shit. It's just that we may have figured out what the copilot saw, seconds before everything went to hell."

Kiki laid a hand on Walter's shoulder. "Please? It's important."

He said, "It might not be safe."

"I can take care of myself. And if worse comes to worst, I can take care of Tommy."

Tommy said, "Right, we— Hey!"

Walter wasn't happy but, truth be told, Kiki Duvall was the most athletically inclined member of the Go-Team. Not that that would amount to a hill of beans if the scaffolding buckled under them. But in the end, Walter's decision was based more on his experience with the carpenters than faith in his teammates. "All right. It should be safe as houses. Just go easy."

## VICTORVILLE, CALIFORNIA

By seven in the morning, the temperature was eighty-five and the wind that whistled up out of the Baja Peninsula was as dry as chalk. Donal

O'Meara had never been much farther south than the 45th Parallel in his forty-plus years. He had a bad feeling about the day to come.

He and Daria had checked into a fleabag motel near the freeway. O'Meara immediately cuffed her to the headboard of the bed, then jumped into the shower. He padded out twenty minutes later, a towel wrapped around his washboard midsection, and uncuffed her so that she could shower. "Don't dawdle," he warned. "We've a busy day ahead of us."

Daria emerged a half hour later, slipping the little floral-patterned dress over her head. It fluttered past her white panties and she adjusted how it fell across her hips. They'd picked up the clothes and mismatched luggage at Goodwill. "Where to, now?"

He eyed her hungrily, but there wasn't time. "We find breakfast, then we steal a car. Are you any good at that?"

Daria ran a hand through her short, pitch-black hair, which fell naturally across her brow. "I can jimmy a lock and I can hot-wire an engine."

"Clever girl," he said, lighting his last Silk Cut. He'd have to switch to American cigarettes. "Ten for ten. Let's go."

## HOTEL, WILSONVILLE

Ray Calabrese was on the floor at the foot of his bed, wearing boxers and halfway through one hundred crunches, when his cell phone chirped.

He rose—using only his legs, his hands not touching the carpet—and crossed to the TV stand where he'd left his cell phone. "Calabrese."

"It's Henry Deits. We got a nibble in Atlanta last night."

Ray listened as the assistant director related the story of the telephone number found in a gum wrapper at the Irishmen's bivouac. "We traced it to an answering machine in an apartment in Georgia. Everything paid in cash. We think the Irish were using it to contact each other and whoever's working with them. Also, we got lucky and caught an incoming call last night. The caller hung up before speaking but we got the trace."

Ray said, "From . . . ?"

"You're going to love this: Oregon."

"Holy shit." Ray squeezed the bridge of his nose, feeling a headache coming on. "Boss, I do not get this. We saw evidence last night that the crash was pilot error. We have absolutely nothing here indicating terrorism. But Daria's sure. And it just . . . it *feels* right."

"I know. I still like the Red Fist assholes for it. That phone call? It came from an airfield in a town called, ah, Valence. It's in—"

Ray said, "Are you shitting me, here?"

"What?"

Ray sat on the bed. "Jesus! I was there! Last night! It's where they put the airliner!"

Henry Deits whistled.

"When was the call?"

"Ah, hang on . . . Eight seventeen."

Ray took a beat. Deits said, "Calabrese?"

"Shit."

"What?"

"We were there. Then. The NTSB Go-Team. We were all there."

"Are you telling me . . . Is this crap connected to the investigators?"

"Maybe. Yeah. I . . ." Ray's mind was reeling. "Yes. One of the crashers called a number that our guys also found in the Irishmen's hideout. That can't be a coincidence."

"So . . ."

Ray said, "We need to background these guys. Got a pen?"

"Go."

"Okay: first guy to look into is Tomzak, Dr. Leonard. Pathologist, lives in Austin, Texas." He spelled the name. "Next. . . ."


## VALENCE AIRFIELD

The carpentry team had built a wooden ladder leading up to the Vermeer, but not connecting to the usual forward hatch, at frame 17, where passengers board and leave. That area was badly warped, the door itself lying on the floor of the hangar, tagged as evidence. Thanks to the fuselage damage, it had been Walter's suggestion to make egress from the midwing emergency exit. That's where the ladder led.

Walter said, "Take it slow, you two. I usually have a steeplejack test that scaffolding first."

"Got it," Tommy said.

He and Kiki were covered neck to foot in the safety suits, complete with sealed gloves. They'd clipped their satellite-phone links to the outsides of their suits.

He paused at the foot of the ladder and touched Kiki's elbow. "Listen, this isn't pretty," he warned. "It's a charnel house up there. It's like nothing you've ever seen before. I puked. Doesn't mean you will, but you might. Here." He handed her the bag her suit had been sealed in. "If you have to upchuck, use this."

Kiki stuffed the bag into the web belt of her suit. "You sure know how to show a girl a good time."

She started scaling the ladder. Tommy followed.

At the top, Kiki waited to let Tommy catch up. He was breathing heavily, annoyed to be so out of shape. "Sorry."

"Well, you got a workout last night," she said. Tommy blushed. Her tone was light but her green eyes glowed with more than a little trepidation. "You ready?"

Kiki flicked on her flashlight. Tommy hit his light and led the way in through the emergency door.

The smell was still bad but not as horrible as it had been in the grassy field. During the drive down I-5, the wind had whipped through the fuselage. Still, blood and viscera gleamed on most surfaces, shiny and tacky. Kiki said, "Oh my," and stopped just inside the door.

"You okay?"

She forced herself to keep her eyes open, forced them to follow the circle of light from her flash. She nodded.

"All right. Watch your step."

Tommy started down the aisle. It was much easier this time; in the field, the plane had rested at an odd angle, the floor pitched thirty degrees counterclockwise. Now it was as stable as the swap-out, which they could see through the shattered windows.

He ignored the blood-drenched magazines and little pillows, and the bits of gristle that crunched under his feet. Stepping over larger articles of debris, he eased forward, Kiki at his heels.

Halfway to the front, the scaffolding that held them thirty feet off the floor groaned ominously. They froze. Tommy's ear jack crackled and Walter Mulroney said, "Are you all right up there?"

Tommy jostled his mike into place. "Think so."

They started moving again. Kiki gasped and Tommy turned. Her flashlight rested on a G.I. Joe action figure. The toy rested on the floor beneath one of the seats. A child's fist still clutched it, the wrist bones glistening white.

"The med techs missed that," Tommy said. "Sorry."

Kiki was very close to panicking. Or puking. She forced herself to breathe deeply through her mouth. She made eye contact with Tommy and nodded. They moved forward again.

Ahead of them was a band of light. The fuselage and the nose cone were near each other, but with a two- or three-inch gap all the way around. They stepped over that gingerly, hearing the scaffolding groan again. Tommy looked through the gap and saw Walter, staring up at them, three floors below.

Tommy approached the flight deck with an odd sense of vertigo. The last time he'd been here, it had been nose down, everything facing the wrong direction. He shone his flashlight on the galley refrigerator. There was a jumble of footprints on its surface, at chest height. Kiki said, "How in the world did those get there?"

"They're mine. Ain't that weird?"

He swiveled the light through the galley, stopping at a drawer that was jammed halfway open. "That's what I thought. See?" He reached in and pulled out a red plastic swizzle stick. "If you get coffee with cream from a stewardess, they don't give you a spoon."

"It's 'flight attendant,' not 'stewardess.' And I know what they give passengers. I want to see what the flight crew gets. Did you check Kazmanski's autopsy?"

Tommy had, surprised to find the Multnomah County Medical Examiner in his office before seven. "Kazmanski's stomach turned up positive for coffee with milk. Thoroughly undigested, too. He'd just swallowed it before he died."

Kiki shouldered past him onto the ruined flight deck. The windows had been smashed on impact and the smells of the hangar—including the aroma of fresh-cut wood—blocked out much of the stench here. The pilot's left-hand seat had been torn apart by Tommy's volunteers on Tuesday, to get to Meghan Danvers.

The copilot's seat had been wrenched off its tracks and hung at an odd angle against the flight controls. Viscera glistened on the remains of both chairs. Kiki knelt and played her flashlight slowly across every surface. Tommy stayed standing, his light shining over her head. He kept it steady so that it wouldn't make the shadows dance.

Kiki scoured through splattered blood and wads of paper that had escaped three-ring binders. She used a pencil to shift detritus aside. Two minutes later, she held up a shard of porcelain. "You don't get coffee in nice cups like this, not if you're a passenger."

"So if the flight crew gets better cups . . ." Tommy left the thought dangling.

Kiki resumed her search. It took another three minutes before she said, "Bingo."

A ventilator shaft behind the copilot's seat had been wrenched partway open. She slipped two gloved fingers through the opening and withdrew a stainless steel spoon.

It held a brownish residue. She held it under her nose. "Coffee."

She stood and turned. Tommy was staring past her at the ruined avionics equipment. "What?"

Without answering, Tommy tapped several numbers into the satellite phone control box on his belt. "Peter? It's Tommy. Where are you?"

"Three stories beneath you," the voice came back immediately. "It was stupid to go in there, Tomzak."

"Good seeing you, too, Pete. Listen, Silverman, the guy from Gamelan? He said the pilots had about three minutes of warning that a reverser had kicked in. Right?"

"Yes."

"Do you know which monitor that would have shown up on?"

Peter Kim didn't try to hide the note of annoyance. "Of course."

"So can you pull that monitor out of here and reconstruct what was on it? I mean, is there any way to know which lights were on and which were off, when it was smashed?"

After a pause, Peter said, "Actually, yes. We can tell if a filament was hot or cold when it broke. Why?"

"Do it," Tommy said. "We've proven the fuselage is safe. Get someone up here and get that monitor tested. Okay?"

Peter sighed loudly. "But of course. You're in charge."

## 42

DONAL O'MEARA CLIMBED OUT of the stolen Jeep and mopped his neck with the palm of his hand. They had arrived in Boca Serpiente, California. It was going on 9 A.M. and already sweat prickled his brow, discolored a V shape on the front of his T-shirt. "This is like some fucking alien planet," he groused.

O'Meara had chosen khaki trousers, hiking boots, and a T-shirt from Goodwill. Daria wore cuffed shorts with hiking boots and a light cotton shirt with epaulets and breast pockets. She wore the tails of the shirt tied off just under her small breasts. She looked perfectly comfortable as the thermometer outside a convenience store hit eighty-six.

O'Meara pointed to a store that boasted GAS, GRUB AND AMMO!

"They better have a fucking beer in here, or I'm shooting someone," O'Meara said.

Daria studied him over the top of her glasses and beneath the fringe of her bangs. "Didn't think you could abide American beer."

"It tastes like a rat pissed in the can, but it gets any hotter, and I'm not going to give a damn."

They entered the convenience store. An air conditioner as old as Daria hacked ineffectually behind a lottery-ticket display and dropped condensation onto the counter. It was maybe two degrees cooler than outside. "Can you at least tell me where we're going?" she asked, pulling a plastic bottle of water out of a refrigeration case and holding it against her breastbone.

"You can stop asking," O'Meara said, his voice muffled because he was half leaning into the open case, the inside of the glass misting with every word he spoke. "We're there."

## KEIZER CHAMBER OF COMMERCE

Susan Tanaka faced the crowd of reporters and their entourages of sound and camera crews. The certain knowledge that pilot error had doomed CascadeAir Flight 818 felt like a deadweight in the pit of her stomach. "All right." She swallowed. "First question?"

## HOLIDAY INN, PORTLAND INTERNATIONAL AIRPORT

Only one of the local television stations was airing the press conference live. James Danvers sat on the couch in his hotel room, his son perched on his knee, his sister to his left, and his mother-in-law—Meghan's mom—to his right, listening to every word spoken by Susan Tanaka.

They were all surprised when they heard a knock at the door.

## VALENCE AIRFIELD

Kiki Duvall and Tommy Tomzak climbed down the wooden ladder, the cartoonishly large boots of their suits sticky with body fluids. They stripped to their underwear, then stuffed the protective garments into a laundry hamper marked HAZMAT. Walter noted that Tommy wore a Star of David on a chain around his neck. With his rough language, Walter had assumed he wasn't a man of faith.

Peter Kim was waving to a deliveryman toting a hand truck and three plastic evidence boxes. Pulling up his Dockers, Tommy nodded in that direction. "What's up?"

"Shrapnel taken from the survivors at Portland and Salem hospitals. I'm still looking for the HIV."

Tommy and Kiki exchanged looks, then stared at the blood-soaked suits they had just doffed. "Wanna run that one past me again?" Tommy asked.

Peter rolled his eyes. "Hydraulic isolation valve. Relax, you weren't wading through any blood-borne pathogens. Well, you probably were, but none I know of."

Kiki knelt to tie her shoes. "Thanks tons."

"Hmm. Find anything?"

She produced the spoon, tucked into an evidence bag.

"The significance of which . . . ?"

She shrugged. "Loose ends. I hate 'em."

Walter Mulroney approached with two of his structures crew, both wearing Tyvek. He began instructing them about which avionics controls to remove first, including the panel that should have warned the pilots of the reverser deployment.

Tommy turned to Peter. "Why are you still looking for that valve thing." He pronounced it *thang*. "I thought the reverser problem was the culprit."

The engineer sighed irritably. "Loose ends," he said, moving toward the evidence tables. "I hate them."

## KEIZER CHAMBER OF COMMERCE

The questions began with the lawsuits that Bud Wheeler—owner of the farmhouse where the starboard wing had been found—had filed against the NTSB, CascadeAir, Vermeer Aircraft, the pilots' estates, the Air Line Pilots Association, Patterson-Pate Industries, Portland International Airport, and, most specifically, Peter Kim.

Susan wasn't happy to be discussing a case that, she felt, had been the product of Peter's arrogance. Mercifully, it delayed discussion of the obvious pilot error.

## VALENCE AIRFIELD

Ray Calabrese arrived from his hotel in Wilsonville exactly as three cars from the FBI's Portland field office pulled into the muddy parking lot. Everyone climbed out and sprinted through the torrential rain for the safety of the hangar.

Ray spotted Tommy and Kiki dashing from the wrecked plane to its unwrecked clone. He wondered what was up.

The agents gathered around Ray. "Talk to security first," he said. "Get the names of everyone who was here last night. You: dust the pay phone out front and any other phones you can find. You: get me a judge who'll cut a warrant. I want to be able to search every room in their hotel by noon."

His agents scattered.


Kiki strapped herself into the copilot's seat of the Vermeer swap-out and pointed to the left-hand seat. "Park it."

Tommy parked it.

Kiki eyed the monitors and banks of equipment before them, deciding which surface of the spoon to tap with. She chose the edge of the ladle. She reached out, tapped the panel nearest her seat. She frowned, shook her head.

She tapped the next one. Her grin brightened the flight deck, her eyes popping wide.

"Tommy," she whispered. "This is it. This is what Kazmanski saw just before everything went haywire. This is the monitor he tapped."

Tommy leaned over to his right, squinted at the panel. He said, "Sumbitch."

Russ Kazmanski had seen something odd on the monitor of the Gamelan flight data recorder.


They couldn't have planned it better if they'd hired a choreographer. Ray marched into the hangar as Tommy Tomzak and Kiki Duvall emerged from the undamaged jetliner and jogged down the portable stairs. Peter Kim, his head down and a plastic bag in his hand, crossed from the other side of the hangar. All four converged in the middle.

"Tomzak." Ray nodded. "Something strange has come up. It's looking like this whole thing is linked to the Irish terrorists, after all."

Tommy said, "We found something weird, too. Hey, Peter. What do you got?"

Peter Kim cleared his throat. He was clearly annoyed about something. Ray had met the slight, intense man only a couple of times, but he always seemed annoyed; just more so now than usual.

Peter held up a plastic evidence bag marked LEGACY GOOD SAMARITAN

HOSPITAL. "I found the hydraulic isolation valve from engine number three. Seems it was lodged in the thigh of a survivor."

Kiki said, "What's wrong with it?"

Peter's face grew darker. He held up the bag for the others to see. "Nothing. It looks pristine."

Ray glanced at his watch. "Can this wait? I—"

"If the thrust reversers kicked in by accident," Peter cut him off, "this device should show scoring, here and here."

He pointed to the device.

Tommy said, "Looks okay to me."

"Yes. Which indicates the deployment was not an accident. It was an ordered deployment."

Kiki squinted at the device in the bag. "That's crazy! You've gone from assuming the pilots were criminally negligent to just plain criminals. I don't buy that they'd purposely crash—"

"Of course not." Peter's imperious tone increased a notch. "I've already accounted for the other valves from engine number three, and they look perfectly normal, too. And that's not logical. If you deploy the reverser and only one or two blocker panels descend, the other valves—the ones governing the parts that fail to descend—should show scoring. If it's an accidental deployment, then the valves governing the blockers that do descend show scoring. For all of the valves to look fine after a partial deployment makes no sense. It means some of the blockers were ordered shut and others ordered to stay open. Engines aren't made to do that. You couldn't sit on the flight deck and orchestrate something like that if your life depended on it. Which, of course, in this case, it did."

Ray said, "Sabotage?"

Peter shrugged his narrow shoulders, rippling the otherwise perfect lines of his designer suit.

Kiki said, "Could the flight data recorder do this?"

"No," Peter said. "It records problems, that's all."

But Ray was shaking his head. "Silverman said his company's recorders are programmed to fix minor faults, if they've recorded them before. The Gamelans can learn. And they're proactive."

"Active," Peter corrected absently, his mind racing. "The opposite of reactive is active."

Without any warning, Tommy said, "Shit!" and reached into his shirt pocket for his ear jack.

## HOLIDAY INN, PORTLAND INTERNATIONAL AIRPORT

The Danvers family sat hip to hip to hip, red-eyed, glued to Susan Tanaka's press conference. Isaiah Grey sat on the bed, watching. He knew what was coming, and he wanted—no, needed—to be here for their questions. And their recriminations.

Neither Tommy nor Susan had sent him. It wasn't his job to be the Danvers' counselor, but he didn't want the family to be alone when the words *pilot error* were spoken. As the only pilot on the primary Go-Team, he felt a link to Meghan Danvers. He felt he owed it to her and her family to be here for this.

"Anything further on a cause for the crash?" an off-screen reporter asked.

Isaiah watched as Susan Tanaka adjusted her microphones. "Ah, yes. Our Go-Team has made a preliminary finding. I repeat, this is preliminary. There's much investigating to do yet. According to our work so far—"

Susan paused, frowned, reached into the pocket of her raisin-colored blazer, and withdrew something. "Ah. Can you hold on a moment, please?" she asked the journalists.

Isaiah recognized her ear jack, identical to the one in his pocket. Susan placed her legal pad in front of the bouquet of microphones and half turned, speaking into the voice wand.

James Danvers leaned around his mother-in-law and made eye contact with Isaiah. The baby on Danvers' leg chirped gleefully. "What's going on?"

"I don't—" Isaiah's comm unit pinged, too. "Hang on." He slipped his on.

The Danvers family watched him (live) and Susan (on TV) doing the exact same thing.

"What's up?" Isaiah whispered into the voice wand.

"Isaiah? It's Kiki. Are you with the Danverses?"

"Yes." On the TV screen, Susan Tanaka's eyes grew wide.

"Tommy's talking to Susan right now," Kiki said. "I hope we stopped you in time."

"Stopped?"

On the screen, Susan pushed back her shoulders, stood a little bit taller, and returned to the press microphones. "Ladies and gentlemen . . ." she started.

In his ear, Isaiah heard Kiki say, "It was sabotage, Isaiah. Not pilot error. Don't tell them Captain Danvers did this!"

"That was my Investigator in Charge," Susan told the media.

It was bizarre, hearing this news from Kiki Duvall (at the Valence hangar) in one ear and from Susan Tanaka (in Keizer) in the other. "I'm sorry, but he says our preliminary findings as to cause have been disproved. So we do not have a standing theory on cause. I'm sorry."

She didn't sound the least bit sorry. Isaiah wasn't, either. He let out a whoosh of air, rested his elbows on his knees.

"Thanks, Kiki. I'll get back to you," he said and signed off.

"What?" James Danvers could hardly stand it any longer.

"Like the lady said." Isaiah nodded to Susan's image on the TV. "We don't know the cause of the crash. Not for certain. But the Go-Team seems convinced it was not pilot error."

He pronounced the last three words with exquisite care. The family began hugging one another, crying. Those three words sounded so much better than the words Isaiah had come here to tell them.

## BOCA SERPIENTE, CALIFORNIA

By ten o'clock it was ninety-two degrees and the wind whipsawed around the creaky little Land's End Motel about three miles outside of Boca Serpiente, population fifty-six. The aluminum siding on the motel, once white, had been reduced to the color of bad mayonnaise by the relentless sun and buffeting dust. The rooms were laid out in a C pattern, with a gravel courtyard and parking spaces in the middle, a single cactus, limp and bedraggled, propped up in the exact center of the parking area. A sign facing Route 45 read LAN S EN MOTE.

The only vehicles in the lot were a Vanagan from Wyoming and two Harleys. Daria Gibron drove up in the stolen Jeep and paused on the roadway, studying the fleabag motel.

Donal O'Meara, sitting in the ripped leather passenger seat, was starting to look a little more acclimated, even though his T-shirt had developed a dark V of sweat across his chest. Daria, born and raised in the Middle East, looked as cool as a lady eating cucumber sandwiches at a cricket match. She had rarely felt truly hot since coming to the States. She almost wept with pleasure with each deep breath, the air raking through her lungs, the taste of dust on her tongue.

They studied the motel for a moment, then turned in, parking the Jeep behind the van and out of sight of the road. O'Meara handed her the dwindling wad of cash and told her to check in. While she did, he circled the building and found a cracked green garden hose with no nozzle. By the time Daria returned, O'Meara's head and torso were drenched in the lukewarm water, his hair, worn short, matted to his skull.

"We're here," he told her.

"Really?" She glanced around at the two-lane blacktop, the crappy clutter of buildings a half mile away, at the sun-peeled paint of the motel. "Where's here?"

"Fucking slice of hell," O'Meara muttered. "C'mon. We've business partners to meet."

# 43

AT THE VALENCE AIRFIELD, Tommy's phone pinged. "Tomzak."

Susan Tanaka said, "Want to tell me what this is all about?" He heard her slam a car door and rev an engine. She was leaving the press conference.

"We know three things this morning that we didn't know last night," Tommy said, waving across the hangar to Walter Mulroney, who was consulting with the carpenters.

"One," Tommy said. "Peter found some kind of framistat that, he says, points to sabotage."

Susan said, "Hoo boy." Tommy could make out frantic honking in the background but didn't ask.

"Two: Ray found something really spooky."

"When did he go from 'that damn FBI mole' to 'Ray'?" Susan asked.

"Ha-ha. Listen, someone tried to call that terrorist cell Ray's been telling us about. He thinks the call came from somewhere in this hangar, just after last night's debriefing."

They were quiet for a time. Walter crossed the hangar to Tommy and said, "Tomzak?"

Tommy covered his voice wand. "Ask Peter to explain it. I'll be right there."

Walter shrugged and walked over to Peter Kim, who'd parked himself at one of the computer stations that lined one wall of the hangar.

Tommy covered his other ear with his palm. The hangar was thrumming with crews and activity. Susan's voice came back over the line, flat, devoid of her usual wry humor. "There were many people in the hangar last night. The airfield crew, the carpenters for the scaffolding. Most of the people in that hangar are not on my Go-Team."

"I said the same thing, Suze. It could be coincidence. But you know how I feel about coincidence, and I know how you feel about coincidence, so . . ."

"Yes," she said darkly. "What else?"

"Kiki isolated that tapping sound on the cockpit voice recorder. The copilot had a spoon with his coffee. He tapped the onboard monitor for the Gamelan flight data recorder."

"Wait a minute. That doesn't make any sense. Last night we were told the Gamelan monitor was showing them a crisis for three minutes and they never noticed it. But Kiki thinks the copilot saw something interesting on that very monitor a second before the crisis started?"

"Go figure," Tommy agreed. "Makes no kinda sense to me, but I'm just a canoe maker. Kiki and Peter have an idea."

"All right, Tommy. I'll be there in ten."


Walter Mulroney said, "That's impossible. I mean, I think it's impossible. Isn't it?"

He looked at Peter Kim, who shrugged.

Walter turned to one of his structures crew. "Ben! Can you get your hands on the ops manual for a Gamelan-type FDR?"

One of his crew jogged over. "Maybe. Why?"

Walter explained.


## BOCA SERPIENTE, CALIFORNIA

O'Meara rapped on the door. A man opened the door a crack and peered out. He had a thick brown beard, sun-baked skin, and a barrel chest barely restrained in a sleeveless T-shirt. His belt buckle was a duplicate of the Harley logo. Daria guessed he was six-six. "What?"

O'Meara said, "Me mates want to do some bear hunting."

With an affirmative grunt, the bearded giant let them in. It wasn't until the door was fully open that Daria saw the butt of an old Smith & Wesson .45 jammed into the man's belt.

The room was a rat trap, with a double bed, a small TV, one hard-backed chair and a tinny air conditioner straining madly. An open door led to a bathroom that hadn't met any state inspection codes, maybe ever. Sitting on the bed was a rail-thin man in torn jeans and boots, his sunken chest bare. He held a bottle of Jack Daniel's by the neck with one hand, a remote control in the other. On the TV, a couple screwed to a dull, throbbing jazz beat.

Without a word of greeting, the big, bearded man crossed to the bed and got down on one knee. He pulled a dilapidated golf bag out from underneath and plopped it down next to his associate, who never took his eyes off the porno film.

The big man upturned the golf bag. Several long guns slid out.

"Your friend paid us up front," the giant said. He grabbed the bottle from his cohort and took a swig, wiped a dirty hand over the top, and held the bottle out to O'Meara.

"Ta," he said, but waved it aside. He began sorting through the rifles.

Daria said, "Mind if I use your bathroom?" The giant just leered at her. Even crossing in front of the TV screen didn't cause the smaller man to notice her.

She closed the door behind her, then quickly riffled through the crackled, plastic toiletry kit she'd spied from the other room. She found a disposable razor. She unscrewed the lid, popping the razor out into her hand. It was double-sided, which made it close to useless, but better than anything else she had to go with. She flushed the toilet and turned on the sink tap, watching brown water gurgle out. She lodged the razor into her boot, sinking it into the leather and away from her skin.

As she returned to the living room, O'Meara was stuffing the long guns back into the golf bag and hefting it over his shoulder. Daria caught only a brief glimpse, but to her trained eye, the weapons appeared to be in good shape.

The giant's eyes raked Daria from head to foot and back up again. "You and the lady wanna stay and party?"

O'Meara made no effort to keep the disrespect out of his voice. "Another time." He hoisted the heavy bag and headed for the door.

"How about you?" the giant asked Daria. The couple on the TV kept fucking to the bad music.

Daria took the Jack Daniel's bottle from his meaty hand and took a gulp. The booze was nauseatingly sweet, closer to cough syrup than the vodka she normally ordered.

"Another time," she said and handed the bottle back, then followed O'Meara out the door.

In their room—equally as squalid as the bikers'—O'Meara helped himself to a cool shower. This time, he didn't bother to chain Daria up. She took the opportunity to examine the weaponry. They were in possession of three Benelli M1 Super 90 shotguns. She hefted one, admired its matte finish. The Benelli was the shotgun of choice in the Mossad, because it could fire eight shells in two seconds. The other item in the case was a Heckler & Koch PSG1, one of the finest sniper rifles money can buy, with a twenty-four-power night scope and a twenty-round magazine.

These were professional weapons, designed for a specific mission. Unlike the handguns Daria had sold "Jack" in Los Angeles.

Whatever was happening would happen soon.

## BEAVERTON, OREGON

Dennis Silverman had been excused from all other responsibilities at Gamelan Industries. One of the co-owners of the company, Alexi Jacobian, had come down from The Tower to tell him in person, and to slap his shoulder and tell him how proud they all were of him.

"Really? Hey, you know that micro-electronics convention in California? I'm having trouble getting a flight out and—"

"Take the Gulfstream," the co-owner had said.

*You're proud now,* Dennis thought, tapping the Romulan Warbird over his desk and making it spin. *Wait until the NTSB report is published and our stock climbs through the ionosphere. They'll fucking give me the Gulfstream.*

## VALENCE AIRFIELD

Walter Mulroney of the structures crew and Peter Kim of the power-plant crew began poring over the operations manual of the Gamelan brand flight data recorder. They called over a half dozen of their top crew members. Ricky Sanchez, day-shift foreman of the airfield, scrounged up a seven-foot-high chalkboard on wheels. Several of the technicians stationed themselves at computers on folding tables and logged on to the Internet, accessing Gamelan's Web page. Others logged on to sites dedicated to NASA's Aviation Performance Measuring System and the federal Center for Flight Operational Quality Assurance, or FOQA. One woman logged on to the Dryden Flight Research Center's big mainframes and Ames Research Center, both operated by NASA. She bounced back and forth between sites and downloaded specs for a 6-DOF flight simulator—standing for six degrees of freedom, the simulator could move a virtual airliner in every imaginable direction: up and down, backward and forward, left and right, testing maximum threshold values and exceedence data.

They began around twelve thirty in the afternoon. It wasn't until close to two that they began to see that it was just barely conceivable that the Gamelan's technology could be used to manipulate an airliner.

## GAMELAN INDUSTRIES, BEAVERTON

Dennis Silverman's IBM T43 went *ding*.

It wasn't supposed to ding.

Dennis blinked at it, wondering, *What the hell?*

"Hey, Dennis," his cubicle mate called out. "I heard you were catching a flight today."

Not bothering to answer, Dennis switched programs. He'd commanded his computer to monitor the Gamelan FDR on board the NTSB's swap-out. Just to keep an eye on those idiots. Now he squinted at the screen, wondering why his spy program had been activated. A three-foot-tall Catbert, Evil H.R. Director, hung by suction cups on his cubical wall, grinning at him.

Dennis jacked in to the Net, the computer opening up on the Gamelan home page. There, he typed in his superuser access codes and began clicking through the active files.

Around the world, eighteen users were accessing Gamelan information that afternoon, either downloading data about the products or uploading the codes for some flights. It took him no time to find the Go-Team's data stream and tap in to it.

In essence, Dennis slaved his terminal to a keyboard being used in the Valence hangar. He could sit back, sip his Red Bull, and observe their every action.

He was so busy doing that, he didn't see the office manager from human resources mounting a plaque by the elevator, announcing that Dennis Silverman had been named employee of the month.


## OVER NEW YORK

The pilot of the Albion Air Flight 326 toggled his microphone. "Ah, JFK tower, we are feet dry."

The tower said, "Roger that," and provided a vector.

The Irish delegates were over North America.


The leader of the Catholic delegation whispered, "This all seems hurried."

Representative Dan Riordan of California sighed. He stood near one of the toilet hubs on the Airbus, along with the Catholic leader and the Protestant leader. Their delegations remained seated.

The delegates had very little in common. Some were ex-cons, some were lawyers. Retired members of parliament and retired snipers. Laborers and academics. They shared only their passion for Ireland and their fervent hope that The Troubles were firmly rooted in history and would have nothing to do with the twenty-first century.

"Yes," Riordan said. "You have raised that point. Repeatedly."

"He's not wrong," growled the Protestant leader.

The three of them stopped talking as a bathroom stall clamored open and a passenger edged out between them. Another passenger entered, activated the Occupied sign.

"I know," Riordan whispered, thinking, *Will this nightmare never end?* "Yes. It's rushed because the latest round of talks has been stalled for months. It's rushed because—and you know this, you know this—there are elements in both of your parties who are happy with the power-sharing agreement stuck in neutral. They fund-raise on the talks being stalled. They write sermons for the pulpit on the talks being stalled. We have to unstall these talks and we have to do something big and dramatic. You know this."

The Catholic and Protestant leaders eyed each other, nodded. They'd heard this speech by Riordan over and over for the last week. He had pleaded, cajoled, lectured. The six Catholics and the six Protestants had eventually agreed to go with the U.S. congressman to his home state of California, partly because they were frustrated at the slowdown of the talks, and partly to get him to shut up.

"It's just," the Protestant leader held up a beseeching hand, "we don't want to get out five kilometers ahead of leadership. Something big and dramatic, aye. Of course. But leadership will have to—"

"And they will," Riordan said, nodding, adjusting his silk tie. His face was blotchy and red. "They will, thanks to you. They'll have to. Trust me. You'll meet with the governor. The media will be all over this story. We'll shake loose the peace talks. Trust me!"

Ten minutes later, with the Irish once again placated, Representative Dan Riordan ordered his fourth scotch and slumped angrily in his seat. His *economy-class* seat, for Christ's sake!

He gulped the new drink in one swig. It was a nightmare. How had he ended up on this goddamn flight with these fidgety Irishmen? It was madness.

Riordan's thoughts grew sullen as he thought back to the confidential, sealed, intergovernmental pouch that had been delivered to him *on the House floor!* He had opened the pouch, half listening to testimony, and let the pictures pour out onto his desk, only to scoop them up in seconds, jam them back into the envelope.

Pictures of Dan Riordan and the guys. Fooling around. Naked.

He always thought of them as *the guys* and sex as *fooling around*. Not *boys*. Not *young boys*. What was age, anyway? An illusion. Maturity isn't dictated by the days we've spent on the planet. Riordan knew this. America's preoccupation with the bedroom was sick, irresponsible. Yes, sure, he'd campaigned on a ban on same-sex marriage and he'd opposed any mention of sexual preference in housing and employment bills. In his district, it's what you did to get elected. Only a moron would have expected him to vote differently. Still . . .

The sender of the photos had waited six days to contact Riordan. Six agonizing days. Riordan had called in sick, missed important votes, told the press and his staff that he had a flu. On the sixth day, he received a call at his residence.

"Did you like the photos?"

Riordan—drunk, unshaved, unwashed, going mad from the anxiety—had screamed into the phone. Had shouted threats and invectives. The caller had waited. In the end, as Riordan ran out of breath, the caller said. "It all goes away. It goes away easily."

Riordan had knelt on the Persian carpet in his Georgetown town house, an empty bottle of rye held loosely in his left fist, and whispered, "How?"

"You will bring a delegation of lawmakers from Northern Ireland to California on the date of my choosing, and on the aircraft of my choosing."

"Why?"

"You don't care. The date of my choosing and the aircraft of my choosing. No media. No one gets a word about this in advance. Use your clout on the House Foreign Affairs Committee. And understand: it's not just photos. There are videotapes. With audio."

Riordan had debated silently for almost two minutes before whispering, "Okay."

That had been five months ago. And now here he was. On the right plane. With the delegates. Riordan doubted that Irish Americans made up 3 percent of his district. Yet, here he was.

He ordered another drink.

## LOS ANGELES

Lucas Bell confirmed that his favorite pedophile, Riordan, was about to put the Irish delegates on the right aircraft.

He'd done his part. It was up to Silverman and the Red Fist now.

## VALENCE AIRFIELD

Peter Kim had taken over the Internet-linked keyboard. Walter Mulroney had been joined at the chalkboard by Isaiah Grey, the only pilot in the hangar with experience in commercial carriers. The chalkboard had been covered by notations and rough-drawn schematics, then erased, covered again, erased again. More than thirty download printouts from the Net cluttered the evidence tables where Peter sat.

Walter had called Dennis Silverman to get his help but got his "I'm out of town until . . ." recording. He was surprised Susan had okayed a trip out of town but guessed that, with last night's presentation of the Gamelan data, Dennis's job was mostly over.

Susan Tanaka was at the human-size door of the hangar, signing a receipt. She motioned toward the Go-Team and three men carried in twelve boxes of pizza and cartons of soda. When the food had been distributed throughout the hangar, Susan returned to the crew leaders working on the Gamelan project.

"This still seems far-fetched," she said, picking olives off a slice of pie.

Tommy Tomzak and Kiki Duvall sat hip to hip on the motorized stairway leading to the swap-out. The pizza smelled great but, after wading through the abattoir of Flight 818, neither of them had much appetite.

Isaiah rubbed the back of his neck. He looked tired, Susan thought. Nothing's more draining than spending time with the bereaved, but Isaiah had volunteered to be with the Danvers family. Russ Kazmanski, the co-pilot on the doomed flight, had no family.

Isaiah studied the chalkboard. "I'm just a jet driver, guys. I can race that Vermeer around the globe and land it on a pool table with room to spare. But all this math is beyond me."

"The amazing thing," Peter said, not looking up from his terminal, "is that Kiki was right. It is possible the Gamelan could have ordered a partial reverser deployment. God knows I've never heard of such a thing, but it's possible."

"Walter?" Another engineer hurried over. The man wore a lab coat, white cotton gloves, and thick, enlarging goggles hanging around his neck. He carried a manila folder and a plastic bin the size of a cigarette pack. Inside were tiny lightbulbs, much smaller than peas. All were broken.

He showed them to the crew leaders. "This is from the monitor bank for the starboard power-plant complex."

He set down the bin, opened the manila folder, and took out slick black-and-white blowups of the bulbs. "You see how the filament is fractured? Here, and here? When these lightbulbs burst, there was no electricity going through them. They were cold inside."

It took a moment for that to be absorbed by the nonengineers. Tommy said, "So, no electricity means no light. No light means no warning from the monitor. And—"

"And no warning means no pilot error," Kiki finished, then high-fived Tommy.

Peter turned from his keyboards. "Grey. Can you fly in this weather?"

"Yes." No equivocation, no doubt.

Peter turned to Susan. "I think we can test this hypothesis in the swap-out. I've done the math. I think I can send a pulse through the infrared input as the plane passes overhead. Something innocuous: turn on the DVD player for the in-flight film."

Susan pursed her lips. "It's all right with me. What's our IIC say?"

All eyes turned to Tommy Tomzak. "Any danger of something going wrong? Accidentally touching off some sort of crisis with this experiment?"

Peter and Walter Mulroney exchanged glances. "No," Walter said. "Either nothing will happen, or it'll do just what we tell it to. But I'm betting good money that nothing will happen. This is feasible, but it stretches believability."

Tommy turned to Isaiah, "You good to go?"

"Let me file a flight plan and find a copilot. Shouldn't take long. Taking off and landing on the same runway—while no other traffic is using it—cuts down on the paperwork."

"I have one on my crew." Walter turned and walk-jogged over to the scaffolding on the far side of the hangar.

Peter stood. "Let me move the recorder out of the empennage and up closer to the cockpit. I can hardwire it directly into the monitor. It'll save time removing it so we can download the data."

Tommy glanced around, sensing a new energy from the crashers, a shared sense of excitement. The idea that a flight data recorder could crash a jet was just this side of science fiction, but all of a sudden, it seemed possible. If they were right, the Go-Team was about to make history.

Tommy grinned. "You know what my daddy would say, times like this?"

Susan Tanaka said, "What?"

"Oy vey."

## GAMELAN INDUSTRIES, BEAVERTON

Dennis Silverman was sweating bullets. He'd watched, sickened, horrified, as his terminal echoed Peter Kim's.

It was unbelievable. Unthinkable. Somehow, those dumb shits on the Go-Team had figured out what every other engineer at the Gamelan company had failed to even guess at.

Dennis had bragged to the investigators about the wondrous qualities of the Gamelan flight data recorder: its ability to check about two thousand aspects of a flight; its ability to fix some small, repeated problems; its ability to be downloaded via a remote infrared beam.

But there was another trick of the Gamelan he'd never mentioned to them. Each machine had a chip in it that let the company headquarters know when one of their FDRs was airborne. At any given minute of every day, the company knew how many Gamelans were in the air, and how many air miles each logged.

As a precaution, Dennis had tapped in to that monitoring system. The second Isaiah Grey began the preflight check of the Vermeer swap-out in Valence, Dennis's monitor pinged.

Dennis, alone in the privacy of his cubicle, said, "Oh, shit, man. . . ." The room had begun to reek with his fearful sweat. The fuckers were going to test the hidden capabilities of his Gamelan. They were going to find their smoking gun.

Dennis shut down his computer and dashed from the room, down the stairs three at a time, through the lobby, and out into the pounding storm. He fumbled for his keys, dropped them in a puddle. His glasses were smeared with rain by the time he finally popped the trunk of his Outback. He rummaged around inside, found his laptop and infrared transceiver.

## BOCA SERPIENTE, CALIFORNIA

By 2:15 P.M., Feargal Kelly and Keith O'Shea pulled off Route 247, shaking off the dust of the Mojave Desert and arriving at the crappy little motel. The temperature hit 105 as they arrived. Overhead, the sky was a too-bright blue, no clouds from horizon to horizon. Two thin condensation trails from commercial jetliners trisected the sky.

Despite the heat, O'Shea looked good. With dark, curly hair and darker skin than that of his associates, Daria assumed he was the so-called Black Irish, descendants of some shipwrecked Spanish fleet.

The men hugged, slapped one another on the back. "The missus is still with you," Kelly said, winking at Daria. O'Shea, more hostile, just glared at her. "And where's himself, then?"

O'Meara said, "Johnser's dead."

The others froze. Just for a second, Daria forgot to be surprised, but O'Meara was looking away from where she sat, perched on the room's one table, next to the TV.

"Ah, the fuck." O'Shea fell heavily into the hard-backed chair. "How?"

"Got himself into a sports bar. Came out with no wallet and a broken neck, near as I can tell."

Kelly, who'd known the big Belfast man for years said, "Tha' prick. Endangering the mission for a fucking bet?"

"It's past," O'Meara said with a horizontal swipe of his hand, as if slicing through something. "We've got a job to think about. I've met our suppliers. Take a look."

He pulled back the thread-thin bedspread, revealing the collection of shotguns and one professional sniper rifle, the Heckler & Koch PSG1. O'Shea went immediately for the PSG, cradling it.

"What about me?" Daria asked, just to see what would happen.

"Aye, and what about herself?" Kelly eyed O'Meara warily. "Why's she still along with you? I'd've thought ye'd shag the bitch and kill her and have done with it." He turned languidly to Daria. "No offense."

She nodded. "No no. It's actually a good question."

O'Meara pointed at Daria's nose and said, "Less of you." He turned to his men. "She shows more brains getting out of L.A. than Johnser did, and you know Johnser was me mate for life. Now shut it. We'll wait for the call."

*Wait?* Daria thought. So this was the final destination. She stirred. "I'm hungry. P'rhaps we should see what's in that little town we passed through?"

O'Meara sat and hit the TV's remote control. "We wait."


## JFK

Airport officials helped Representative Riordan and the Irish delegates make it to the gate for the next leg of their flight to Los Angeles. Nobody had told anyone at the airport why these officials were important. They just did as they were told.

The delegates may have had little in common but they did share this one thing: none of them had flown before on the gargantuan beast known as the Airbus A380. The wide-body double-decker so vast that there are four aisles on both the upper and lower decks.

The delegates gathered at the windows of the international terminal at JFK and marveled at the size of the new jetliner, which had come off the line six weeks earlier at Jean-Luc Lagardère, Airbus's facility near Toulouse.

# FBI, LOS ANGELES FIELD OFFICE

Assistant Director Henry Deits got the call from a team of Ireland watchers in New York. Catholic and Protestant leaders had left Dublin on an Albion Airlines flight, although no one seemed to know why. No further talks in the power-sharing agreement had been scheduled, as far as almost everyone knew. Even the State Department was in the cold. Deits was told that the delegates had all arrived at JFK and were en route to Los Angeles via Albion Air.

He issued an interagency alert. Soon, every law enforcement and intelligence organization in the West would know that a prime, grade-A threat magnet was airborne, heading to California.

## 44

DENNIS SILVERMAN BROKE EVERY traffic law known to man, heading out of the metropolitan area, southbound on Interstate 5. He couldn't let the swap-out take off before he caught his own flight south. Praying that he wouldn't hit a speed trap, Dennis screamed off I-5 at the Valence exit and stomped on the brakes, swerving to a stop. He cut quickly into the town, calculating the direction the airfield's one runway stretched, relative to the community.

"Jesus, God, please," Dennis prayed, not feeling the slightest bit odd about what he was praying for. All he'd wanted to do was crash a couple of airplanes and get paid handsomely. In return for which, he'd vastly increase the profitability of his company. And since, in his heart, Dennis knew that the Gamelan FDRs were superior to every other competitor's, why, in the long run, he was actually making airline travel that much safer.

Was that so bad?

## VALENCE AIRFIELD

A copilot named Burke, certified in visual and instrument-aided flight, was picked from Walter Mulroney's structures crew to assist with the test flight. He cinched himself into the right-hand seat as Isaiah Grey began walking them through the preflight.

"Shoulder harness," Isaiah asked.

"On."

"Parking brake."

"Set."

"Fuel quantity."

"Ah, let's see." Burke fiddled with a monitor. "Twenty-two three."

Isaiah nodded, he knew that 22,300 pounds of fuel should be much more than enough for Peter Kim's mad-scientist experiments. He said, "Twenty-two three, check. Pneumatic cross feeds?"

Burke said, "Open."

"Anticollision light."

"On."

"Fuel-boost pumps."

"Got 'em."

"Ignition."

"On."

Isaiah peered down at the tangle of cords and wires that ran from the Gamelan monitor to the orange "black" box, now secured in first class. The English ex-cop, John Roby, had supervised as crews moved the Gamelan from its place in the empennage, to make it easier to download diagnostic information after each test.

"Is that thing ready?" Burke asked.

"Guess so. Let's get upstairs."

He eased the Vermeer 111 out of the protection of the hangar and into the rain.

In first class, Tommy Tomzak sat down in a randomly selected seat. Kiki Duvall, John Roby, and Ray Calabrese had come along, too. Tommy and Ray exchanged glances. They both knew that if they could prove sabotage, the title of Investigator in Charge would be handed off like a baton.

A bundle of yellow and black wires led from the flight deck to first class, where John had organized four technicians. Under Peter Kim's direction, they'd established a series of monitors that would "ambush" information coming in and out of the Gamelan flight data recorder. Techies had disassembled a bookshelf—a bricks-and-boards affair—in the pilots' lounge of the airfield and carted the boards to the Vermeer. Laying them across the tops of three seats, they had a fairly stable platform for the black box, as well as their computers and monitors, situated right at stomach height if you were standing in the aisles. John had volunteered to monitor the black box.

The Vermeer crawled slowly out of the hangar and into the rain. Kiki had chosen a seat across the aisle from Tommy, both of them two rows behind Ray, and all three of them behind John and the Gamelan black box.

"Nervous?" Kiki asked.

Tommy nodded. "A little. We just crawled through a jet that looked an awful lot like this one, except . . ."

Kiki reached across the aisle, palm upward. Tommy took her hand. She said, "I know."

Two rows forward, Ray pretended he couldn't hear the couple—and hell, they were clearly a couple—behind him.

"November Tango Sierra Bravo One, you are cleared for takeoff. Don't suppose I got to tell you which runway. Over."

Isaiah adjusted his voice wand. "Thank you, tower. Be advised, this is a test. We'll be returning shortly. Over."

"Roger that, November Tango. See you soon. Valence tower out."

## VALENCE AIRFIELD

Dennis skidded to a stop in the parking lot behind a Glidden Paint store. If he'd calculated right, he should be lined up with the runway.

He scrambled out of the car. The parking lot, and that entire end of Valence, sat on a little hill, maybe ten feet higher than the valley floor where the airfield lay. Dennis dashed to the end of the parking lot, stared through a chain-link fence and between two bedraggled yew bushes. He was looking down and almost directly into the mouth of the single runway, which was separated from the hillock by maybe a hundred yards of flat land and low brush. The Vermeer was just now turning onto the path.

One hundred feet away from Dennis, one of the ubiquitous rented Sentras idled. Two figures in NTSB windbreakers stood behind the car, their identities obscured by an umbrella.

Sitting on the trunk was a Gamelan infrared transceiver.

"You shits!" Dennis hissed to himself and scrambled back to his car.

Isaiah Grey toggled the switch for the intraship communications. "Can you folks hear me?"

John Roby's voice came back. "Oy! There's a baby crying. Can I get an upgrade?"

Isaiah said, "Tourist. We're about to leave the ground. Peter called in. They're ready."

John said, "We're ready as well. Let's give it a go, mate."

With a nod to his copilot, Isaiah throttled forward.

Next to the rented Sentra, and under one umbrella, stood Walter Mulroney and Peter Kim. Walter was leaning over Peter's shoulder, staring at the infrared transceiver. "You know what you're doing?"

"Yes, Walter," the engineer replied with an irritated sigh. "I do know a little something about computer programming."

"I'm just asking. Here comes Grey now. Let's hope he's as good a pilot as he brags."

A hundred feet away, Dennis Silverman had his laptop and transceiver out. He'd set them up on the driver's seat of his Outback, the driver's door open, then perched himself sideways on the passenger's seat, thus protecting the equipment from the slanting rain. He had no idea what set of instructions the Go-Team was about to send to the Gamelan in the swap-out jetliner. It didn't matter. He knew what signal he'd send.

The plane rolled forward, rain drumming on its aluminum skin. Ray was on his cell phone in the back of first class. He hung up.

"L.A. says Irish delegates are in the air, flying from New York to Los Angeles, right now."

Tommy and Kiki twisted in their seats. "Catholic?" Kiki asked.

"Catholic and Protestant both. Show of hands: who here likes big, fat, whopping coincidences, when we're right in the middle of this shit with the Red Fist of Ulster?"

Tommy said, "So who on Flight Eight One Eight had ties to Ireland?"

Ray said, "Not a damn soul. We've triple-checked them."

Tommy rubbed his neck, still aching from hours at the autopsy tables. "This makes no sense. I like what you're saying about a delegation heading to Los Angeles. That's gotta fit in somehow. But downing the Vermeer on Monday? The telephone call from the Valence airfield? I got nothing, Brooklyn."

Kiki stood to face Ray and put one knee up on her seat, her arm resting on Tommy's shoulder. "If the Gamelan is involved, I wish we could have reached Dennis Silverman. Doing this without our designated expert is a handicap."

Tommy was not aware that he touched her arm. "Pete and Walter know what they're doing. My money's on them."

Ray said, "For what it's worth, the brass at the L.A. field office agrees with you about the Irish delegates. We're promoting them to most-likely target."

John Roby took five paces back to their little party. "Best take your seats. Isaiah is about to take off. This works, Peter should activate the screens, show us a movie."

"Yeah?" Ray piped up. "What's playing?"

"Dunno. Something with Will Ferrell."

"Jesus." Tommy winced. "Couldn't Petey just crash the fuckin' plane instead?"


Dennis reached into the glove compartment of his Outback and pulled out his home-built radio rig. He slid it into the gaping hole in his dashboard, where the factory-original radio would have gone. Normally, when he drove, Dennis took advantage of his technical skills to entertain himself. He'd extensively modified it to scan the frequencies dedicated to cell phones. Over the years, he'd listened to hundreds of calls around the Portland area. The vast majority had been dull. A few had been hilarious. Occasionally, some were pornographic: his favorite.

The night before, while they'd been sharing a beer, Dennis had asked to see Tommy's comm unit. He'd noted the frequency and, now, adjusted his radio to match. He was immediately rewarded by a harsh squawk and then the voice of Susan Tanaka.

"Walter? They're rolling."

Dennis quickly turned down the audio before the two men under the umbrella heard something.

"We have them visually, Susan." It was the voice of Walter Mulroney. "Here they come."

The Vermeer reached takeoff velocity and the front wheels lifted off the tarmac, marked with thick stretches of melted rubber. The aircraft rose smoothly, passing directly over the stretch of low brush, then over both parked cars and both Gamelan transceivers.

Peter tapped the Return key. "Message sent."

A fifth of a second later, Dennis hit a knuckle-buster combination of keys. It was his own get-out-of-jail-free card, a program he'd plugged in to the Gamelan, just in case. His message traveled at the speed of light to the Vermeer roaring overhead.

The message: Abort all changes. Maintain status quo.

Whatever message the NTSB boys sent, Dennis just erased it.

In the cockpit, Isaiah peeked at the Gamelan monitor, sitting at two o'clock relative to him. A red warning light blinked twice on the monitor screen in less than half a second.

Tommy, Kiki, and Ray watched the movie screens in the front of first class. If this trick worked, the DVD player would blink on. John Roby was busy watching oscilloscopes attached to the Gamelan.

The trio behind him continued to watch the movie screens.

Tommy raised his voice. "Are we there yet?"

Isaiah Grey's voice came back over the PA system. "Yeah. We're there and well beyond there. Did anything happen?"

"Oh, poo," Kiki said. "We missed the dinner show."

Susan Tanaka was standing in the simple, unadorned box on stilts that served as the Valence tower. From the hasty cleaning job and the dust-free squares marking the walls, Susan suspected that the tower crew had quickly squirreled away any girlie pictures before she arrived. She appreciated the gesture.

Ricky Sanchez had tuned the ATC radio to the speaker mounted on the wall. Isaiah's voice piped up. "Ah, ATC, this is November Tango One. Negative, repeat, negative results on Gamelan test."

As the tower controller responded, Susan hit the controls of her belt satellite-phone unit.

"Nothing, Walter. It didn't work."


Dennis Silverman chanted, "Yes! Yes! Yes!" as softly as he could, not knowing how well sound traveled in the rain.

He'd done it. He'd beaten the NTSB's best. And there was still time to catch his flight out of McNary Field, in Salem. He'd be late getting to the rendezvous, but he'd make it.

He reached for his homemade radio, which was plugged into the cigarette lighter, and turned it up. Walter Mulroney's broad, Plains accent sounded. "Okay, Susan. Tell them we're a go for test number two."

Dennis blinked. He stared at the radio as if daring it to retract that statement.

"I'll tell them," Susan said. "Be advised, this storm is getting worse. They just closed Portland International. Isaiah's only got about another thirty minutes for these tests. That's, what? Ten passes, tops."

*Shit!* Dennis slammed a fist into the dashboard.


It was Dennis's worst nightmare. He'd driven like a bat out of hell and had gotten to the parking lot behind the Glidden Paint shop with seconds to spare. He'd managed to negate whatever signal the Go-Team had sent to the swap-out, thus making it look like a Gamelan flight data recorder couldn't be used to sabotage an aircraft. Everything was going his way.

Then the wide-body began wheeling around for another pass.

Only this time, the jet would fly over his position first, then the NTSB rental car. That meant the FDR would catch his signal first, then theirs. It was simple physics. There was no way he could order the Gamelan on board that jet to belay their orders if it hadn't received them yet.

The jetliner finished its arc. Even with the leaden sky and the rain, Dennis could see it out there, a faint blob amid the clouds. It was maybe ninety seconds away, headed right for him.

He hadn't wanted to do this. He'd set out just to discredit their theory about the Gamelan. But now he needed a stronger move. With the Vermeer sixty seconds out, he slipped a flash drive into the port of his laptop, watched the programs pop up on the screen.

A prewritten set of instructions began scrolling across his screen.

John Roby turned around. "I know we didn't get our test right, but something happened. This monitor shows a double spike of energy to the Gamelan."

Ray, Tommy, and Kiki digested that, not sure what it meant.

John gave them a shrug.

"Second pass. Gonna try the same test," Walter relayed to Susan via their ear jacks.

"Excuse me." Susan touched the air traffic controller on the shoulder. "Can you tell the pilot we'll try the same test on this pass?"

In the cabin, Tommy, Kiki, and Ray began concentrating on the blank movie screen.

The flicker of light blinked onto the screen. About a third of a second after the Vermeer began shaking itself to pieces.

# 45

ALBION AIR FLIGHT 326 passed through a minor bit of turbulence over Nebraska. Normally, Captain David Singh wouldn't have thought twice about it. But normally, he wasn't playing chauffeur to high-ranking officials—or so Captain Singh had been assured—of the Irish government and a sitting U.S. congressman.

Teddy McCoy, the jovial navigator, unlocked the flight-deck door and let himself in. He carried three cans of soda pop and his hands were so huge, all three fit in one. The Scotsman stood over six-two and was as thin as a hockey stick. He also had a constant smile plastered on his long features.

"Here you go, then." He handed a Coke Zero to the captain and a Diet 7UP to the copilot, Eloise Pool, who nodded her thanks. Even on a long, dull cross-Atlantic flight, Eloise didn't say three words other than the count-off checklists. It wasn't that she was shy, it was that she was the world's worst conversationalist. It was the same in the pilots' lounge or taking a cab from the airport hotels. The woman seemed incapable of making small talk.

Daya Singh, fifty-five, had started calling himself David in his teens. He'd been born in London of Indian parents and he wanted to be as much a Londoner as every other kid at school. He'd excelled at cricket, which had gotten him into King's College on a scholarship. From there, he'd joined the Royal Air Force with one goal in mind: to fly. It was David Singh's one true passion; or it had been until meeting his wife and the birth of their three now-grown girls.

But even today, after all these years, all those cockpits and flight decks, David Singh was never happier than riding the left-hand seat of *his* aircraft.

He removed his watch and adjusted it for Pacific Time: it was 3:30 P.M. in California.

Teddy McCoy took his seat, which was behind Eloise's, and turned ninety degrees from the other two. He adjusted the four-point harness before opening his Coke. "Are we flying anywhere near that Vermeer that went down Monday?"

Captain Singh slid his soda pop into the holder to his left, which was fitted with a gimbal to be steady even in turbulence. "That was in Oregon, north of California. I've heard naught about a cause yet."

"Aye, it's early days." Teddy checked his state-of-the-art navigational equipment. He also had the assignment of handling internal and external communications for the mammoth aircraft. "These things take bloody months, don't they."

"I'd met the pilot," David said wistfully. "Black girl, 'bout your age. It was just about, I don't know, eight months ago. She spoke on a panel about wake vortices. Very keen, that one. Told her so, after the conference. That's why I remember her. Shame."

"Damn shame," Teddy agreed.

Eloise Pool, it seemed, had no opinion on the topic.

## OVER VALENCE

For every flight that Tommy Tomzak had ever been on—every single one of them, without fail—an attendant had instructed the passengers to wear their seat belts. The one time he'd boarded an airplane with no flight attendant, he'd forgotten.

The Vermeer quaked like an epileptic in a grand mal seizure. Tommy went flying, landed hard in the aisle, his head ricocheting off an armrest. He caught a half-formed glimpse of Ray Calabrese, also airborne.

Tommy scrambled for a purchase, anything solid would do. But as his hands reached for a seat back, the plane's lurching increased. He went skidding backward down the aisle.

. . .

"Dammit!" Isaiah Grey shouted at the yoke as it shivered badly in his hands. The Vermeer careened crazily, the nose too low, the fuselage vibrating like a tuning fork. He could feel the wings "slipping"—the port wing falling back, the starboard wing moving faster than the fuselage.

"What do we got!" he bellowed over the roar.

"I don't know!" The copilot, Burke, sounded panicky. "Telltales are green! Monitors green! We—"

The stick shaker rattled, warning of a stall.

Isaiah glanced out at the lights of downtown Valence, a retail region maybe two blocks by two blocks with nothing but fast food, motels and gas stations. A commerce zone aimed entirely at the drivers of Interstate 5. He didn't like seeing the lights so well, so close. His hand reached for the lever that would dump his fuel. But something made him stop. It was a thought—too low, too primal to be called a plan. More like a gut reaction, his hominid fight-or-flight instincts grafted to a lifetime's experience in cockpits; especially in fighters.

Isaiah reached to cut off engine number three before he realized he'd done it.

"Three off!" he shouted.

"There's nothing wrong w—" Burke started to protest. But the buffeting stopped. The yoke no longer vibrated.

Isaiah wiped sweat off his brow. Outside the cockpit window, the city of Valence was perilously close. He was only ten or twelve stories off the ground—and the cockpit stood three stories high with wheels on tarmac.

With one of the two starboard engines out of the show, the Vermeer began angling to the right. The tip of the left wing scythed through the afternoon sky, barely clipping a tall Burger World sign on a long pole. It exploded, electricity from the lighted sign rippling off its surface.

Isaiah tried to correct. Dropping power to the dead engine's counterpart—interior engine, portside wing—would have balanced the thrust. But at this altitude and speed, the Vermeer would stall out and drop like the hammer of a gun.

Instead, he boosted power to the right-hand outboard engine, redlining the Patterson-Pate turbine. A warning whistle sounded as he pushed the engine beyond its maximum stress load.

With one engine on the right putting out almost as much thrust as two engines on the left, the flight straightened out. The right wing missed a Taco Magnifico sign by seven inches.

That was the good news. The bad news: they were flying directly away from the only runway Isaiah knew in the region.

He vectored toward Interstate 5 and away from the residential and commercial developments of Valence. He could see details on the tops of farm trucks on rural roads beneath him. He needed some altitude. Out of the corner of his eye, he noted the close-clustered, dark purple clouds roiling over Portland, not thirty miles north of his position, and gave thanks that he was only clipping the edge of the storm. He crossed the highway at a thirty-degree angle, heading for the Willamette River with its twin corridors of tall evergreens along both shores. Beyond the river lay—what? Isaiah didn't know the region. Something flat, he prayed.

Either that, or get this beast to stay in the air long enough to get back to Valence.


The boards perched on the tops of seats had been an ideal place to put the black box and monitors, as long as the flight remained relatively smooth. When the Vermeer began to buck like a rodeo bull, the wood went flying, equipment smashing into the fuselage or the floor.

Kiki got to her feet first, as soon as the violent shaking stopped. "Tommy!" she shouted, and edged back toward his prone form. The jet was swinging in weird patterns; in a car, she would have recognized the motion as fishtailing. A flash of lightning flickered outside the left-hand windows, and bits of metal and plastic pinged off the fuselage. Kiki winced and stumbled, banging her knee against a seat. She pitched forward as Tommy sat up. She landed atop him, nose to nose.

"Are you all right?" he asked, surprise and worry in his voice.

"Am I?" Kiki rose to her hands and knees above him. She touched his forehead, her fingers coming away slick with blood.

Tommy sat up and touched his skull. Bleeding, all right, but it wasn't hurting much. "It's okay," he said, rising. "Superficial."

Ray Calabrese's face came into view over Kiki's shoulder. "You two all right?"

They scrambled to their feet. Tommy said, "The fuck's going on?"

Ray glanced out the windows to the right and saw a fast food sign slide by, almost close enough to touch. "I think we're screwed."

Tommy sidled past him, toward the flight deck. "John, did you get a reading on—"

Tommy stood for a moment, blinking as a trickle of blood reached his right eye. He wiped at it with the back of his hand.

Kiki moved forward. "Tom—"

She stopped, seeing the limp, dead body of John Roby, his neck snapped, his eyes glassy and unfocused.

Just as Kiki started to cry, the crazy buffeting started again.

The Vermeer was losing altitude. Normally, it could run on three engines just fine, but the buffeting that followed the crisis had chewed up way too much forward thrust. They had been within seconds of a stall-out.

The jet screamed over a high, dense cluster of trees and was suddenly above the Willamette River, choppy and gunmetal gray in the overcast weather. The buffeting increased.

Isaiah Grey shouted, "Calabrese! Get up here!"

"Dammit!" the copilot screamed. "The board's green! What the hell's happening!"

The door to the flight deck banged open and Ray Calabrese stumbled in, his face pasty and slick with sweat. He'd climbed over the body of John Roby to get there.

Isaiah cut the power to engine number two—the inboard engine on the port wing. It was a wild-assed guess but it proved to be right. The bucking stopped.

And the Vermeer sank lower.

Isaiah pointed to the Gamelan monitor and the twisting vine of cables leading to first class. "Calabrese! The wires! Shoot 'em!"

Ray knelt, pulled his Glock 9 from his belt holster, and aimed at the bundle of wires. He fired from an inch away. The noise was deafening in the enclosed space. The wires shredded.

Ray said, "Will that help?"

Isaiah shrugged, his fists squeezed around the sluggish yoke. "Damned if I know."

The stick shaker sounded. Isaiah goosed the two remaining engines, avoiding the stall yet again. He glanced out at the dark gray river and the tree-covered hills beyond and said, "No good."

He turned the jet back, a nice, soft roll to port, sacrificing speed and precious altitude. The copilot said, "Oh, Jesus . . ."

Ray said, "We got a plan?" He couldn't be positive—Isaiah's face was cheated three-quarters away from him—but he could swear the pilot was grinning.

"Wouldn't call it anything as fancy as a *plan*." Isaiah spat the words through gritted teeth.

# 46

Dennis Silverman's Outback hydroplaned onto I-5 south to a symphony of horns. He missed a Subaru by inches. His windshield wipers slapped madly at the rain and he leaned forward, his face just inches from the steering wheel.

A produce truck pulled into the middle lane and Dennis skittered between it and a Ford F-110, drawing a blaring horn from the truck, as he juked the Outback into the fast lane and hit the gas.

He prayed that the company's Gulfstream was ready for him in Salem and that the weather wasn't too bad for a takeoff.

## OVER INTERSTATE 5

The Vermeer swap-out hung in the air reluctantly, maintaining all the aerodynamics of a refrigerator. The stick shaker rattled twice, and twice Isaiah Grey cajoled the wounded bird into staying aloft.

Burke, the copilot, moaned. "Where are we going?"

Isaiah said, "Gonna find us a runway." The tendons in his neck stood rigid and extended, but his voice was casual, calm.

Standing behind their seats Ray watched the pilot carefully, looking for signs of tension. Mostly, Isaiah looked energized.

Isaiah forced a quick smile over his shoulder. "Ask," he said, "and ye shall receive."

Ray peered out the rain-spattered window. "That's . . . a runway? Jesus, that's the highway!"

Isaiah said, "Six of one," and hauled with all his strength, forcing the jet toward the six-lane ribbon of asphalt.

Conchata Menchu was singing along to the soundtrack of *West Side Story,* belting out the Sondheim lyrics at full volume. She couldn't carry a tune worth a lick, but singing by yourself in the cab of a long-haul truck had its advantages.

Conchata was so caught up in the refrain from "I Feel Pretty" that it took her a moment to realize that the great gray blob in the air, dead ahead, wasn't an extremely dense cloud formation. Conchata's voice faded away, leaving Marni Nixon to handle the tune alone.

The gray blob grew larger, took on a shape. It was a plane. No, a jet plane. No, a really, really big jet plane.

And a really, really low one.

"Holy Mary," Conchata whispered. She hit her powerful air horn, prayed the other drivers around her had seen what she had, and began yanking on the massive steering wheel with all her might.

Tommy and Kiki looked out through side-by-side windows in first class, then looked at each other, then out the windows again.

Tommy said, "Well, shit."

"This is the oncoming lane!" Burke bleated from the copilot's seat.

Ray rested a hand on his shoulder. "We don't want to be sneaking up on those drivers. Better they should see us."

The plane was still bucking badly and Ray braced himself against the copilot's seat.

Isaiah shook his head. "Overpass."

"Yeah." Ray sighed. "I see the bitch."

About two miles ahead, a rural road crossed over the highway, just barely visible in the gloom.

Burke said, "Our father, who art in heaven . . ."

Ray said, "That's not funny."

Isaiah said, "He's not joking."

Dennis Silverman switched lanes and his wheels spun without traction for a split second before catching. The Outback lurched forward.

Peering through the arc of the windshield wipers, he activated the Bluetooth hands-free controls on his steering wheel. He'd preprogrammed in the number.

"Scarlotti Aviation."

"This is Dennis Silverman! I'm with Gamelan Industries! Our Gulfstream Three is scheduled for a flight to California! Is it ready?"

"Sir, I gotta tell you, we've got a nasty storm front moving south. We've got considerable wind shear and lightning cells all over the place. They just shut down Portland International and McNary Field could be next. Are you sure y—"

"Yes!" Dennis bellowed, blinking as sweat dripped into his eyes. The *Battlestar Galactica* model dangling from his rearview mirror danced as he swerved around a sky-blue Caddy. "I have to fly out today! I'll be at the airport in twenty minutes. Have the engines running. We'll take off the second I'm on board!"

He disconnected. Around him, cars started honking. *Fuck you all,* he thought, speeding up.

The cars across the median from him, heading north, started honking, too.

The Vermeer 111 was hobbling along on two engines and the stall-warning stick shaker sounded yet again. Isaiah hauled back on the yoke, scrambling for every inch of elevation he could get. The rural road overpass slipped beneath them, clearing the belly by three feet.

"Landing gears down."

"Please, God, oh please . . ." Burke chanted. He didn't touch the landing-gear controls.

Isaiah casually stretched far to his right, hit the controls.

The great plane began dropping again. "Seat belts!" he shouted.

Ray folded down the extra seat behind the pilot's and reached for the wall-mounted shoulder straps.

In first class, Tommy and Kiki scrambled for the nearest seats and strapped themselves in.

A long-haul rig zoomed down I-5, carrying three tiers of the new line of Lexus LS 460Ls, one atop the other on their tracks. The driver was searching through his books-on-tape collection. He glanced up as the Vermeer screamed over his cab.

The driver panicked. He wrenched the wheel as hard as he could to one side, even though the jetliner had already passed. The truck glided into a right angle relative to the trailer, blue smoke erupting from the wheels as momentum dragged it sideways down the highway. The trailer crabbed over onto its side, covering all three lanes, and the right-hand wheels left the ground. It teetered for a moment, then bucked over. The sedans were wrenched from their tie-downs, rolling over and over across the highway like monstrous dice. Three of them bounded through the air and barrel-rolled across the median, landing in the southbound lanes.

Oncoming northbound cars screeched and swerved to avoid them and hit one another instead. One minute they had been seven individual cars driving for seven individual destinations; the next they were a kinetic sculpture of rent bumpers, hoods accordioned in and steam hissing from engines.

In the southbound lane, a school bus carrying the girls' basketball team from Sprague High School belched blue smoke from its tires as the driver stomped on the brake and brought the mammoth yellow vehicle to a full stop. Girls screamed. The nose of the bus barely kissed the chassis of an on-its-side Lexus, moving at less than a mile an hour, making the sedan rotate slowly on its doors like a clock hand.

A mile south of that accident, Dennis Silverman glanced over and realized that every single northbound car had pulled off the road, onto either the median or the shoulder. *There must be one hell of a fender bender back there,* he thought. Which was when he saw that some of the cars heading in his direction were veering to the shoulder of the road, too.

What could—

The gigantic wheels of the Vermeer touched the pavement almost exactly parallel to Dennis's Outback, belching black smoke and leaving melted-rubber patches as it shrieked past him in the same direction, roaring south in the northbound lanes, the wing span so great that the starboard wing stretched across the median and hung over two of the southbound lanes.

Dennis screamed. The Outback swerved as if under its own power, shifted two lanes and back again, but not before it clipped the left-front quarter panel of a Civic, sending it into a spin. Dennis's heart slammed in his chest. *"Fuuuuuuuuuuck!"* he keened.

The Vermeer shot ahead of him, engine reversers howling like werewolves, its wake vortex made visible by a solid tube of swirling rainwater, twin, horizontal tornadoes stretching out behind it.

The plane disappeared into the thick rain ahead. Dennis regained control of his car, tears running down his face, and plunged after it, slamming his fist into the ceiling of the car, over his head, again and again. *"Fucking . . . I killed you! Fuckers! Fuck! I . . . FUCK!"*

The reversers screamed at Isaiah, straining to slough off the magnificent momentum that let a bucket of metal 230 feet long and 63 feet high defy gravity. At that speed, Isaiah's vision was limited to ten seconds ahead of the nose cone. If another overpass was waiting for them, or if any of the drivers failed to get their cars off the road, he wouldn't have time to swerve. But then, he didn't have any space to swerve anyway.

How far to the next overpass? He'd driven the route out of Salem twice so far, but he couldn't remember where the overpasses were.

He gauged the speed of the highway stripes. The reversers in the two functioning engines were doing their job. The Vermeer began to slow down.

Not only had every car abandoned the northbound lanes to avoid the Leviathan bearing down on them, but most of the cars in the southbound lane had either pulled off to the side, or had been hit by one of the flying Lexus sedans. The highway behind the Vermeer remained empty of all traffic.

•   •   •

As cars pulled off the road ahead of him, Dennis shot into the fast lane and stood on his accelerator. The Outback fishtailed, the tires caught, and he raced ahead.

It took him two minutes to catch up to the Vermeer and zoom past it, crossing under the starboard wing. By now, the jetliner was crawling toward a complete stop.

He had thrown the greatest technological monkey wrench in history at the airliner. His Gamelan had fucked over one engine for sure and was prepared to fuck over the others, as need be.

There was no possible way to bring that jet down for a safe landing. It had been doomed.

Dennis continued to cry. *"Dammit! Goddammit!"* He pounded the steering wheel with his fist, tears streaming down his face.

The doomed craft was on the ground, not so doomed after all. And the fucking Go-Team had survived.


Tommy Tomzak forced himself to look out the window. The rain-slick highway wasn't moving. He turned to Kiki. She was staring at him.


Ray Calabrese said, "Where the hell did you learn to fly like that?"

Isaiah pried his fists off the yoke. "I learned how to do that about thirty seconds ago."

"Fucking Jedi." Ray clapped him on the shoulder.

Ray stood up, his legs almost buckling under him. Burke sat, bent forward, lips moving in silent prayer.

"I thought that guy Kim was going to make the projector flicker? What the hell went wrong?"

"That wasn't Peter's doing. There's no way." Isaiah unbuckled his harness, pointed to the Gamelan monitor, now dead. "See this? This light blinked as we flew over Peter and Walter's car. Less than half a second later, it blinked again. I didn't think much about it at the time. On the second flyby, I was watching. It blinked twice again."

"One blink, as it received Peter Kim's signal," Ray cut in. "One from someone else?"

Isaiah nodded. "What I'm thinking."

"Okay. Then who?"

Isaiah shrugged.

"How well do you guys know that Silverman guy?"

"Dennis Silverman?" Isaiah shrugged. "We don't. He's our liaison with Gamelan. But, really? The nerdy guy? You like him for your mastermind?"

Ray thought about it for a minute. "Nah. Not really. But he is the expert with the Gamelan. He was at the airfield when someone called the Red Fist's phone in Atlanta. . . ."

The thought of the out-of-shape geek with the bad glasses and goofy grin as the villain behind this plot seemed pretty unlikely. But Ray had to admit, there was a case to be made.

# BOOK THREE

CRASH

## 47

REACHING MCNARY FIELD, IN Salem, Dennis Silverman scrambled from the Outback, carrying his overnight bag and his laptop with infrared transceiver. He scampered across the tarmac to the big, corporate Gulfstream III, running beneath its thirty-five-foot-long wing. The ladder/door was out, and a man in a captain's peaked hat and a slicker was waiting for him.

"You just about didn't make it," the captain said. "Word is, they're shutting down this airspace in twenty minutes."

Dennis stood at the top of the stairs and peered owlishly through his rain-soaked glasses. "Can you get me to Southern California ahead of this storm?"

The pilot winked. "We got a couple of Rolls-Royce turbofans out there that can hit five hundred eighty miles an hour without breaking a sweat. We can get you there all right. Go get yourself buckled in, sir, and we'll see what this bird can do."

## INTERSTATE 5

Ray moved back into first class to tell Tommy Tomzak about the new theory: that Dennis Silverman of Gamelan Industries was behind their near crash.

He found Kiki Duvall sitting on the arm of a seat, hands on her knees, watching as Tommy knelt, pushed John Roby's head into a more dignified position, and closed John's eyes. Kiki looked like she was close to passing out.

"Doc," Ray started, then looked over Tommy's shoulder. "Ah, man. I'm sorry."

"Cervical," Tommy said, not turning around. "Clean break. Immediate cessation of the central nervous system. He didn't suffer."

"Jesus." Ray scanned his brain for something to say, came up with nothing new. "I'm sorry."

Nobody spoke for a while.

On the flight deck, the copilot wordlessly unbuckled himself and shoved his way out. A second later, Tommy, Kiki, and Ray stepped in.

"Everyone okay?" Isaiah asked.

Tommy held a handkerchief to his bleeding forehead. "John died. We have abrasions, contusions, nothing serious. We—"

Isaiah almost fell back into his chair. "John? Ah . . . Jesus. John?"

"Yeah. I know." Tommy wiped tears from his cheeks. Then he suddenly threw a bear hug around Isaiah. He pulled back, kissed the pilot on the forehead. "Seriously, that was one kick-ass piece of flying. We owe you our lives, man."

"Yes." Kiki kissed Isaiah on the cheek. "Thank you."

He and Kiki left Ray and Tommy, who sank into the copilot's chair. Ray leaned back, his head against the wall, eyes closed.

"The Englishman. You two were friends?"

Tommy nodded, wiped his cheeks again. "Worked together three times. He's brilliant. Very funny."

They waited, quietly. Tommy dabbed the still-bleeding wound on his forehead. He nodded at the avionics. "That was spooky."

"No shit." Ray opened his eyes blearily. Only then did he realize that Tommy was bleeding. Ray reached into his jacket pocket and produced a travel pack of Kleenex. He tossed it to Tommy.

"Thanks."

Ray activated his cell phone. His hands were still shaking. Ray called Henry Deits in Los Angeles.

"Calabrese? I'm glad you called. What's going on there?"

"Oh, not much," Ray said, his voice almost cracking. "How about on your end?"

The assistant director told him about the Irish delegation en route to LAX. "They'll be there in under four hours," he said.

"I still like them as the target."

Deits said, "I have my doubts. I don't like coincidences any more than you do. But still. There are Sinn Fein members on board, true, but also Ulster Unionists. They're not likely to sacrifice the same number of their friends, are they?"

"I don't know," Ray said honestly. "Everything we've seen points to them bringing down that Vermeer. Daria says they're moving into position for another play. Look, there's something else. Guy named Dennis Silverman."

Ray walked Deits through it, including the emergency landing on the highway.

"Holy crap! You're okay?"

"Yeah, but we heard Silverman was leaving town for a conference. If I'm remembering correctly, it's in California. Have someone from the Portland field office check with Gamelan. Find out where he is. Also, look into this guy's background. He sure doesn't come across as a terrorist, but you never know."

"Okay, we're on it. Ray? Wow, I hope to hell you're wrong."

Ray nodded. "I know why. If I'm right, this schlub can drop airplanes out of the sky. At will."

Across the cockpit, Tommy called Susan Tanaka at the Woodburn tower and told her about John Roby.

Susan allowed herself five seconds to mourn John, then filed it away for later. There would be plenty of tears. Now wasn't the time.

"It was Dennis Silverman," Susan said, even before Tommy broached the subject.

"Whoa!" Tommy reached out and backhanded Ray's shoulder to get his attention. "Susan. She says it's Dennis Silverman."

Ray said, "Call you back?" and folded away his phone.

"Suze?"

"Walter heard a car near where they were parked. As it pulled away, he got a good look at the driver. Peter surmises that he sent a message to your Gamelan, screwing up your flight."

"We figured the same thing," he assured her. "Call the cops and—"

"We did. I, ah, may have used Agent Calabrese's name a bit liberally to get the police to report back to me. They called about thirty seconds ago. There's no sign of him at his office or his home. And a receptionist says he was scheduled to fly to California today."

"He's in California," Tommy repeated, watched Ray nod his understanding.

"Stick close to the swap-out," Susan told him. "From all reports, you guys have clogged traffic in both directions. Walter is calling in the flatbeds that hauled Flight Eight One Eight here. We'll get an ambulance for John. They'll be there in about two hours to tow you guys off the highway."

"Okay," he said.

"Tommy? I am so sorry about John."

"I know. Me, too." He rang off, glanced at Ray. "California?"

## BOCA SERPIENTE, CALIFORNIA

The three Irishmen and Daria sat in the stifling motel room, watching TV. The men had found the ESPN Soccer Channel and a football match. Manchester United versus Arsenal. None of them cheered or groaned, they all just watched stoically, waiting for something.

Everyone twitched when a knock sounded at the door. Donal O'Meara slipped his hand around his Colt Python and moved to the side of the door. "What is it?" he shouted without opening it.

"Are you Jack?"

"Yeah."

"Got a phone call for you in the office."

O'Meara slipped the gun's safety back on, then tucked it into his belt, throwing on a work shirt to cover it. He unlocked the door and stepped out.

Contact. In the time Daria had been with the Irishmen, this was the first time O'Meara had received a direct, real-time contact with anyone. Always before, he'd left messages on answering machines. But a true, living human and a live telephone conversation meant that this was their final destination after all. Whatever was going to happen, this motel would be the staging point.

Which meant it was time to call in the marines.

A plan came to her fairly quickly. "Hope he remembers to get towels," she said, eyes on the telecast.

Keith O'Shea said, "What?"

"Towels. We don't have enough for everyone to shower, and I'm afraid in this heat, we'll all want one."

The men exchanged looks. "I'm sweating like old nitro," Feargal Kelly said to his partner. "And you smell like shite."

O'Shea waved the back of his first two fingers at the smaller man.

Daria shrugged. "Just hope he remembers."

The door opened again. Both men rested their hands on guns, but it was O'Meara.

"Good news?" O'Shea asked. O'Meara shrugged. "Well, did you think to grab some extra towels at least?"

"Towels?"

Sighing, Daria dragged herself to her feet. "I'll go get them. Right back."

"Oh. Ta, then," O'Meara said, and stepped aside so she could pass.

As she did, he swung his right fist from his hip, catching Daria in the jaw. Lights burned bright in her eyes. She hadn't seen the blow coming, hadn't rolled with it in the slightest. She spun, her head cracking against the wall.

Her vision was useless, her balance worse. She slid to the floor, nauseated with pain, barely aware of O'Meara's boot. He kicked her in the side, not with his toe but with the bottom of his heel. A rib cracked, the sound reverberating through her body.

Consciousness slipped away.

## 48

AN OFF-DUTY MARION COUNTY sheriff's deputy in a four-wheel Land Rover cut across a blue fescue field, bounced over the median, and screeched to a stop next to the emergency gangplank of the Vermeer, which Isaiah had deployed from the midsection hatch. Isaiah and Susan stood under the port wing, shielded from the rain. The deputy gawked.

"What the ever-loving hell . . . ?" He produced his badge.

"Long story," Kiki said. "We're NTSB. We're investigating Monday's crash."

"By reenacting it?"

"That's the part I meant when I said 'long story.' We have a fatality on board."

"I'm off duty, but I can help." The deputy nodded down the highway, where the copilot, Burke, stalked away, hair and clothes plastered by the rain. "Who's he?"

"A man who's had enough for one day."

Kiki and Isaiah returned to the cockpit, soaking wet, after stopping to check out the engines. "Amazing," Isaiah said, water trailing down the back of his windbreaker. "Engine number three doesn't even show any signs of wear. The wing didn't sustain any damage when we hit that fast food sign, either. Fortune favors the foolish."

"You shut off the Gamelan just in time," Tommy said. "You reacted faster than Meghan Danvers."

Isaiah shook his head. "No. If I'm right, she and Kazmanski would have had no way of knowing that shutting down engine number three would save them. And the Gamelan was programmed to create a cascading failure. If the first two engines didn't knock us down, I'm sure more nastiness was about to erupt. But everything reset itself as soon as the Gamelan was offline, erasing evidence of sabotage."

"This is perfect," Ray said. "Silverman's scheme. Think about it. A plane with that whatchahoozit crashes, and you guys call in the guy who programmed the—"

"Gamelan," Kiki cut in.

"Gamelan. Right. He knew he'd be called in and handed the fucking evidence. It's perfect. Set up a crime in such a way that you have to bring the bad guy into the tent. Genius."

"Let's admire the prick later," Tommy growled.

Ray nodded, then updated them on the situation of the inbound foreign delegation, Dennis Silverman's unknown whereabouts, and the Red Fist of Ulster. Tommy just sat there, pressing the now-red wad of Kleenex against the cut on his temple.

Kiki said, "So. The Irish delegates will be in California in less than four hours. The terrorists are in California. And Dennis Silverman is on his way to California."

Tommy finally spoke. "Us, too."

"Agreed," Isaiah said. "As soon as they get us back to the airfield, I'll find out about this storm, see when they're reopening the fly zones. We can probably be gone by morning."

"No," Tommy said. "We can't wait that long."

Kiki frowned. "What do you recommend?"

"Can this plane fly?"

The others stared at him and shifted uncomfortably.

"I'm not concussed," he assured them. "The bad guys, the delegates, and Silverman are converging in California. They'll get there in four hours. And we know that crashing a jet is part of their overall plan, which means they'll try to kill the delegates as they arrive in L.A."

"Wait a minute," Kiki cut in. "Didn't Ray just say there are Ulster Union guys on that flight, too?"

"According to one of my bosses," Ray said. "But we're talking about terrorists. Don't use logic. It's the wrong tool for the job."

Isaiah cleared his throat. "Doc, this storm? This is serious as shit, man. It's pouring buckets out there. If we had a healthy beast, the FAA probably wouldn't let us fly in this. And she's not all that healthy. Plus, we had a forced landing on a highway, people. Do you have any idea how many regulations we'd break if we left the scene before—"

"Before what?" Tommy cut in gently. "Before the NTSB gets here?"

"The FAA's gonna yank my ticket, at a minimum. We're all on contract with the NTSB and we can kiss that goodbye, too. Also, the jet could have sustained more damage that I don't know about. We—"

Ray said, "Daria."

All eyes turned to him.

He sat upright, rubbing his eyes. "She was with Israeli intelligence. She was ordered to take part in an assassination and she refused. She was shot for that, almost killed. I was there. Now, because she wants to help, she saved the life of a friend of mine, Lucas Bell. She infiltrated this group of psychotic thugs. Her name's Daria Gibron."

They waited.

"It's happening all over again. She's risking her life to save others. Again. And I'm responsible for her. She's my asset. So there it is. She's in California and I have to go get her. Dennis Silverman pretended to be one of you and tried to kill us all. He did kill Roby. And we have to go get him. Now, it's up to you guys. I'm invoking no privileges here. Tommy's still IIC, as far as I'm concerned. But I'm going to California if I have to car-jack the next fucking Mini Cooper I see."

He stood wearily and left the flight deck.

The other three were quiet for a while. Tommy daubbed at his fore-head wound. "*Asset.* Man, that guy's in love."

Kiki reached out to run her hand through his hair and nodded.

Finally, Isaiah Grey flopped down heavily in the left-hand seat and began going through the preflight sequence. He muttered, "There are no crazy people like crazy *white* people. . . ."

## BOCA SERPIENTE, CALIFORNIA

The glare of sunlight in her eyes revived Daria. She was outside. She tasted blood, and she moaned as someone shoved her to the side. Her arms were yanked back and handcuffs clicked.

Fully conscious, the pain in her side blazed. She was lying on the ground behind the hotel. She forced herself to sit up, hissing in fine agony when she leaned back. Her hands were cuffed behind an old iron clothesline pole, which canted five degrees off true. Atop it were five steel arms spread like fingers, with rope looped lazily from arm to arm, creating a spiderweb for hanging wet laundry. Most of the ropes were gone now. The pole was so hot to the touch that it would leave blisters after sustained contact.

Donal O'Meara knelt beside her, on his haunches, head tilted to one side and studying her through sunglasses. Sweat trickled off his forehead and glistened in the hair on his forearms. The Python revolver hung easily in his right hand.

Daria tried to lean forward, not touching the red-hot pole. Her side ached and each breath was agony, but she wasn't coughing up blood. He hadn't punctured a lung.

O'Meara said, "You're FBI, then."

"I saved you from the F—"

He reached out languidly and poked her rib, hard, with the four-inch barrel of the Colt. The rib creaked. Daria gasped, leaned over, and vomited. Black dots blinked around her peripheral vision. Groaning, she sat back up again, blinking the sweat out of her eyes.

"I didn't make many rules," O'Meara said, his voice casual. "Just one. Fuck with me and I'd kill ye."

She squinted at him.

"I have a contact who says you killed Johnser, back at the hotel. Dunno how."

She waited.

"My contact says you're working for an FBI agent. I need to know what you've told him."

Daria leaned forward and spat a gob of blood on the ground. The blow to her jaw had split her lip.

"I've a friend in high places, Daria me love. I've learned enough to know you've screwed us, but not the fine details. And the devil's in the details, isn't he. Now, I've more friends you haven't met yet. They're on their way here. And when they arrive, I'd like a few more details from you, if you please."

He stood. "I'll give you a little time to consider the error of your ways, my girl."

He left her there, squinting into the sun of the Mojave Desert.

## FBI HEADQUARTERS, WASHINGTON, D.C.

Assistant Director Timothy Perdue ignored his phone without taking his eyes off the field report. It was a security analysis of Quantico itself, and Perdue was pretty sure he'd reread that last paragraph at least three times. He still didn't know what it meant.

The phone kept ringing. He checked his desk clock, which read WORLD'S GREATEST DAD! It was almost 6 P.M. Eastern. *Who calls at this hour?*

He scooped it up. "Perdue."

"Tim? Lucas Bell."

The assistant director smiled. "Hey! How's La-La Land?" He leaned back and reached for a stress ball. He and Bell had worked together on the Ireland Watch for years before Perdue had moved up to the highest echelons of the Bureau. They had been the best of friends for a time.

"Bad," Lucas said. "Very bad."

Perdue removed his reading glasses and glanced at the clock again.

"Are you up to speed on the Red Fist of Ulster problem?"

"More or less. I can't hear you very well."

Lucas whispered, "I can't speak up. I have proof, positive proof, Tim, that agents in the Los Angeles field office are running interference for the terrorists."

Perdue reached for a pad and pen. "Go."

"Ray Calabrese, for sure. He's our point man on the investigation!"

"Shit! Anyone else?"

"I think Assistant Director Henry Deits has been covering for him. They—"

"Henry? I know Henry. He's—"

"Tim, I'm telling you, I don't want to believe it either, but I can't explain the lapse in security, the protocols we've blown, the secret conversations. I don't think we can afford to gamble on Deits. You know about the Irish delegation . . . ?"

"Yes. We have bad clock here, Lucas. What do you suggest?"

After a beat, Lucas said, "Jesus, Tim. I don't know. What do you think?"

"If you're right, we have to raise the firewall."

"Whew. It's a big step. But until we get the delegation on the ground and into a secure location, I guess you're right. I don't see any other choice."

*Raising the firewall* meant isolating a field office. It meant cutting off everyone's communications for a period of time—their phones and computers; cutting them off from other FBI field offices, from other federal law enforcement agencies, and from the intelligence community. It would mean routing some of their duties through another office, like San Francisco. If, by some chance, Lucas was wrong, well, nobody's career would be eighty-sixed by his taking this precaution.

Tim Perdue stood. "I'll talk to the director himself. He hasn't gone home yet. I'll also recommend we reroute the delegation from LAX to Frisco."

"That's good thinking. I'll keep nosing around here."

"Lucas? You keep your head down, my friend. Cavalry's coming."

"Thanks, Tim. Good luck!"

Timothy Perdue depressed the tine, then stabbed three buttons. "Director's office."

"It's Tim. I need him. Now."

## INTERSTATE 5

"No. No. No! Absolutely no way."

Susan Tanaka didn't seem too keen on the idea, Tommy observed.

He stood in the open midway hatch of the swap-out and watched the rain fall outside.

"Sorry," Tommy said. "Overruled."

"You can't do that!" Susan snapped across the satellite phone.

"Look, it sounds stupid, but we don't have a better choice. I'm going to need your bureaucratic sorcery. Keep the FAA off our backs. And keep Del Wildman from firing my sorry ass until we find these terrorists."

When she replied, he heard the concern in her voice, overriding the anger. "Tommy, this breaks every rule. You're screwing with a vital piece of evidence! You're fleeing a crime scene!"

"I'm following the instructions of the senior law-enforcement official on the scene, so it's not fleeing. And we're trying to solve the downing of

CascadeAir Flight Eight One Eight, not the swap-out. So this bird isn't evidence." It sounded like pure, unadulterated horse crap, even to his own ears, but he no longer cared. "Look, I gotta go. This is insane and stupid and impetuous and reckless and just plain nuts. I'll stipulate to all of that. But he killed John. He's gonna kill more folks."

Susan didn't reply, not right away. "I disapprove of this and recommend against it. That goes in the official record."

Tommy said, "Agreed."

"Good luck. I'll keep the dogs off your heels as long as I can."

Isaiah Grey stood beneath the wing of the swap-out, the hood of his NTSB windbreaker up. He and the off-duty deputy had transferred John Roby's body to the Land Rover.

"You sure about this?" the cop asked.

"Yeah. We're pulling out. Can you take care of John until the rest of the police get here?"

"Um, well, yeah. But . . ." The kid, all of twenty-seven, was way out of his league. "You sure it's okay, you taking off in that thing?"

"This?" Isaiah reached over and patted the portside landing gear, smiled at it. "Yeah. She'll take care of us."

"I don't know. . . ."

Isaiah said, "You ever hear of anyone flying a crashed airliner away from the scene?"

The cop gulped. "No, sir."

"Me, neither. Can't be a law on the books if nobody's ever tried it before. Right?"

And—absurdly, amazingly—the cop agreed.

Isaiah returned to the interior of the liner.

"Okay. John's in good hands. We ready?" He brushed back his hood. Tommy, Ray, and Kiki gave him appreciative looks.

Ray said, "Yeah. Thanks—"

"You can thank me if I don't turn this bird into the world's biggest corkscrew. For now, you and Tommy take a seat and strap your asses in. And if you've never given any thought to a personal relationship with Jesus of Nazareth, now would be the time."

Kiki started to sit down.

"Not you. You're copilot."

Her jaw dropped. "What are you talking about? The last plane I piloted was mounted outside the grocery store in my hometown and it rocked for a nickel a minute!"

"Burke walked. Proving at least one of us has the sense God gave a hamster. Sorry, Kiki, you were a bridge officer on a nuclear submarine. That makes you the closest thing I've got to an aviator. C'mon."

He stormed onto the flight deck. Kiki turned to Tommy, her eyes narrowed. The temperature in first class took a dip. "You owe me, Tomzak."

And she followed Isaiah.


"This is the part where we go through our preflight mantra," Isaiah said, tightening his shoulder straps. "But since none of that stuff will make any sense to you, we'll just skip right along to the next thing: getting airborne."

"Isaiah." Kiki reached over and touched his forearm. "We're doing the right thing."

Isaiah said, "Famous last words," and kicked over engine number one.


Turning the Vermeer around involved crossing the median. If they got stuck in the mud, their harebrained stunt would be over before it began. But they didn't get stuck.

The giant jetliner turned slowly, creaking onto the empty southbound lanes of Interstate 5. The road ahead was still empty of moving vehicles. People who'd pulled off to the side sat in their cars, eyes glued to the spectacle they'd be telling their grandchildren about in decades to come.

Lining up on the fast lane, the Vermeer's wings hung over the shoulder of the road to the left and over one of the northbound lanes to the right. Isaiah goosed the engines and began rolling back down the highway.

The plane picked up speed, spraying a V of rainwater in front of it, two horizontal tornadoes of swirling water forming behind it. Isaiah's hands nudged the throttle controls forward, nodding to himself as if he'd done this a thousand times on a thousand different highways.

"Looking good," Kiki shouted over the roar. She wasn't fooling either of them. She had no idea how it was looking. Isaiah appreciated the cheerleading nonetheless.

*Of course,* he reminded himself, *she doesn't know about the overpass lurking in the gloom ahead.*

## MARION COUNTY

Walter Mulroney was at the wheel of one of the Sentras as Peter Kim pored over a badly folded map, trying to find his way through a labyrinth of twisting rural roads that connected downtown Valence to Salem without getting on the clogged I-5. The men careened around a muddy corner and Peter said, "Left here. Left! Your other left!"

Walter cranked it to the left. Visibility was pretty bad, and it took him a moment to realize that they were crossing an overpass above the highway. "There are straight-shot farm roads on the west side of I-Five," Peter explained. "We should be able to get even with those idiots, then hike to the highway on foot. Then, we'll just talk them out of this stu—"

Walter stomped on the brakes. The Sentra skidded, the nose coming around. They stopped, halfway across the overpass, facing the wrong way.

"What the hell?" Peter spat. He knew Walter didn't approve of obscenities, but he didn't much care. "Are you out—"

The shriek of the Vermeer's four massive engines battered the car like a physical force. The wide-body rose from the south, blotting out the clouds, hurling its shadow across the raised roadway and the Sentra, blocking the rain, if only for a second.

Walter leaned forward, mouth open, eyes staring up at the retracting landing gear. He could see wear patterns on the treads of the great tires.

Peter stared up, too. The sliding, floating mass of metal over his head reminded him of a scene from *Close Encounters of the Third Kind*.

The Vermeer passed on by.

Its thrust tube of rainwater hit the Sentra a second later, rocking the car, maxing out its shock absorbers, lifting both right-side wheels off the road for just a second.

Then the jet was gone, the wake vortex dissipating into the clouds. The Sentra quaked back down onto its shock absorbers.

Walter and Peter sat there for a while. Finally, they looked at each other.

Walter Mulroney's voice cracked. "Fuck! Me!"

# 49

THE SUN WAS BRUTAL. Even Daria's Middle Eastern complexion and upbringing couldn't alter that fact. At least, by being cuffed to the clothes pole, her shadow had cooled it enough so that she could lean back against it without blistering.

Every breath was a fine agony. Her tongue played along the teeth on her left side, found a cracked tooth.

Sweat discolored the ground beneath her. Pretty soon, she'd stop sweating. That's when heatstroke would set in.

Grunting with pain, she curled her legs up against her butt. She twisted, reaching for her boot. The razor blade was still there. Big deal. If there was an old spy trick for defeating a regulation pair of FBI-issue handcuffs with a double-sided razor, they hadn't taught it in the Mossad. It didn't even make a decent weapon—being sharp on both sides, she'd be as likely to slice open her own hand as any attacker.

Her mouth was dry and she tasted dust on her teeth. Between each labored breath, her thoughts fell morbidly on her case agent, Ray Calabrese. She'd failed him, and she knew with icy certainty that failing Ray meant dooming some airliner.

As the thought fermented in her head, the sound of another jet fought through the fog of fury and recrimination. She glanced up, squinting. A twin-engine aircraft cleft the cloudless sky. Two more old vapor trails were visible.

Daria didn't know any of the details, but she suddenly realized the strategic value of this festering excuse for a motel. It sat beneath a bustling air corridor leading to the airports of Southern California.

## OVER ROSEBURG, OREGON

The swap-out sliced through silver-gray clouds, soaring into the bright blue sky of southern Oregon. It was going on 5 P.M.

Isaiah Grey relaxed his grip a little. When he looked over, Kiki winked at him.

He reached for the intraship PA system. "You boys can get up now. This bus is so light, it'll only take us about two hours to reach L.A."

He clicked off the system and leaned back. "So. You and Tommy, huh?"

Kiki's face burned a bright pink. "Isaiah!"

"Oh, please." He rolled his eyes. "This morning was the first time that man has smiled since he hit Oregon. Go get him. I'll hail regional air traffic, declare an NTSB emergency and let them know why we're in the air. Honestly? I think we're the only craft flying today. Should have the sky to ourselves until we clear this weather."

## OVER CHICO, CALIFORNIA

Dennis could barely feel the thrum of the engines of the luxurious Gulfstream. He'd been in Cadillacs that had bumpier rides. He leaned back, admired the burnished wood paneling of the fuselage, the big-screen TV with satellite feed, the well-kept furniture, the full bar. This, he thought, was the life. Soon, it would be his life.

The pilot's voice drifted over the PA. "Sir? We're about an hour out of LAX. Is there anything we can do for you?"

"Yes. Divert to Victorville Airport."

He listened to the hiss of the PA system. "Ah, we can do that. It's not much of an airfield. Are you sure?"

"Yes," Dennis said, and snuggled deeper into the fantastically comfortable seat.

## OVER TWIN FALLS, IDAHO

David Singh swiveled in his seat. "Can I have the PA, then?"

Behind him, Teddy McCoy pulled on his Mickey Mouse ears and flicked the appropriate toggles, activated the PA system, then nodded to David.

The captain adjusted the microphone attached to his headset. "Good evening, ladies and gentlemen. The good news is, we're facing less head wind that I'd anticipated. We should be reaching Los Angeles in a little under two hours."

The Sinn Fein members exchanged looks. The Ulster Unionists exchanged looks. They sat on the upper deck of the double-decker jet—actually higher than the flight deck, which was located forward and directly between the upper and lower seating areas. The delegates occupied seats in the first ten rows of the jet, and, if it had been configured differently, this definitely would have been first class.

As it was, the A380 had been configured to make the most money possible for the first five years of its life. That is: it was all economy seating throughout the vast fuselage.

In this configuration, the jet carried 838 passengers. They, plus the 9 crew members, accounted for a staggering 847 souls.

Almost six times the number of people who'd been on board Cascade-Air Flight 818.

## BOCA SERPIENTE, CALIFORNIA

It hurt like hell doing it, but Daria edged herself around the pole. She was no longer facing the sun. At least she didn't have to squint, and the sunburn would cover her arms and legs and midriff evenly. *It's important to keep up appearances,* she told herself. She tried to approximate a smile, which just opened her split lip again.

"Lovely day, isn't it."

Keith O'Shea, the dark-haired Irishman, had sauntered up behind her. Daria bent forward, covered her mouth with one arm stretched around the pole, and coughed dryly into her fist.

O'Shea circled in front of her and lowered himself to his haunches, close enough that their knees touched. He wore a wifebeater and a red bandanna around his neck. A Glock model 27 was stuffed in his belt. He held a bottle of water and a long military knife with a serrated six-inch blade and a handle made of black polymer.

He grinned at her, a handsome rake of a man who knew, in his heart, that every woman desired him.

"Drink?"

Daria stared up at him, breathing shallow.

"No?" He took a long gulp. "He shouldn't've trusted you. O'Meara, that is. He was always a wanker."

Daria said, "Think so?" but her voice was husky and as dry as gunpowder, the words slurred as if her tongue had swollen to match her parched, cracked lips. Her hair hung lank in front of her eyes and she stared at him through the straight, black locks.

"Johnser, too," O'Shea said. He reached over and ran the tip of his knife along the muscles of her calf. The tip left a soft red trail as it passed.

Daria stared at him through her hair. O'Shea smiled languidly and shifted his weight, one hand down on the ground, shoulder softly touching Daria's shoulder. The knifepoint drew along her exposed thigh. He sipped more water.

"Why here?" she asked, the words more or less intelligible.

He shrugged. "We've a friend who can drop an airliner in our laps. The only reason we're here is, sometimes people walk away from plane crashes, don't they. Our job's to make sure no one walks away from this one."

And this far out into the Mojave Desert, Daria knew, they could swoop in and take care of any survivors long before rescue crews could arrive.

"There are . . . Catholics . . . aboard?" It was difficult to understand her, her words were so slurred.

O'Shea winked at her. "Ye need to speak up, lass. Catholics? Oh, aye. There're IRA butchers on board, to be sure, but we could kill those fuckers at will, and twice on Sunday. No, we're aimed at the Protestant delegates."

Daria looked confused.

"Jay-sus, girl. Killing a Catholic is something any of us could do—did do—by the time we were seventeen. But these fucking delegates? They're talking about giving the land to the pope. They're pissing away Ireland, a bit at a time. When we crash this jet and kill the Catholics, we'll show them the respect any soldier shows his enemy. It'll be a military death, dignified-like. But the Protestants? They're bugs. I'm hoping they survive the crash. I'm hoping to kneecap them and watch the desert take 'em."

*He'd enjoy it, too,* she thought.

"Plus, fucking the Good Friday Accord on American soil, destroying an airplane, it'll be 9/11 all over again. Remember how badly the Yanks screwed Iraq? We'll finally be rid of their meddling."

He took a hit of the water, his Adam's apple bobbing. Wiped his lips with the back of his hand. "Look, lass. This is crap, this. Chaining you up like a dog, in this sun. O'Meara has no idea how to treat a lady. That's always been his problem."

Daria dredged up enough saliva to say, "Oh?"

O'Shea winked at her. His hand rose and the knife danced along his knuckles, flipped easily end over end and returning to his palm, like some sort of conjurer's trick. He handled it like a virtuoso, studying her eyes for fear.

"We need to know who you are and who you work for. Where your mates are. What they're planning. All of that. But we'll get fuck-all doing it O'Meara's way. It's ham-handed."

Daria raised the outer curves of her eyebrows in question.

The knife flashed and the shirt button between her breasts spiraled away, landing in a puff of dust. Only the knot of her shirttails held the cloth together under her breasts.

"My way's better," O'Shea whispered. The knifepoint glided along the inner curve of her breast.

Daria let her torso edge forward, leaned into the knife. "Give us a kiss," she slurred.

O'Shea didn't know if it was heatstroke or a trick, or if she got off on it. But he was no fool. He reached around, tested the cuffs on her wrists. They were secure.

The knife danced easily over his knuckles again. He slammed it into the ground, half the blade disappearing into the dirt. He leaned in, grabbed the back of her head, and kissed her. It was a hungry kiss, openmouthed. He felt her tongue, dry as sandpaper, slip past his lips.

Daria took the deepest breath she could and exhaled for all she was worth, as if giving O'Shea CPR. Her rib made a creaking noise and spots danced before her eyes.

She had no spit to give, but when she'd coughed into her fist, she'd slid the two-edged razor onto the dry surface of her tongue. When she blew into his mouth, it shot off her tongue and lodged itself in the soft tissue at the back of Keith O'Shea's throat.

O'Shea's eyes flared open and he pulled back. He had absolutely no idea what was happening. It felt like a live electrical wire had touched the back of his skull. He tried to say something but the act of moving his tongue filled his mouth with hot, sticky blood.

His hands rose to his throat. He gagged, the gag reflex increasing the pain in his head a hundredfold. He leaned forward, blood drooling from between his lips. He tried to close his mouth and felt like his tongue was caught on fire. The water bottle fell to the ground, water gurgling onto the hardpan.

He rose to his feet.

Daria kicked out her legs, caught O'Shea at the ankle. She cried out, the broken ends of her rib grinding together. O'Shea fell like a brick, landing on his ass, hands around his throat, eyes wide with terror. His chin, neck, and chest were coated in blood. Air bubbles popped around his lips as he tried to speak.

Daria braced herself on one elbow, knew that this would hurt them both, maybe equally, and drove the heel of her boot into O'Shea's balls. He grunted and rolled into the fetal position, his face red and puffy, eyes wide.

Daria was crying from the pain as she used the toe of her boot to nudge the Glock out of his belt. It hit the dust and she used her boot to crab the gun closer.

A car pulled into the parking lot and Donal O'Meara was on his feet in an instant, his Colt drawn. He moved the curtain a half inch and snuck a peek.

The newcomer drove a Lexus Coupe, a rooster tail of dust following. The door opened and Lucas Bell stepped out, wearing a casual, button-down shirt, untucked, sleeves rolled up, and sunglasses.

O'Meara smiled. "Friends in high places."

"I hope Keith doesn't kill that bitch," Feargal Kelly said, eyes on the football match.

"Sod it. O'Shea's a pro. And he's good at getting information from people. Especially women."

O'Meara unlocked the door. In truth, he didn't have much use for rapists. But then again, this was war. Soldiers didn't always get to pick the tools of their trade.

Daria heard a car door shut. She thought about yelling for help but squashed that notion immediately. It was either another ally of O'Meara's or an innocent bystander she'd manage to get killed.

It would have been easy enough to take O'Shea's gun and shoot the cuffs. Easy, but loud. Instead, she kept kicking him in the balls, paralyzing him until he asphyxiated from breathing his own blood. Then, grunting in pain, Daria used her feet to drag him closer. She undid his belt and removed it. As she had hoped, the tine of his buckle was almost exactly the right shape to pick the lock on her cuffs.

That took a couple of minutes. It took two more before she could rise shakily to her feet. Her head swam, bile rose in her throat. But she didn't fall over.

Picking up the empty water bottle, she let a few drops fall on her tongue. Tossed it aside, found the Glock. Daria stumbled toward the front office.

## 50

SHE PEEKED AROUND THE first corner. State Route 247 was vacant, little dust devils prancing across the tarmac, heat ripples distorting her vision.

Daria limped to the next corner and glanced into the parking lot. The motorcycles were gone. So was the van, leaving only two stolen Jeeps and a sleek, black sedan. She snuck around the corner, keeping her shoulder against the faded aluminum siding, and slid along the wall until she reached the office. She opened the door carefully, remembering that it had squeaked when she'd checked them in.

There was nobody behind the counter. Daria circled the counter, one hand holding the automatic, the other pressed gently against her snapped rib.

The manager lay on his back behind the counter, a neat hole in his forehead. From the pool of sticky blood and the buzzing of flies, she doubted that the exit wound was as tidy. He must have been shot while she was unconscious.

She stepped over the manager and into the apartment behind. Turned on the light. Conway Twitty began twanging from a cheap radio plugged into the same wall socket that worked the lights. She turned down the music. There was a rocking chair next to it and a pile of *Reader's Digest*s. Other than having a tiny kitchen and a bedroom, the apartment was every bit as soulless as the rooms for rent.

Daria spotted the phone but, first things first, limped into the kitchen. The floor tiles were mushroom gray and peeled back at places. There had been a pattern to the wallpaper but it had faded into near nothingness. Daria found a cup of lukewarm coffee and tossed out its contents. She turned on the tap. Dull gray water gurgled out. She filled the cup, took a sip, gently letting it seep down her throat. If she drank too fast and coughed, her rib would punish her. The kitchen smelled of bad vegetables. An almost full pot of coffee had been left plugged in, the coffee obsidian black and smelling like it had been cooking for half the day.

She poured more water into the cup and dumped it over her head. It felt fantastic on her tender, red skin. She cupped water in her hand and splashed it softly onto her face, chest, and neck.

Revived, she limped back to the living room and eased herself down onto a stained sofa. She set down the gun, reached for the aged Princess phone. She thought about calling Ray Calabrese's cell but remembered that he was in Oregon, at that crash site. Daria's Mossad training had included memorization techniques. She tried the number to Ray's office.

The Irishmen turned when Lucas Bell's cell phone chimed. Lucas reached for it. He had rigged a call-forwarding from Ray Calabrese's office.

"Ray Calabrese's office."

"This is Daria Gibron."

His eyes went wide. He made the finger-to-the-lips gesture to shut up the others. Her voice sounded chalky.

"What? Wow. We'd given up hopes of hearing from you. It's me, Lucas." He put his hand over the phone, but lightly, and said, "It's Ms. Gibron. Get Ray on the line, now. And trace this." He removed his hand. "Ms. Gibron?"

A snarl on his features, Donal O'Meara drew his Colt and moved to the motel room door. Kelly followed, heading toward the front of the motel.

"Yes. We're outside a town called Boca Serpiente, in California.

Somewhere north and east of Los Angeles, in the desert. The Irishmen are here. They're making their stand."

"I understand," Lucas said. "Are you all right?"

"I'm fine. One of them told me they plan to crash a jetliner that passes overhead. I don't know how. They're armed to the teeth, handguns, shotguns, and one sniper rifle. And they said more cohorts are on their way. But this is the staging area. It happens here."

"Got it," Lucas said. "How'd you get free? Are you armed?"

"Yes, I have a gun. Where's Ray?"

"He's still in Oregon, checking out that crash. I'm leading a crack team your way right now. Are you in the same building as the Irishmen?"

"They're in a motel room. I'm in the front office."

"And they're both armed?"

In the manager's apartment, Daria said, "Yes. I'm . . ."

And a certain, uncanny dread crept through Daria's skin, the chill almost counteracting the sting of the soft burns on her arms and stomach.

*Both.* Lucas had known there were only two Irishmen left.

The door to the office squeaked. She caught a glimpse of fair hair. She raised the Glock and flicked off the safety in one motion, fired once. The head ducked back out the door.

She slammed down the phone.

In room 3 of the Land's End Motel, Lucas Bell hurled the cell phone onto the bed. "Goddammit!"

O'Meara and Kelly entered. O'Meara's eyes were narrow and cold. "You were right, O'Shea's dead."

Kelly nodded. "Aye, and she's got his gun."

"You fucking incompetents!" Lucas hissed.

O'Meara ground his teeth, the muscles along his jawline twitching.

Lucas pinched the bridge of his nose, willed himself to calm down. He looked at the two Irishmen. They looked back.

Lucas sighed. "Would you for God's sake cut the damn phone lines? Please?"

.   .   .

Daria lifted the receiver, heard a dial tone. She hit 911.

She kept the stolen gun aimed at the door, but was aware that she had windows to her left and right to worry about. Damn old-fashioned phone, she felt hobbled by the wire leading to the wall socket.

"Nine One One. Police, fire, or—"

The line went dead in her hands. She tossed the useless thing aside.

*Took them long enough,* she groused to herself. *Amateurs.*

## 51

THE SWAP-OUT VERMEER CRUISED along at 550 miles per hour, making splendid time. All four people on board wished the wide-body could go twice as fast.

Tommy and Ray had joined the other two on the flight deck. It was crowded, but they'd quickly grown bored, sitting in first class and waiting.

Kiki had been given a crash course on how to fly the jet, and then had asked Isaiah not to use the word *crash* for the rest of the flight. She didn't understand a tenth of the avionics equipment in front of her, but the global-positioning-system monitor was kith and kin to the locator system installed on her last nuclear sub. She quickly typed in their position and speed, and the screen glowed with a map of the western United States, a dotted line marking the route before them, a solid line the route behind.

After ten or fifteen minutes of listening to the engines rumble, Ray said, to no one in particular, "We're in good shape here. Right?"

Tommy shrugged. "I guess."

Ray stuck a stick of gum into his mouth, waved the pack at Tommy, who took a slice.

They rode for another minute.

Ray hefted his right pant leg and exposed a small leather holster. He withdrew his backup weapon, a thin, matte-black Kahr K9. He checked to see that it had a full load and returned it, saying, "So how come I feel like we're still in it up to our ears?"

"I've got that feeling, too," Kiki said. "Like we're forget— Hold it. Got 'em." She pointed one unvarnished fingernail at the GPS monitor. "Albion Air Flight Three Twenty-six. There are the delegates."

Isaiah let his eyes flicker away from the mass of dials and sensors before him. "Holy crap."

The others looked at him.

"Look at the transponder numbers. That's an Airbus A Three Eighty."

"I've read about them," Kiki said. "Supposed to be gargantuan. Holds five hundred people or more."

"More," Isaiah said. "The first generation is geared for all-economy flight. Shoehorn as many people aboard as possible and pay off the debt that it took to build these beasts."

"Okay." Tommy thought about it for a moment. "So how many folks on board?"

Isaiah said, "Full flight? Figure eight hundred plus."

"Are you shitting me?"

"Nope." The pilot shook his head in awe. "I've lived in towns with smaller populations than that bird. They're lining up with the Rapids. We'll get to L.A. almost a half hour ahead of them."

They rode along a little longer. Tommy rubbed at a kink in his neck. "You're right," he said to Ray. "I got the feeling, too. What have we forgotten?"

## VICTORVILLE AIRPORT

When Dennis Silverman stepped down from the Gulfstream III, his first impression was the heat. It seeped into his lungs and made his eyes water.

"Oh, man," he whined.

He dashed to the rented Jeep awaiting him, his shirt beginning to stain around the armpits before he stepped down to the bottom of the ladder.

## GAMELAN INDUSTRIES, BEAVERTON

Gamelan co-owner Alexi Jacobian reached into a desk drawer for an industrial-size bottle of Tums. He tossed five into his palm and popped them into his mouth, chewing.

"I do not believe this," Jacobian moaned, eyeing the Employee of the Month wooden plaque just outside his office. "Are you positive?"

Susan Tanaka said, "Yes. Absolutely."

He cradled his head in his hands. "Maybe you missed something. Maybe—"

Peter Kim said, "Do you own a corporate jet?"

"Yes. A Gulfstream."

"Does it have a Gamelan FDR?"

"Of course."

Peter said, "Then I can crash it. Want to see?" His tone was brusque, unfriendly. That's why Susan had brought him along. In the land of the Geek Gods, engineer-speak was the lingua franca.

Jacobian groaned and threw three more Tums into his mouth. "The irony is, Dennis has the jet. He flew to California this afternoon."

Susan cursed herself silently. She should have suggested looking for a private jet, after the police had failed to find Silverman at any of the regional airports.

"This is insane. Do you know what this will do to my company?"

Susan's eyes narrowed. Her first instinct was to blow up at him for being so unfeeling. Instead, she said, "Of course, your assistance with this investigation will be duly noted. I'll make sure the media is aware of your help."

He brightened a little at that. "Anything. Name it."

"We need to find Mr. Silverman. Do you know where he went?"

Jacobian said, "Sure. California."

Peter's voice dropped half an octave. "Could you be a little less specific? We'd like this to be a challenge."

Jacobian reddened. "I don't know where his conference was. I didn't ask. But I know where the Gulfstream is."

"You do?"

"Sure. I told you, it has a Gamelan recorder on board."

Peter rolled his eyes. "Of course. They can track the Gamelans. I should have realized that."

Jacobian rose. "Come on. I'll show you."

## OVER CALIFORNIA

Ray Calabrese checked his watch. It was going on 6 P.M. He knelt and yanked a box from under the flip-down seat. It contained a variety of survival equipment, including a flare gun, heavy field glasses, a portable compass, and military-style food rations. He sorted through the inventory, hoping not to need any of it.

Tommy's satellite-comm link chirped. "Tomzak."

"Tommy, Susan. We tracked down Dennis Silverman. He landed in Victorville."

Tommy pointed to Kiki's ear. She adjusted the controls on her belt and tapped in to their frequency. "Susan? It's Kiki. Say that again."

She did, and Kiki punched data into the GPS monitor to her left. The airfield outside Victorville, not far from George Air Force Base, glowed.

"Why there?" Tommy asked. "Why not L.A.? We thought that's where the ambush was planned."

Susan said, "I don't know. Maybe they know something we don't."

"Like that'd be a fucking change of pace."

He rang off and told Isaiah Grey the news. "Should I head there?"

Ray said, "Seems as good a place as any."

As Isaiah began calculating for the course correction, a thought tickled Tommy's brain. "Hey. What'd you mean earlier, when you said the delegates were lining up for the Rapids?"

"A little pilot humor. There's a corridor of airspace in the middle of California, over the Bristol Mountains. Everyone flying from the Midwest or the East Coast flies the same route. Commercial pilots used to call it the Rapids. The traffic can get a little busy around there."

Ray perked up. "Can you show us?"

Isaiah turned to his alleged copilot. "Bring up a display of the whole state, will you?"

She tapped keys. California came up on the GPS screen.

"See that little blob of yellow, east of San Bernardino?" Isaiah pointed. "That's a combat training center for the marine corps. And that blob of yellow up and to the right? That's Fort Erwin and—"

"China Lake," Kiki cut in. "It's the Naval Air Warfare Center. Part and parcel with White Sands and Point Mugu. I did six months at China Lake. We were testing a new sonar array."

"They're all restricted airspace," Isaiah said. "No-fly zones. So every commercial job bopping in from the east climbs to thirty thousand feet and flies the Rapids, right between those two bases. After you get out, TRACON—the regional air-traffic control—lines you up for LAX or John Wayne or wherever you . . ."

The words died on his lips.

"That's it," Tommy said. He reached over Kiki's shoulder and prodded the map monitor. "That's where the ambush is. Right in the middle of the Mojave Desert."

Tommy ran his finger from the bright dot that was Albion Air Flight 326, just leaving Nevada airspace, between the two military bases with their no-fly zones, on to L.A. On the way, his finger slid directly over the cross that represented the tiny Victorville Airport.

And five miles to the west, the tiny hamlet of Boca Serpiente.

## BOCA SERPIENTE, CALIFORNIA

Lucas Bell said, "Would someone tell me why the hell that bitch is still alive?"

O'Meara glowered at him. "Mind telling us how she kicked your ass in L.A.?"

Lucas turned his reflecting sunglasses toward the Irishman, no emotions on his face. He didn't even look all that hot. "I entered the apartment building to warn you that the FBI was onto you, but she clocked me. Also, as I've told you, she killed Riley."

O'Meara nodded.

"I tried to get that damn message machine in Atlanta back online, so I could tell you about her. But I'd hoped you'd taken the initiative and killed her long before now, just to be on the safe side."

"Shut up, you." O'Meara's fist squeezed the butt of his .357. "The situation's devolved and I fucking well know it, don't I. But the geek is on his way with his flipping box of wonders. The delegates are on their way. Everything's going by the book, except this lot."

He waved the revolver toward the motel's office. "Believe me, Bell. Everything's under control."

They heard the low rumble of a car engine, heard gravel crunch under tires. Lucas turned and pushed aside the faded, filthy curtain.

A California Highway Patrol unit rounded the building, pulled into the parking lot.

Lucas Bell said, "Everything's under control? Well, that's a relief."

## OVER CALIFORNIA

"Albion Air Three Two Six. Three Two Six. This is November Tango Sierra Bravo One. Come in, Three Two Six. Over."

Isaiah waited for his hails to be acknowledged. Tommy said, "What are you gonna tell them?"

"To divert to Las Vegas. Once they get between those two bases, there isn't enough room to turn these big wide-bodies around."

## OVER NEVADA

Teddy McCoy activated the communications array and reached forward to tap the copilot, Eloise Pool, on her left epaulette.

"November Tango, this is Albion Three Two Six." You wouldn't know she was from Cardiff because she almost never spoke, but when she did, her elongated vowels gave her away. "We know about your situation. You are ordered to leave this airspace. Over."

After a crackle of interference, the Vermeer responded. "Say again, Three Two Six. Over."

"November Tango, we have been alerted to your status," Eloise said. "You are in a stolen airliner, and you're on some sort of renegade mission. LAX has informed us to ignore your hails. As one pilot to another, sir, I advise you to land that aircraft as soon as possible and turn yourselves in to the authorities. Three Two Six out."

In the left-hand seat, David Singh made the throat-cutting gesture and Teddy disconnected the call.

"Cheeky bastards!" the captain marveled. "Stealing an airliner!"

## OVER CALIFORNIA

Silence held court in the cockpit. Ray reached for his cell phone. "Taking this bird was a risk, but someone's overreacting. I'll take care of it."

## 52

ANOTHER CAR ENTERED THE parking lot but Daria couldn't get close enough to a window to see who it was. She looked around the apartment, counted one doorway and three windows, one each in the living room, bedroom, and kitchen. Each was a potential threat.

Keeping low, she returned to the kitchen and gulped more water. She'd begun sweating again; a good sign. She'd been perilously close to heatstroke. She returned to the living room, kept low, and hit the light switch, cutting off the room's only lamp and the country music radio station.

Now the only question was, would they lay siege to the office, or would they trap her in there and go on about their business? After all, they had the advantages of numbers and weapons. It could go either way.

She started to worry about how Agent Bell had known that there were only two Irishmen left. It had to mean he was there, and that he was running with the villains. How was he involved? Who else in the FBI could be trusted?

*No.* She waved those thoughts away. How didn't matter. Time enough to worry about that when Ray got there.

*Get here, Ray.*

. . .

Lucas Bell presented his FBI credentials to the trooper who stepped out of the dusty prowl car and donned his wide-brimmed hat. "Got yourselves a situation here?" the trooper asked.

"Situation and a half," Lucas admitted sheepishly. "And I've only got these two undercover agents with me. How soon can you get us some backup?"

The trooper puffed up, excited to be asked. Other than traffic tickets, this had been the dullest of weeks. "Nearest station is in Barstow. That's thirty-five minutes away. I can scramble half-a-dozen units."

"Thirty-five minutes?" Lucas said. "Great. That's all we need."

He shot the trooper in the forehead.


## OVER CALIFORNIA

Ray drew his cell phone and balanced himself as Isaiah eased the jet into a soft, portside turn. He hit speed dial number two.

*Ding.* "Under the auspices of the Patriot Act, this number has been temporarily disconnected." *Click.*

*What the hell?* The others didn't notice the confused look on Ray's face. He hit speed dial again. Got the same message.

He dug out his wallet and found a laminated card. He called Henry Deits's direct number.

*Ding.* "Under the auspices of the Patriot Act, this number has been temporarily disconnected." *Click.*

He tried Lucas's direct line.

*Ding.* "Under the auspices of the Patriot Act, this number has been temporarily disconnected." *Click.*

"Guys?" he said, and the others turned. "We have a complication."


Kiki went online and found the number for the nearest FBI field office, in San Francisco. Ray reached a voice tree and asked the computer for Dale Hiroda. They'd worked together before.

"Hiroda."

"Dale? Ray Calabrese. Hey, there's a problem in L.A. There's either been an earthquake or someone's drawn a firewall. Can you—"

The man on the other end hissed, his voice low to avoid anyone else hearing, "Christ almighty, Ray! What the hell do you think you're doing?"

Ray said, "I'm on a tight clock here. Something's wrong in L.A. Lucas—"

"D.C. has transferred operational authority to San Fran. Now get that damn jet on the ground! This stupid incident will cost you your job, but if you come to earth now, it doesn't have to land your ass in prison."

"There isn't time for this shit, Hiroda! The ambush isn't in L.A. It's out in the Mojave. You've got to tell that Albion Air flight to turn around and head to Vegas. Tell them—"

"Get out of the air now, Calabrese. That's a direct order."

"Get Lucas Bell! He'll—"

"Shit," the agent on the ground cut in. "Bell's the one who told D.C. you went rogue. We don't know who in L.A. you've dragged into this, but as of now, that field office is in the tall grass. San Francisco is in charge. And we're not listening to your shit. I don't know how you hooked up with these terrorists, but you've had your last warning. Land. Now."

He hung up.

Ray almost fell into the fold-away chair behind Isaiah.


## BOCA SERPIENTE, CALIFORNIA

Daria duckwalked to the kitchen, holding her side. She dug around under the sink and in the cupboards and found an old, mustard-yellow blender. She tossed the lid aside and emptied the entire pot of bitter, burned coffee into it. She found glass salt-and-pepper shakers with tin tops, unscrewed them, and emptied them into the blender.


Lucas Bell climbed into the prowl car and came back out with the trooper's Remington 870 magnum shotgun, plus a box of shells. Kelly emerged from their motel room with two of the Benelli shotguns. He tossed one to O'Meara.

Lucas said, "Where the hell's the geek?"

"He should've landed in Victorville by now. He's cutting it close."

"Where's the ambush?"

O'Meara pointed to a mesa, a half mile away. It was perfectly flat and roughly the size of a soccer pitch, only twenty feet higher than the land where they stood. As he did, a Jeep appeared, right where he was pointing. "That's him, now."

. . .

On the mesa, Dennis shut off the engine and squinted down at the motel, half a mile away. "What are they waiting for?"

He climbed out, stunned again by the heat, and began to set up his transceiver.

Lucas watched Dennis climb out of the Jeep. "We don't need surprises from the Gibron woman," he told O'Meara and Kelly. "I'll take this side. You guys go around to the other two. Fifteen shells each. Let's see if she's awake."

The men stationed themselves to the east, south, and north of the office and began firing shotgun shells. Thick, ragged holes appeared in the aluminum siding and the poorly insulated, thin wooden walls within.

The sound echoed and reverberated for miles in every direction. Nobody in the nearby town of Boca Serpiente, less than a mile away, was stupid enough to go see who was shooting what.

Daria cried out in pain when she shoved the refrigerator away from the wall. She created an opening maybe a foot wide and knelt there, head buried in her arms. Theirs wasn't a bad strategy, she admitted. It lacked subtlety but, as the kitchen began disintegrating all around her, subtlety seemed a cheap commodity. A shotgun blast slammed into the Formica countertop opposite her and a sleet storm of debris wafted down from the ceiling.

Horizontal shafts of late-afternoon light began filling the apartment, dust and smoke and shrapnel glittered in the beams. *With my luck,* Daria thought, *it's probably filled with asbestos.* A hail of shot pocked the fridge, made it rock back against her, knocked the freezer door off its hinges. It clattered to the floor along with a half brick of Neapolitan ice cream.

On the mesa, Dennis twitched as the first shot echoed past him, falling on his ass. "What the hell are they doing down there?" he groused, rubbing dirt off his palms.

## OVER CALIFORNIA

Ray sat in the fold-away seat, a crease bisecting his forehead. He punched Lucas Bell's personal cell-phone number for the fourth consecutive time. There was no answer.

"This guy's your friend?" Tommy asked softly. He was leaning against the right-hand seat, his hand absently resting on Kiki's shoulder.

"Yeah," Ray said. He couldn't take his eyes off the phone. "He is."

The others were quiet for a time. Isaiah said, "We'll pass Albion Three Two Six in about ten minutes, folks. Do we have any options?"

Ray just stared at his phone.

"Could John use his . . . ?" Kiki said, then blanched, a hand over her mouth, eyes wide. "Oh God. I forgot."

Tommy squeezed her shoulder. "Wish to hell the Mad Bomber was here. Ray, I'm sorry, I know this Lucas fella is your friend, but he screwed us royally."

Ray just stared at his phone. "Yeah. He did."


Lucas Bell and the Irishmen fired their last shells into the apartment, then drew handguns and approached the perforated remains of the motel manager's apartment. No window was unshattered, no wall complete. The tiny office and the apartment had been separated by the front desk and a door. The desk had been chewed into kindling, revealing the dead manager's body behind it. The door had been blown off its hinges. A haze of dust and smoke hung in the building, glistening dully in the air.

Kelly entered the office, sweeping his Springfield Armory V-10 automatic in front of him. It felt good to be out of the sun, but his eyes weren't adjusted to the gloom inside.

Lucas and O'Meara stepped carefully up to the holes they'd blasted in the outer walls. A stream of water gurgled up from a broken pipe in the bathroom. Dust obscured their vision.

In the front office, Kelly stepped over the manager's body, the V-10 leveled in front of him. He peered into the apartment, his throat tightening as he inhaled dust. He slipped halfway into the door, reached for the light switch.

The light of one unbroken bulb blinked on. Clint Black began warbling, midsong, from the radio at his left. At his feet sat the lidless blender, ratcheted up to its highest setting, plugged into the same socket as the radio. It kicked on, shooting up a geyser of coffee and pepper and salt. The mixture burned his skin, injected itself into his mouth and nose, blinded him.

Kelly bellowed, stunned by the blistering concoction.


Daria kept her head down until the radio and the blender came to life, followed by a cry of shock. She'd established the angle before the shooting started, knew where the door was relative to her hiding spot. She rose, one knee in the ice cream, and fired twice.

Feargal Kelly screamed.


Lucas Bell peered through a hole in the south wall, saw the light of the dim bulb go on, saw Kelly hit twice in the chest. From his angle, he couldn't see Daria's muzzle flash.

He ducked back, checked his watch. "Damn," he swore softly, holstered his Glock and circled the building, finding O'Meara peering through another hole. "Come on," he said. "They'll be overhead in no time."

"Fuck you," O'Meara shouted. "Kelly! Kelly!"

"He's dead, man. C'mon."

O'Meara stood his ground, an almost feral rage darkening his face. Lucas touched his shoulder and O'Meara yanked his arm back, teeth bared. "Fuck you. She's mine."

"Is she your enemy, or the delegates on that jet?" Lucas asked.

*"She's my enemy!"*

"Good. Fine. Here's a compromise."

Lucas marched to the cop car and popped the trunk. He found what he'd expected: a red plastic container with a gallon of gasoline, plus flares. He marched back to the devastated apartment and said, "Cover me," as he passed O'Meara.

He opened the container and set it on the floor of the front office, tipping it over. Gas began glugging out. He took the safety cap off a flare, lit it, and tossed it deep into the apartment. He launched four more, their sputtering flames flickering in the darkness. He lighted the last one and tossed it into the gallon of gasoline, backpedaling fast before it caught.

The front office went up like dry hay, the fire gusting quickly to the apartment beyond and the other flares.

Lucas said. "Done. Now come on."

## 53

TOMMY SAID, "I'VE GOT an idea. We catch up to the Albion Air flight, then fly directly beneath them, covering their Gamelan receiver thingamabob."

Isaiah said, "They're heading west, Tommy. We're flying east."

A beat, then Tommy said, "Oh."

Ray was still staring at his cell phone. He said, "Did you get Silverman's cell number?"

Tommy rummaged through his shirt pockets and pants pockets, came away with five ripped-up pieces of envelopes or magazine edges. It was his personal filing system. "Um . . . yeah. Here it is."

He handed it over. Ray punched the numbers into his cell phone.

"The customer you are trying to call is out of range," a recorded voice said. "Please try again."

Ray hung up, hit Redial. "The custome—"

He hit it again. "The cus—"

Kiki said, "What's the range of a cell phone?"

"It depends on the power of the cell tower," Isaiah said. "It could be hundreds of miles."

"The custo—" *Click.*

# ABOVE AND AROUND BOCA SERPIENTE

Captain David Singh lined up Albion Air Flight 326 directly between China Lake and the marine weapons center, his four engines purring like contented lions, holding a cruising speed of 900 kilometers per hour; about 560 mph. Behind him, 838 passengers—including Representative Dan Riordan, Republican from California, and the delegates from Northern Ireland—waited patiently.

David Singh had been assigned as captain even before the massive airliner had been assembled at the sprawling, fifty-hectare Jean-Luc Lagardère facility. He'd overseen the assemblage of the central fuselage by the team from Alenia Aeronautica. Had watched the crews from Eurocopter install the three cargo doors and sixteen passenger doors. Had watched the stress testing of the wing-surface composites, courtesy of Hexcel.

He'd even run the initial tests of the state-of-the-art Gamelan flight data recorder.

He'd even blogged and Twittered about it. For a guy in his fifties, David Singh was proud of his social-media skills.

Because he'd been assigned even before the Airbus was built, Singh had unlimited faith in his bird.


"The customer you a—" *Click*. "The cust—" *Click*. "The custom—" *Click*.

Tommy said, "That's a long shot, Ray. It's a big fucking state."

Ray didn't even look up. "The customer you—" *Click*.

"Let him try," Kiki said. "I can't think of anything better."

"The cus—" *Click*.

Tommy rested a hand on her shoulder and she laced her fingers in his. She reached up and back, tousling his hair.

"The custo—" *Click*. "The c—" *Click*. "Hi! This is Dennis! I can't come to the phone now—"

"Got him," Ray said. "We're within range of the same cell tower as Silverman."


Dennis Silverman yelped when his cell thrummed near his kidney. He yanked it off his belt, scanned the LED. One missed call.

He turned, wondering where his cohorts were. It was the first time he'd noticed the column of black smoke rolling out of the hotel, a half mile distant.


Daria realized that remaining holed up in the manager's apartment had pretty much run its course, now that they'd set it on fire. A fire that was spreading quickly, licking the popcorn ceiling and snaking up the curtains in the living room.

The smoke was building. With her broken rib, Daria didn't especially want to do much coughing, so she hunkered low, her head not much higher than her knees, and scampered out of the kitchen and across the living room. She expected the men to be waiting at the holes along the walls, and to fire at her as soon as she became visible. But no shots were fired and she made it all the way to the bedroom and the bathroom.

The shotguns hadn't just shattered the window in the bathroom, they had knocked the window frame out of the wall. A geyser of water splashed up from an exposed pipe. Daria aimed out the hole in the wall, squinting into the sunlight. No one was visible. A fire was the perfect way to drive her out of her hiding spot, but she didn't see any options. She leaned out of the hole in the wall where the window had been, sighting down her barrel to the left, then snapping her head back inside. No one had been waiting to the left. She did the same to the right, surprised to see that no one was there, either.

She heard the Jeep's engine roar to life, gravel slapping against the wall of the motel.

They'd abandoned her to go after their real quarry, she realized.

Daria dipped her head and shoulders into the geyser of water, relishing the cold for a moment, then eased herself out of the hole and onto the hard ground, just as smoke began filling the bathroom.


Kiki studied the GPS monitor. "There's a little town ahead. Boca Serpiente. No airport or anything."

Isaiah said, "Fire," and pointed out the window. Directly ahead of them, they could see a tiny pillar of black smoke rising from what looked like some sort of building. They were twenty thousand feet up in the air and maybe twenty-five miles away from the fire.

"That's got to be them," Ray said. He rummaged through the emergency rations and found the powerful, heavy binoculars. "No such thing as coincidences."

"Dammit." Tommy made a fist and punched the top of Kiki's chair. "Who the hell do we tell? Nobody's listening to us."

"My bosses in the L.A. field office know I haven't gone crazy. I just don't have any way to reach them! Maybe, if I can get a call in to someone else, an agent's spouse, someone who could drive over—"

Isaiah said, "Flight Three Two Six is less than four minutes from Boca Serpiente. And we're only about two minutes away. If your bureaucracy is anything like the air force . . ."

"Shit!" Ray spat. "We can't block their signal. We can't convince the authorities in time."

He turned to Tommy, his face almost purple with rage. "I don't know what to do."

Tommy stared at the column of inky smoke, drawing ever closer.

On the spacious flight deck of the Airbus, Eloise Pool leaned as far forward as her four-point restraints allowed. She turned to David Singh and pointed out the windshield. "Smoke up ahead. Looks like some sort of building on fire."

Singh nodded. He'd seen it, too. He turned to the navigator. "Are you tracking November Tango?"

Teddy McCoy nodded. "Aye, sir. They're heading right at us, holding at two K." That put the renegade jetliner a thousand feet lower than the Airbus. *Good,* Singh thought. *The farther we are when we pass, the better.*

Donal O'Meara and Lucas Bell raced away from the burning building, the Jeep cutting cookies in the gravel.

"Bitch." O'Meara said the word through clenched teeth.

"You're striking a blow for your nation," Lucas said. "I'm striking a blow for my numbered bank account in the Cayman Islands. Think positive thoughts."

A few seconds into the drive, O'Meara shouted, "What about the congressman?"

"Riordan?" Lucas, too, shouted to be heard over the engine, "You can kill him, I guess, but not if it means wasting ammo. I leaked that shit about his being a pedophile to the media three hours ago. Alive or dead, he's of no consequence. Alive will be funnier to watch on CNN."

.    .    .

Kiki held the binoculars pressed against her eyes, scanning the ground before them.

Tommy said, "Oh, hell."

"What?" Isaiah cast a quick look back at him, then returned to his monitors.

Tommy said, "I know what to do."


Dennis Silverman had brought field glasses. He held them against his eyes, peering directly away from the sun, and caught a glint of light off glass or metal, maybe twenty miles away and very high in the air.

He checked his watch. "That's it. Come to papa."


Isaiah said, "Are you out of your goddamn mind?"

Tommy said, "Probably." And admittedly, his suggestion was the stupidest thought he'd ever had. It was the mother of all Hail Marys. "Anybody got any better ideas? Kiki?"

"It's . . ." She shook her head. "Isaiah? It's insane, but it would work."

Tommy said, "New York?"

"Damn, Doc. It's . . . Shit. If I had something better, I'd put it on the table."

Tommy said, "Isaiah?"

He turned in his seat as far as his shoulder restraints would allow. "Just for the record, Dr. Tomzak? I really hate you."

Tommy said, "Line forms on the left," and offered his hand. Isaiah took it.


Now that Daria's adrenaline was backing off a bit, the pain was back. She hobbled to the prowl car and circled the dead officer, then leaned against the sedan and tried to catch her breath. She was badly dehydrated, despite the few gulps of water in the apartment, and her rib was killing her. Her vision blurred for a moment, a wave of vertigo knocking her to one knee. She shook her head hard. "Up, bitch," she growled in Hebrew, and remembered something she'd heard an American television announcer say: "Get your game face on."

She didn't know what it meant, but it sounded right.

Daria tossed the half-empty Glock into the back of the cruiser, in favor of the fully loaded Sig Sauer in the trooper's holster. She knelt and began searching for the keys.

Isaiah Grey drove the swap-out down to one thousand feet to let his spotter have a better chance at seeing the players. He was vectoring on the curling, inky smoke rising from the building, everyone on board assuming that Ray's Rule—no coincidences—meant that the smoke indicated the bad guys' basic location.

"That's them, over there," Kiki said, lowering the field glasses and pointing. On a small rise sat two vehicles of some kind. Three men stood beside the vehicles; it was too far away to identify anyone, but they looked exactly like Walter Mulroney and Peter Kim standing outside their car in Woodburn, Oregon, and waiting to send a signal up to the swap-out.

"I can hear it," Dennis said, grinning, as O'Meara and Lucas Bell stepped out of their Jeep.

*Oh, man!* Dennis thought. Dropping the first bird had been a hell of a lot of fun but—by far—the worst part of it was that he hadn't been there to see the plane crash! Not this time. Front-row seats at half court, Jack Nicholson and Spike Lee. Besides, this time he'd be bagging an A380! Bigger and better. He'd forever be known as the first guy to down the high and mighty Airbus A380. Now that the fucking NTSB knew how he'd done it, he'd have to skip the country. But that was okay. Lucas Bell, his FBI buddy who had first connected him to the Red Hand, would be on the lam, too.

*It'll be like a buddy flick,* Dennis thought.

Tommy, Ray, and Kiki dashed to the back of the jetliner, taking three seats in the very last row, closest to the tail cone. They buckled themselves in, then bent over, their heads in their laps.

"Damn," Dennis said. "It's really loud. Must be the desert."

Lucas lowered his field glasses. "Come on. Let's get the shotguns."

He and O'Meara turned. A hellish image, vectoring in low and swift from the west, made their legs freeze up.

Because the sun was directly behind them and low, the gargantuan shadow shot up behind Dennis, eclipsed his position, and fluttered on like winged death. He jumped, startled. The engine noise was much, much louder now. He turned.

The Vermeer 111 was flying as slowly as possible without stalling. It was twenty feet off the ground and three hundred feet behind the three men.

At that speed, the jet chewed up all three hundred feet in less than two seconds.

Dennis screamed. He recognized the jet. He'd tried to kill it a few hours earlier.

Lucas and O'Meara made last-ditch dives for the cover of a Jeep, knowing it would be like hoping that a Japanese paper screen could stop a freight train.

The landing gear was still stowed. The curved belly of the jet hit the hard-packed sand, skipped once, came down again, and crushed the other Jeep, an axle flipping into the air, slinging into the Vermeer's number-two engine, which exploded.

The nose of the plane gouged a divot in the mesa, then slid off and down the far side, a drop of only twenty feet, but enough to shred the undercarriage of the liner. The Vermeer tipped to the right and both engines were wrenched from the wings, fuel catching fire, the right wing itself snapping and spiraling away from the fuselage.

The jet turned sideways on the slide down the mesa, hit the desert floor at an angle, and cracked in two, just aft of the wings, the latter end of the jet spiraling clockwise as the nose and remaining wing spiraled counterclockwise, away from each other.

A ten-story-high wave of dirt and rock and smashed cactus flared across the desert.

In its wake, one Jeep survived.


David Singh said, "My God!"

The laconic Eloise Pool rose as far as her restraints would allow, peering over the dashboard. "Did you see that, then! That plane pancaked into that mesa! Is that our Vermeer? What the Christ?"

Teddy McCoy toggled the RAIMS communication gear. "You've general broadcast, Captain."

Eloise yelled into his mic, "Mayday, mayday! We have just seen a jetliner crash into the desert, due west of the Cady Mountains and south of Barstow! Repeat: a jetliner is down!"

## VALENCE AIRFIELD

Susan, Walter, and Peter were hunched over telephones or computers, each working feverishly to help their airborne cohorts. Peter had linked one of the other computers to monitor the Radio-Audio Integrated Management System of the Airbus.

All three of them froze, stunned, as the copilot's voice echoed in the vast hangar. "We have just seen a jetliner crash into the desert . . ."

## BOCA SERPIENTE, CALIFORNIA

"No!" Daria pounded on the steering wheel of the patrol car so hard, she almost broke a bone. An airliner was on the ground, smoke rising from its shattered hulk. Tears flowed down her cheeks and she pounded on the wheel again. "Nooo!"

She was shrieking, not caring how much it hurt her side. She stood on the gas pedal, the police car bouncing off a culvert, rising airborne for a moment, then racing after the Jeep.

If she was so damn incompetent she couldn't save the passengers of that jetliner, Daria thought, she'd at least claim vengeance in their names.

Lucas Bell and Donal O'Meara rose from near the remains of the second Jeep, coughing, stunned. The nearby crash had punctured one of Donal's eardrums, but he hadn't realized it yet. The Jeep had been tossed ass-over-teakettle, landing on its side, amazingly missing both men who had dived behind it.

They glared at the carnage. There was no sign of the other Jeep or of their coconspirator. No survivors were stumbling out of the jet's fuselage. At least not yet. Every window was shattered, and the undersection of the jetliner, where the luggage and much of the flight mechanisms were housed, had staved in, leaving a trail of debris beyond. The tail cone, with its empennage, lay thirty feet back and to the left.

O'Meara stuffed his Colt Python into his belt and added a Para-Ordnance

LDA P14, with a five-inch barrel and a black polymer grip. He also grabbed one of the Benelli shotguns lying in the sand, its barrel still warm from decimating the motel's office, and began shoving three-inch shells into it.

Lucas found the Heckler & Koch PSG1 rifle under some sagebrush and slapped home a twenty-round magazine.

"B . . . Bell . . ."

Lucas glanced around. Under what looked like it might once have been an engine block for the other Jeep, he saw a smear of blood and torn cloth. He stepped forward. Dennis Silverman was half buried in sand, his right arm missing, his legs and hips under the tortured, twisted gob of metal.

He was alive. Stunningly, he hadn't lost his glasses.

"Bell . . . get me . . . I can't feel . . . my legs. . . ."

Lucas fell to his knees. "It was a hell of a plan, Dennis. Really. You are something else. You're in a league by yourself."

Dennis spat up blood. "Th . . . thank you. Help me—"

Lucas shot him in the forehead. He rose to his feet, turned to O'Meara. "Let's go."


They still hadn't seen any survivors, which was a good sign. They approached the front of the jet, peered into the gaping maw where the fuselage had separated. The airliner's skin had torn in ragged patches, and two dozen seats had been tossed out, strewn like a giant's discarded toys.

None of those seats had bodies in them.

They climbed up and into the fuselage, weapons trained ahead of them.

There were no bodies inside. All the seats were empty. Pillows and blankets had been tossed about, but there were no books, no coats, no shoes. No signs of life.

"Oh, shit," Lucas whispered. "This isn't our jet."

Donal couldn't hear him. "The fuck is this?"

The men glanced at each other.

Behind them, someone said, "Lucas?"

He turned. Ray Calabrese stood in the twilight gloom, his Glock raised in the two-handed position, feet spread, one eye staring down the barrel at his friend. The left side of Ray's face was tacky and glistening with blood, his hair spiky with it. Beside him knelt a badly shaken man, hands on knees, trying to catch his breath. A woman stood to Ray's left, also armed.

She held a short-barreled Kahr K9 and, even in the dim light, Lucas recognized it as the gun that Ray kept strapped to his right leg.

"Jesus . . . Lucas," Ray said, his voice catching.

Everyone heard the sound of a car screeching to a halt somewhere on the far side of the fuselage. It startled Kiki, who turned. Lucas Bell did, too. But Donal O'Meara was an old hand at poker. Nothing distracted him when he was working.

He swung the shotgun up, ratcheted a shell into the pipe.

Ray Calabrese's first bullet caught him in the clavicle. The second one tore through his jaw. O'Meara was dead before his body landed in seat 18-C.

Lucas leaped to the side, landed, and rolled behind a charred seat from the jetliner. He continued his roll, coming out the other side, the seat blocking him from Ray and Kiki.

Lucas had a clear shot at Tommy, who knelt in the sand. And the others knew it.

"Walk away, Ray!" Lucas shouted. "I will kill this white boy!"

"Put it down," Ray said. He began moving sideways, but his left leg almost gave out. He stumbled, his vision swimming.

"You're in no condition for a fight," Lucas shouted. "Walk away, Raymond. Walk into the desert. We don't have to see each other ever again."

Ray tried to answer but his brain wouldn't catch gear. He realized that he was concussed. Tommy couldn't catch a decent breath, didn't have the strength to rise. He was bleeding from his forehead again. Kiki had no experience with small arms. She didn't know what to do.

"You got options, Ray?" Lucas shouted. "Seriously. Look, let's talk about your options. You can decide to be Dudley Do-Right here, make your arrest, Mirandize me. But before you do that, I will have shot this lovely white boy by your side—hi, lovely white boy."

Lucas edged to his right. Maybe, just maybe, he could slide out from cover and drop Ray Calabrese. All he needed was for the big man to look at his friend kneeling by his side.

"Or, and this is the better plan, you let me walk out. Just hike back to my car, give me an hour head start. And you never see my fucking ass, ever again." The kneeling guy moaned and Ray let his glance flicker toward him. Lucas tensed to roll and fire, but Ray was giving him the dead eye again.

"You win, Ray. You saved the Irish delegation. You got the Red Fist. You got that fat turd Silverman. You'll make the cover of *Stoic Hero Quarterly*. Seriously. Do you have options?"

The kneeling guy tried to stand and Ray turned fully to him. Lucas rolled out of position, surprised when his hip hit something solid.

He turned. He'd run into the boot of Daria Gibron.

She slammed the butt of the highway patrolman's gun into Lucas Bell's skull. The cracking sound echoed. Lucas sprawled, his rifle clattering away.

Kiki moved forward, picked up Lucas's gun, but kept the Kahr trained on the strange woman before her eyes. Lucas lay on the ground, not moving.

"Wanna put that gun down?" Kiki asked the stranger.

"No," the woman replied, her voice hollow, emotionless.

Ray limped between them, gently nudged Kiki's handgun aside. "'S all right," he told both women. "Daria?"

With Kiki covering Lucas, prone on the ground, Daria stepped back. Ray limped to her side. She all but fell into his arms.

He didn't stop hugging her until she gasped in fine agony. He didn't stop trembling for a long time after that.

Tommy watched it all. He almost jumped out of his skin when someone rested a hand on his shoulder.

Isaiah Grey smiled at him, his left sleeve soaked in blood, arm dangling limp from his shoulder. Tommy raised his hand. Isaiah took it and lugged him to his feet. Tommy kissed the pilot, an inch over his ear. "Hell of a job."

"This is the Daria we heard so much about," Isaiah said, leaning on Tommy.

Tommy leaned equally on Isaiah. He squinted into the setting sun, took in the smashed airliner, the front section to his left, the rear to his right, the smoldering debris in between.

"'Kay," Tommy said, and nodded. "That worked pretty good."

# EPILOGUE

**EIGHT DAYS LATER**

In one of the conference rooms at the National Transportation and Safety Board headquarters in D.C., one entire wall, floor to ceiling, had been painted with chalkboard paint. That particular Friday afternoon, much of that wall was covered with chalk—outlines of a Vermeer airliner; a diagram of a partial deployment of blocker panels for a thrust reverser in a Patterson-Pate engine; a rough outline of how the Go-Team's engineering crews had worked out the trick with the Gamelan flight data recorder.

The long conference-room table was covered with folders as well as white paper boxes of Chinese takeout and water bottles and coffee cups and a few Diet Cokes.

The room's television was turned to CNN but the audio was off. The media had dubbed the three incidents—the CascadeAir disaster, the rough landing on Interstate 5, and the crash in the desert—the Black Box Blood-bath. MSNBC even created a graphic of a jetliner broken in two.

Susan Tanaka sat at the head of the table. It hadn't been planned like this—there was no seating chart—but to her left sat Kiki Duvall and Isaiah Grey. Kiki looked good as new, a week since the crash, but Isaiah's arm was in a cast and sling.

To Susan's right sat Walter Mulroney and Peter Kim. Delevan Wildman, director of the NTSB, stood, leaning on the far cabinet, which held a coffeemaker and accessories, his raincoat tossed over a chair.

"It's your call, people."

Isaiah dug the last bit of sticky rice out of a box using a plastic fork. "Sir, the board has to recommend pulling every aircraft fitted with a Gamelan-brand flight data recorder out of the sky, now."

Peter Kim raised his hand. "No. Look, the Gamelan is a game-changer. It gathers so much raw data, so fast, that it will alter crash investigations forever. We're used to working on a twelve- to eighteen-month calendar. We knew the cause of this crash in one hundred hours."

Kiki moaned. Of the four investigators on the swap-out, she was the only one without a scratch on her. "The cause of the crash *was* the Gamelan!"

"No." Peter was adamant. "The cause of the crash was one crazy sociopath, plus one bent federal agent, plus this guy we're reading about, the pedophile congressman ripe for blackmail, plus the Red Fist of Ulster. So, who believes that particular set of dominoes is likely to reoccur?"

Walter addressed Susan, partly because he knew that she held Tommy Tomzak's proxy vote. "The data from the FDR wasn't at fault. The X factor in all of this was Dennis Silverman's soul. He was, simply, an evil man. Take that away, and this Gamelan makes other flight data recorders look like toys."

Peter agreed. "In technological revolutions, it's like going from the abacus to Texas Instruments overnight."

"Peter." Kiki picked up her chopsticks and helped herself to the last of the lemongrass chicken. "How many engineers on earth, today, right now, could MacGyver the Gamelan and create another crash?"

Peter frowned. "What? I don't know. Not many."

"Two? Ten?" Kiki chewed the succulent meat. "A hundred? How many engineers are as smart and resourceful and driven as you and Walter? Because, when push came to shove, you and your crews brainstormed this problem for, what? Two hours? Two and a half? And you made the Gamelan gimmick work. So what I'm asking is: how many other people on earth can do what you did?"

Peter waved her off but Walter frowned. "A handful," Peter said. "You could put them in this room. It's—"

Walter turned to him with a rueful smile. "A handful?"

"Yes. Absolutely. Fifty. A hundred, tops."

Walter tossed his pen down on his legal pad. "Dang. I hadn't thought of it in those terms."

Peter threw up his hands in disgust. "Come on!"

Susan Tanaka turned to Del Wildman. "Until the fix-it function of the Gamelan is detached, permanently, from the software, we should ground every aircraft with that technology. *Just* till then. If it takes months, fine. If it takes weeks, all the better. But until then, I'm afraid Kiki and Isaiah are right."

She turned to Walter and Peter. "And the day after that element is removed, we recommend *every* airliner gets a Gamelan. Because you're not wrong: the data is tremendous."

The vote was five to one to ground the Gamelan-fitted airliners. Wildman picked up his raincoat and loosened his tie. "I'll take it to the board tomorrow morning. Thank you, folks. You did a hell of a job out there."

Isaiah said, "Did anyone check on the Israeli woman? Daria? Is she okay?"

Susan nodded. "She apparently is healing from her wounds. Ray said she'll be fine and that she was debriefed by the FBI in Los Angeles. With her help, the FBI knows all about the Red Fist's plot. She's getting some kind of civilian commendation from them."

"She's also going to get a commendation from us," Del Wildman said. "Way I heard it, she saved you all."

As he walked to the door, Kiki said, "Sir? Have you heard anything about Tommy?"

"Not yet. No."

Peter, angrily jamming papers into his leather portfolio, snorted a laugh. "The Intelligence Committee hearing? This time tomorrow, Tomzak and what's-his-name will be on the unemployment line, best-case scenario. Worst-case: they'll be in Leavenworth."

Kiki glared at him. "His name is Ray Calabrese, you horse's ass. And what he and Tommy did was heroic."

"Good." Peter stood, buttoned his suit coat. "Because *heroic* looks really good on the old résumé."

Wildman cut in. "Tommy's methods aren't by the book, Peter. And what he did was pretty damn stupid from my perspective. But I swear to God almighty, no matter what the congressional investigation shows, that's the last time I let that man resign from the NTSB. While I've got a job, he's got a job."

Peter sneered. Kiki laughed. "Think positive, Peter. It's not like they're facing a lawsuit from a farmer whose lawn and white picket fence they destroyed."

Peter Kim stormed out of the room. Isaiah stood. "Want to head over to Capitol Hill, see if we can lend some moral support?"

Susan had an official report to finalize but Kiki jumped at the chance.

## CONGRESS

Tommy Tomzak and Ray Calabrese sat on a wooden bench outside the hearing room of the Joint Intelligence Committee. Tommy leaned back, ankles crossed, legs stretched out, his tie loosened. Ray leaned forward, elbows on knees. The doctors had shaved his head to get to the scalp wound that had resulted in a mild concussion. A week on, it was growing back in but still looked weird.

They were quiet for a time.

"So." Tommy scratched his chin.

"Yeah."

"I was thinking. I could murder a steak."

Ray looked his way. "T-bone?"

"Sure."

"Where do you stand on the issue of side dishes? 'Cause it's important."

Tommy thought about it. "I'm inclined toward the steak fry but I have never said no to garlic mashed potatoes."

"I'm an onion-ring man."

Tommy said, "I am not doctrinaire."

"Okay."

They were quiet again. About twenty feet down the corridor, Kiki Duvall and Isaiah Grey rounded the corner and spotted them.

"Hey!" Kiki ran the last bit. Tommy surprised her by grabbing her wrist and dropping her down onto his lap.

"Tommy! It's Congress!"

Isaiah said, "So, are you still waiting?"

Ray shook his head. "It's over."

A beat, and Kiki said, "And . . . ?"

Ray shrugged. He stood and Kiki did, too, followed by Tommy. "We were talking about getting a steak. You guys in?"

Kiki had had enough. She held her ground and, as she was holding Tommy's hand, he did, too. The advantage of being taller and more athletic than your guy. "What happened!" Tommy responded by kissing her.

Ray said, "Look, I got concussed last week. But near as I can tell, we just get, what . . . ? The oral equivalent of the Congressional Medal of Honor?"

Tommy ran a hand through his hair and puffed out his cheeks. "It was a might confusing. They talked a lot about valor and *thinking outside the box*. One of them used the word *gumption*, which is something my grandmother used to say and I can't rightly claim I know what the word means. So . . . yeah. Maybe."

Ray rubbed his eyes. "Look, would someone just buy me a damn steak?"

Isaiah threw an arm over his shoulder as they walked off. Tommy kissed Kiki again.

She separated, looked him in the eyes. "You got kudos for stealing a jet?"

He smiled. "Didn't see that shit comin'."